Maxwell looked down. Vronsky's and Nella's faces were pebble gray against the darker boulder. The red of Nella's jacket seemed the same hue as the rock, and Maxwell's own hand was like slate. Snow on the high peaks set the light end of the color range; the gun in Maxwell's hand the dark. A black-and-white photo. An old movie. When he pulled the trigger, black lines would trickle down from the corners of their mouths.

And then Technicolor again for him! Blue skies; vibrant green grass; flowers in every hue; golden sunlight to sit in while he looked at the violet mountains, the orange and magenta sunset. . . . He would be free.

Maxwell stared at them for just over thirty seconds. Then he slipped the safety on the pistol.

A Good Death

A Good Death

Philip Ross

TOR

A TOM DOHERTY ASSOCIATES BOOK

A GOOD DEATH

Copyright © 1983 by Philip Ross

Reprinted by arrangement with Dodd, Mead & Company, Inc.

First TOR printing: March 1986

A TOR Book

Published by Tom Doherty Associates
49 West 24 Street
New York, N.Y. 10010

ISBN: 0-812-58798-7
CAN. ED.: 0-812-58799-5

Library of Congress Catalog Card Number: 83-11611

Printed in the United States

0 9 8 7 6 5 4 3 2 1

For Sharon

1

MAXWELL SAT at one end of the bench, staring as
though trying to make out something in the distance. Corchran
was just close enough, just far enough away. He kept his left
hand steady in his lap, holding the folded *London Times*, and
his right inside the fold, his forefinger curled around the trigger
of the Baretta pointed at Maxwell's stomach. Without looking
away from Maxwell, he nodded toward the phalanx of daffodils
marshaled on the bank between bench and pond. "Glorious.
Have you been down to Kent to see them growing wild in the
woods? The entire forest floor carpeted. One of the wonders of
the world."

Maxwell kept his hands in his raincoat pockets, fisted,
bunching the coat over his middle. Not for protection; even on
a subconscious level, he knew there could be no protection.
His hands were cold. "No, Corky. That's another one of the
things I've missed."

"Pity."

Maxwell's fists tightened momentarily. He was contemptuous of his fellow Americans who affected British speech.
"Yeah," he said, to end it. He thought, *I should have worn a
heavier coat*. It had been drizzling and warm in the morning,
but he should have been prepared for the sudden clearing and
cold: the tile-blue sky, the trees sharp with anodized leaves.
He'd been in England often enough to know about changes in
the weather. He should have been prepared. Instinctively, he

clenched his teeth, precluding the already remote possibility that his being cold could make them chatter. Corchran thought the bunched jaw muscles made him look even more like an earth-moving machine than usual.

Two elderly men strode briskly in step across the lawn in front of the bench, speaking loudly at each other in a language without consonants. Clear of the daffodils, they unrolled their long green canvas parcels and produced cloth kites of complex design.

Leaning forward, Maxwell watched intently as stretcher rods were inserted between cross-braces.

"Nice to have a hobby," Corchran said.

Maxwell spoke without turning. "I used to fly kites when I was a kid." To fly: it had seemed like flying, he remembered, as though he himself sailed upward on that March wind—chill, yet warm with promise; soared at the end of ball added to ball of string and looked over the whole world. "I won a contest once." He said it matter-of-factly, to hide the pride he still felt. "I made it myself."

"Fascinating. You should have brought one today for cover."

"I guess I should have done something."

The first of the flyers snapped the string onto his kite, held it at arm's length, and let it rise. Blue and pink panels, green and yellow, fluttering. It seemed to Maxwell that the kite lifted in an arc, not pulling against the string so much as propelled by a ray of energy from its master's fingertips, guided aloft on some errand. "Would it have done any good? I mean, did you know about me before you came?"

"Would we have planned it this way? We followed Algernon here—"

"Algernon?"

"That's what I call him. What do you call him?"

"Boris."

"Why are they all either Boris or Ivan? It must get awfully confusing for *them*. Anyway, when I realized it was *you* he was

2

sitting down by—Charles Maxwell, ace agent of the CIA—well, I was so dumbfounded it must have taken me five or six seconds to realize you had to be his source."

"That long."

"You see how astonished I was."

"You must have been, to let me see you."

"That answers your question. Of course, we hadn't expected anyone who would recognize us, but that's no excuse. We should have been far enough back so we could let you go on and then just called you in later. How long did it take *you* to realize that I knew?"

"I knew."

"Instantly? I wouldn't have thought your reactions were quicker than mine, Max."

"Corky, I'm so much older than you, I don't have to react anymore."

"I'll bear that in mind."

"You know, Corky, the English can be pretty stuffy; they don't like scenes, like shooting people in Kensington Garden. Bad form, not the done thing."

Corchran looked at Maxwell without any expression breaking the fine joinery of his facial planes for a few seconds, then smiled quickly. "Don't think about it, Max. Sure, it would make a nasty flap. Telephone calls. Notes. *Admonitions*." His eyebrows arched momentarily in mock horror. "You know what they call us: the Cousins. You know what we call them?"

"The Poor Relations."

"Well, there you have it, Max. You try anything, and I'll fill ya fulla lead."

What the hell, Maxwell thought, *what the hell? Why not now and get it over? It's a pretty place. All washed clean after the rain. Go out clean. Just go out . . .* He tried to hunch tighter into his own bulk, away from the breeze. The second kite went up on a gust, and, despite himself, Maxwell shivered. "That's a nice overcoat you've got, Corky."

3

"Thank you. I've been pleased with it."

"You know, you ought to watch that kind of expense. The main office may begin to wonder about *you*."

"Just the opposite. My tastes show I have a vested interest in the success of our side."

"You really as rich as they say?"

"I don't know what they say, but probably so. I don't take any salary, and the office knows no one is going to buy me."

"A dedicated soldier in the war to make the world safe for plutocracy."

Corchran tipped his head, as though to see into Maxwell sideways. "Is that it, Max? *You* turning ideological in your old age? I really can't believe you've been a mole all along. Were you? Or did you have a sudden vision, a little trip along the road to Damascus?"

"No."

The two kites paused in the sky, then swayed and swept to the left. Maxwell felt them as animate beings, moving for the sensuous delight of moving. Corchran let the moment hold. Then he cleared his throat discreetly. "We are all going to be interested in knowing why. Of course, you don't have to tell *me* . . ."

"For the money."

"For the money," Corchran repeated flatly.

Maxwell turned to him. "For the money, Corky. *You* should understand that. From what you just said, I guess you're doing it for the money too, aren't you? You've got it, you want to keep it. Well, I didn't have it, and I wanted to get it." He felt the burning in his stomach again. His hands warmed, and the places inside him that had frozen when he saw Corchran began to thaw.

Corchran assayed Maxwell as though he were a curio at a stall on Portobello Road. "I don't believe it. You must have bought that raincoat in Macy's basement ten years ago. What's your idea of a good meal? A steak and French fries? And, to make it especially fancy, some catsup? You're not a spender, Max.

You're not a person who wants money. You don't have a wife; no kids." He paused. "Are you keeping a woman?"

Maxwell looked again at the kites as they turned and swung together slowly in a broad sweep. "No."

"Well, you don't have to tell me." Corchran believed in refinement as a way of life, so, after a moment, he put it in as gentle a voice as he could. "You will have to tell, though. You know that."

The burning in Maxwell's stomach increased. "Yeah," he said. "I'll tell. There won't be any problem." Anger and fear and loss within him flamed. He looked at the pond, at the cool, cloud-filled sky reflected there. Shame burned hottest of all. "I hadn't wanted anybody to know . . ." He'd think of the shame as pain too. That would be the way to handle it, because he didn't let pain affect him. "But now . . ." He looked at Corchran from far back under his heavy eyebrows and spoke firmly. "I'm going to die." Like having the bullet dug out of his arm, that time, down in a wine cellar: shout. Shout, and you don't scream. "Cancer. Six months, I've got about six decent months, they figure. I'll be able to get around pretty normally. Not too much pain, not too weak. After that it goes down fast. It's inoperable, all through me. And the treatments didn't work."

Maxwell let his attention be caught by the daffodils tossing in the breeze. The brilliant yellow, it came to him, was like a single, clear trumpet note.

"I'm sorry, Max." Of course, it was not possible for Corchran to touch Maxwell. Apart from the circumstances, apart from their being men who did not know each other that well, Corchran knew Maxwell would not want, would not tolerate, to be touched in sympathy. And Corchran didn't like Maxwell, had never liked him in any of their brief encounters. He disliked the short cropped hair, the big-boned, coarsely creased face, the determined insensitivity that Maxwell appeared to consider true masculinity. Corchran held Maxwell in contempt for having played college football casually for money instead of viciously for sport, and, in the same way, despised him for being the perfect professional doing his job skillfully with no apparent concern about what ideal or ideology originated his orders. Still, perhaps because he was *not* like Maxwell, Corchran wanted to make some gesture to show he understood the suffering that the other man gave no sign of feeling. "Truly, I am sorry." He cleared his throat. "But you'd have been taken care of."

"I didn't want to be taken care of."

"Yes, of course." Corchran was aware of an impulse to look away but was not distracted by it. "What did you want, Max?"

Maxwell continued staring. "You're right, Corky. Those flowers really are beautiful. I've been in and out of London a lot of times in the spring before, and this is the first time I've ever just sat and looked at the flowers."

"You didn't need money for that."

"Well, there were some other things like that I wanted to look at. You know, I've been all around Europe for the past thirty-eight years, and I've never even seen . . . And I've been to the Far East a couple times. But I haven't seen the Taj Mahal, or anything. I thought—in the time I've got left—I thought I'd like to go somewhere and look. Somewhere I'd like to be when . . . When I look back, Corky, I don't see that I've had much of a life. I'd like to have a good death. After the treatments, I didn't have any savings left."

"You could have had the treatments free."

"Sure. And been taken off duty and put into a hospital and kept there."

"They'd have let you—"

"They'd have let me go anyplace I wanted *in the States*. Well, that wasn't what I wanted."

Only for himself. No goal, no principle . . . Corchran's sympathy was obliterated. "So you sold out, so you could see the Taj Mahal and die, huh? The Grand Canyon wouldn't do, it had to be the Taj Mahal."

"That's right, Corky. That's exactly right. I didn't sell much,

6

nothing that's going to get anybody hurt. You'll have to shake up some offices and close some accounts—"

"But it's a price we can afford." Corchran's voice went sharp. "*You* decided we could afford that. For *severance* pay? So it's not treason, it's severance pay!"

Will he shoot me? If I goad him, will he shoot me? Maxwell looked to the pond again, and beyond it to the long stretch of golden-green lawn and the century-old beech trees. *Now?*

"You're a shit, Max. I'm sorry you're dying, but you're a shit." Corchran realized his hands were clutching the gun in his lap. He should release the tension. "OK, never mind. Prescott should be back in a few minutes with the car, and then we'll just stroll down the path, and you can take it all up with the home office."

Now! Maxwell set himself to move, then hesitated at the thought, *But what if he doesn't kill me?* He saw himself bleeding into that green lawn, turning his face to the flowers, letting the yellow trumpet note fill his head, the last sight and sound, and then . . . And then taken away. White sterile walls, clicks, metal and glass. He would be strapped down. And then offices, small plain rooms, grilles on the windows. If he didn't die instantly, if Corchran only wounded him . . . But it would all happen that way if he didn't try. *Worth the chance*, he decided.

Maxwell set himself to move, but suddenly there was a glowing orange globe on the ground at his feet. Both men snapped looks out from the bench. Corchran's was barely a flash, and he was back on Maxwell instantly.

A boy, perhaps two years old, stood fifteen feet away, regarding the men intensely. After a moment, he gave a high-pitched scream and jumped from foot to foot. His chubby, chapped knees jerked up and down.

"Randolph!" A woman's voice called from somewhere at a distance behind Corchran.

Maxwell leaned forward and took up the ball. The child stopped his side-to-side dance. Maxwell tossed the ball lightly, bouncing it so the boy could catch it.

He did, with both hands, against his chest. He squealed with delight. Raising his hands together above his head, he ran forward three steps and hurled the ball at Maxwell. Maxwell had to lurch backward to catch it.

"Easy, Max. Don't make anything of this."

"Randolph!"

Maxwell looked for a moment at Corchran and nodded slightly.

The child wore a knitted hat, a sort of balaclava tied under his chin. Gray wool, with a red pom-pom on top that bounced and wobbled as again he hopped from foot to foot and screamed.

"That is an unpleasant child," Corchran said.

Maxwell leaned forward, put the ball on the ground, and pushed it. It rolled slowly toward the boy, who ran to meet it. Though it was a near thing, the child managed not to fall as he bent over his fat belly and between bowed legs to take up the ball. Again he raised it over his head and threw. Maxwell caught the ball directly in front of his chest. He held it there.

"Randolph!"

"Max . . ."

Both Corchran and the boy stared at Maxwell, who sat steady, relaxed, not moving. The child shrieked. He waited. He shrieked again.

"Randolph!"

Maxwell could see a woman about fifty yards away. She was sitting on a blanket on the grass, in the lotus position, but straining upward from the waist, looking at them. He held steady.

Randolph could endure it no longer. He ran to Maxwell and tried angrily to seize the ball from his hands. Maxwell scooped up the boy to his lap.

"Max!"

"You shoot this kid or any other civilian and nobody's going to fix the ticket, Corky!"

Corchran froze, waiting. Holding the child against his chest, Maxwell put the ball down and rose from the bench. The boy was temporarily astonished. He frowned, considered smiling, then deliberated.

Corchran rose too. He and Maxwell faced each other at opposite ends of the bench. Moving precisely, Corchran swung his clasped hands to his side, used the newspaper to cover his slipping the pistol into his overcoat pocket, and dropped the paper onto the bench.

Still facing him, Maxwell sidestepped to the broad path behind the bench. He shifted the boy more to the crook of his arm and began walking past Corchran toward the gate onto Kensington High Street.

Corchran took a breath, then also stepped out onto the path, falling in two steps behind Maxwell. "This isn't going to do you any good, Max. You can't carry that kid forever. You're going to have to put him down."

"Randolph!" The young woman rose. Her hair was like a copper scouring pad, and she wore tight trousers made from a mosaic of blue denim patches. She came toward them from the lawn ahead and to their left.

Maxwell closed on two elderly women in Queen Mother hats who were coming up the path toward him. He stepped to the right to pass them, shifting the child to his left hip, putting Corchran on the other side of the women.

Randolph's shock was beginning to wear off. As the novelty of being served by a new large person faded, he reverted to customary behavior. He squealed.

Corchran kept his distance. He preferred not being too close. "Any time, Max. I'm right here. Later's the same to me as sooner."

Randolph shrieked and kicked his feet against Maxwell's thigh. His mother waited on the path just ahead. Randolph took a great gulp of air and howled.

Suddenly Maxwell half turned, lifted Randolph in both hands much as the boy had lifted the ball, and hurled him at Corchran. The woman screamed.

Instinctively Corchran snatched his hands from his pockets

and caught the child. He was thrown off balance, stumbled a step backward, but avoided falling. He set the screaming child onto the path. Randolph immediately sat, shrieked louder, and kicked his heels into the gravel. His mother swooped down upon him.

Maxwell was already twenty yards along the path, sprinting, dodging strollers as he had dodged linebackers on those crisp Saturdays nearly forty years gone by. Corchran raced after him.

I'm faster, Corchran said to himself. *I'm younger, I'm faster! I'll catch him! I'll catch him! Catch him! Catch him!*

A heavyset man with a walking stick strode along like the nineteenth century in front of Maxwell, but a woman halted in surprise. The gap between them closed. Maxwell couldn't get through. He crashed into the man's back, careened away, spun 360 degrees, and ran on.

Ahead of Corchran a boy stood gaping after Maxwell. His huge sheep dog heard Corchran, saw him coming, lunged half forward, half back, then cowered directly in Corchran's path. Without pause, Corchran hurdled the animal and drove himself faster.

Maxwell was at the park gate, but Corchran was gaining. *Catch him! Catch him! Catch him!*

Maxwell cut to the left onto the High Street sidewalk. He struck a young woman with his shoulder, sending her sprawling. Just ahead, a bus pulled away from the curb. The great gasps of breath he took were raw in his throat. His legs were leaden, but he forced a final surge of effort. He sprinted still faster after the bus.

Corchran saw the woman on the sidewalk just in time to leap to the side past her. His eyes swept ahead, searching. He saw Maxwell. He dashed on.

The bus picked up speed as it moved into the road. Maxwell pounded after it. Brakes shrieked from behind, a horn blared. Maxwell closed the distance and stretched for the pole at the rear platform, touched it with his fingertips, lunged and grabbed it. The speed of the bus almost pulled him off his feet, but he leapt forward, using the acceleration of the vehicle to help him, and landed on the platform.

Corchran's momentum kept him running for several steps, but he felt every particle of energy flush out of his body. *No! Don't stop! Traffic. He may get caught in traffic.* Corchran loped on, dodging and bumping into people on the sidewalk, until he reached the Queen's Gate. The bus was far ahead, beyond the Albert Memorial. It had stopped at a traffic light. Corchran's chest heaved, his head rang, but he pushed himself to run on. The bus started again. Corchran caught himself up against a lamp post. *No good. No good.* Sweat soaked him. Everything he looked at seemed two-dimensional and faded. *No good.*

At the next stop, Maxwell got off the bus. The conductor had not yet reached him to collect the fare. He shouted after, but Maxwell was gone.

2

FEEDBACK SCREECHED as the technician rode his gain too high, trying to compensate for Vronsky's mumbling. The chairman, sitting to the left of the podium, motioned for a higher vocal level. Vronsky nodded and spoke louder, but he kept his eyes focused on his notes and gripped the lectern as though it were the Rock of Ages set amid eternally sweeping seas.

Constantin Vronsky was used to lecturing. He had been regarded by his students as an excellent lecturer (when he was still teaching, before he was forced to leave the university). Once he was warmed up, he liked lecturing. But every time was the first time: all those faces turned to him, the minds behind them expectant. Would he reach them? The logic, the order of his thoughts was so clear to him. Would his audience see that structure? Had he sketched so few lines that they would be recognized only by those who already knew what he had drawn, or had he illustrated in such detail that embellishment obscured essence?

In this instance, Vronsky's anguish was worse than usual. He felt a fool, reviewing the current state of knowledge and theory on subatomic particles for the benefit of the very people who had discovered them. He had wanted only to present his own material and be finished, but Semoilov had insisted.

Vronsky ached for a cigarette. He felt willing to give up everything and go back to his tiny room with its narrow window framing eight hundred miles of emptiness, because he could smoke one cigarette after another there. He knew smoking was rationally and scientifically wrong. He was only thirty-two. If he stopped smoking, he could increase the length of his life by ten or twenty years. Vronsky now felt willing to die in ten or twenty minutes if only someone would give him a cigarette. He licked his thin lips.

Semoilov, Vronsky's director, had insisted on ten minutes of background for two reasons. First, he knew that Vronsky would take at least five to warm up, and, second, he believed that the most important scientific construct since Einstein's theory of general relativity should have some dramatic build to it and should take more than only four minutes to present.

The members of the congress understood. None knew what Vronsky would say to them, but everyone knew what sort of thing it would be. For two days, brilliant young researchers had detonated papers that should have set off fire storms of controversy; distinguished professors had summarized, synthesized, and hypothesized, and both groups felt they were chewing on sand. If any of the rumors were true—and they must be, if the Russians had let Vronsky out—then half the world community of physicists might be proved wrong, and all of them would be redundant.

And then there were the other things he might speak of. Most of those at the congress—all those from outside the Communist bloc—had been on committees or signed petitions to free Constantin Vronsky. Most of them, including many within the bloc, were almost as eager to hear the results of Vronsky's political thinking as they were his scientific ideas. Though he had published nothing on the subject for seven years, his colleagues had no doubt that he pursued the principles of social organization with the same quality of intellect as he did those governing matter, and that his statement, if ever heard, would be as profound.

Vronsky hurried down his outline toward the end of the beginning. He became more at ease. His audience was not restive, and he was approaching the part that would be new and interesting. He spoke more clearly, with growing authority, although his light voice never dropped below medium pitch. The moment was historic and filled with drama, but that he would be established as one of history's scientific giants did not arouse his emotions. What did excite him was the presentation of the idea.

He could survey his audience but not yet with more than an unfocused scan. Now that he kept his head erect, glare from the lectern lights on his owlish spectacles no longer screened his eyes.

Vronsky was struck by the number of bald heads scattered throughout the audience. Because he would be having slides to illustrate the essential part of his presentation, the lights over the audience were dimmed, and their subdued glow was reflected on each pate. Without attempting any actual count, he sensed that nearly a third of the delegates were bald. Their disposition intrigued him: although no pattern was obvious, the distribution did not seem random. He formed a new image, shifting all the bald heads to the right side of the hall. Then he imagined them separated and spaced evenly. Mentally, he moved heads from place to place, creating clusters of glowing domes and dark hirsute expanses. None of the imaginary pictures matched what he saw in actuality. What hypothesis might explain . . . ?

Vronsky was amused and annoyed with himself. Distribution of bald heads! Of course, it was an escape mechanism; he recognized that. A relief from the excitement of the occasion and from the humiliation of having to listen to what he was having to say. And, most of all, from the excruciating tension over what would be attempted that evening: defection.

He had not promised not to defect. He supposed they hadn't asked for that because the probability of his trying was so obvious they preferred simply to accept and guard against it. The man from Moscow had been clear about the other conditions.

Vronsky had been called from his room while attempting to

understand why, when a particular proposition could be proved true, its contradiction could not (apparently) be proved false. Being summoned abruptly to Semoilov's office had disconcerted him, so he had never quite heard the name of the man from Moscow.

The man had been straightforward. He had not offered to shake Vronsky's hand. He had simply nodded once to acknowledge Semoilov's introduction and a second time to indicate that Vronsky should sit opposite him in the other tubular-steel chair. Semoilov himself had sat behind the desk, as though he were presiding, put his right hand up over his gray beard, and said nothing until the interview was ended.

Vronsky had remained silent.

The man also had said nothing at first. He sat with one black-trousered leg over the other, long hands dangling limply from the chair arms. He regarded Vronsky for over a minute, then began directly. "The highest authorities have decided that you should go to the congress in Geneva to present your work in person."

Vronsky terminated thought about his equations, about his fear, about his sorrow for poor old Semoilov, who seemed always caught and ground between his basic decency and his directorship. Vronsky focused. "Oh?"

"While you will be congratulated and honored by leaders of the State when your work is made public, it is felt you should receive in person the acclamation of the entire world, and particularly of the world scientific community."

"You mean that there should be a demonstration that, despite what I have written, scientific thought is still possible in the Soviet Union."

The man from Moscow was annoyed that this pudgy-faced boy should attempt to taunt him, but he sucked in his cheeks for an instant and held his temper. After all, whether he liked Vronsky's tone or not, the statement was accurate.

"That is true. And against that truth is another."

"I am not permitted to appear in public."

"You are permitted to speak in public on those subjects

which are in the field of your genius. You are not permitted to speak on matters about which you have demonstrated incompetence."

Vronsky resisted the urge to argue. There was no point debating this person at this time.

Again there was a period of silence. The man had large eyes set deeply, close to his narrow nose. He imagined that he looked rather like a bird of prey; his stare seemed to disconcert people.

Finally he said, "The question comes to this, Vronsky: will you go to Geneva *to talk about your work*, or will someone else present it for you? Director Semoilov will be willing, I'm sure."

Vronsky was not skilled at hiding his feelings; he simply was not expressive, so the jolt of hope that surged through him did not register in any external sign. "I would like to go to Geneva," he said, "but I have written to decline."

"Yes. 'I am not permitted to go.' 'I am not at liberty to go,' neither of which we would send, and 'I am unable to go because of poor health,' which you would not write. I believe the compromise was simply, 'I am unable to attend.' Now you can write again and say you are able."

"I can?"

Another thirty seconds went by. The man from Moscow twitched his lips to one side in what might have been a smile. "In one of the papers you wrote before coming here, you spoke of morality, of the importance of truth and honesty. If you are permitted to go to Geneva, will you promise to make no statements of any kind of a political nature? Will we have your word?"

To dissemble was alien both to Vronsky's nature and to his system of belief, but he managed to avoid revealing his eagerness by taking a moment for apparent consideration.

"Very well," he had said.

Vronsky now wiped out that memory along with the bald head problem.

"And now," he said, "I should like to present work of my own which may serve to explain some of these phenomena." He gestured toward the projectionist, and the first slide flashed onto the screen behind and above him.

Someone later remembered the next four minutes as beginning with a roll of thunder and a sigh, as though the veil of the temple had been rent and the ultimate mystery revealed. The sound was actually that of three hundred physicists shifting their feet and sliding forward to the edges of their seats.

Vronsky was using a small flashlight that projected a yellow beam to point to the more significant symbols in his equations as he ran through them. His voice was firm, and he looked back and forth from the screen to individual members of the audience. His presentation was dramatic only in its calm assurance. Vronsky was speaking the truth as he knew it, and that was enough. In ninety seconds, he reached the point of showing where the line so far developed could be turned in a promising direction. Several viewers were heard to hum their assent. Vronsky then proved the trail false, and someone gasped loudly. Vronsky returned to the point of divergence, where he inverted the equation and introduced a hypothetical constant. Two or three men whispered to their neighbors and were shushed. In another minute the next-to-last slide was flashed on. As Vronsky worked through it, one soft, sharp intake of breath followed another as the implication was grasped. Vronsky's voice, still calm, rose in intensity just enough to carry and then fell back again as he called for the final slide. He no longer needed to be heard, and the applause began even before he completed his last words. The rumble of thunder returned as the audience surged to its feet.

Vronsky had not thought about the moment after his presentation. He had imagined vaguely a scene including polite applause. Perhaps there might be more reaction, given the significance of his theory. Although the theory would not be accepted without study and experimental verification, the audience's reaction was unlikely to be one of instant disagreement, requiring him to debate, so Vronsky had not envisioned it. The tumult of an ovation stunned him. He blinked. He looked from side to side. He almost clapped his hands, too, like a circus performer, but stopped himself and let them flop awkwardly out of too-long shirt cuffs.

The chairman came up and seized Vronsky's hand, shaking it so that Vronsky's elbow flapped. Members of the audience started toward the podium, but suddenly Vronsky's assistant, Suvanov, was there. He took Vronsky by the upper arm and led him through a door.

Vronsky was weak with gratitude, and when Suvanov gave him a cigarette, Vronsky almost wept. He forgave Suvanov for being more a guard than an associate physicist; forgave the younger man for his strong jaw and curly hair, his ability to wear clothes well. Vronsky sucked smoke down to his toes with every third step as they walked, and as Suvanov guided him through corridors and passageways, Vronsky even forgave the exaggerated respect with which Suvanov patronized him.

Back at his hotel, Vronsky forgave all of them: Suvanov again, big Dobrinsky, the ones in the corridor and lobby who were never introduced, and even the unsmiling Nev. Suvanov answered the telephone (it rang again every time he replaced the receiver) and told Nev who was calling. Nev checked the list and said yes or no. Dobrinsky opened the door each time and told the two outside to let the visitors enter or not.

And the visitors came in a stream, in a torrent. No, Vronsky thought, that was inaccurate: the visitors were the steady drip of a water torture. He wanted to writhe away from them, but his hands were held in one effusive clutch after another. Yet in his torment, he recognized the more excruciating agonies his guards did protect him from. Nev gave orders, and Suvanov and Dobrinsky were polite but unyielding: a press meeting in the morning, no statements, interviews, certainly no photographs until then. Only the senior or most distinguished representatives from each nation present at the congress could visit. And no more than three at a time, no more than five minutes each group. Vronksy imagined his eternal dream realized: all his keepers vanished, himself alone. The real vision was that of a swimmer being devoured by piranha fish.

Vronsky was so agitated throughout the entire afternoon that none of the security men could have noticed any difference in the way he had greeted Professore Bentivoglio. Vronsky did take Bentivoglio's thin hand firmly, instead of merely offering his own, but the gesture was too small for its significance to be read.

Bentivoglio laid before Vronsky a tribute of compliments like a treasure chest laden with golden *molto*s and sparkling *issimos*.

"*Grazie, grazie, molto grazie,*" Vronsky replied, "but please, Professore, since you do not speak Russian, let us talk in English. I have not spoken Italian for a long time."

"Ah," said Bentivoglio, looking down his distinguished nose, first at Vronsky and then at Suvanov, Dobrinsky, and Nev, who had gone to "red alert." "And your friends do not understand Italian at all, yes?" He shrugged, then went on, speaking more loudly as though trying to compensate for the inferiority of English superlatives.

As Bentivoglio's time neared its end, Dobrinsky moved discreetly beside Vronsky.

"Ahhh!" Bentivoglio threw up his hands and sighed in desolation. "I see I must leave you." He clasped Vronsky's hands with both of his own. "Dear Constantin . . ." He paused, looked into Vronsky's eyes, then clutched Vronsky to him, called again on the expressiveness of Italian, and gave his benediction. "*Aspetti Paolo,*" he said heavily, and in a voice quivering with emotion added, "*e non bevi caffe!*"

Then he thrust Vronsky from him, turned abruptly, and hastened to the door before his feelings could overcome him completely.

Dobrinsky and Suvanov let their eyes meet, but out of respect for the old man's gray hairs, they did not smile.

Vronsky stood transfixed. The words sounded over in his head: "Wait for Paul, and don't drink coffee!"

When they came in, the Canadians were astounded to find Vronsky so vague a person, but they put it down to genius or fatigue, the symptoms of which often are similar. Next in was Dr. Kenzo, who assumed the problem was language, as usual, and decided he would make his point simply by bowing more deeply and smiling more widely. Vronsky managed to get himself back together a little for the Scandinavians who, as always, were brought through as a unit.

At ten after six Nev closed the show, not out of humanitarian concern for Vronsky, but because the impression he was making had deteriorated so badly. The switchboard was told to accept no further calls; the men outside were ordered to allow no one to knock.

Nev was not exhausted; he was excited. Now it was beginning. He had not expected any attempt at defection before Vronsky made his little speech. That would have been a good trick, but not in Vronsky's character. But now . . . if defection was to be attempted—and Nev assumed it was—it would come tonight or tomorrow. Nev was not troubling himself over the possibility that Vronsky would pretend to go to the W.C. and flush himself down to the American embassy (although precautions would still be taken). The little twerp could be kept from going anywhere on his own simply by smudging a thumbprint onto his glasses. Vronsky would have to be snatched. He would cooperate, but the initiative would come from outside.

Nev ran his hand around inside the top of his trousers. He liked to have his shirt tucked down smoothly, and he liked to feel the hard muscles of his back and abdomen. A thrill of tension ran through his chest. If he failed on this job he would probably be sent to guard a pile of camel dung in Turkestan—if they didn't just shoot him. If he brought Vronsky back there would be some equally impressive reward. Nev thought little about either prospect. The exhilaration of the moment was all he cared to feel. The challenge was superb: to achieve maximum security with minimum display. Nev understood completely that the appearance of freedom for Vronsky had to be conveyed. Guards would be stationed on the pretext of maintaining Vronsky's privacy, but the place could not be

20

isolated. He was not working in a country where he could exercise absolute control through local authorities.

"Heigh-yo!" Dobrinsky yawned and rubbed the back of his neck. He grinned at Vronsky. "Doctor, I think meeting all those people was harder than thinking up your idea, huh?"

Vronsky smiled weakly back at him.

"You must be very tired," said Suvanov. He turned to Nev and said in a tone that might have been genuine even if he had not been ravenous himself, "The Doctor must be very hungry. Shall we call for dinner to be sent up?"

Nev nodded.

Suvanov went to the phone.

Vronsky started for one of the adjoining rooms.

"Comrade?" Nev stopped him.

Vronsky turned, gestured vaguely with both hands. "The W.C."

Nev nodded again. Vronsky went on through his bedroom and into the W.C. As he had been instructed, he left the door open. Dobrinsky positioned himself in the bedroom door so that he could watch Vronsky, so that Vronsky knew he could be watched, but then Dobrinsky looked away.

It was being handled well, Nev thought. Two of them were awake at all times. The adjoining suites were occupied by others of the Russian delegation, the one below by the Czechs, and there was only the roof above. Two guards were outside the door, another two in the corridor—one at either end. There were two more on the roof, two in the lobby downstairs, and two outside the service entrance at the back. The hotel was of moderate size, old, with character but no duct system. The suite on the fifth floor faced over a little park. Nev narrowed his eyes as he felt the satisfaction of knowing how well it had been done. Complacency was dangerous. Satisfaction at knowing he would not be satisfied and recognition of continuing danger made Nev's blood race as though he had taken a drug.

He ran his fingers against the grain on his jaw. He needed to shave again, which pleased him. He went to his own bathroom, took off his jacket and shirt. He admired his pectorals in the mirror. He ran hot water into the basin. He dipped and wrung out a cloth, tossing it in the air to cool it slightly, then held it over his face. He would have loved to soak in a hot bath, but would not take off all his clothes until after the next day, when they were back. Then he would boil himself red for an hour. And then have Luba. He would have been gone five days by then, long enough for her to have gorged herself. He had forbidden her to gain weight, and she would be guilty for having disobeyed, and for having gotten ugly again. She would want him to punish her but still desire her. On the plane back to Moscow he would think in detail of how he would punish her. But for now he must use the relaxation of the hot water to think about the ever-present danger. He breathed in deeply of the steam and set the problem: reverse roles. If he wanted to get Vronsky *out*, how would he do it?

When Nev returned to the center room, slipping his thin necktie up to his collar, the room service waiter was setting the round table at which the four of them took their meals. Dobrinsky and Suvanov had already moved it away from the windows. Nev stopped, his arms still at chest level. Without thinking about the movement, he took his hands away from the necktie and turned them palms down in front of him.

"Who are you?" he said. He had learned the trick of projecting his commanding baritone without actually using much volume. When Nev spoke, all attended.

Dobrinsky turned from the window. Suvanov, sitting on one of the couches, snapped his eyes up from his magazine. Even Vronsky peered out of the clouds in his brain which seemed thicker than the cigarette smoke always around him. The waiter froze for an instant, holding a fistful of silverware.

"*Signore?* Sir?" he said.

"Who are you?"

"Your waiter, sir."

"No. You are not our waiter."

"Beg pardon, sir. I am your waiter tonight. Giovanni does not work tonight. It is his night to rest."

Without taking his eyes from the waiter, Nev inclined his head toward Suvanov.

Suvanov went to the phone, called down to the desk. The waiter put a fork at the place where he was standing, but as he started to move around toward the next place Dobrinsky took one step toward him. The waiter halted.

"Good evening," said Suvanov. "We have a new waiter from room service. Is this correct?" He nodded affirmatively to Nev. "Giovanni is off Tuesdays. And what is the name of the new waiter?"

"What is your name?" asked Nev.

"Paul."

Suvanov nodded. "Thank you very much. Yes, everything is—"

Nev interrupted. "Ask him to describe the waiter Paul."

"Excuse me, would you describe Paul?" Suvanov repeated the manager's words. "Medium height, stocky, dark hair, moustache. Yes. Yes, everything is fine. We must be careful, though. You know these newspaper people will do anything, and Doctor Vronsky is so tired. Yes. Yes, of course. Thank you."

Nev nodded, and the waiter continued to set the table.

Vronsky watched in fascination, then caught himself and stared down at his fingers in his lap. His heart hammered, and he felt giddy. It was happening. But how could it happen? How could this Paul, alone, possibly get him out of the hotel? One of the conditions set two years ago, when Bentivoglio had visited the Institute, was that there should be no violence. No one should be hurt because of him. Heat from his cigarette reached his fingertips. Vronsky pressed the stub into an ashtray and lit another. His hands shook. He told himself he must gain control. Otherwise they might see and wonder. He visualized his situation as a point in the center of a box and began to imagine what qualities the walls of the box might have in order for the point to pass through them.

A helicopter swinging someone in through the window was too farfetched, Nev thought. And they would be able to hear one coming far in advance. Yes, it was farfetched, but if he heard a helicopter he would move everyone into the corridor and put Vronsky into one of the other suites. No, if he were doing it, he would try outside the hotel. Sometime tomorrow.

Tomorrow was the important day, from the official point of view. It had been decided to keep the remainder of the day on which Vronsky gave his paper low key, while the news of his theory was published. On the next day, once the attention of the world was focused, the minister of science and the ambassador would arrive, and the press meetings, interviews, and official reception would be held. Vronsky would be outside, surrounded by people, moving from place to place.

After he had eaten and disciplined the corridor guards for admitting a new waiter without checking, Nev decided, he would spend several hours with maps and plans, thinking again through every moment of the coming day.

"Gentlemen?" Paul bowed slightly toward the table and uncovered the serving dishes on his rolling tray.

Nev discouraged conversation. Dobrinsky always gave his full attention to eating anyway, and Vronsky seemed especially distracted, so Suvanov also was forced to eat in silence. This security work was less interesting than he had expected, but he believed it would yet prove of value to his career.

After serving, Paul had withdrawn. Vronsky watched him leave with the horror of a castaway seeing sails sweep close by and then away over the horizon again. But even as the door closed, Vronsky understood.

Of course! But what then? Still inside the box.

He realized he was not eating. Had they noticed? He fell to as though starved, but in three mouthfuls felt as though he had swallowed lead.

Outside the hotel, Nev thought. *But not necessarily tomorrow.*

If *he* couldn't get in to Vronsky, he would try to get Vronsky out to him. *A fire.* He had already thought of that, but he would go over the drill again with the outside men as soon as supper was finished.

Knives and forks clicked. Dobrinsky smacked his lips as he ate.

"Water and air and earth are *not* separate elements," Vronsky said suddenly.

The others paused in mid-mastication.

"What is solid at one moment can become a gas and . . ." Vronsky looked around him, flushed, took a mouthful of potato.

After ten minutes Paul returned bringing coffee. He put the pot onto his serving tray and began clearing the supper plates.

"That was really very good," said Suvanov. "The sauce was especially fine."

"Thank you, sir."

Vronsky stared at the ceiling. He could feel perspiration soaking his shirt.

Paul began to place fine china cups before each of the men, white cups with roses and gold trim.

"No, thank you," said Vronsky. His voice was tight and high. He cleared his throat. He smiled nervously at Suvanov. "I'm very tired. I'm afraid it might keep me awake." He cleared his throat again and looked at the smoke as it rose from the point of his cigarette.

"Sir?" Paul poured for Nev. Then for Dobrinsky. Then for Suvanov.

"Excellent coffee," said Suvanov.

Vronsky had to do something. He rose from the table. The three men turned to him questioningly. Vronsky's lips twitched into a momentary smile. He walked over to a couch, sat, stared again at the ceiling.

The waiter worked quietly at his tray, stacking dinner plates and silver slowly and with care.

Suvanov stirred his coffee. It was not too hot, but he liked to hear the ring of good china. "The food here is really very good."

Nev ignored the remark. He was trying to think of a device other than fire.

"Ahhhhh-ah!" Dobrinsky yawned. "Who sleeps first tonight?"

"You can," said Nev.

"Good." Dobrinsky yawned again. He slipped down into the Louis XVI armchair, put his head back, blinked once, and slept.

Suvanov was staring directly ahead. He didn't know exactly what, but something was very strange. First there had been a little bell tinkling far away, and then Dobrinsky's voice had sounded hollow, as though he were speaking from the end of a long tunnel. A tunnel. Yes. That was it. Suvanov was looking down a tunnel. How had he gotten into a tunnel? He didn't understand.

Nev understood. As soon as he felt himself moving while he knew he was sitting still he understood. He was not surprised when Suvanov toppled forward smacking his head on the table.

Nev was already in action. The drug was fast working, so he could not expect to fight. He must contact the men in the corridor before passing out. It was very clear: no fuzziness, no fading. He knew exactly what he was doing. He rose from his chair and started toward the door, which he perceived in its true size and correct location. It would take him only six carefully placed steps to reach it. He was strong and strong willed. He would be able to hold on for those six steps. His head rang, and his dinner was about to come up, but he walked steadily along a precise line toward the door. He would have reached it easily, but on the third step the room tipped sideways and the brilliant red and orange carpet swung up and would have hit him full on the left side of his face had not Paul caught and lowered him gently.

"Quick!" Paul was peeling off his white jacket. "Quick!"

Vronsky sat pinching his cigarette between the thumb and forefinger of his right hand; his left was clasped between his knees. What was he to do? No image came to mind. "Are they all right?"

"Only sleeping. Come here."

Yes! He must get up. Vronsky rose. He would be leaving. He stubbed out his cigarette.

"Come here!"

26

Vronsky crossed to Paul. Without realizing, he stood at attention, a correct little scholar at the teacher's desk.

Paul had thrown the skirts of the white cloth that covered his rolling tray up over serving dishes and plates. He lifted off the entire top of the tray.

Vronsky's mind functioned again. He stood motionless, waiting for instructions. The false tray top made a thin secret compartment. Lying flat on the true top were some straps and a yellow coil.

Paul lifted the straps and turned to Vronsky. "We must be quick. The Czechs are all down to dinner, but one might come back. And the guards outside will expect me to come out soon. Take off your jacket."

Vronsky pulled away his baggy, gray suit coat. Paul stepped behind him, placed the strap affair against Vronsky's back, dropped one strap over each shoulder, came around, and began snapping hooks into rings.

"No!" Vronsky saw it, felt it. He felt himself falling from the window toward the street below, screaming higher than the pitch of audible sound, begging, praying to strike and die and end it, and still eternally falling. "No! I can't do that! I can't!"

Paul was on his knees, hooking straps from between Vronsky's legs to the harness belt. His eyes snapped up to Vronsky's face, incredulous and then furious. He swore violently in Italian. He snapped a hook, sprang up, smacked Vronsky's left shoulder with the flat of a huge hand. "Move! Four, five minutes, that's all we got!"

He smacked again, spinning Vronsky around, snapped the nylon rope to the ring between Vronsky's shoulder blades, grasped the harness there, and half pushed, half lifted Vronsky over to the window.

"Ten minutes for serving coffee, cleaning up. That's what they expect outside. I got about two minutes to get you down."

Two parts of Vronsky's mind tore at one another. Going through the window was the logical, the only possible way out of the room to freedom, to life. He must go out the window. But out the window was sure death. Falling to death. The most horrible death.

Paul pushed open two adjoining windows. Around the post between them he slipped the strap that was already attached at one end to the pulleys hooked to Vronsky's harness.

"Right," he said. "Now out."

Out. Vronsky stared out over the tops of the trees in the park. Just over them. Not high, not really high. He looked down and felt the entire building tip forward. He gasped and pressed his knees against the wall under the windows, leaning back into the room.

Not high! As a child, he could be terrorized by being lifted up onto a table top. *Five floors not high!*

Paul grabbed Vronsky's shoulder and pulled him half around. He clutched Vronsky's trouser leg just above the left knee and jerked the leg up. Only the hand still on his shoulder kept Vronsky upright. Paul released his hold on the trousers and before the leg could fall again, seized Vronsky's ankle and thrust it out over the low windowsill. Then he began forcing Vronsky's torso after the leg.

Vronsky gasped again and again, each intake of breath vocalized, a rising screech in his throat. He tried to flail his arms, to hit Paul, to find a hold.

Paul snapped the line with his left hand, caught it, wound it once around his fist. Vronsky was supposed to climb out the window so the strain would come onto the rope gradually. He was not supposed to be thrown. But he wouldn't go!

In the little part of his mind over which he yet had control, Vronsky understood. He knew he would be safe, that the rope would be strong, that all had been planned for. He shook his head up and down and bowed his whole upper body over and up in a gesture of affirmation to Paul and himself. Yes! It would be all right. He would be safe. He would do it. He swung his own left hand around and clasped Paul's right, which still held his shoulder, pressing the hand to assure it would not be taken from him. Then Vronsky put both palms on the window ledge

28

and turned toward the room as he lifted his right leg over and out. He lay half in, half out across the ledge, then eased himself down backwards. He hung from his armpits full length down the facade of the building. He felt a pull at the back of his neck and realized that Paul was taking strain on the rope. With most of his weight carried by the rope, Vronsky lowered himself to arm's length, his hands still clutching the stone ledge outside the window.

He concentrated on immediate sensation—the texture of the facade before his nose: stucco, chipping off from stone underneath. White islands, an archipelago. What made stucco chip in one place instead of another, he wondered. It was working. Despite a coolness from the breeze on his ankles dangling below his pulled-up trouser legs, Vronsky was comfortable. Yes, the strain of the harness between his legs was an acceptable substitute for pressure against the soles of his feet. He had no feeling of height at all. In another instant, he would release his fingers from the window ledge, calmly.

With a sense of detached amusement, as though coming across in a family album the photograph of an elderly aunt whom one had met once in childhood and been frightened by, Vronsky turned his head to look down at the vertical space that no longer troubled him.

There were only another three minutes, Paul knew, before he would be overdue in leaving with the dinner tray. No one was timing him exactly, of course, but there was a rhythm. He had to lower Vronsky, retrieve the rope, close the window, put on his jacket, pull Nev out of the line of sight from the door—all within about three minutes. That was to deal with the danger inside the hotel. Outside . . . ? They had not spotted any security in the park, and the tree tops screened the upper floors from anyone there, but who could be sure? And any passerby who might look up and see a man hanging from a rope five floors up might naturally make that fact known. It had to be done quickly!

Even the little part of Vronsky's mind that was still rational snuffed out. He stared down in fascinated horror at the street below. The building he lay against seemed to sway and lean. Chill air wafted along the facade and cut through his sweat-soaked shirt. His teeth chattered. The harness no longer lifted him up—gravity drew him down against it. It would break. He would fall at ever increasing speed. Every piece of matter hungered for the energy in every smaller piece. The earth wanted his. It was insatiable, irresistible. Fingers would slip, lines would snap. He would fall, and then—because one's last moment is his eternity—he would fall in horror toward that oblivion yet never be conscious of reaching it.

"Let go!" Paul called, trying both to shout and whisper.

Vronsky never heard. His pudgy fingers were white with strain. Paul let out the rope by inches, putting more of Vronsky's weight onto those fingers, but that only seemed to temper and transmute them into hooks of horn or ivory that would cut into the stone before they would bend.

"Let go! Let go!" In desperate fury, Paul smashed at Vronsky's fingers with his fist.

Vronsky dropped suddenly, but less than a foot before the rope jerked him. Paul's rope hand was snubbed painfully against the pulley and held there. Carefully and deliberately he took the line with his right hand as well, released himself, and began to lower Vronsky.

Looking down, Paul could see the open windows two floors below. He paid out the line quickly until he reached the warning marks taped around it. He felt a sudden, then a steady pull.

White jacket neatly buttoned, sweat wiped away, hair in place, Paul opened the door. One of the guards stood in front, facing him, about to knock. Paul smiled and forced the man to move by pushing the tray into the corridor. He closed the door quickly behind himself before either man could see in.

"Good evening, sir. And sir," Paul said. He rolled the tray down the corridor, smiled and nodded to the guard at the end, and went down in the service elevator.

3

THE LITTLE, yellow car skidded to a stop. Its gears crashed, and the souped-up sewing machine motor that powered it whined as the car reversed. The car stopped again opposite the cottage. A man and woman bounded out. Sunglassed, permpressed: obviously tourists. They went to the low stone wall and looked over.

Maxwell watched from behind a bush diagonally across the lane. He had hidden himself there when he heard the car far behind him. It seemed foolish to hide even from tourists, but Maxwell was always careful. As a small child he had always looked left and right before crossing the street even when being chased by Fat Freddie. That natural inclination to be careful had kept him alive in his profession long enough for the instinct to be developed and toned like the hard muscle over his stomach.

Of course, nobody's perfect. Maxwell reminded himself of that from time to time whenever he began to feel smug about how careful he was. *And letting myself get caught bare-assed in the park by Corchran sure proves the point,* he thought.

Maxwell always tried to have some reserve options, something ready in case he hadn't been careful enough. The something ready in this case had been a carryon bag already packed and stored in the closet of a bed-sitter near Brompton Cemetery. Maxwell had rented the room there for over ten years. He, Mr. Pemberton, the landlord, and the gray, flowered wallpaper had passed into late middle age together. Maxwell had tried to sleep in the room at least one night every time he was in London—four times a year, on average. Sleeping there reestablished a nominal need for the room or made a gesture at doing so. If Mr. Pemberton wondered why an American machinery company kept a room for such occasional use by its European representative instead of having him book into an inexpensive hotel, Mr. Pemberton kept his curiosity in check. There certainly was nothing curious about the American himself: bluff, open, a ready smile. They always had a good chat together about football, and—if the American accepted Mr. Pemberton's invitation for a glass of ale—about politics. Maxwell was quite knowledgeable about English football, and if he did not discuss as much as listen to Mr. Pemberton's hope for a return to the policies of Good Queen Anne, he was nonetheless interested. Maxwell had few friends; by compensation, everyone he met was an acquaintance whose ideas he sincerely enjoyed hearing. Maxwell always looked forward to seeing Mr. Pemberton, as he did the owners of the very similar rooms he kept in Frankfurt, Berlin, and Vienna.

The carryon bags were similar, too: neither very old nor new, each containing two changes of underwear and one of outer. In the thin compartment under the handle, each bag had two passports with pictures of Maxwell but different names, and a book of twenty hundred-dollar traveler's checks for each name. Everything was renewed from time to time.

If any of his colleagues or superiors had found out about those rooms and bags, Maxwell would have been in trouble. On the other hand, he would not have been in his *current* trouble. He would have been pulled back and reassigned or dismissed, because he would have been unable to give a satisfactory reason for what obviously were bolt holes and wherewithals for escape. Since his superiors provided those as Maxwell needed them in his official duties, the inescapable conclusion would have been that he was planning or doing something unofficial.

But he hadn't been planning. Until he discovered his illness, Maxwell had never planned anything in the sense of establishing some long-range goal and working out a series of steps to reach it. There was a story he liked: One Pilgrim says to another, "Why dost thou carry thy musket to Meeting? Dost thou not believe in predestination? Thou canst not save thyself when thy time is come." "Yea, Brother," answers the other Pilgrim, "but it may be that on my way I will be attacked by an Indian, and *his* time will have come." Maxwell had survived for thirty-eight years in a hazardous occupation, without ulcers or nervous breakdown or drinking too much, because he had never really thought about being caught or dying. Much less had he speculated on any ultimate end. He thought only about not being caught, about staying alive from day to day. He was, perhaps, like the desperate poor, so busy subsisting as to have no time to consider whether life is worth living. Pressures built, of course. Fear had been with him continually for so long that he no longer was aware of it. The rooms, suitcases, passports, and money had been acquired, not out of any recognized fear, but because Maxwell came to feel that he wanted a reserve, a private resource. Of course, when he came to consider selling (he didn't say to himself *selling out*), having that resource contributed to his decision.

When he got off the bus, Maxwell cut south from Kensington Road, then through backstreets to the Knightsbridge underground station. He took the underground to Earls Court and walked to his secret room.

He checked the contents of his suitcase and took out the soft cap and horn-rim glasses. He turned his raincoat inside-out to the brown plaid side. He picked up the bag, locked the room, and went downstairs and out of the house forever. He had paid for a year in advance. Mr. Pemberton would not care whether the room was used before November, and by then Maxwell would be dead.

It was nearly five o'clock, just over an hour since he had run from Kensington Garden. They would have the air and hovercraft ports covered by now. And the ferries to Ireland. Maxwell imagined Corchran back at the branch office; no one would say anything to him yet about having lost Maxwell. All of them would be standing, looking at the map of England, checking ways out of the country, guessing what Maxwell would do.

Maxwell knew that England is a fine country to escape into. It has a free society: no identity cards, no showing of passports or filling-out of a fiche before checking into a hotel. As long as he has money and is willing to move from place to place—in a leisurely way, like a tourist—an American can probably hide there for years and be safe from discovery by anything short of a picture-on-the-front-page manhunt. But Maxwell didn't want to die in England. That gave him his problem: how to escape from an island.

From Earls Court he took a cab to Paddington Station. He didn't believe they'd have the rail stations covered—special police and all; not like the embarkation points where there was already a screening process. Still, at another time of day he would have found another way from the city. By the time he reached Paddington, though, the evening commuter rush was under way.

He had to wait forty-five minutes for a train to Bristol. He bought a copy of *The Guardian* (he thought it went with his glasses) to read in the station and a new book on the Thirty Years' War for the train. He went to the station bar and ate a sandwich made of two slices of pasty bread and a transparent shaving of roast beef. The sandwich did double service by fortifying him and by removing any incipient appetite. He allowed himself only a half pint of bitter. He read his paper as best he could in the press of those drinking the ritual pint of passage between the cares of the business world and semidetached suburban bliss. Maxwell always felt a curious mixture of contempt and envy for such lives.

There was no sign of police activity. Maxwell boarded the train. The car was of the older type, with compartments. He sat next to the aisle, away from the window. Once past the suburbs and exurbs, he was alone in the compartment. He knew he was safe for the forseeable future. He took off his raincoat and glasses, loosened his tie. As the train rolled along he did fifty pushups in the narrow aisle. If he had not been alone, Maxwell could have used a less active method to dissipate the flood of nervous energy released after stress.

It was late evening when the train reached Bristol, but Maxwell had no difficulty in getting a room in a hotel near the station. Its Grille Room took orders until midnight, so he washed quickly, changed his shirt, and went down.

A cellar restaurant, cozy with candles, red tablecloths, exposed brick. Maxwell felt warm and secure seated in a corner, his back against a cushion on the wall. He felt good. He decided to order a steak, then thought of Corchran. "Tournedos Rossini," he said, looking at the menu again, "and could I see the wine list, please?"

Maxwell knew a little about wine. Not as much as Corchran, perhaps, but something. He ordered a Chambertin. It was the second most expensive wine on the card, but he thought *what the hell*. In fact, the more he thought about it, the better it seemed. It had started. *Today is the first day of the rest of your life, as they say*, he thought. He hadn't planned to start the rest of his life until he'd got where he was going, but . . . why not? He swirled the wine in the long-stemmed, large-belled glass the restaurant management provided to assure customers who bought the more expensive wines that they had indeed received something of value.

The tournedos were not really as good as a prime rump steak from Scottish beef might have been, but the wine was excellent. Maxwell looked through the glass, and the candle at his table became a ruby from the Arabian Nights, burning with magic fire in the center of the liquid.

At the end of the room a party of four men batted witticisms back and forth as though they were playing handball and roared inaudibly with laughter as well-bred Englishmen can do. Maxwell enjoyed their companionship. Two tables away a young couple leaned on their elbows toward each other, speaking very earnestly and smiling little smiles. Maxwell looked at the couple with his own smile. He liked lovers. He had never married. Wife, home, children: he thought of them occasionally in the way a happily married banker might think about being a secret agent. The young woman caught Maxwell's stare, spoke to her young man, and both of them looked at him. Unembarrassed, Maxwell broadened his smile, and raised his glass slightly in a toast. His intention was so obviously benevolent that they accepted the intimacy and nodded back.

Maxwell let himself get just a little drunk. *I'll have a good bottle of wine,* he thought. It would be evening, and he would eat slowly, and drink a really good red wine. *That'll be part of it. The last of the wine.*

He had a headache the next morning; not a hangover, really, but a dull headache for a few hours. It passed with fresh air coming through the open windows of the car he'd rented from the Godfrey Davis Agency at the station.

He drove through Somerset and into the long, green hills of Dorset. He thought of Thomas Hardy—with distaste. Maxwell was not a reader of literature, although he read a great deal. Much of his life had been spent simply waiting, and customarily he had a paperback in one of his pockets; non-fiction, usually. Once, though, for want of anything more interesting among the offerings at an air terminal, he had bought *The Mayor of Casterbridge.* He had read it through to the end, growing steadily more irritated at the deepening gloom, hoping at first for some change, finishing only to be done with it. Not that Maxwell expected happy endings, but he saw no point in anybody's writing—or reading—a story that was totally and merely depressing.

So, when he reached Dorchester, he simply left the car in a public parking area, where it would collect tickets for a day or two before anyone bothered about it, and sat on a bench reading instead of sightseeing. He was lucky: he had only two hours until a train came through on its way toward Bourne-mouth. Maxwell got off at the village of Wool.

He was sure he had left a cold trail. He would have at least two days, probably longer. They would not have been able to trace him to Bristol, although they might pick him up again there (despite his minimal disguise) if they checked every car hire agency in England. But they would lose him again until the car was found. And then again, unless the ticket seller remembered. And then again at Wool, because he had walked from there. That four-mile walk was probably ridiculously unnecessary, like hiding behind bushes from the two or three cars that passed him, but Maxwell was very careful.

The tourist couple had gotten cameras from their car—an Instamatic for her and a Canon with many lenses for him—and they photographed the cottage in a variety of poses. It was remarkably photogenic, of course: the heavy, thatched roof scalloped over diamond-paned windows; whitewashed walls barely visible behind the flowers; and the flowers. *The platonic flower-covered cottage*, Maxwell thought.

A great wisteria vine draped with lavender blossoms clutched an entire corner of the house. It was like seeing the fingers and forearm of a tough old woman through a lacy sleeve. The other corner was claimed by another vine with a similar flower but yellow. It looked just as determined. Maxwell was reminded of his two grandmothers, and he wondered what would happen when the vines reached each other over the doorway. Whatever, he was sure the roses trellised on either side there would not count. Obviously, they had no inner strength, however youthfully pink they might be; they had to be supported from the base of the house and led around the lower windows.

The tourists should have come later in the summer, of course, when the flower beds would have had real color and variety. In keeping with off-season rates there were only yellow daffodils, blue and pink hyacinths, and crimson tulips—all in proper clumps—and a rabble of miscegenated pansies helter-skeltering between. Not realizing the delights of delphiniums and dahlias, the glories of gladioli they were missing, the couple recorded everything they did see in three f-stops and two depths-of-field. Then they went on down the lane, like Cromwell, to capture Corfe Castle.

Maxwell crossed the road and paused at the gate in the clematis-covered wall. He smiled to himself. It really was as pretty as a picture from an old book of fairy tales. One hoped to find in the garden a plump gray-haired woman with apple cheeks and sparkling but very shrewd eyes. As Maxwell expected, when he went in through the gate, he found James Newlands.

James was lean, but he did have steel-colored hair and flushed cheeks, and his eyes did sparkle, because they were pale and watered easily.

"I have coddled these hyacinths," he said. "I have kept them under cover all winter. And now when they are asked to stand up for themselves through a chilly night or two, they wilt."

James was on his knees, just to one side of the door. He prodded with a small trowel at the ground around the stalks of the offending plants.

He really is top of the line, Maxwell thought. *Haven't seen him for two years, just appear in his garden. No reaction, not a flicker.*

"Tell them England expects them to do their duty," he said.

Although Maxwell knew how it was done, he admired James's technique. Most people would try to cover themselves by talking about the weather.

"That doesn't seem effective anymore," James said. "It's this music they hear all the time. I play Elgar and Vaughan Williams for them, of course, but the Rolling Stones go up and down the lane at all hours. I blame myself mostly, though. I didn't want them to suffer the cold as I suffered when young; but my headmaster was right: it was cold showers made England great."

James poked the trowel down into the ground and stiffened his left arm as a crutch while he rocked back onto his haunches and then got to his feet. He paused for a moment, still on three points.

A septuagenarian left tackle, Maxwell thought.

James straightened slowly and stood still for an instant while his head cleared. He pulled off one worn driving glove and offered his thin hand to Maxwell. "Good to see you, Charles. I'm so pleased you've come. And that you can stay for a while this time."

He said the last without having seemed to notice Maxwell's suitcase.

"Only overnight, James. If I may."

"Of course you may. Longer, I would have hoped. You're sure?"

"I'm sure."

"Then we'd better get to visiting."

James unbuttoned the bottom of his baggy cardigan sweater and extracted a thin gold watch from the pocket of his baggy tweed trousers. "Time for tea, I think."

James meant high tea, with which he served beer. They sat at one corner of a Jacobean walnut table. Never a piece of fine furniture, made for the kitchen where it stood, it nevertheless carried the grandeur of that age on thick, turned legs, dominating the whitewashed, stone-floored room. They ate Irish ham and Welsh cheese and coarse bread and pickled onions.

"You're looking very well, James."

"Thank you. Fresh air, wholesome food, clean living. You know, the sorts of things a man my age is reduced to. You're not, Charles. You've lost weight. Drawn about the mouth and eyes."

"I haven't been well."

"Sorry."

"I'm getting over it."

"Good. Busy as ever, I suppose?"

"Always. I expect to take a vacation soon, though."

Instantly, Maxwell was annoyed with himself. No harm done, but saying that wasn't necessary. But he felt he wanted to say something true in response to James's true concern. James Newlands was one of the few people—certainly the only person in the past twenty years—with whom Maxwell had ever been open. Maxwell valued that.

"How are *you* getting on?" Maxwell asked.

"Well. Quite well. I remain content with my circumstances and myself."

"You holding out against inflation?"

"My pension is beleaguered, but the cottage has proved a gold mine. I've sold sixteen watercolors and two oils already this year, and the bulk of your countrymen won't arrive for another three months. The postcards do well—price and my royalty rise with inflation. Best of all, British Air has paid me a tidy sum to permit Mr. Robert Morley to have his picture taken in the company of my hollyhocks. And I receive a small honorarium from time to time from the old firm for consultations."

Maxwell raised his eyes to register nothing more than genuine but mild curiosity, though he felt like he had been touched by a live wire. "I didn't think you were still in the trade."

"Only now and again."

"I wouldn't think they'd keep you up on the plays."

"Oh, they don't. Thank the Lord. I don't want to know anything. It's always very hypothetical. The adventures of Mr. A and Mr. B. Rather the sort of thing some of those communications specialist fellows do. You know, make interesting conjectures on the basis of who is talking to whom, without ever knowing who either of them are or what they are saying. You know my knack for brainteasers."

"Yeah. And your real name is Sherlock Holmes."

"I have a good one for you, Charles. Four spies in a railway carriage—"

"I've seen it."

"No you haven't. Not this one, because I made it up just

Wednesday last. There are four spies facing each other in pairs in a compartment in the Orient Express."

"The Orient Express doesn't run anymore. It's just a tourist train now."

"*My* Orient Express will run forever. Now pay attention. One of the spies has the secret documents on microfilm. Now, the German has a handlebar moustache. The Chinese is sitting across from the man with the wooden leg. The Englishman is to the German's left. His cover is being a football player. The man with stainless steel teeth is Russian. The Chinese is dressed in gray. At the Bulgarian border the train is stopped by the authorities, and all of the men are searched. But the microfilm is not found! Who has it?"

"There's not enough information."

"Yes there is."

"You haven't told me anything that relates to hiding the film."

"Yes I have."

"Well, you'll have to tell me more."

"Charles, you will never be successful in this business unless you develop your ability to reason logically."

Maxwell laughed. It was a joke because James said it with fogyish pomposity and because Maxwell *was* successful. But it wasn't a good joke, not a joke completely, and James knew that. Maxwell was a successful field agent, renowned for tactical ingenuity, though he seldom knew what strategy his tactics served. Sometimes he was called into the large offices with glass-topped desks and maps under shades, into the conference rooms where men wrote on single sheets of paper—never pads—if they took notes at all; and he gave information or received instructions. He was never invited when (as he imagined it) they drank black coffee, and looked over papers in red binders and decided what it all meant and what should be done about it. Maxwell didn't mind not being invited. He knew what he was good at and what he wasn't. He accepted that the men behind the desks should have higher salaries and greater prestige. What he didn't accept was the implication that he shouldn't feel successful.

"James, I *am* successful. But that's not the way I work."

"Work any way you like, but tell me who has the microfilm."

"I don't know!"

"I have means of persuasion at my disposal," James said, narrowing his eyes cruelly. He leaned back in his chair, raised his head, and sang, "There was a jolly miller who lived on the river Dee." He sang the words with great force to a seemingly random selection of pitches.

Maxwell clamped his hands over his ears. "I give up! I give up! Not that, James!"

James allowed himself a small smile of self-congratulation. "Very well, Charles. Are you ready to tell me?"

"I would if I could, James. But I'm no good at those things."

"I mean why you've come here."

It was done very well, James thought. He'd caught Maxwell inhaling and so could see the momentary freeze of breathing and the infinitesimal widening of eyes. James hadn't planned to do it that way, but he knew the moment would come sooner or later and was prepared when it arrived. Of course, Maxwell would tell him eventually; tell him something. James did not always believe what people told him, especially when they did the telling on their own terms. Not even Charles Maxwell, whom he knew as a sincere and decent young man. James did not consider himself cynical for holding that view. One simply must use one's understanding of the world to best advantage.

It was enough of a jolt, James thought, to put Maxwell on notice, so he went on to ease the moment.

"No car. Dusty shoes and trouser bottoms. Longish walk from the village—or somewhere. Not just for exercise. Not just to pass the time. And you can stay only the one night. He squinted his right eye and tapped his temple with his forefinger. " 'aven't been on the force for three-hundred-'n-fifteen years for nothin', m'lad. You'd best come out with it."

"I want to go to France."

Maxwell was relieved. Now he didn't have to think how to get around to it. But he would have to be careful. James would probably be able to tell if he lied. "I want you to take me to France in your boat. You still have your boat?"

"Why? Why in my boat?"

"That ought to be simple for you, James. I don't want anybody to see me going."

"I did grasp that fairly readily, Charles. It was the point of my question."

James sat very still against the carved slat back chair. His left forearm was on the table, his right hand lay open on his crossed knees. He seemed totally relaxed. His eyes were neutral, but they never left Maxwell's.

He will be able to tell if I lie, Maxwell thought. And he felt strongly that he didn't want to lie to James. They had never lied to each other, not even in small ways for politeness. "James, if I told you, you'd know."

Outside, in the oak, a bird to whom Maxwell had not been introduced sang the same six notes over and over as though they were the distillation of all music.

Finally James nodded slightly. "Obviously it is important that you do it this way. Will tomorrow morning be soon enough?"

"Tomorrow will be fine."

They cleared the tea dishes and then went back outside and looked at the garden. James told Maxwell in detail about each of the plants.

"This is King Alfred. One of the older varieties. Large, bold, true yellow. Exactly what a narcissus should be."

"I thought they were daffodils."

"Only to the culturally deprived, like yourself, who do not have their Latin. As I was saying, King Alfred is an exemplary narcissus. Would you believe that some of the Irish—those *hybridizers*—are developing pink narcissus? Pink! Proves we never should have permitted the Free State."

"Yeah. Without a strong foot on their necks those Irish are capable of anything."

"The Dutch are now recommending the use of sewage sludge instead of bonemeal under the bulbs. I may experiment with some when I divide in the fall. I think I shall put some of the Alfreds with Lord Nelson, which should be good company for both of them."

Maxwell did not pretend to be interested. James liked talking about his flowers, and Maxwell liked looking at them. Maxwell simply stood, or trailed James from one group to another, smiling slightly, letting the colors flood his eyes, wash through him, carry off every thought, every other sensation. Maxwell had always considered flowers pleasant to look at, of course, but seldom had he really looked at them. In that evening, with a rose sky deepening to violet twilight, it seemed to him that he was looking truly for the first time. He saw the color not as bright paint on objects, but realized it as emanating from living things. He marveled that a soft and fragile petal could have within it a force of life so intense that it glowed with those colors. He seemed to share that life. Although he did not detach himself from the sensation in order to think about it in connection with his own coming death, feeling such vivid life satisfied his need. When he did think about it later, the justification for all his acts seemed confirmed.

James and Maxwell sat outside until after nine, despite the chill, because it was light so late into the evening. Then they went back into the house and supped on omelets and bacon. They looked at James's paintings of the house and garden and agreed that the paintings were terrible but faithful, and that anyone who liked that sort of thing would like these very much. Finally, they sat in a room with windows under the wisteria, a room lined with books. It was James's library and parlor and studio and anything else except kitchen and bedroom.

"Roddy Lovecraft died a fortnight ago. Had you heard? Cerebral hemorrhage . . ."

". . . Vaclav Pojarsky is a grandfather again. I think that makes sixteen or . . ."

". . . ah, yes, sitting for hours at the Cafe Mozart. Ersatz coffee and that wonderful zither."

"Vienna wasn't like that at all, James."

"Of course it was. I see *The Third Man* on the telly every year or so, and I say to myself, That's just how it was. I remember . . ."

"England may do OK up through the semifinals, but the DDR team is going to cut your heads off at the ankles. I hear they . . ."

". . . it will be the French Revolution all over again. First they will guillotine the old regime, then 'sympathizers' and anyone who did not exercise revolutionary principles in choosing his grandfather, then each other."

"I don't know what the hell's going on down there, James, but I think we're at it again buying fancy harness for an old nag who won't make it to the third turn. But it's not my area and . . ."

"As an old person, I take my privilege of harking back. It was different. It was better. You were there at the end of it, Charles. You were very young, but you know what I mean."

"I don't think I ever felt about it the way you do, James."

"You must have. You are an intelligent and sensitive man, Charles, despite your poses. I remember when you were a young lad, first attached to work with us, in '44. We all worked hard, but we were tired. But you drove yourself. I remember Commander Holstone confronting you one day with the fact you were sleeping in the back pantry so you could work with the 'dawn patrol,' too. He didn't rebuke you for it, but you blushed scarlet."

"I don't blush much anymore."

"I dare say. The point remains: we had an *enemy* then. Thank God for the Nazis. That's a terrible thing to say. But they were totally, definitively evil. They provided for all time a positive answer to the question, Can there be a just war? And the Russians, too, back then. Stalin was just as bad as Hitler. Perhaps worse. Oh, we may have done some nasty things ourselves. Dresden. And smaller things that you and I know

45

about. But our hearts were pure. No, I mean that seriously. There were acts we knew were wrong. We didn't do them except in extremity, and we carried guilt with us ever afterward. We fought for a cause, a set of values laid down by all of the greatest moral teachers of history. That's not true now, is it?"

"I don't know, James. Probably not. I never thought about it that way. I guess I'm just for mom and apple pie and the American way. I mean, my mom and her pie. It's always been just us versus them, and I'm for us."

"How do you tell us from them nowadays?"

"See who likes apple pie. Well, come on, James, what else is there? The more you tell me we're all the same, the more the only thing that matters is which side you were born on."

"That's a curious principle for you to base your loyalty on, Charles. You seldom go back to America, do you? I think the last time you did you told me everything had changed, that you couldn't find your boyhood home anymore. I shouldn't think the place you'd been born would mean that much to you."

Suddenly the subject had turned again to Maxwell himself. He rested his head against one corner of the wing-chair where he sat beside the dark fireplace and said nothing. James couldn't *know* about him. Maxwell wondered if he suspected, or if he were simply pursuing a concept to its logical conclusion. *Probably both*, he thought. James had built a career on spinning out threads of abstract speculation and making them into webs. Maxwell had known it would be this way with James. It was a chance he had to take.

James sat in the other wing-chair, his hands clasped, and regarded Maxwell. He had merely been discussing an idea, but he was aware of striking home. First Maxwell's desire for a secret departure, now . . . He felt two emotions, a combination he found increasingly and depressingly familiar: exhilaration at having sniffed out and followed a trail, and dismay at what he expected to find when he reached its end.

Both men knew how to wait. They sat, quiet in the dim

room. Only one light had been turned on, a small lamp made from a ship's decanter. It had a parchment shade, and the brown glow soaked into leather bindings of the books like oil. Encyclopedias—several sets, atlases, dictionaries in a dozen languages, great books—Plato, Cicero, Plutarch, Shakespeare, Goethe, and their fellows—heavy on the thick oaken shelves around three sides of the room. In contrast with the serious-mindedness of those walls, though, the fourth was scatter-brained with short strokes of color. James adored mysteries. He would not dignify his vice by buying hardback books, nor try to hide it, but acknowledged it in the garish spines of paperbacks.

A clock behind Maxwell chimed softly. James allowed himself to yawn. "Bedtime, I should think. We shall be wanting to make an early start in the morning."

"Right."

Maxwell leaned forward, about to rise, but stopped as he saw James still looking at him.

"Not to pry, Charles, but I did wonder how far you were going."

Maxwell met the old man's eyes steadily. They were very pale, and the flesh around them was soft and sunken, so they never had seemed shrewd. Maxwell still felt embarrassment when he remembered how long it had taken him as a young man to realize the truth.

"I'm not going too far, James."

"Good. I should feel rather badly to think I were speeding you on your way to one of those awful places where the women have hairy armpits."

"I wouldn't like a place like that. That's not where I'm going."

Maxwell slept badly. He went off to sleep at once; he was very tired. But he woke again after an hour or two and immediately felt waves of guilt go through his stomach like nausea.

I didn't lie to him, he told himself. *Not one thing. Everything he asked I answered truthfully. I did not lie to him.*

Maxwell tried to think about where he was going. He tried to think about sex. He tried thinking about which spy had the microfilm. But what he thought about was James taking him around to the pubs and to the parties behind blackout curtains, and being totally charming as he pointed out when Maxwell had made a fool of himself, and how he could avoid doing it in the future. And Maxwell thought how James, who liked to read and think about those heavy books, unaccountably liked him. Finally, as he began to be able to see the crisscross leading of his window against the lightening sky, Maxwell got himself under control. He had not told the whole truth, but he had not flatly lied, either. It was a compromise, but it was the best he could do. He had to do it. He hadn't had much of a life, so he had a right to the last six months and a good death. He wouldn't do *anything*, but he had a right to a few compromises. It was the line he had developed when he had found out about himself a year before. He had gotten it well organized while working with Boris. Now it flowed smoothly and lulled him back to sleep for an hour, until he heard James moving in the next room.

James cooked scrambled eggs and smoked fish for breakfast and ate them with apparent gusto. Maxwell imagined that the gusto was one of the burdens of being a British gentleman. He ate his own fish quickly because he knew he would need the nourishment.

They got into James's venerable Humber (which always made Maxwell think of the dowager Queen Mary), and drove out of the driveway. White fog covered the earth up to the tree tops, but the sky was pale blue above, and a few rays of the most tentative yellow sunlight were venturing to touch the flowers. James paused, and they looked back at the cottage.

"It's a beautiful place, James."

"Yes. I wish you would stay longer, Charles."

"I'd be tempted, but . . . I can't really see myself potting begonias. But thanks."

They drove down to Lulworth Cove, where James kept his boat. It was a sloop, and James sailed whenever the weather was good and he was tired of his flowers and he could get a local boy to crew for him. For this trip they would leave the sails stowed below and use the auxiliary engine.

It was an early workday; few people were about the harbor. The fog was lifting but still hung over the water, giving only a quarter-mile visibility. Despite the morning stillness, the engine made little noise, and Maxwell slipped away from England unnoticed.

The men spoke to each other very little throughout the day. As the fog persisted, James concentrated on his compass, and Maxwell stretched out in the cockpit and dozed.

Maxwell did not want to speak. Guilt made his insides burn, as all stress had begun to do. Even at the end of the long day, at the Norman fishing village, they talked tersely of practicalities and simply shook hands. Maxwell knew that he had betrayed James and that James would find out.

Maxwell turned and went away.

4

VRONSKY FELL. He never knew how far, since by that moment his fear had driven out all sensation. In fact, he did not fall so much as crumble.

Nella and Bentivoglio had swung him in through the open window. It was harder than they had anticipated, because Vronsky didn't help at all. He could neither clutch at them nor at the window to pull himself through it. They had to hold him erect to pull slack on the rope and detach it, and as soon as their support was gone, Vronsky collapsed. He had not fainted. His eyes were open. He sat half upright, leaning partly against the wall under the window and partly against Bentivoglio's leg, but he had no awareness.

"Constantin! Constantin!" Bentivoglio leaned over, tapping Vronsky's cheek with the flat of his fingers.

Nella dropped to her knees, put her hands on Vronsky's shoulders and shook him.

"Is he dead?" Bentivoglio's voice was thin. He was again an old man with prostate trouble, not the Scarlet Pimpernel.

"No. No, he is breathing."

Nella rose quickly, went to her case, which was open and ready on the table, and brought back a bottle. She held it open under Vronsky's nose.

"Ammonia?"

"Solvent."

Vronsky coughed. He blinked, coughed again, looked

around him. "Where am I?" Since he spoke in Russian, he did not get a reply.

"Merciful Jesus, thank you, thank you!" Bentivoglio had been an atheist for forty-seven years, but at times of stress only the old words seemed adequate.

Vronsky answered his own question. As he began to see again he perceived that he was in a room identically organized to the one he had left. Another room in his hotel. As he remembered how he got there, he shuddered, and his mind almost shut again.

"Constantin, are you all right?"

Vronsky recognized Bentivoglio's voice coming from above him but did not look up. He looked straight ahead at the woman kneeling in front of him and saw a face of exquisite beauty. That impression was one of the rare ones that he didn't try to consider objectively. Such a consideration might have conceded that she had striking eyes: large, brown, skillfully made up. But they were striking also because the lower part of her face was narrow, with a small mouth and a slightly receding chin. The disproportion was actually greater than it seemed, since her forehead was high and broad. She hid it with dark hair waved at either temple and cut in bangs. Altogether, a pretty face but hardly beautiful.

Vronsky stared into her eyes and felt his heart ache with wanting to relieve the anxiety and pain he saw there. It really did not occur to him that she was concerned about *him*. "It will be all right," he said. He did not know what he was talking about, and because he still spoke Russian, neither did Bentivoglio or Nella. But Nella grasped something of Vronsky's intent and smiled. She did have a lovely smile, too. Again, it was more a matter of what happened with her eyes than her mouth, but the effect was delightful.

Vronsky was so delighted that he repeated himself, and Nella smiled more broadly, and the circle of cause and effect might have continued indefinitely, except that Bentivoglio interrupted it.

"Are you all right? Are you injured?"

Vronsky answered automatically in Italian. "No, I'm fine, thank you." Then, for an instant, he felt as though his lungs had frozen, partly as he remembered hanging outside the window, more from shame. "I'm sorry. I am so stupid . . . I have acrophobia."

Naming it helped. His weakness had a name, a medical name, in Greek. Perhaps it was like being blind or deaf: something for which he was not *responsible*.

"Constantin! Forgive me! I did not know!"

Bentivoglio was desolate, and Nella's eyes widened with horror as she understood Vronsky's experience by imagining herself locked in a room full of spiders.

"It doesn't matter," Vronsky tried to obliterate the thought for all of them, "it's over."

"Ah! Yes! We must hurry." Bentivoglio helped Vronsky to stand. With Nella's help, he unfastened the harness. "We must get you out of here. Before anyone discovers you are not in your room. We must disguise you. Quickly, take off your clothes."

The pictures in Vronsky's mind blanked out. He stood dumbly.

"You must change your clothes!"

Vronsky flushed. His eyes darted toward Nella, then back to Bentivoglio.

Bentivoglio threw up his hands. "Constantin . . . ! Holy Mother of God! This is no time. . . ! Signorina Galucci is a professional person. She is an artist! She works in the cinema! She is accustomed to seeing men . . . *You must change your clothes!*"

It was the final blow, and Vronsky's emotional being surrendered. They had thrown him out of a window; now they were stripping him naked (only to his underwear, in fact, but the principle was established); they could do what they wanted with him. It was necessary to his freedom. His rational mind accepted it, and though he blushed from his knees and elbows to his hairline, he took off his clothes and let them lead him to a chair by the table.

Nella wiped his face with a cool, wet cloth and began smearing cosmetics over him. She worked with sponges and little brushes. Vronsky kept his eyes closed through much of the process. At one point, when Nella had not touched him for some time, Vronsky looked again and saw her studying a photograph propped up on the table beside her case. The details were blurred, but he could see it was the portrait of a man, rather plump in the face. Vronsky comprehended at once that he was being made up to look like the man in the photograph. The face seemed so different from his own that he found it difficult to believe the exercise could be successful.

"Do you recognize him, Constantin?"

"No. Who is it?"

"It's you!"

Vronsky leaned forward and stared at the photograph.

"It's a copy of the photo I took of you two years ago. Nella has transformed it."

Vronsky held his glasses in front of him. The face in the picture was middle-aged, florid. There was a mop of curly black hair streaked heavily with gray, and a bushy moustache over heavy lips. Vronsky could see that the photograph had been retouched, with shadows and highlights painted over the contours of his own features to deepen and exaggerate them. He looked up at Nella in wonder.

She shrugged. "It is an easy makeup. A real change, for the close-up camera—that would take hours to do. Please." She took Vronsky's glasses from him again.

Vronsky leaned back in his chair and gave himself to the swift strokes of Nella's fingers. This was the way one becomes free, then: by becoming a new person. Yes. Freedom must be the ability to change oneself whenever, however one chooses; whenever the old self is a prison uniform. But can one truly be so transformed? Can one pull on a new hairstyle over one's ears and then no longer put on the left shoe before the right, change one's taste from honey to jam on morning toast, and cease to be the man who, as a puny boy, was bullied? Exhausted from tension and soothed by Nella's caresses, Vronsky let his mind drift with these contradictory currents. It was a dream, anyway, he thought, all a dream: the chair would turn into a laundry basket floating him down a river of stars inside an oak tree. Finally Vronsky gave up any attempt at thinking. He let himself be made up, dressed, and led from the room.

He was incorporeal. The body in which he moved was not his own. It was not merely chubby, it was fat. The silk suit he wore (unlike the baggy wool ones he owned) fit that body snugly, yet never touched him. His face was changed—not only to those who saw it but inside. Nella had put some sort of dental plastic inside his lips and cheeks. The world looked much the same, yet slightly different, too. Glasses made to the prescription Vronsky had sent hidden in a page of computations were correct for his vision, but their shape framed the world strangely.

It was all a dream, the ultimate dream: full of suspense and hope, not only terrifying but erotic. Nella's arm linked through Vronsky's. Her hip touched his. Sometimes her breast brushed against his elbow. All along his side—even where they did not touch, even through the padding—he could feel her warmth. He could smell her wildflower perfume like a tantalizing veil over half-hidden muskiness. Vronsky dared to press the woman's arm with his own, and felt them drop together through a humming, flashing, isolated corner of the universe.

When the elevator door opened, Kusnich stared Vronsky up and down. Unconscious of any incongruity, Kusnich sat hulking in a pink-flowered armchair just beside the entrance to the dining room. He was no more than five meters on a diagonal from the elevator, positioned so that he could watch both it and the entrance to the hotel. Grabov sat across the lobby from the elevator, by the front entrance. Neither of the guards even pretended to read a newspaper. They sat with their feet under them, never crossed, so that they could spring up. Sometimes they placed their palms along the tops of their heavy thighs, sometimes they rested their elbows on the chair arms and clasped thick fingers across their stomachs. Other than that, they seemed never to move except to swivel their heads as they watched every person who entered or crossed the lobby.

Vronsky was vaguely aware of other people: a clerk behind the desk on his left, two or three guests; but he focused only on those two watchers. Like carved stone temple dogs, they would see him, spring to life, and tear him to pieces if he tried to pass.

With a pressure of her arm, Nella urged Vronsky forward. They stepped from the elevator onto the long carpeted pathway that ran to the door so far away. The sides of the carpet seemed to converge, like railway tracks disappearing on the horizon. Vronsky fixed his eyes on the doorway and tried to march toward it steadily. He knew Kusnich's eyes followed him, his head rotating slowly. Vronsky felt perspiration running down his forehead. Panic began to seize him. What if the makeup ran? He pictured himself under the heat of Kusnich's stare, his false face beginning to melt, streaming away, dissolving. Vronsky struggled to control himself. The makeup was good. The door was only ten or twelve meters away. He had only to focus on it, to be determined. He tried to ignore the eyes of Kusnich and Grabov. Only a few steps more. It would be all right. But they were staring directly at him! Their pig eyes were fixed, they would see! His breath came shorter. Only such a few more steps. But any second they would see and jump up! If only he and Nella could walk those few more steps more quickly!

Nella dropped her purse.

"Don't pick it up," she squealed.

She went to the floor herself, dropping onto her left knee. Her tight skirt rode up, and as she twisted to grab the purse and then get her balance for rising again, both Kusnich and Grabov were treated to a panoramic view of her inner thigh.

"Now help me up and speak to me. They don't understand Italian. Say anything!"

"Are you all right?" Vronsky was not skilled at improvisation.

"I'm fine. Say more. Say the alphabet!"

Vronsky was able to do at least a little better. "Monday, Tuesday, Wednesday . . . Good morning, good evening. Is this all right? I can't think of anything . . ."

"Never mind. It's fine." Nella laughed gaily and took Vronsky's arm again, pulling him toward the door.

Vronsky finally caught the spirit. He giggled. He turned back toward Kusnich and called out, "Good night, Hogface." He laughed aloud. "Good night, you retarded gorilla, you imbecilic orangutan."

Vronsky's Italian words were meaningless to Kusnich and Grabov, but his calling out was strange. Anything strange was suspect. Their eyes tracked away from Nella's neat bottom and up to Vronsky's face.

Nella's hand was on the bar of the glass door.

Vronsky could smell cold air outside, the smell of freedom. "Goodbye, you hind ends of rhinoceroses!"

Grabov put his hands on the arms of his chair.

Vronsky breathed the free air. It was intoxicating, hallucinogenic. Vronsky felt his chest swell and his heart grow huge within it. He was a balloon filled with laughing gas, rising clear of the earth, soaring. He waved back down to Grabov and Kusnich and shouted, "Goodbye forever, you brontosaurus-brained—"

Nella clutched Vronsky's arm frantically, dragging him out after her through the door. He went, roaring with laughter, not even realizing that Grabov had started to rise.

5

"WHERE THE HELL can he have gone?" Corchran stood looking at the map of England on the side wall to the left of Minelli's desk.

"Look at the other map," said Minelli.

The maps were the unmarked, unclassified ones, barefaced on the wall for anyone to see, three of them—England, Europe, and the world.

"Not that one," said Minelli, as Corchran glanced to the next. "The big one. He can be anywhere by now."

"Three days. We had every airfield and port sealed to him within an hour of the time he got on that bus."

Corchran struck the map of England with the back of his hand, came away, and dropped himself into a chair facing the desk as though depositing garbage into a barrel. "Well," he said, "obviously he's gone to ground somewhere. That would be easy enough. But he's got to come up again. He wants to go someplace. There's something special he wants to see before he dies. He didn't say much, but that came across clearly. He's a tough old bastard, but he can't swim the Channel. Sooner or later . . ." Corchran's hands were on his thighs. He stretched his fingers as though he were imagining Maxwell's neck between them.

Minelli picked up a paper clip from his desk top and leaned far back in his green leather swivel chair. He held himself back by putting his foot onto a lower desk drawer which he kept

57

slightly open for the purpose. He was not wearing a jacket. His shirt had pale blue stripes, and the collar points were short and buttoned on either side of a dark blue tie. Minelli always tried to look neat and in order but relaxed. He knew that Corchran would have more to say, so he waited.

"He's under pressure. He said only six months, so he can't try to outwait us." Corchran's need for reassurance finally overcame his shame, and he looked directly at Minelli.

"He's bound to try to get out of Britain, and if we keep watching . . ."

Minelli appeared to give the idea serious consideration, then shook his head. "Probably not, Corky. Oh, it was good exercise to get up the watch for him; proves the system works. And we'll keep it on for a while just because we'd feel like dumb shits if we didn't and found he'd walked through. But I don't think we'll get him that way. By now old Max has probably got himself shipped to Hong Kong disguised as a bolt of Harris Tweed."

"Can't we do something? Can't we get out the constables? Somewhere there's going to be a boat stolen, or a fisherman or private pilot who picked up some cash for a quiet trip. Give them immunity—"

"In the works. My 'opposite number' is being very cooperative." Minelli smiled with one corner of his small mouth. "The son of a bitch is really enjoying this. Maybe we'll find how Max got out, which will be interesting, but we won't trace him on the other side."

"Frank, Max is good, but still—"

"Corky, Max is the best. Did you hear about his little junket to Prague two years ago?"

"Prague!"

"Yeah."

"I heard gossip that he was in trouble with the home office about that time, but no one knew what, or wouldn't say."

"Max was in trouble, all right. They snatched his ass straight back to Langley and just about chainsawed it off. Or they were about to. I mean, Max isn't supposed to get involved in direct actions anymore. In the first place, he's fifty-nine years old— fifty-seven then—and in the second place, he's been around so long every counterespionage division east of Long Island must have a file on him. He's just supposed to be a District Field Supervisor and travel in crowds. They would have pulled him back years ago, except that he wouldn't go, and he really is too valuable here. For years, if Tito had a chest pain, Max knew before anyone else whether it was the big one or just gas. If you wanted to put a whoopee cushion on Giereck's chair, Max knew somebody who knew somebody who could do it.

"Well, to get to the point, two years ago, Max is in Berlin when he hears something he doesn't like. So he sends word to the local office, like a good little agent. Then he flies straight to Vienna, which is more than called for, but still OK. And he finds he's just missed the courier for a net in Prague. The guy is on his way back in. Well, the point is, Max had gotten onto a double. So the deal is that the courier is going back with—in effect—a 'kill-the-bearer' letter. It would have been a full technical interrogation. The net would have been blown, of course, but more than that, when the back-bearings were taken. So, without checking with anybody, Max goes in after the courier.

"Of course, it was a stupid, criminal thing to do. He was bound to get caught, and with all he knows, they'd have been pulling his brains out through his nose for the next five years.

"I don't know what he did, probably put on a false moustache, or another one of his ridiculous disguises. He must have gotten an ID someplace. Well, I don't know what happened on the trip, but Charley Maxwell, the well-known spy, gets himself from Vienna to Prague, intercepts the courier, deactivates the net, sends them back into the woodwork for a rainy day, and then gets himself and the courier out. They turned up in Linz five days after he left Vienna."

"Wow," said Corchran.

"Yeah. I hear he was marched all the way up to Chief

HUMINT himself. But I guess Max just asked them whether they would have liked it better if he'd let that courier be caught. And then he must have asked if they'd like him to resign. So, he probably got some bad marks on his chart, and he came back. You see why I don't think we're going to track him?"

Corchran was silent for a moment, in awe of Maxwell's exploit and despondent over its significance. All he could think of to say, after a moment, was, "If only I'd shot the bastard in Kensington Garden."

It was rumored that Frank Minelli could lose his temper, a prospect that terrified his subordinates, although none had ever seen the phenomenon. Probably they never would see it, because Minelli had found anger to be pointless, except as a self-indulgent release for himself. When he found incompetence, he removed it, but he knew that a good man who made an honest mistake seldom needed help to feel badly about it. "You did the best you could, Corky."

"Yeah. That's what hurts most."

"Don't sweat it. Max was right. You couldn't chance killing the kid or somebody else. And we'd be almost as badly off as we are now if you'd killed him and we couldn't have talked to him. What could you have done?"

"I could have shot him in the kneecap the first time he picked up that ball."

"Yeah. I guess you're right. I hadn't thought of that. Experience is a great teacher, Corky. Learn from it, don't regret it. Nobody likes what happened, but it's OK. The point is, what now?"

"I don't know. I'll get some sleep, and then maybe I can take on another assignment, something more my form, like carrying out the unclassified trash."

"What about Maxwell?"

"Frank, I shock myself when I think what I would do to Max if I could find him."

"Any ideas on how you'd find him?"

"As I said, if we could find his tracks here—even if they're cold . . ." Corchran trailed off as Minelli continued to look at him without response.

"You don't think we will."

Minelli remained expressionless.

Corchran's shoulders felt leaden, and his eyes gritty. He had slept little for three days, going home to his flat from time to time to shower and lie down and toss and drop into deep sleep for ten or thirty minutes, and then waking suddenly and showering again, dressing in clean clothes, and going out. He had been to Heathrow four times, although he knew it was pointless. He couldn't be at the international gate for every departure, and it was covered anyway. Besides, Maxwell wouldn't try to go that way. But Corchran kept expecting a certain moment when he would look up and see Maxwell in the line. Corchran would have gone down to Dover or Folkstone, too, except that it would have taken so long and been even more patently absurd. He might as well have gone to Liverpool or over to Harwich. For three days, though, he had continued to hope *the* phone call would come into the office.

Minelli wasn't going to let him hope any longer, and Corchran felt an immense desire to let himself slide from the chair and curl into a ball under it. But Minelli wouldn't let him do that either. Minelli just kept looking at him.

"We're going to have to come at it some other way," Minelli said.

"How?"

"I'm the executive, Corky. I *pose* the problems. Nobody expects me to be able to solve them. Go over it again. What did he tell you?"

Corchran punched the button in his head again. He was weary of hearing himself tell the same story, but he began it and tried to find something new in what he said. "He's got six months to live. No, he didn't say how long—six months before he starts to deteriorate badly." Corchran paused, a thought coming to him. "Would Max have any of those cyanide pills we're all believed to carry?"

"He could have."

"I think he intends to kill himself when he starts to decline seriously. I could tell it almost killed him right there in the park to tell me he was sick. He won't be an invalid."

"In character."

"But there's something he wants to see before he dies. He'd been in India and never seen the Taj Mahal. I don't think that's it, but we should have him watched for there."

"What do you think it is?"

Corchran began to sense an idea. It seemed to germinate near his stomach and bore him up straighter in his chair as it grew. He stared at the world map, not really seeing it. His right hand ran down his necktie unconsciously, making certain the striped silk was straight and properly tucked inside his jacket.

"A place. Not a *thing* like the Eiffel Tower or the Acropolis. I can see him, the way he sat on that bench looking over the park. A place, a kind of life—for what life he's got left. Tahiti! I'll bet we find him under a palm tree, surrounded by brown-skinned beauties, eating a mango. Or . . . Rome. Has Max ever been to Rome?"

"Probably. I don't know. It was never his district, but he's probably—"

"Can we find out? Was he ever sent there? Did he go on vacation? Where did he go on vacation? He's been entitled to thirty days leave every year. Where did he go?"

"You said he wanted to go someplace he hadn't been."

"Right, Frank. So we can eliminate places where he's been for any length of time. But possibly we can get some idea of what he likes to do and where he hasn't been to do it. Who are his friends?"

"I don't think he's got any. I mean, everybody knows Max, and most of us like him. But I don't know that he was ever close to anybody."

"Well, the people who've known him the longest must know something about him. Look, Frank, if I could get his file and then get in touch with some people . . ."

Minelli took his foot from the drawer, leaned forward, and

put his forearms on the desk. "I've been through to Langley every six minutes on this, and they think we ought to proceed along two lines now. Of course, we'd most like to get Max back and find out exactly what he's given them. But since we don't know when or if, we have to assume he's given anything he could give. We've already started a full-scale review going of everything Max has touched that could be compromised—and I hate to tell you how long it's going to take to get that all together and what it's going to mean when we see it all in one place. So, the situation is this: we've got to assume we're not going to find him, and put our major effort into dealing with that. We want to try to find him, but it has to be the minor effort. We're just going to task one man with it—with support, of course—but just one man full time until something turns up. I was hoping that might be a job you'd like to have."

Corchran was sitting fully upright. He pulled his trouser creases up at his knees and leaned forward. "Yes, I might like that, Frank. I just might."

"Good. I think you've got the kind of motivation we want, Corky. I think you'll do a good job."

"Thanks." Corchran rose, buttoned and smoothed his tweed jacket. "When can I get his file?"

Minelli opened the top drawer of his desk, took out a thick packet and offered it to Corchran. "Why don't you use the conference room?"

Corchran took the file, started briskly across the room, then paused.

"He did it for the money." He turned back to Minelli. "He had to have the money. Where do spies have their money?"

Minelli leaned back in his chair again. He spoke in a tone of bland innocence. "In Swiss banks, from what I hear. But you don't have to go there to get it out, do you? I mean, naturally, I've never had occasion to use one of those accounts for myself, but I understand you can just write a letter and transfer funds. Isn't that how it works?"

"Not for Max. Max wouldn't take the chance that somebody

else could write a letter, or make him write a letter, and get his money. Max would insist that it be paid out only to himself in person, on presentation of proper and secret identification."

Still semi-reclining, Minelli reached to his right and pushed a button on his intercom. Nodding his head up and down as though following a complex idea, he went on speaking to Corchran. "But there are an awful lot of banks in Switzerland."

"There is a treasury of banks in Switzerland, Frank. But didn't Max go in and out of Geneva regularly as he made his appointed rounds?"

"Yes, Mr. Minelli?" said the intercom.

"Margaret, I want to send a flash to the Geneva office."

6

MAXWELL DIDN'T GO to Geneva; too many people there knew him. He would have preferred that the money were deposited at one of the smaller cities, like Thun or Sankt Gallen, because they were out of the way and he had never been there. But those advantages had obverse sides. He wouldn't know his way around or be able to get in and out quickly in an emergency. So he had settled on Zurich, where there were plenty of banks and no branch office. Technically, there is no branch office at all in Switzerland. Switzerland may well be the espionage center of Europe, but because of the Swiss passion for avoiding anything so unprofitable as taking sides, it is all handled unofficially and with discretion. There were some "monetary specialists" and "manufacturers' representatives" in Zurich, of course. They, and the trade commission and disarmament talks team "staffers" from Geneva or "liaison officers" from the embassy in Bern, could be called up at need. But low-grade fieldwork—such as speculative surveillance—was handled in Zurich through an accommodation office. It was staffed by a local rep (who really did export carved-wood figurines) and some stringers.

It was one of the stringers who spotted Maxwell.

Maxwell had slept late that morning. That was not his plan. He had intended to get up and be at the bank just after it opened. But when he first awoke he was too heavy. Pushing himself too much, he knew. He tired more easily now and felt the rottenness inside. Lying there in the soft bed, between smooth, wholesome sheets, it was easy to persuade himself of the good sense of going back to sleep. Whether from weakness or prudence, he decided he ought to let his batteries recharge.

It was after eleven when he got to the bank and was conveyed to Herr Hotz, who was gracious, if reserved; a tall, thin, sandy-haired man wearing a suit color-coordinated with the bank's sooty walls, and a silver tie that matched its vault. Maxwell judged him to be about thirty-five, but already he had set his expression for the formal portrait that would one day hang with those of his predecessors on the office wall.

Herr Hotz established his client's identity by taking a thumbprint to compare with the one mailed in when the account was opened. He seemed to regard this as a perfectly normal business procedure.

Probably is, Maxwell thought to himself as he washed the ink from his finger in Herr Hotz's private lavatory.

Maxwell took the equivalent of fifteen thousand dollars cash in Swiss francs and had a check made out payable to Herr Julen to cover the first month's rent beyond the deposit already sent. He wrote permission for future transfers to be made upon receipt of letters from himself, rather than in person only.

Unlike some bankers, Herr Hotz seemed to accept philosophically letting clients take money away, and his correct cordiality warmed to downright pleasantness as he suggested shops where Maxwell might buy certain items he asked about.

Probably seeing the cash going 'round and coming back in again, Maxwell thought. Then he felt ashamed as Herr Hotz heated toward enthusiasm, throwing in a recommendation for a restaurant nearby.

It was after one when Maxwell finished lunch. Although his spirits were rising steadily, he had still been uneasy in his gut, so he had ignored Herr Hotz's suggestion and gone instead into a small ground-floor stubli on a sidestreet, because the blackboard menu outside listed chicken soup. The choice amused Maxwell, but the soup was exactly what he wanted, and he felt better after eating it.

Then he went to W. Koch Optik, where he bought a huge pair of 10x50 Zeiss binoculars, a more compact and lightweight 8x30 pair, and a magnificent telescope. The telescope cost eight thousand dollars and would (he was assured) allow him to see the moons of Jupiter and the rings of Saturn quite clearly, along with many other marvels of the heavens. Maxwell took the smaller binoculars with him and paid for the other purchases to be delivered where he was going.

Next, he went to Och's, where he bought warm, rugged outdoor clothing and a medium-sized pack, which he equipped with plastic water and wine bottles, a compass, and other items. Then he bought a pair of beautifully made medium weight hiking boots. It took him half an hour of fitting, walking, and refitting before he was satisfied with them. Maxwell had not hiked in twenty-five years, but he knew the importance of good boots fitted correctly. These things made a bulky and heavy bundle, which he took back to his hotel. Then he set off again.

He went to Grieder and outfitted himself with everyday casual clothes. Again he had a big and awkward package, so he bought two large suitcases at a department store and took a cab back to his hotel. Unlike his other purchases, the suitcases were cheap, but Maxwell expected to use them only once.

In his room, he packed all his acquisitions into the two suitcases. He handled each item again slowly and carefully, running his hands over them, hefting, examining stitches. These were more possessions than he had owned in one place at one time in many years. He imagined himself wearing the boots and carrying the pack up through clear air; then, later, sitting in the warmth of soft wool and a fire. As he packed, Maxwell felt he had gotten his money's worth. He felt rich.

But he regarded the closed baggage with dismay. Maxwell never liked to carry large pieces of luggage: they tied up your hands, slowed you, made you vulnerable. He decided not to take them with him on the train but to send them ahead. He would have the hotel porter deliver them to the railroad station.

He reached for the phone, but paused. As Maxwell had imagined using his new possessions, they had seemed to become the end of his life made tangible—a short life, but a good one. He had never cared much about possessions; now every moment spent with them was precious. Impetuous as he had never been before, he ignored the little voice inside him. He had the man at the desk call a cab, and went himself to the railroad station.

That was where Handelsmann picked him up.

Handelsmann had mixed feelings about being given the Bahnhof. When assignments were made, Hans Fuchs had gotten Kloten, which Handelsmann had wanted. He considered it far more likely that a man would come by jet than by rail after he had sold information for at least two million francs. (Handelsmann was a young man, an up-and-coming young man, he liked to think, and he never thought in less than seven figures.) Still, Maxwell was tricky; he might sneak in by train. And the Bahnhof was certainly better than having to walk all day, making a circuit of every major bank in the city, which was what Gerd Rechsteiner was having to do. Of course, Gerd might be the lucky one, because if Maxwell was coming to Zurich at all, he was coming to a bank.

They all knew why they were watching for Maxwell. At first there had been some discussion between the home office and London branch about how much to say. But they had to say that Maxwell was to be picked up if seen. They had to warn that he would try to avoid being picked up—that is, that he would be highly dangerous. And they had to say that all of Maxwell's known contacts had to be notified not to give him any further assistance. After they had said all that, what was left to hide? Besides, the other side already knew.

Handelsmann had had a long, boring three days. The local rep, Aeschliemann, had told them the full-time watch would last for one week only, but already Handelsmann was sick of it. Drinking far too much coffee had jittered his nerves and upset him internally to the point that he had almost missed the arrival of the express from Paris that morning because he was in the W.C. The job had been exciting at first, as he moved around the Bahnhof finding strategic vantage points from which he could monitor arrivals of trains on the various tracks without being exposed himself. He planned how he would fall in behind Maxwell, shadow him undetected by keeping between them the newsstand, a row of columns, the baggage area. He considered whether he should dress in something more ordinary, but decided his Italian cut light blue suit, cream shirt, and wide polka-dot Cardin tie were perfect cover since he saw a number of smart young entrepreneurial types in similar clothes cutting through the plodding crowds with controlled swiftness on their way to inevitable directorships. Handelsmann considered getting a slim briefcase for himself, too, but decided he should keep his hands free, in case.

Between trains, Handelsmann drank coffee. He did not permit himself alcohol while on duty because he knew what it could do, and he intended to be in top form when he met Maxwell. He evaluated the women going in and out of the station—early shop girls and secretaries (probably poor, but often cute), and then the fine-tuned young matrons come to shop. He scored his mental card on two criteria: the relative perfection of feminine beauty, and what he imagined they would be like in bed. He kept the latter speculations under control because he knew they were deadly to professional concentration, but by the middle of the third day he was so bored that he found himself drawn back again and again to the newsstand where the girl behind the counter wore a tight stretch top and no brassiere. Handelsmann judged that he could pick her up with little difficulty. Women liked him, at least that type did. He was good looking, and if his upper teeth protruded slightly his moustache covered the defect well. A beard might have done the same for his narrow jaw, but beards were not in fashion in the business world. Women didn't seem to mind his jaw. They liked his big blue eyes, and they all said he had a nice smile. And he knew how to smile at them and make clever little compliments about their hair and to treat them like ladies in public. He considered making contact with the newsgirl so she would be available after this surveillance was over, but decided she was not his type: too full-blown, and worse, low class. But she did look better to him every hour.

The newsgirl's breasts and a Lamborgini that was driven up and parked for fifteen minutes in the no-parking zone in front of the station late on the second day were the sole external sources of excitement. The only real stimulation Handelsmann could give himself from time to time was to plan how he would spend what he got of Maxwell's money.

He would buy a car, of course. Deciding which kind was a subject he could return to frequently when the quarter-hours were thirty minutes long. His first choice was a Ferrari, naturally. Blood red. Or possibly that deep blue they used—it was more restrained, and the car made enough of a statement by itself. There was no need to be vulgar.

Handelsmann despised vulgarity. His contempt for the vulgar was bred from extensive familiarity. He often wondered at his own taste. Surely it did not come from his father, whose characteristic manner of expression was to clear his throat and spit; nor from his mother, whose sense of the beautiful was a four-color print of Jesus with chest opened up and heart exposed, bleeding. Even before Handelsmann was old enough to earn his own transistor radio he had tuned the family set to concert music and listened, transported, until some older sister or brother came in and laughed or swore and spun the dial to find a heavy beat.

No, he would not be vulgar. The circumstances of his past were tar, filthy and smelling, but he would scour every patch he found sticking to himself. The car would be blue.

Or silver. Patrician, the ultimate in understatement practiced by those who want to call attention to truly great wealth. But thinking of it that way, perhaps the whole idea of the Ferrari was a bad one. Perhaps he should just get a Mercedes. That would be dull—everybody had one—but then, the very solid uniformity might be an advantage while he was moving up. A Mercedes, then, but the SLC. After all, he was a young man, energetic, daring. It would be all right—it would be *exactly* right for him to drive a sporty car.

The car would be his only extravagance. That and some clothes. Not many—he wasn't going to waste his fortune on fripperies. But he would allow himself a few small indulgences. And he would have to look good, too. Making the right impression was critical in business affairs. Maxwell's money would be only his stake, only the means to allow him to operate on the higher level for which his intelligence and talent were suited.

He would be smart with the money. A third would go at once into some blue-chip investment. Never again would he be a fake, presenting himself as a man of affairs while hiding frayed shirtcuffs, negotiating a fee quickly before his stomach growled and revealed he would settle for the price of soup. Currently, he was dressed and fed well enough. Aeschliemann paid his bond and arranged assignments as a commercial courier for the sake of cover. But Handelsmann was wise for his age and looked to the past and the future. He liked taking risks, he triumphed when carrying off a bluff; but he detested the degradation of being a fake. Always he believed the others knew, and laughed at him, and patronized. The money he would invest would not provide a living, but it would be a life preserver. He would never sink again.

The rest of the money would be his venture capital. He liked that term, which he had learned from the financial pages of the *Neue Zuricher Zeitung* he read every morning. He pondered the areas into which he might venture.

He was still pondering when Maxwell passed him on the way to the baggage counter. It was over half a minute before Handelsmann recognized him, partly because of Maxwell's appearance—thinner, older looking, with his normally short hair cut farther down to a half-inch brush—and partly because of the unexpectedness of an occurrence long awaited.

The evening migration had already begun and the station

was becoming crowded. Maxwell had difficulty making his way to the baggage room with the two great suitcases. He did not see Handelsmann.

Handelsmann stood at one of the snack tables, drinking a Coca-Cola. After the moment of explosive shock, he drained his paper cup without abruptness, wiped his neat moustache with his left forefinger, turned, and went several steps away to the other side of one of the large columns supporting the floor above. He could not see Maxwell from there, nor did he peer around. Instead, he looked back toward the vaulted concourse and the tracks beyond. Trains came and went regularly at that hour. There was a continual hum and whine from their electric engines and a pulsating rumble. People streamed across the concourse and down the platforms. It was like a rush of blood inside him as he watched. Maxwell would have to go that way. Several minutes later he did. But to Handelsmann's surprise he did not go toward the trains. He turned and passed out of sight heading again toward the main entrance. Handelsmann was not disconcerted. He felt the thrill of the chase and smiled to himself as he slipped away from the column.

Maxwell knew he should go directly back to his hotel, eat nearby, and stay inside until time to leave the next day. He had already been on the street far too much, and coming to the station was particularly risky. Not that he knew he was watched for, but it was obvious that he might be. Still the sense of release was so great, and the thrill of having gotten some of his money and spent it and begun to enjoy it was so exhilarating that Maxwell indulged himself further by deciding to walk through the Old City and have a good dinner.

At the third street down he turned to the right off the Bahnhofstrasse, where traffic was becoming even more hectic. He followed the square-cut, stone-paved street as it curved upward.

Although it was bright, and sunlight still poured into the Bahnhofplatz behind Maxwell, the three- and four-story buildings close on either side made the street a shadowed canyon. Here and there a stuccoed facade was painted pink or ochre,

72

but most were gray, like the stone that faced each building up one level.

Maxwell did not find that shadowed, slightly lavender gray depressing; rather, it was the perfect neutral background for the treasures displayed in every window. Here, fine leather: handbags, rectangular, thin, with an absence of decoration only much money can buy; there, watches: stainless-steel machines to measure microseconds, and some with unmarked faces for people who care not what the hours are, only that they be golden. Not only the clocks said it was late in the day: shops were closing. Maxwell passed a jeweler's, where a woman's hand—exquisitely slender—was removing from the window a tray of rings, none of them as finely carved as that on her finger.

Maxwell stopped outside a cutler. On night-blue velvet were knives of all descriptions. A circle of knives in the center: carving knives, boning knives, chef's knives, hunting knives. Around them, other circles of pocket knives, scissors, and devices for cutting Maxwell couldn't imagine what. He hadn't wanted a handbag or a ring, but it came to him suddenly that he would like to have a fine pocket knife. He went into the shop.

The shop was tiny. A narrow aisle for customers, a long counter, a narrow aisle again for the shopkeeper, and shelves lined with thin boxes. Samples of all the wares were displayed in the window.

"I'd like to buy a pocket knife," Maxwell said.

"Indeed, sir, yes," replied the shopkeeper. He was quite bald, with a thin, short fringe of white hair behind his skull from ear to ear, but his eyebrows were prodigious. He looked up at Maxwell from under them; he had to, as he was a good eighteen inches shorter. "We have an excellent selection. Highest quality. Would you care to see?" He directed Maxwell back to look from the inside at the window display.

That was when Maxwell first saw Handelsmann. He didn't truly see him, though. Looking at the knives, Maxwell was aware of a figure in his field of vision: a man across the street looking into another window.

"That one, I think," Maxwell said.

"Ah, yes!" the shopkeeper said, bobbing his head like a spring-necked doll in delighted agreement with Maxwell's good taste. "Solingen steel. Will sharpen like a razor, keep its edge under heavy use. Stainless. A special formula." He peered at the circle of knives again. *"Nummer zwei, zwei, eins, und sechts,"* he said to himself, turning back and scanning along the shelves. "Ah!"

He pulled down a box and placed it on the counter. He slid over to himself a board wrapped in the same blue velvet, removed the box lid with both hands, placed it reverently on the counter, lifted out the knife carefully, unclasped it, and laid it on the board for Maxwell's inspection.

"No, that's not the same one," Maxwell said. "I wanted the one with the straighter blade." He motioned the shopkeeper back to the window. "There. I think you got the one next to it."

"Ah, so. Excuse me, please. One moment. *Zwei, zwei, eins, und sieben.*"

He replaced the first knife with care, took another box from the shelves.

Maxwell remained at the window. He often noticed things without realizing that he noticed, such as the lack of change in the picture that was background to the window display. Across the street, the man continued to look into the opposite window. That lack of change would have disturbed Maxwell to some extent in any case, but since the window contained a display of three ladies' hats hung on wires before a yellow cloth, and as the man persisted in staring at those hats in fierce concentration, Maxwell was more than disturbed.

"Here, now, I believe this is correct," the shopkeeper said. He opened the second knife and laid it as though it were crystal upon the velvet. "The same steel, of course. And the handle is African ebony."

Maxwell walked down the counter, looked at the knife. "Yes. I'll take it."

"Very *good* sir. *Very* good. An excellent knife!"

The shopkeeper closed the blade carefully. It made a soft but

74

solid click. Then he took a sheet of white paper from underneath the counter and began to wrap the box.

Maxwell stood across the counter from him, away from the window, but looking through it. The man across the street was still absorbed in the hats.

"Would there be anything else, sir?"

Maxwell looked down at the display again. "Yes. I think so. I suppose they're just toys, but I've always wanted one of those." He pointed.

"Ah, yes, sir!" Again Maxwell had proven himself a customer of great discernment. The shopkeeper turned back to his shelves. "An amusing novelty," he said, "but very well made. Italian, genuine mother-of-pearl inlay on the handle. Here." He opened the box, took out the knife. "If I may?" He pressed the button, and a four-inch stiletto snicked into place faster than the eye could follow.

The Solingen clasp knife was a dangerous machine, of course, but it was a machine of many admirable uses. A sense of the one thing the stiletto could do well—more than its highly polished gleam and iridescence—made it as fascinating and repulsive as a cobra.

Maxwell pocketed his purchases, one on either side in his raincoat, left the shop without looking across the street, and turned uphill again.

After fifteen seconds, Handelsmann followed.

Maxwell did not place the situation in a mental list of possibilities, the way James Newlands or Matt Corchran would have done. Maxwell worked more intuitively. Though the method differed, the conclusions were the same. He had been spotted. Either the man following him was alone or there were others. Maxwell needed to know about that first of all.

He reached a corner, turned left, then left again at one side of Pelikan Platz, and walked as straight as the curving street would let him back toward the Bahnhofstrasse. He walked slowly, windowshopping. He passed an alley and continued on his way. When he checked again, he saw that Handelsmann must have ducked through the alley. Either Handelsmann was alone, taking a chance and getting ahead so that he would not be spotted by being continually seen behind, or he was not alone, and confident that Maxwell was boxed.

Reaching the Bahnhofstrasse, Maxwell turned right—toward Handelsmann. Maxwell had not recognized Handelsmann at first, but he did so as he passed him standing in line for a trolley, facing away and talking to someone.

The broad sidewalk was as packed as a school of herring, all headed toward the Bahnhof. Maxwell had to stay close to the building line and use his considerable bulk to oppose the tide. He was not the only person moving in that direction, of course, but none of the others he could see behind him were likely to be agents closing in on him, except Handelsmann, who had changed his mind about the trolley.

Maxwell turned right again into the next sidestreet. He was forty yards up, looking into a shop window at a garden of floral-embroidered handkerchiefs when Handelsmann popped out around the corner—the force of effort against the crowd making him overshoot into the quieter street.

Handelsmann was furious with himself. He had, he thought, managed it all so well thus far, the trick of getting ahead of Maxwell had gone off perfectly. Then to have failed to slow at the corner . . . He might as well have jumped around shouting *look at me!* There was no doorway near the corner for him to duck back into, so he crossed diagonally to the other side of the small street and went into the first shop he came to. It was a tobacconist, fortunately. He half expected it to be selling lingerie, the way his luck was going.

Maxwell did not seem to notice him and went on slowly up the street. Handelsmann let him get around the corner to his right before following. He saw Maxwell turning left around the opposite side of the Pelikan Platz from where he had passed before. Handelsmann backtracked, crossing the street that marked the far side of the rectangle that he believed Maxwell was going around. In three minutes, Maxwell appeared, turning the corner and coming back down the hill toward the Bahnhofstrasse again.

The pattern was clear: Maxwell, like any tourist with time to kill on a pleasant evening before dinner, was working his way up one street and down another through this quaint old quarter filled with chic new shops. Handelsmann walked quickly down his street, at an angle away from the one where Maxwell was strolling. He turned at the Parade Platz, reached the Bahnhofstrasse before Maxwell could, and got inside a tea room two doors down from the corner.

Handelsmann was breathing heavily. He tried to control himself, taking deep breaths, slowing the rhythm. It was not so much from the hurrying as from his excitement over the chase and his growing anticipation of the prize at the end. Fragments of the dialogue he had composed for himself and Maxwell sounded in his head like a radio being switched abruptly between stations.

Although the tea room was crowded with people having a snack before staying in town for the evening, there was a table vacant in the rear. The hostess offered to seat Handelsmann, but he said no, he was waiting for a friend.

He waited five minutes.

It should have taken Maxwell less time, even at his leisurely pace, to pass the tea room. Handelsmann's stomach began to tighten, and he felt a tingle all around his hairline that he knew was sweat. He waited another two minutes. His stomach was now leaden, and his legs felt weak. He went back out onto the street, standing first in the doorway, peering through the corner of the window in case Maxwell were even then approaching.

Maxwell did not approach. He watched Handelsmann from his vantage across the Bahnhofstrasse, behind a divider used to isolate those waiting for trolleys from the stream of pedestrians. There were posters in bright colors on the divider. On the inner side, Maxwell stood in front of a very attractive girl wearing an infinitesimal bikini who wanted him to satisfy her by drinking Cinzano. On the street side was a row of six identical posters advertising Gauloises. Each showed an abstract rooster smoking a long cigarette. Had Maxwell known, he might have moved, for the stylized smoke from one of them rose and ended directly below his eyes as he looked over the top.

Question one had been settled. Handelsmann was alone. Question two was for how long? More exactly, had Handelsmann called in as soon as he had spotted Maxwell and then bird-dogged to point the game when the hunters arrived? Or had it all happened so quickly that he had not been able to call yet? He should have called as soon as he had established that Maxwell was in the area, on foot, and moving slowly. He should certainly do so now that he had lost the quarry but knew approximately where.

Handelsmann rubbed his hand back and forth over his upper lip to take off the moisture, then automatically smoothed his moustache. He should call in. He could alter the story just a little and still get credit for having spotted Maxwell, even if they never found him. But if they never found him—or even if they did—Handelsmann would never get any of that money. A large man, hurrying, knocked him off balance and into a pretty girl who was trying to cut between him and the building.

"*Entschuldigen, Fräulein,*" he tried to say, but she had already gone on, scowling.

"*Bitte!*" and "*Pass auf!*" Two young executives brushed against him, one on either side.

Handelsmann pulled himself together and started to move with the stream, back in the direction of the Bahnhof, looking into stores as he went. Most were officially closed; a doorman or salesgirl stood behind the locked doors to let out the few remaining customers. Many of the establishments sold only articles for women, so there were few places where Maxwell could be.

Handelsmann was torn between anxieties: that he would not

find Maxwell again and that he would—face to face, not as or where he had planned it.

Across the avenue, Maxwell moved with the stream of pedestrians. He kept toward the inner side, letting the faster-moving crowd screen him.

Handelsmann reached the corner. Could Maxwell be inside a shop? Could he have crossed the Bahnhofstrasse into the quarter on the other side? Could he have come to the corner, feared being pulled under by the crowd, and sought higher ground again? Handelsmann was not a ditherer. He turned up the sidestreet.

Maxwell stepped back into a doorway opposite the mouth of that street and watched Handelsmann move with deliberate speed up the hill, checking shops as he went. In that space, out of the rush of people, Maxwell took off his raincoat and turned it around to the plaid side again. He took out his packages so that he could replace them in the same pockets where they had been: the box with the clasp knife on the left, the other on the right. Before putting the stiletto back into his pocket he broke the string around the package and removed the wrapping paper, which he wadded and dropped behind him. He put the box into his pocket, opened it there, and took out the knife.

Maxwell had no intention of killing Handelsmann, and he did not normally use a knife. He had bought the knife when he saw he was in danger: securing a weapon was an instinctive response. Getting his weapon ready was an equally automatic part of taking the initiative.

He moved back into the stream, going with it again, but forcing his way across to the curb at the crosswalk. There was a litter container there, and he dropped in the empty knife box. Glancing at the basket again, he pulled out some folded pages of newspaper. He waited patiently until the light changed to Walk, then went across quickly with the surge of people. He was lucky: there was an empty cab stopped for the light.

"Right here, up the hill," he said in German.

The driver was not pleased. Business was good at that hour, excellent if one could keep to the main avenues, but there were fewer people now on the back streets. He spun around the corner with one hand on the steering wheel while fishing for a cigarette, which he hoped would irritate his fare.

"Where to?" he asked.

"I'll give you directions as we go," Maxwell said, and settled back with his newspaper.

When they reached the first corner, he guessed left, then right at the third cross street, and right again for another two blocks. One more right, and they passed Handelsmann in the middle of a block.

Handelsmann stood looking at his reflection in the window of a darkened shop, a solitary figure surrounded by precious objects intangible to him. He faced facts: he had lost Maxwell. He tried to console himself. He hadn't really lost his big chance, because he'd never really had it. It had only been a possibility. Something else would come. He walked briskly down to the corner, considering what story he would tell.

A good story should contain as much truth as possible. He had not called immediately from the Bahnhof out of fear of losing Maxwell. This was the first chance he'd had. He paused at the corner, looking both ways. There was a telephone box to his left, down farther at the next intersection. As he went toward it he continued to scan the figures on the street ahead of him: departing shopkeepers who finally had locked their doors, arriving town dwellers who could afford to live in the apartments on the floors above. Handelsmann checked them automatically, but with no hope that Maxwell would appear among them.

Handelsmann stepped inside the phone box, fished in his pocket for a coin. He dialed Aeschliemann's number and heard it ring twice. Aeschliemann came on, the beeps sounded, and Handelsmann was about to drop the coin into the slot when someone banged on the panel behind him. He released the coin, heard it fall and the line clear as he turned.

"Aeschliemann hier. Hallo? Hallo? Wer ruft? Hallo?"

Handelsmann replaced the receiver without turning back. He felt as though he had been struck by a car. He had been, once, so he knew the force of shock that knocked breath out and made the head ring, and simultaneously the disbelief that it was happening. The impact was so great that he did drop his jaw, and his eyes bulged as he stared at Maxwell through the glass panel.

Maxwell pushed with two fingers against the door. It stuck for a moment, then began to fold inward in the middle.

Handelsmann's first impulse was to push back, to hurl his shoulder against the hinge. But you don't get to the top if you let yourself panic. He pulled on the handle and helped to open the door. Maxwell filled it.

Maxwell smiled. "Hello, Eric. *Wie gehts?*"

Handelsmann licked and bit his lower lip. "Pretty well, Max. And you?" He said "vell" and "und"; but his English was good, and he spoke firmly.

"OK, OK. Nice place you've got here," Maxwell said, looking into the upper corners of the box.

Handelsmann managed a thin smile in return. "Won't you come in and have a drink?"

Good kid, Maxwell thought. *Sent him up for a second, but he landed on his feet.* He said, "I think it ought to be my treat. Why don't we find a nice quiet place and—"

"Not on the first date. Why don't we just take a walk?"

"OK, Eric." Maxwell stepped aside to let Handelsmann out of the booth. "Fine by me."

They started back down toward the Bahnhofstrasse. Neither spoke for the first minute. The sky was still bright blue directly overhead, a blue even more intense as the glare went out of it. Handelsmann's suit seemed to glow as they walked down the narrow, now somber, street.

"How did you do it—get behind me?" Handelsmann asked, finally.

"Didn't go down to the Bahnhofstrasse the way you figured. I knew you were trying to get ahead of me again, so I just went along behind you and crossed the street."

"Ah," said Handelsmann, nodding abruptly in appreciation. "And you followed me back up again. I never saw you."

"Taxi."

"Ah. And so when did you first spot me?"

Maxwell told him. "You have to keep changing the picture, Eric. Remember that. It doesn't have to be much, just some little thing to make it *seem* different."

"*Ja.* I remember from now on. You have given a good lesson. Thank you."

They reached the Bahnhofstrasse once more.

"I think we did this side pretty well. You want to cross?"

"*Ja.* Whatever you like."

Handelsmann's stomach kept trying to tighten, but he breathed carefully and kept control. Actually, he felt good. His whole body tingled with excitement, and though images flashed through his mind of the treasures heaped before his hands, he was pleased that he was patient about reaching for them. He was content to stroll with Maxwell and let the moment come when it would.

The rush had crested and subsided. A few late leavers hurried to catch the last commuter trains; a few strollers looked into lighted windows. Cars still swished in both directions, but not frantically. When the traffic light changed they seemed to wait good-naturedly as Maxwell and Handelsmann crossed and went into the small street on the other side.

"When did you pick me up?" Maxwell asked.

Handelsmann told him.

"Damned suitcases. Never carry baggage, Eric."

"*Ja.* I was surprised . . . Why didn't you have the porter from your hotel take them?"

"I knew I should have. I guess I didn't want to let them out of my hands."

"Oh? So valuable?" Handelsmann tried to be ironic so as not to be obvious, but his faith was confirmed. A thrill surged through his chest as he felt himself racing along the autobahn in his open car.

"Not really," Maxwell said. "There were a couple of things, but . . . No, it was just something personal." He thought about the end of his life so carefully folded and so neatly packed. "Just being foolish."

They passed a little restaurant. A man and woman were entering, although it was too early for dinner. Both Maxwell and Handelsmann looked in through the lighted window as they went by, and each felt a longing to go in too.

"You know, Eric . . . That business with the suitcases. It shows you. In this trade you can't ever let down. You know that? You ever really think about what kind of business you're working your way into?"

"*Ja*. I know, Max. So what else am I going to do? Put hands on cuckoo clocks? Be a waiter? I didn't go to the university. I am of a family with eleven children, the eighth. And—I tell you the truth—I am not so good in school, anyway. Not in *Mathematik* or some of the other *Akadem* . . . What is it?"

"Academics."

"Academics. *Ja*. Thank you. I have not good examinations. So I have no . . . *Stipendium*."

"Scholarship."

"Scholarship. Thank you."

"You speak very good English. Almost perfect—you still let your w's slip to v's, but your English is good."

"*Ja*. That came easy in school. And I go to the cinema, the same picture maybe five times, so I can speak the words with the actors. And I talk with people—we could be speaking German, you can; but always I speak English."

"You could do something with that."

"I could, perhaps, work at a small desk in a travel agency. But I can not be an engineer or a medical doctor, and so on."

Abruptly, Handelsmann stopped walking. Maxwell stopped too. Handelsmann put his hand on Maxwell's arm and looked directly into his eyes.

83

"But I will be *something*, Max. I do not accept a little job and a little house and a fat little wife and a little pension at the end of my little life. And I do not feel sorry for myself, give up, smoke dope, fall out of the world. I will work up to the top, Max. I will!"

After those isolated seconds, the men went back into time and walked on toward the river.

Although it was like seeing a high school photograph of a self he hardly recognized—smooth face and slicked-back hair— Maxwell recalled his own foolish ambitions. *Does everybody have to make the same mistakes?* he thought. "You know, Eric, I've been in this business for thirty-eight years. Since '44. I was younger than you, enlisted right out of college. They let me get through because I was in engineering, then put me into intelligence because I had the languages. G-2, OSS, CIA: thirty-eight years. Take me as your example. Am I what you want to be?"

"*Ja.*"

As Maxwell looked at him incredulously, Handelsmann went on.

"*Now. Ja.*" Now you are a good example, Max. You show me what a man can do in this business. With the information he gets, with the contacts he makes. I am not good with the academics, Max, but I am pretty smart. I don't take thirty-eight years to see what is possible." *More than possible*, he thought. *I have it.*

"Eric, if you're really smart, go into another trade. If you're really smart you'll make it anywhere. But people who think they're pretty smart don't last in this one."

"You sound like my grandpapa."

Maxwell felt a great weariness come upon him.

They reached the river and turned right toward the lake. They came up behind a young couple walking hand-in-hand, the girl leaning her head against the boy's shoulder. They made a nice picture, Maxwell thought, against the evening river. The men were silent as they passed the pair. Handelsmann looked back over his shoulder, then grinned. "Lucky boy. That girl is a real bed-bunny."

"How do you know?" Maxwell suppressed the sharpness enough so that Handelsmann took it only as a request for credentials.

"I know the type."

They came to the Münster Bridge and had to wait until the traffic light changed. Beyond the bridge, stairs led down from street level to a pedestrian quay. The men descended. There were benches at intervals, facing the river.

"Do you mind if we sit? I'm kind of tired." Maxwell let himself down. For ten seconds he let his whole body sag, and experienced a sensation of such physical delight as might have imperiled his soul had he indulged himself further. He was glad of the bite of cold air flowing with the river. Handelsmann sat beside him, on the left, at a discreet distance.

The couple had come up behind them while the men waited at the bridge. They passed. Maxwell didn't want to embarrass them, so he made a point of gazing away, but Handelsmann stared steadily at the girl as she approached. Her young man, looking toward the river, didn't notice, but the girl was aware, and blushed. They went by but stopped thirty yards farther on, where two swans floated. The girl spoke; the boy found some crumbs in his jacket and gave them to her. She took them as if he were giving her diamonds, and he watched her feed the swans over the parapet as though she were healing the lame, or so it seemed to Maxwell.

"Ja," said Handelsmann, "you see how she swings that schwanz?"

"Let's get to it, Eric. I really am bushed."

Handelsmann looked at Maxwell and thought over what he had planned to say. He decided that directness was best. He spoke with the authority of one long used to the power of wealth. "One million francs."

The demand—if not the amount—was what Maxwell had expected all along. Still, hearing it saddened him.

He kept his own voice light. "How did you arrive at that amount, Eric? I mean, aside from the roundness of it?"

"For everything you know, Max, you must have gotten a million dollars, at least. At least that. I don't hit you too hard, Max. I want less than half. And I get myself started, I make something, I pay you back."

Maxwell shook his head in astounded amusement. "Eric, you've gone to too many movies. You have got a wildly exaggerated idea of the kind of money involved in the spy business. If I promised to go to Moscow tonight and talk nonstop for the next three years, I couldn't hope for more than half—maybe three-quarters of a million. I mean, I do know a lot of things they'd like to know. Sure. But not the strike positions of the Trident fleet or how the stealth bomber works. I'm not in that class."

Maxwell looked directly into Handelsmann's eyes. He was still amused at the young man's foolishness, but at the same time felt a sadness in having to reveal it to him. "It's true, Eric. I wanted a certain amount of money. I told them just enough to get it. It's the truth."

Handelsmann looked back at Maxwell and knew he was not lying. He also knew Max was laughing and—the worst—knew his sympathy. He felt his hopes and ambitions wither. There would be no car, no clothes, no ventures, nothing. Never. He suddenly knew there would never, ever, be a fortune. He felt cheated and ashamed. And rising out of all those feelings came anger: at his mother for not having him first and then stopping, at his father for not being rich, at his landlady for cooking cabbages under his bedroom; anger at all the sleek women who would not sleep with him, and at the silly, stupid, vulgar tramps who did—and anger at Maxwell, who had failed him.

"How much did you get?"

"Two hundred thousand francs. Around a hundred thousand dollars, but I asked for it in francs."

"Thirty-eight years, and all you get for yourself is two hundred thousand francs?" Handelsmann could have gagged as he named the sum. His hand clutched the slats of the bench at either side of his legs. He suddenly despised Maxwell.

"I want it. All of it."

"You said half, before."

"I want it all."

Handelsmann hated Maxwell, not for denying the money, but for having gotten so little. He wanted that money, all of it, to throw into the river, to hurt Maxwell by showing him how loathsome he was.

Maxwell continued to look at Handelsmann for a moment, then turned to stare across the river. Orange sunlight still colored the western sides of the cathedral's twin towers. Down the quay the young couple were walking away, and the swans had turned upstream toward the men.

"I need it myself," Maxwell said.

"I don't care for shit what you need! You give me that money or—"

"Or what, Eric?"

Maxwell snapped his head back to look at Handelsmann out of slightly narrowed eyes. That narrowing, and an edge to his tone were the only signs he gave of any change within himself. Handelsmann was too furious to notice. Maxwell went on, speaking softly and calmly. "Suppose I just get up and walk away. Are you going to try to stop me?"

"No. I go straight to the telephone. I call Aeschliemann. I get the others here and—"

"I'll be sure to wait."

"You will wait, all right. I will call the police. I will tell them you robbed me, I will tell them anything, so they hold you for long enough until your people get here to pick you up. I'll tell them I saw you kill someone. You try to run now, I tell them so they will close the airport, the Bahnhof, everything. I get you, Max, you cheap bastard! You pay me, or I screw your ass!"

The swans were close to the bench. They glided in circles, always facing the men, the bigger one cutting ahead of the other.

Oh, God, thought Maxwell. *All I want to do is go off and die.*

"OK, Eric, OK." He said it only to get Handelsmann's attention. The burning was coming again to fill the hollowness inside him. Why wouldn't they just let him die? OK, he would humiliate himself, if that's what it took.

"Eric, I've got cancer. I've got six months to live. That's why I didn't want more money. And that's the only reason I wanted any at all. I need that money so I can go off and—"

"Die now! Die now, Max! Go die in the shithouse!"

Maxwell looked as though he had been struck, then he dropped his eyes. He sighed heavily, put his hands into his raincoat pockets, bunching the coat over his lap. "OK. OK, I'm old and tired, Eric. And I'm sick. I just don't care anymore. We'll work out something. Tomorrow I'll . . ." *Offer a deal: I'll go for the money, arrange to meet him, give him the slip. . . .* Maxwell's mind raced to put together a plausible sounding plan.

"Now! Now! Don't 'work out'! We get the money now. I go with you, every step. I know you're a tricky one, Max. One trick—I don't care, on the street, anywhere—I shout for police."

Maxwell sighed again. "I understand how you feel, Eric. You're a good kid, ambitious. I can see how it is." He ventured to raise his eyes to look at Handelsmann again. "When I was your age I probably would have felt the same."

He put his left arm out along the bench back, just touching the shoulder of Handelsmann's jacket, a gesture across the generations. "But when you get older . . ." Overcome by the shame of age, Maxwell looked down again.

Handelsmann was sharp enough to be wary, but not fast enough. Startled by the movement, the swans exploded into flight with frenzied wing beats and frantically churning feet as Maxwell's fist swung from just outside his right pocket. The blade snapped and locked the instant before plunging into Handelsmann's chest at the exact spot to which Maxwell had dropped his eyes. The point hit the top of a rib but was deflected in the right direction. Maxwell drove in all four inches, then rocked his fist.

For some little time, Handelsmann knew. Knowing, as much as the pain and shock, kept him still until—as though covered gradually by mist—the multicolored buildings across the gentle river all went black.

Maxwell held him upright and checked each direction again. There were strollers down the quay, but far away. Maxwell let Handelsmann slip down and against the back of the bench, his head supported as though he were dozing. He pulled out and closed the knife, buttoned Handelsmann's jacket over the spreading blotch on his shirt, and walked up the stairs toward the bridge. He kept his bloodstained right hand in his pocket.

An elderly couple—both shawled—were up the quay, walking slowly toward the bridge, and well beyond them was a jaunty man with a poodle. Maxwell guessed he would have at least five minutes to get clear. No telling how long until the young couple were found and gave a description of him; probably a matter of hours at the quickest; perhaps a day, perhaps never. Even an hour would be enough.

Maxwell looked back quickly at Handelsmann's body. It remained as it had been, in repose. Blood had not yet soaked to any place where it could show. The suit that had gone so well with Handelsmann's eyes still seemed crisp and new.

7

A WARM WIND BLEW from the southwest all the next day. The sky was as solid and gray as cast iron. By noon it was raining. Maxwell's feet and shoulders were damp. Overheating of the trains made the coaches steamy, and he and all the other passengers sat together stolidly, smelling like wet dogs.

He had walked back to his hotel in Zurich quickly and checked out at once. With his carryon bag, he went directly to the Bahnhof and took the first available train, which happened to be destined for Rome. He got off at Luzern. He spent the night in a small hotel, destroyed the Waterhouse passport he had been using, and switched to the Pennington from the carryon. Before traveling on in the morning he put on an ascot, a tweed cap, and a false moustache. The moustache was a mistake in that weather, and he removed it when he changed trains in Bern.

By the time he reached Visp the clouds were so low that Maxwell could have believed he was traveling across the Baltic plain again, a feeling that depressed him greatly. The last little train, climbing up into the last valley, seemed to move through a long, gray tunnel. When it arrived at the village he could see nothing beyond the tops of the buildings immediately around him.

Herr Julen, his landlord, suggested that Maxwell might like to stay in town for the night. In fact, he suggested, Maxwell would have to, as the lift was not running. But Maxwell felt compelled to end his journey. He would have walked. Finally, a deliveryman was found who would take Maxwell and his luggage, which had arrived a few hours earlier, and several boxes of groceries in his electric truck up over the winding dirt road. The fee was outrageous, but Maxwell paid it.

On the way up they saw nothing but narrow strips of green hillside spattered with drained-looking flowers on either side of them as they moved. There would have been few sounds anyway, and the clouds muffled those, so they heard only the constant high whine of the electric motor. The jolting from the rocky track, and the passing flowers, proved they were moving; yet they never had a sense of being in a different place until, suddenly, the house materialized in front of them.

Maxwell spent the evening getting settled. He chose the main room on the second level as his living room, and the room with the small balcony above for sleeping. The house was cleverly designed: it could be used as a single dwelling—as Maxwell had hired it—or divided among several tenants, one set on each upper floor, two below. Maxwell could have saved himself steps by sleeping in the spacious bedroom at the rear of the second level, but by going up, he obtained the forward view. It was from his bedroom that he first saw the mountain.

He had unpacked, putting his belongings away carefully into the tightly crafted, built-in drawers. He made note of more things he would need—some books, some kitchen staples, perhaps a radio. He fried two pork chops for his supper and ate them with potato and cabbage salads he had bought ready-made. After the gray fog deepened to black he stopped going to the window. Very tired, he went to bed early.

Light woke him at four-thirty. He started up in his bed, which he had moved so that it faced the large window. There was fog, still, but he sensed a lightness just above. He lay down again and drifted off for another hour and a half. When he came back to consciousness, he was suddenly fully awake. The room was bright. He sat up. Framed by the mullioned window, set off by a slope to the left in the middle distance, the mountain stood white against the clear blue sky. The Matterhorn.

Maxwell sat up in bed for five minutes looking at it. Finally, he got up and swung open the windows, ignoring the bite of chill air, so that he could have the view unobstructed.

He dressed, went downstairs, and prepared his breakfast, trying to do everything while still facing the mountain. When the coffee was ready, he carried it out to the small table on the main floor balcony.

Maxwell had planned this breakfast. He had brought up fresh, flaky croissants from Herr Julen's bakery in the village and sweet butter and marmalade and apricot jam. And coffee beans roasted black. Although the morning was cool, the sun warmed his balcony. Wearing his new Icelandic sweater, which still smelled of sheep, he was quite comfortable.

He was, in fact, ecstatic. The Matterhorn was exactly as he had expected it to be. It looked like every picture of it he had seen. It reared up, it towered, it was majestic; it fulfilled and transcended every description, every cliché written about it. It was not the highest mountain or the largest, but it was what Maxwell wanted to find: the ultimate definition and spirit of *mountain*. Maxwell had found few things in life to be as expected. Secretly, he had feared the Matterhorn might prove to be like any other peak, save for having better public relations work.

Maxwell ate slowly, made a second pot of coffee, and drank it slowly. After a while, he let his gaze move away from exploring every face and crevice and ledge of the mountain itself, and looked down to the tiny houses on a shoulder below it, to the mountains on either side of the valley that the great peak blocks, to the other chalets nearby, and to the collection of buildings comprising the hamlet of Findeln just half a mile below him. But mostly he looked at the Matterhorn. He sat looking throughout the morning and thought, *Yes, this is the place*.

8

PAUL DROPPED into second gear, simultaneously accelerating and slipping the clutch so the speedometer needle never wavered from exactly eight kilometers per hour, despite the increasing incline. He had to admit the BMW was good machinery. No style, of course; no spirit. When driving it one felt oneself to be an engineer, not an artist. Nonetheless, it fulfilled the requirements of its job.

Like me, he thought.

He bent the car through a left-hand curve, went up to third and fourth, and—with a long straight in front of him—flicked his eyes first to the rearview mirror, then to his right. He couldn't see Nella. She must still have been curled up on the rear seat. Vronsky was as before: upright, staring ahead, pinching a cigarette at chest level between his thumb and forefinger. Smoke was pulled out in a thin stream through the window cracked open beside him.

One does one's job, spirit or no spirit, Paul thought. He lay against the sharply canted seat, his arms stretched almost horizontally to the wheel, his elbows just bent. He snaked the car through a chicane while accelerating further. He felt himself in perfect control. He liked to drive, especially at night.

There had been light traffic on the autobahn out of Geneva. Now the empty highway created itself just ahead of his lights as he hurtled along. It played its game with him, now running straight ahead, now twisting, rising, dipping, changing its surface—anything to make him act with less than perfect control.

The game was not serious tonight, not life and death. Nothing must stop them or call attention to them. Above all, there must be no involvement with police, no law broken—not even a traffic violation. Paul hadn't minded. Driving full speed was more exciting, but making the best time possible while never exceeding the speed limit was entertaining, too. He concentrated on the game, on the elation it gave him, and tried to ignore the disillusionment—even disgust—hanging around him like the stink of Vronsky's cigarettes.

Our hero, Paul thought with scorn. *Our Great Man. Our Savior!* He ran his tongue over his front teeth as though cleansing them of a bitter taste, and pushed out his upper lip to make a rude noise.

Vronsky seemed not to notice.

Our new inspiration, our new shining spirit. The man who will bring us courage, and the energy and vision to make a new world. Paul remembered Bentivoglio's voice shaking, his eyes filling with tears as he said those things. Paul remembered his own hope—and his surprise that he still could hope. He made the noise again.

Courage! Paul saw Vronsky clawing at him in terror at the window. *All right, he has no head for heights. Everybody has something. We didn't get him to lead us out of windows. But energy? Vision? Like a plate of overcooked pasta.*

Even though it was four A.M., Paul obeyed the road sign while they passed through Stalden. He would do his job well. If there was no other reason, there was at least his own pride.

Vronsky was aware of Paul's annoyance but ignored it. He would have tried to do so in any case. He had leaned to shield himself from what others thought of him. But he was far more distracted than usual. Exhausted physically, mentally, and emotionally, he was tense beyond any hope of rest.

At first, as Nella had half-dragged him down the sidewalk and away from the hotel, everything had been exhilarating,

94

vibrant, and vivid—if not understood. Spots of light had streaked and spun over the surface of the black car that had driven up alongside them. Nella had opened the rear door quickly and pushed Vronsky to make him enter. As he climbed in, he looked back and saw Grabov standing just outside the hotel entrance, staring after them as they pulled away.

Sparks from passing trolley cars and garish colors from neon signs flashed around them. *Fireworks!*, Vronsky thought. He grinned foolishly. *To celebrate! All the colors . . . Yes! Freedom is colors!* His mind was too charged with sensation to allow him to speak coherently, but he turned to Nella, smiling and laughing, bobbing his head. He saw her face: red, then orange, withdrawn again into darkness, then half-revealed in violet contour. She was a spirit-guide, a genie transporting him past white dwarfs and red giants, through whirling galaxies into the vibrating center of the universe.

Nearing their destination, after they had left the first car, it seemed to Vronsky that they were passing through the chambers of time: their steps echoed as they walked down a long corridor through bands of darkness and shafts of light from overhead. Nella led, one step ahead of him. She was bright when he stepped into darkness, gone when he appeared. They were pulses, quanta, energy. It was as Vronsky had always known: to be free was to become pure energy.

Nella took a key from her purse and opened a door. She paused to let Vronsky enter. He was unsure. "It's all right," she said, "we are safe here."

Vronsky's fantasy vanished as he stepped through the door. The apartment was so ordinary. The rooms were small. Everything was patterned: walls covered with a figured plastic material, garishly splotched curtains, flowered slipcovers over shapeless furniture. Vronsky stood in the center of the living room. There were pictures on the walls—scenes cut from magazines and calendars, with postcards stuck behind them, children's crayon scribbles, paper flowers in little baskets. Every surface was covered. Vronsky stared around him.

"My grandmother had hands like paper," he said.

"There is no one here," Nella said. "They have all gone away until tomorrow."

Vronsky nodded vaguely. "Will the Professore come?"

"No. Not here. Someone might recognize him."

"Who?"

"From the press."

"The press?" The word crashed in Vronsky's ear like a gallows trap being sprung.

"You must make a statement to the press. Didn't the Professore tell you?"

"No."

"There was so little time. Yes. You must make a statement. The Russians will say you were kidnapped. They will say that; they will call on the Swiss authorities, the police, to help find you. You must show you go by your own choice."

"Ah." Vronsky nodded. "Of course." He closed his eyes momentarily. "Of course."

Nella sensed his dismay. She went to his side and touched his arm tentatively. "It will be over soon." She was unsure of the gesture. Important people were often temperamental, didn't like familiarity. But Nella believed that those who were truly great always were kind, and she knew that Vronsky was great. She had read his writings—the few smuggled out of Russia—and Professore Bentivoglio had told her word for word of the conversations he and Vronsky had held during the Professore's visit while they had pretended to work.

Vronsky felt the weight and warmth of Nella's touch in his heart more than on his arm. "Thank you," he said.

"You must wash off that makeup. And change your clothes again." Nella went to a closet and brought out a small suitcase. "Would you like to bathe? There is time. I think a hot bath would be wonderful for you. Relaxing."

Vronsky was disconcerted. Take off all his clothes? Bathe? In a strange place? With a strange woman in the same apartment?

"You will feel better. Here." She offered the suitcase. "Take these with you. It will be all right. The reporters were not being contacted until nine o'clock. It will be over an hour until they are brought here. It will be all right." She nodded her head and smiled.

Vronsky took the bag and let Nella guide him toward the bathroom.

The hot water *was* relaxing. Vronsky let himself sink into it and almost giggled, partly because of the relief from physical tension but more because of the incongruity. To sit soaking in a hot tub in the midst of an escape! In one day to have announced to the world a theory of the essential nature of the universe, to have escaped from prison and worn the face and body of another man, and, now, to paddle in a bath!

On the shelf of the tub was a small, yellow, plastic duck. Vronsky took it, held it under water, let it shoot up and fall back to the surface. He wanted to shout Eureka! That duck was the human spirit. It could not be suppressed. The more deeply it was pushed, the higher out of the water it would jump. Its buoyancy was his own. The chains that had bound him so long were broken—his spirit would spring up and in its force would tear the bonds which held other men. Vronsky held the duck down and demonstrated the truth again.

He giggled. He pushed the duck.

Incongruity, insanity. Vronsky laughed and laughed, making ripples and sending the duck bobbing away from him. He laughed until tears streamed down his face.

In the other room, Nella was startled. She hurried to the bathroom door. "Dr. Vronsky, are you all right?"

"Yes, Signorina. Thank you."

Instinctively Vronsky nodded his head up and down, and the motion caused more ripples, and the duck, which had met the edge of the tub, turned back to face him and nodded too. Vronsky exploded into laughter again.

"Later," he managed to say at last, "I will tell you later. All is well."

Nella was unsure at first, but the laughter was so deep and

open that she smiled too and went back to wait, her anxieties lifted.

After a while the water began to cool. Vronsky added more hot—it came from the tap at nearly scalding temperature. He sat back. He would have lain at full length soaking away all tension, except that the bath was only halfsize. Made of green plastic, the tub, walls, ceiling, curtain rod, shelf and soap dish all were formed in a single casting. Vronsky saw that it was mass-produced, cheap. He regretted that it would not permit his lying in the water at full length. But he also marveled at it, and at the fact that hot water flowed the instant he turned the tap. Perhaps there were such fixtures in Russia. In some of the newer apartment blocks in the larger cities there well might be, but they would be for the upper echelons: the government, the technocrats, the artists and athletes, perhaps for himself if he had limited his ideas to science. But this bathroom, this apartment clearly was for the lower classes. For workers. Vronsky held the spray-nozzle in his hand, felt its weight, and admired the coiled metal sleeve that protected the hose connecting the nozzle to the faucet. His own bath had such a nozzle, but the hose had sprung a leak the second time he used it.

The sense of contradiction swept over Vronsky. Switzerland—from all he had heard, the most extreme example of capitalistic materialism—could provide common workers with such facilities, while his own country—the fountainhead of communism—reserved them for an elite. And couldn't even give that elite a spray-nozzle that worked!

The Swiss, the West, capitalism produced these things—produced them for all, Vronsky would grant them that—but at the cost of their people's souls. *Can we have good plumbing only if we believe good plumbing is the height of man's aspirations?* he wondered. *That is as wicked as saying that a classless, free society can come only through rigid obedience to a heirarchy!*

No! He would not accept either choice! There were other

possibilities. He knew it. He would say so! Now he would be able to say so, and people would listen—at first, because it was he who spoke, because of what he had done that day in science, because he had purchased their attention with his seven years of silence. Then they would listen not because of *him*, but because what he said was true!

Suddenly Vronsky could stay in the bath no longer. He had to be about his work.

He dried himself and dressed hurriedly. Another set of clothes had been provided, clothes which fit him more nearly than those of his disguise. The trousers were snug; perhaps he had gained weight since Bentivoglio's visit. They were brown trousers, and there was a light tan dress shirt. Vronsky found that strange; he had always worn white. There was no necktie. He looked several times, then buttoned the collar anyway and went out without a tie.

Dealing with the press was not as bad as Vronsky had expected. There were only three reporters, representing the wire services, and one photographer. Bentivoglio had arranged it carefully. Before the reporters came, Nella gave Vronsky a paper with a statement written out, as a "suggestion" for him, that said that he was defecting voluntarily in protest against the lack of freedom in Russia. Vronsky would have liked to say more about that lack of political freedom, but Nella said Bentivoglio had advised that the statement should be simple. Elaboration could be made at a more appropriate time. Vronsky was to say nothing about where he would go.

Nella had answered the knock and then gone directly to the bedroom, out of sight. The man who brought in the reporters was the same who had picked Vronsky up outside the hotel. When he took the reporters away again he disappeared from Vronsky's life forever. Therefore, Vronsky had had no discussion with anyone about his destination. He had merely assumed.

That assumption was soon shattered.

Paul came five minutes after the reporters were driven away

and took Vronsky and Nella immediately to his car. In ten minutes they were on the autobahn.

"Are we going now to Italy?" Vronsky asked hopefully. It was not merely tension and the longed-for release from fear that made his tenor voice high and eager as a child's. A sense of mission, of destiny, ran through his body like electricity. Vronsky knew Bentivoglio had been right to advise making a simple statement to the press. Had he begun to express all of the thoughts exploding in his mind in multiple chain reaction, there would have been no leaving for hours—for days. He realized that what he had to say must be written first, then spoken about at another time, in another place.

"Will we soon be in Italy?" Vronsky asked again, since his first query had received no response.

"No," Paul answered. He kept his eyes on the road ahead. "We don't go to Italy tonight."

"Tomorrow?"

Nella sat in the back of the car. She leaned forward, putting one arm on the back of Paul's seat so that she could be closer to Vronsky when she spoke. She knew he would be upset. "Perhaps the Professore should have told you . . . There was so little time . . . We cannot go directly back to Italia. We must wait a little while."

Vronsky was stunned. He licked his lower lip.

Nella went on. "It is the plan. For you to come to Italia to live, you must have permission, papers. All is arranged—oh yes! But the Professore says that it must not *seem* to have been arranged. The Professore says that would be very bad diplomatically."

"Diplomatics!" Paul considered several words that might have expressed his feelings but didn't use them in deference to Nella.

She went on. "The government—the important people— they agree to let Dr. Vronsky come to Italia. But they say they cannot admit they knew before tonight that he would come. If we had the papers now, if we went to Italia tonight, it would show the government was involved. This would be bad trouble between Italia and Russia."

"So? Who cares? Why do we bring the Dottore at all? To kick the asses of the government and the Russians, both of them!"

Vronsky dragged at his cigarette. The coal glowed close to his fingers. He crushed the stub in the ashtray on the dash.

Nella tried to smile reassuringly, but this time Vronsky did not respond.

"The Professore says there will be only a short delay. We are to wait only two weeks, then people will come with the papers and take you to Italia safely."

"I think we should go tonight." Paul consciously had to keep his foot light on the accelerator. "I think we should go over the border in the mountains. We should go straight to Rome. You should stand up in front of the Palace of Government and call the people out into the streets. Those government fascists wouldn't dare send you back. What kind of revolution are you going to make if you start by waiting for permission?"

Vronsky was trying to get another cigarette from his pack. His hands shook, and he spilled half a dozen into his lap.

Nella was aghast at Paul. "The Professore said—"

"So, the Professore! The Professore, he is maybe a captain, right? But here we have got a general. Isn't that right? Isn't that the whole point of this? So, General, what do you say? Cross the Rubicon?"

Vronsky clutched the handful of cigarettes.

Paul pushed in the dash lighter. He was astonished by Vronsky's blankness. *Considering strategy,* Paul explained to himself.

A truck came around a curve toward them, its lights sweeping through the car. Vronsky screwed his eyes closed, then blinked. The lighter popped out.

"What do you say, General?"

Vronsky licked his lips. "I . . . I . . ." *Yes!* The sense of destiny drove inside him, the thrust and roar of that automobile hurtling itself through the night multiplied to an infinite power. "But . . ." To stand in a street, haranguing the crowd? He could not imagine it. Instead he would . . . What? To whom would he speak? If he defied the instructions of his friends, who would help him? What, specifically, would be his objectives? He had no idea, anymore than he knew what practical applications might be made of his Force Theory. He never thought of such things. He had never needed to. He assumed that he could not. Often that made him ashamed, but he accepted it as concomitant to his genius. "I . . ." Could he explain? "No."

Removing his hand from the wheel for as little time as possible, Paul snatched out the lighter and handed it to Vronsky. Although his hand was quivering, Vronsky seized the lighter, pressed it against the end of a cigarette and dragged smoke into his lungs.

Eyes darting from the road and back, Paul watched Vronsky. He felt as though concrete were setting in his guts. "Ah, shit," he said at last.

Throughout the night, as they skirted Lake Leman and drove up the Rhone Valley, Vronsky sat tense and silent, chain smoking. The wild desire to let Paul speed him into confrontation with Fate was caged inside iron logic. He had waited for years; he could wait two more weeks.

By the time they reached Herbriggen, the sky had lightened, transforming the blackness around them from void to jagged-topped mountain walls. "Nella?" Paul spoke quietly. "Hey Nella." A little louder but still gently. "Nella, wake up."

"Oh?" She came awake suddenly. Her neck was stiff. "Are we there?"

"Soon. The next town."

"What time is it?"

"After four."

"How long do we have to wait for a train?"

"About an hour. But there may be a bakery open. We can get something to eat."

"Where are we?" Vronsky's voice surprised Paul.

"Randa."

"Is this where we're going?"

"No." Paul was abrupt. He offered no further information.

Nella explained. "We have to leave the car here and go by train. It's only a short journey. We're going to a very safe place."

"Where is it?"

"High on a mountain. It's supposed to be beautiful. It's called Findeln."

9

A SLIGHT MOVEMENT behind the window, perhaps just the white of a face, far back in the room. Maxwell would never have seen it if he hadn't been looking exactly at the window at exactly that moment.

He was below the chalet, coming up the path from Findeln. He was hungry and tired. Not as tired as the day before, not nearly as tired as on Thursday. He was getting used to the altitude, and to hiking up and downhill. His legs were in shape, of course. One hundred deep knee-bends nearly every day for the past forty years had seen to that. But he knew that mountain hiking took more than being in shape. There was a rhythm of pacing and breathing. He had to relearn the rhythm.

Maxwell told himself it was his not quite having gotten the rhythm, and being hungry too, that made him tired. He still did his pushups and pullups and situps and all the rest every morning. The same number as always. If doing them seemed harder . . . well, it was going to get harder; but for now, he was still doing them.

Should have had something to eat, he thought. *Knew it.* He was annoyed with himself. He had planned only to look around the hamlet for an hour. Then he had seen the stream flashing over rocks below and had followed cowpaths down to it. The stream was blue and white, bright between its mossy banks. Where sunlight struck through broad evergreen branches, diagonally down across tall trunks, water sparkled and sent up mists.

Maxwell had sailed stickboats over the cataracts, then sat cradled between huge, gnarled roots, almost hypnotized by the motion of water over gleaming stones. He had spent an hour and a half in a state of transcendent delight, not thinking, hardly aware of himself at all, until his stomach growled. He was returning more than two hours later than he had expected.

Nothing turns out exactly the way you plan. That's what you have to plan for. The necessity of telling himself one of his own basic rules irritated Maxwell.

It might have been the tiredness and hunger that made him look up at the chalet every fifty yards or so, instinctively checking to see how close he was to rest and a good lunch. When he saw the flash of movement he looked away from the window and continued walking steadily up the path. In another situation he might have hit the dirt or bounded zigzagging downhill. In this instance he had no sense of being in immediate danger, as from a sniper. Whoever was inside his house would be waiting for him to come in.

He restrained himself from looking back up at the window again. Knowing someone was inside was an advantage for him. Keeping the person unaware that he knew would double it, no matter what he did when he reached the house.

What now?

Maxwell did not feel like avoiding the situation. Running away would have been impracticable—his money and passports were inside the chalet—and he had no inclination to run. This was the place he had run to.

The muscles at either side of his jaw began to bunch with his growing anger. There was an intruder in his place. He wanted to find out who it was and to get rid of him.

The path reversed, turning west. Maxwell climbed the next leg at the same steady pace. He stopped directly south of the chalet. He looked intently at the ground to one side, then bent over and picked a yellow gemswurtz. He walked a few steps farther and found another. Then he went on up the steep slope until the path turned east once again. He picked two sprigs of yellow rattle and proceeded on the final leg, which rose northeast and would take him up to the dirt road running across the northern, uphill side of the chalet.

The chalet was set into the steep mountainside. There were no windows facing the road on the main floor, and a decorative balcony projecting out on the third made the section of road below a blind area to anyone standing back in the room.

Still in view to anyone looking through the side windows, Maxwell stopped, turned, and gazed back over Findeln and off to the Matterhorn. Then he continued into the blind area. After a moment he reappeared, going back a few steps to pick from a clump of toadflax. He straightened, looked at the view once more, and ambled toward the house.

Maxwell threw down the flowers. He ran down the slope beside the house, fast but quietly on the heavy grass. He ducked under the west window of the lower floor, came around the corner to the downhill side and flattened, still crouching, beside the large window. He peered in at the lower corner.

Empty.

Still doubled over, he sprinted across so that he could look into the other bottom floor apartment.

Also empty.

He spun back around to the door into the hall between the two rooms.

Empty.

Quietly he pressed the thumblatch. He always left the door unlocked so he could come into the chalet without climbing to the main entrance. The door was heavy, its hinges oiled. It swung without sound.

He stepped into the hallway, closed the door behind him silently, and waited, his head turned to one side. His ears twitched.

Silence for a moment, then there were quiet footsteps above him. Someone crossed from one side of the room to the other, as though going from the west window to the other side to see why Maxwell had not yet come into the house. There was a click.

The Vibram soles on Maxwell's boots were resilient enough to make no sound as he crept down the hall to the stairway at the far end. Keeping his steps to the outer edges where the treads gave most support and were least likely to squeak, he began to ascend.

He paused at the landing, still on the lower flight. Footsteps moved across the room, coming from the bathroom side and going away from him, toward the main window. There was another metallic click.

He crouched again, moved onto the landing and around to start up the second set of stairs. The door at the top was open, as he had left it.

He had no plan—there was not enough information to make one. Who was there? How many? Maxwell assumed they would be armed—if so, did they have guns in hand? The footsteps crossing suggested only one person waiting for him—one person having to check each window. And there had been no query to another watcher on the upper floor.

Maxwell's eyes came above floor level.

A figure was silhouetted against the window, holding a casing upright with one hand, the other arm extended up and pressed against the glass.

Maxwell straightened. "Good morning," he said in German.

"*Ach!*" The girl screamed, whirling around. Fright made her clench her fist, and water from the sponge dripped onto the floor. Maxwell regarded her steadily. He could not see her face well because there was light behind her making her curly, yellow hair shine like a halo. She wore a bulky sweater, sleeves pushed up, but her jeans were very tight.

"Herr Bergmann?" Her voice was breathy with fright.

Maxwell nodded. He continued to stare.

"*Ach*, you startled me. I did not hear you come in. You came from below." She said the last as though taking assurance from the explanation. She became aware of the wet sponge in her hand and dropped it into the bucket beside her. She looked back at Maxwell. "Why do you look at me?"

"I didn't expect anyone to be here."

"It is Saturday. I clean. Has Herr Julen not told you?"

"Ah." Maxwell remembered. "Yeah. You are. . . ?"

"Excuse me. I am Renata Tauber."

"I am pleased to make your acquaintance, Fräulein Tauber." Maxwell made a slight bow, using the phrase-book formality with a straight face.

Renata was unsure how to take him. "And me, too."

She looked down, noticed the puddle of water on the varnished floor. "Oh!" She went down to her knees, squeezed out the sponge, wiped up the water.

Maxwell came up the remaining three steps into the room. He took off his windbreaker and hung it in the closet.

The presence of another person in his house—his refuge—was unsettling. But the person was a woman. What was he imagining after a year of continence? Did the heat he felt come from sunlight through the window behind her, or did it come from *her?*

"You have been walking?" Renata asked.

"Yes. Down to Findeln, and then down to the stream."

"Ah. It is a very pretty day for walking."

"Yeah."

Maxwell realized he was staring again. "But now I think I'm ready for some lunch. Do you mind. . . ?"

"Please. I have finished in the kitchen."

"I'm just going to have something cold."

"It does not matter. I have yet only these windows to wash, and all will be ready."

Keeping his attention away from Renata, Maxwell got a slab of paté from the small refrigerator, some cheese, and a pickle. He cut several chunks of crusty bread and peeled and sliced a cucumber. He had planned to eat on the balcony, as he did every meal unless the air was too cold, but when he turned with his food and wine and saw Renata bending over to rinse the sponge, he put the lunch on the table near the kitchen instead.

Renata stretched to wipe one of the upper panes. While pouring a glass of wine, Maxwell admired her.

She stretched up to the right, her left foot extended and off the ground. She glanced over her shoulder and noticed Maxwell studying her. She continued to sweep her arm back and forth across the window. "Do you like the view?" she asked.

"I find it a source of great pleasure. Inspiring. But I guess everybody says that."

"Yes, they do."

"You must get tired of hearing it."

"No. We are proud of our attractions."

She dropped the sponge back into the pail and carried the pail back to the bathroom.

"One of the wonders of the world," Maxwell said without taking his eyes from her as she passed.

"Thank you."

Maxwell heard her pour the washwater into the john and flush it. She came out, put the pail into the cabinet under the kitchen sink, and picked up a small rucksack.

Objectively, Maxwell realized that she could never have been as beautiful when seen clearly, closely, as she had been at the window. It was unlikely that any woman whose every feature matched the perfection of that incandescent hair and that figure existed at all, much less that she would work as an Alpine chargirl. Nevertheless, he was slightly disappointed to see that her nose was sharp and the flesh under her chin full.

She slipped the straps of the rucksack over her left shoulder. The movement pulled at her sweater and pushed her breasts forward against it. Maxwell forgot whatever it was he had been thinking about imperfections, especially since Renata was facing him, looking at him directly. Although her movement with the rucksack was natural, he was certain she knew and intended its effect.

"Would you like some lunch?" he asked.

"Thank you. I have something with me."

"Would you like to eat it here? Have some wine?"

She paused for a moment, regarding him with her head tipped slightly to one side. "Please," she decided.

He started to rise. "I'll get you a glass."

"I can get it." She put the rucksack down again, brought a glass from the kitchen, sat at the table to his left. From her pack she took an orange.

"That's your lunch?"

"Yes."

"You're never going to get fat that way."

"Ever there is hope."

"Have some paté?"

"Thank you, but it is very rich."

"It's very good."

"From which shop?"

"Brendel."

"Then it is very good. And very rich. And very expensive."

Maxwell shrugged. He tore off a piece of bread, spread paté on it, put it in front of her.

"You think I look better if I am fat," she said.

Maxwell let his eyes drop over her body and brought them back up to her face. "I think this wine will taste terrible if you drink it right after eating that orange."

"Ah. No. First I will drink the wine, then I will eat a little piece of bread, then I will have my orange for dessert."

"Plan everything you do."

"Yes. But it is nice that the little piece of bread will have some paté. Sometimes things turn out better than planned." Renata smiled and sipped her wine.

Maxwell took another swallow from his own glass. The wine was a Fendant, a light red wine, pleasant but a little sharp. The sharpness was good on his tongue. All of his senses were keen.

"You are here all alone?" she asked.

"Yes."

"That must be very nice, to have such a fine big house all for yourself." She took another sip of wine. "Does your family come later, in the summer?"

"I don't have any family."

"Ah. That is too bad." It was almost a question.

"I don't think so."

"Well, good then."

Renata finished the glass of wine. She ate the bread and paté, making two bites of it. "Mmmm. This is very good. And what do you do by yourself all the time?"

"I walk. I admire the scenery."

"And at night?"

"I read. I go to sleep early."

"That is good for the health."

"Yeah." Maxwell said it without expression. "And what do you do when you're not cleaning house?"

"I work at the Tenne. I pretend I am my great-grandmother in her quaint native costume, and I carry food to the tables and set it on fire. Meat, cake, ice cream, coffee: I put the torch to all."

"Sounds cheery."

"Yes. It is not a bad job. The more I burn, the more the diners tip me. And I practice my languages."

"What do you speak?"

"Italian I am learning for myself. I have French and English from school. Would you like to speak English? You are an American, yes?"

"Canadian."

"You have a German name, and you speak German very well. I did not at first realize."

"My grandfather spoke German. I learned it at home. And I have . . . I had a lot of business in Germany."

"I see. And now, no more business?"

"I'm retired."

"That must be very nice for you. And you are so young." She said it looking directly at him as she peeled the orange.

Maxwell kept his customary blank expression, but he smiled to himself. He found Renata's obviousness charming.

"Do you look at the stars?" she asked, nodding toward the telescope set up by the window.

"Yes. The air is clear here."

"That must be very interesting."

"Yes. Beautiful."

"How many stars can you see?"

"I don't know. Millions, a billion."

"And they are all so far away." She shuddered.

"What's the matter?"

"It is too big. Does it not make you feel small?"

"No. Well . . . Oh, I think it's a good thing not to take yourself too seriously, if that's what you mean."

"What should one take seriously, if not one's self?"

"Oh, I agree with that. I mean, not take yourself too seriously in the ultimate scheme of things. I mean, what you think is important may be important to you, but don't think . . ." he raised his hand in a vague gesture toward the telescope and beyond, ". . . it's important to them."

"Ah." She regarded the telescope appraisingly. "It is a fine machine." She turned the same look to Maxwell. "Do you look at the Matterhorn?"

"No. The telescope's too powerful. Too narrow a field. You can't see the whole mountain with it, only details."

"I must remember to close the curtains of my room when I am undressing."

"I wouldn't look into your room, Fräulein Tauber."

"You are too shy?"

"I don't know where you live."

Renata separated a segment from the orange. She held it between thumb and forefinger and put it carefully into her mouth while looking at Maxwell. She bit slowly with her front teeth and let the juice run around her tongue. Then she chewed deliberately and finally said, "I would think you are a man who finds what he looks for."

Maxwell discovered himself pleased with the flattery: not what Renata said, but that she should be interested in flattering him at all. Surprisingly, that pleasure did not seem diminished by his suspecting the reason for her interest. "You get what you want, too, don't you," he said.

"One tries."

"And you want a rich husband."

Maxwell saw her eyes widen for a fraction of a second. She had not expected him to see that much of it, or at least not to say it that way, but she recovered instantly. "No." She put another piece of orange into her mouth.

"No?" Maxwell smiled slightly.

"No. Oh, if I should want a husband, then it would be good that he should be rich. But I do not want a husband. I could already have a husband, even a rich one—for Zermatt. That is not what I want."

"What do you want?"

"To be rich from myself, not from my husband. To go away from Zermatt."

"Where?" Maxwell was astounded at the notion anyone could want to leave there.

"Anywhere I want to go."

"You won't find anyplace more beautiful than here."

"Oh? When I have seen them all and I know that, then perhaps I will come back. And be retired. And live in a large chalet all by myself. And have someone clean it for me."

Maxwell put his glass back onto the table. There were two wet rings there, overlapping. He made the third, interlocking them into a perfect trefoil. "How old are you?" he asked without looking up.

"Twenty-two." She was starting another segment of orange. She paused. "What is wrong?"

"Nothing," said Maxwell. "You remind me of someone."

"A woman?"

"No. A young man. Also ambitious."

"What happened to him?"

Maxwell lifted his eyes to the Matterhorn. It still took his breath away every time he looked. "He came to a bad end," he said.

"I am sorry."

"I hope you won't be."

"I hope. Many people come to a bad end. My mother came to a bad end."

"How?"

113

"She married my father and had seven children and scrubbed floors and cooked and did laundry."

"I see."

"Yes. She died of it. In another ten years she will lie down and we can bury her."

Maxwell poured more wine.

"What does your father do?"

"He is a guide. He takes tourists up the Matterhorn."

"He must make good money."

"He does. He has a large bank account. But no paid servants. He believes in work. We all work—my mother, my brothers, my sisters. Perhaps I would not mind if I were a man and could be a guide, too. It is pleasant to walk in the mountains. But a woman cannot be a guide. I know all the pathways, but a woman—"

"You've climbed it?"

"The Matterhorn? Oh, yes. Four times. And Dom, Dent Blanche, Weisshorn, all of them. My brothers take me for practice. And I am better than they, but . . ."

She shrugged. "But I must earn money by carrying food to the table and cleaning houses." She stared at Maxwell intently. "But I will do more!"

Maxwell disliked the way the conversation had turned. He looked away and drank some of his wine.

Renata ate a piece of orange, watching Maxwell as he drank. "And now you are retired from business and ready for a life of pleasure," she said. She always spoke with the faintest irony, choosing each word carefully, which suggested laughter suppressed beneath the surface of what she said.

"Or at least a pleasant afternoon now and then," Maxwell said.

Renata smiled at him, then gathered the orange peelings into a pile and rose from the table taking them and her glass. "I must go now."

"Must you?"

"Yes. I have another house to clean."

She continued looking into Maxwell's eyes for a moment before going to the kitchen. She returned, picking up the rucksack as she came. Again she put it on, slipping her left arm through one strap, her right through the other, facing him. There was no coyness. Her movement was not ostentatious, but neither was there any pretense as she thrust her breasts toward him and twisted, getting the pack into place.

"Thank you for the wine," she said.

"Please. Sorry you have to eat and run."

"I come again next week."

Maxwell raised his glass in salute. He felt full of savoir faire.

By the end of the afternoon he felt ridiculous. First came a suspicion that he had invented the incident, that Renata was only an innocent, outgoing girl whose naiveté he had twisted into innuendo. That idea was easily dismissed, but the one that followed naturally from it was not: she was making fun of him. He *was* old enough to be her father. But his initial inspection of her had not been paternal, and she had paid him back by leading him on like an old goat. Which he was. He thought about that sense of hidden laughter when she spoke. Maxwell felt he had made a fool of himself.

Trying to escape that feeling led to a conclusion which—though perhaps accurate—was hardly more satisfactory. She wanted to become rich "from herself." That, in the context of her frank sexuality, could easily mean she was a whore. She saw that he admired the goods, so she displayed them—making sure he understood there was a price.

To be seen as a mark—an easy mark—by an amateur hustler; to have played along without even recognizing the game, made Maxwell disgusted with himself.

Nevertheless, just before dawn on Sunday morning, Maxwell had a vivid dream in which he cupped Renata's buttocks in his hands while she twisted under him, brushing enormous breasts back and forth against his chest.

* * *

Both dream and disgust stayed with him through a shower and breakfast. To escape, Maxwell set out to reach as high as he could on the mountain behind the chalet. He hiked up the footpath to Sunnega, rode the cable-gondola up from there to the Blauherd station, and changed to the other line up to Rothorn. Then he walked higher, along the narrow hiking path.

It was another fine day. Fog lay in the valley far below, making a white lake around the bases of the peaks. After a while the fog burned away without a trace, unless, perhaps, it was lingering moisture that gave an intensity—almost a sheen—to the blue sky. The Matterhorn appeared in a dimensionality that made Maxwell remember his grandmother's stereoscopic slides, taken with lenses set farther apart than the eyes so that subject and background had a separation more than real.

Maxwell had to wear his sunglasses to look at the snow- and ice-covered mountain. Even so, its brightness hurt his eyes. It seemed right that gazing on such magnificence should cost some pain. In recompense for his willingness to mortify his flesh, the mountain healed all other hurts.

He had ridden above the trees and grass, climbed higher, beyond matted alpine shrubs and moss. Now, only rock—the peaks themselves: the bones of the earth with all deceits and vanities stripped away. He had come to the place of the gods; not those petty spirits of stream or wood which interact with humans, which can be offended or propitiated, but the great gods. Maxwell did not believe in gods, but he sensed a truth in all the primitive legends he had read while waiting in carbolic-reeking railway stations, fly-specked cafés, hotels with peeling wallpaper. There was a presence in the high mountains. If any being did exist among the stars, between the galaxies, Maxwell thought, its nature might be sensed on earth most truly at the tops of mountains.

He sat lost in contemplation through half the day. Thoughts, memories from his life, drifted into his mind: the banister in a

116

house where he had lived; catching a long pass on a particular smoky October afternoon; the polished shoetips of the second man he had killed. They were like the buildings of Zermatt below. He could see them clearly, individually, but they were far, far away and tiny.

Always his eyes were drawn up again to the Matterhorn. It took him into itself, took *him*, freed, purified of all concerns, of regret. He would die—that knowledge never left him—but his little death hurt him no more than it could hurt the mountain.

In midafternoon he walked all the way back down to his house. The trail was steep in places, hard going, and it was long. He arrived back late, tired and hungry. He drank a bottle of dark beer while grilling two wursts, and another bottle when he ate them with bread and kraut, and then he went to bed.

He had hardly thought of Renata at all, and when he did, it was only as one of the hundreds of attractive women whom he had met once and never again.

There were high clouds across the sky when he awoke on Monday, a whiteness. Maxwell decided to go up to the glacier at the head of the Findeln Valley anyway.

The road that wound up from Zermatt and passed the chalet went on eastward to a small dam that controlled the flow from the glacier into the stream that Maxwell had sat beside on Saturday. He enjoyed the walk up to the dam, seeing the valley and the mountains. He was disappointed, though, when he reached the end. Gravel excavated when the dam was built was piled to one side. It made him think of a slag heap.

He went up the footpath skirting the small lake behind the dam and rising to the top of a ridge. The glacier began below, on his right—a wall of gray and blue ice; the blue was not deep but looked as though a stain had been splotched over the surface. The sky was now completely overcast, and the ice seemed dull and dirty. It reminded him of elephant's skin. The side of the bank on which he walked ended below him in debris

117

shoved aside by the glacier and left in long, irregular piles.

Maxwell found himself becoming more and more depressed. He had expected purity, origin. Instead, he found decay. He cut his excursion short and went home. Even before he got there, a drizzle had started.

He spent the afternoon moping, perversely unwilling to light a fire that might have cheered him. He told himself it was only his mood, but he felt ill. At suppertime he cooked half a chicken and drank a bottle of good St. Emilion. He knew the wine would be too heavy to go with the meat, but he wanted something good to make himself feel better. It didn't work.

He slept heavily for a while, then dreamed about Handelsmann and woke suddenly, covered with sweat. There was something sharp burning in his stomach. He got up, took some bicarbonate, tried to go back to sleep. He thought about James and of writing a letter to him. It could be delivered afterward. He lay in bed working on the letter word by word until after four o'clock. By then it seemed well composed. He was sure James would understand. Maxwell drifted off to sleep while repeating the letter to himself.

He woke again at 5:30. It was the jelly dream, and he never was sure whether he woke because of his screaming or because he could not scream loudly enough.

The rain continued all Tuesday. Maxwell had spent most of a lifetime by himself. He knew how to handle his moods, damping any dangerous exhilarations, pulling up his socks if he slipped toward despondency. Yesterday had been inexcusable. He did not intend it to happen again.

He ate a solid breakfast, lit the fire, and set himself up in front of it. He oiled his boots and sharpened his knives—all except the stiletto; its blade had gone into a bin in Luzern, its handle down a grating at Bern. He checked his hiking gear, taking every item out of the pack, inspecting, replacing. He went through the refrigerator and kitchen cabinets, taking inventory. In the spirit of getting things done, he considered writing the letter to James but realized he had no stationery. In the afternoon he finished a book on Schliemann and the discovery of Troy.

Maxwell didn't go outside all day. He hardly looked out the windows. There was no point; he could barely see a hundred feet. He was shocked, then, when he did glance out to the west, early in the evening, to discover lights in the neighboring chalet, which stood to the side and uphill of his house; he was rarely aware of it when looking across toward the Matterhorn.

His hackles rose slightly. There were so few visitors this early in the season, Maxwell had come to think of the entire slope between Findeln and Sunegga as his own territory. Obviously, the house next door—and all of the others scattered over the mountainside—would be occupied sooner or later by vacationers. He had understood that. But he resented the intrusion.

There was more rain on Wednesday, light but steady. After breakfast, Maxwell cleaned the top of the small electric range. It was not really dirty, but the cleaning gave him something to do. It made him think of Renata. He winced slightly at the memory yet found seeing her in his mind pleasant, too.

He decided to go down to Zermatt for his weekly shopping, despite the rain. Assuming that the chairlift to and from Sunegga would not be running, he walked down the path through Findeln, into the forest beyond, and on to the bottom.

Aside from the pleasure he got while shopping for groceries and anticipating good meals, Maxwell disliked going to Zermatt. He was contemptuous of its commercialization, and he had come to dislike being among people. Yet he spent the afternoon going from shop to shop simply to be occupied. He found some new books, one on the Khmers and one on Disraeli which seemed well written.

The newspapers on their racks near the door all showed

pictures of Constantin Vronsky, with headlines about his defection and disappearance, but Maxwell now avoided looking at papers as scrupulously as he had previously read them.

He did notice a copy of *Der Stern* with an artfully photographed nude girl on its cover. Maxwell did a double take, because she was blond and at first glance looked like Renata. He paused for an instant, almost at the point of buying the magazine, then laughed at himself and went out.

It rained again on Thursday. Maxwell went for a walk along the road, to be out of the house, but it wasn't pleasant. He couldn't see anything, the air was raw, and he was getting his boots soaked. After ten minutes he came back.

There was a man outside the chalet next door, taking trash to the garbage can. The man stopped to watch Maxwell. Maxwell had no particular suspicion—he was only curious about who had entered his territory—and accepted the man's stare as being the same as his own.

"*Guten Morgen,*" Maxwell said. He preferred to be thought of as Swiss or German.

Paul simply nodded.

Before lunch, Maxwell decided to repeat the whole series of his morning exercises to keep his joints from mildewing. He got through the first fifty pushups with only a little more effort than usual, but halfway through the situps, he felt ill. Not in pain or nauseous; he simply had no more strength. For a few seconds he tried to raise himself, sure that an act of will would keep him going. But he had no will either.

He lay on the floor, his toes hooked under the foot of his box bed. He stared at the boards of the paneled ceiling. Their edges were beveled, making V grooves. The grooves were painted red. Maxwell lay looking at the boards, noticing how straight they were, how well they were joined. He did not think. For a moment he had the feeling that comes before crying. He took a very deep breath and let it out. He rolled to his side and got up without straining. He looked toward the window for several seconds, seeing nothing but gray cloud.

On Friday morning, it rained again, but the fog seemed thinner; it was whitish instead of dull gray, and Maxwell felt lighter. *Barometer going up*, he thought. He should buy a barometer. He would get one next week when he went back down to Zermatt.

After breakfast he washed his underwear and socks. They wouldn't dry, of course, but it kept him busy. He left them draped around the bathroom.

He walked up the road for fifteen minutes, then back. Moisture from the clouds stood on his clothes, but the rain had stopped.

He read about Disraeli until noon.

While he was making lunch he noticed some dust and a few grains of spilled rice between the stove and cabinet. He was about to sweep when he remembered that Renata would be in to clean the next day. The realization went through him like an electric shock.

After lunch he read, but Renata kept coming into his head. He put down Disraeli, picked up the book about the Khmers and thumbed through it. There were a few photographs. One was a detail from a temple: a female figure, a dancer, narrow waisted, with breasts like grapefruit.

Maxwell looked up from the page and stared at the blank window. He knew with an intuition he had long ago learned to trust that Renata would be very good in bed.

The only question was whether he wanted to pay for it. He had not paid since those two years after the war when it had seemed fun to go with some buddies and as much whiskey as they could come by on the black market and spend an entire weekend in a whorehouse. Those had been parties. The girls seemed to enjoy themselves, too, and the bill at the end covered food, lodging, and entertainment all together. When he shifted out of the army into fieldwork, he no longer had buddies.

Maxwell realized he was breathing shallowly. He took a full breath and shook his head at himself. He did not often indulge in sexual fantasies, not because of his age, but because he found them ultimately to be frustrating. So he would not dwell on whether Renata's breasts would be hemispherical, like the dancer's, or conical, or how soft and smooth they would feel, or. . .

He put the screen in front of the fire, changed into his boots, and went for another walk. He gathered more wildflowers for his table, this time making the bouquet all reds and pinks.

The weather was changing, no doubt. Clouds still covered everything, but it was even paler. In late afternoon it took on an amber tone. In the evening, just as Maxwell finished eating, the clouds began to disperse.

He went out onto his balcony. The sun was setting behind the ridge to the west of the valley. The clouds had thinned to veils. They began to glow pink, then an intense rose. Maxwell stood amazed. The scene was magical, a fantasy. After days of grayness the world gleamed and sparkled with vibrant color. Through rifts in the drifting mist he could see the valley below and the lower shoulders of the Matterhorn: emerald green above, sapphire and amethyst below. The Matterhorn itself still was mystical, shrouded in horizontal folds of cloud, layered peach-colored and violet.

Maxwell heard voices behind him. On the balcony of the neighboring house he saw a man and woman. The woman called, "*Paolo. Paolo? Paolo, veni, veni,*" and more that Maxwell couldn't understand.

Italians.

The man Maxwell had seen the day before came out on the level below the balcony. The three people spoke together, then stood gazing.

Maxwell turned back to the view. He had no more resentment of his neighbors. On the contrary, he was grateful for them, as though that soft and glowing beauty was more than he could bear to witness alone.

When he woke in the morning, Maxwell decided not to have sex with Renata. He still felt distaste for the commercial aspect, but more than that, he did not want to become involved. He was free, finally, of people, of obligations and responsibilities, of concern for others: free now—for as long as he lived—to live for himself. The beauty of the previous evening, which he had watched until every dusky-purple shade had faded into black, reminded him of the sense of isolation and purity he had sought by coming to that place.

The Matterhorn was still behind cloud. Clear air would come with the center of the new weather system, but further showers still seemed possible before then. Maxwell decided to be gone from the house while Renata was there. He walked west along the road, keeping to the high branch instead of taking the one that dropped down to Zermatt.

He got back to the chalet at 1:30, after the time when Renata had left him the previous week. He came in through the front door, hung his jacket in the closet, took off his boots, and went into the living room.

Renata was still there.

"Oh."

"Good afternoon, Herr Bergmann."

She stood in the kitchen. Her trousers this week were light blue, made of stretch fabric, even tighter than the jeans had been. Instead of the bulky sweater, she wore a white shirt.

"I didn't think you'd still be here."

"I changed my schedule. I have first cleaned next door."

"I see."

Renata's shirt was of a thin cottonlike material. It fell against her upper body, then bloused softly where it tucked into her belt. As Maxwell looked, he saw her nipples reveal themselves through the fabric as they hardened.

"I can go out again," he said. He felt himself flushing.

"Please stay. I will not bump you when I vacuum."

Maxwell felt foolish staying while she worked, but he would have felt equally so if he made a point of leaving. He went to the chair by the fireplace and took up his book.

"You have been walking again?"

"Yeah. Just down the road and back."

Renata brought the vacuum cleaner out from the closet, plugged it in, and began sweeping the carpet at the kitchen end of the room, behind Maxwell.

He tried to read about the Khmers, being careful not to look at the photographs.

He glanced up as Renata worked along the side of the room opposite him. He could see into the front of her shirt. Every time she pushed the cleaner forward with her left hand, the right side tightened, the left bloused downward, and Maxwell could see her breast. Not merely the inner rise, all of it.

Hemispheric.

She knows exactly what she's doing, he thought. *She's excited about it. And so am I.*

Maxwell sucked in his cheeks to wet his mouth, and found he had to shift position in the chair.

Renata continued sweeping around the edge of the carpet, crossing in front of him over near the windows. Then she began working toward him.

He gave up any pretense of looking at his book.

Renata stood in front of Maxwell, smiled, looked down at his feet. He raised them, and she leaned over again to sweep back and forth up to the chair. He could look directly through the perfect arch between her breasts and see her navel.

She looked up at him, smiled again. The smile was open, and Maxwell remembered the tone of sincere pleasure in her voice the week before when she had said, "We are proud of our attractions."

She moved around behind the chair, and Maxwell lowered his feet. She finished and put the cleaner by the stairs.

Maxwell stared out of the window. He looked as much like a

boulder as ever, but he knew if he raised his hand and held it out, his fingers would tremble.

Renata went to the kitchen and got the pail. She filled it with water and crossed to the window.

"The windows don't need washing," Maxwell said.

"Not the others. But this is streaked from the rain. You do not want this view to have streaks, yes?"

She went out onto the balcony, smiled at Maxwell, and began wiping it.

Maxwell watched, expressionless, as she bent and stretched, swayed and twisted. None of her gestures was exaggerated more than was necessary to do the work, but each movement displayed the litheness of her body. From time to time she glanced at him, without archness, as though acknowledging their participation in an activity they both enjoyed.

She finished the window and came back inside. "So, isn't that nice?"

"That is very nice."

"I have hung your clothing on the line outside."

"Thank you. I'm sorry if they were in your way."

"No matter. If you like, I would be happy to do your washing for you."

"I don't mind doing it."

"Good. It is good that a man should not mind to wash his own clothes. But it is not necessary. I would be happy to wash for you."

"Is that included in the cleaning fee I pay Herr Julen?"

"No. That would be an extra. To me."

"Ah."

"Would you like for me to shop for you? If you do not like to come down into Zermatt, you can give me a list. Each week you give me a list for the next week, and I bring what you want when I come."

"I suppose you have other services, too?"

Despite the speed of his heartbeat and the tingling all through his body, Maxwell felt detached, as though watching

125

himself playing a role. It was a situation he had often experienced. Sometimes there were lines that had to be spoken, gestures to be made, as though rehearsed. It didn't matter whether the actor believed in the part; the scene was written and had to be played.

Renata smiled brightly and nodded, then suddenly moved away. "I clean upstairs now."

She hefted the vacuum cleaner and went to the floor above. After a moment, Maxwell heard her over his head running the sweeper.

I'll be damned, he said to himself. Evidently he and Renata were not working from the same script. But, no, he was not making it up. And he didn't believe she was only teasing him.

Maybe she just likes to finish one job before she starts another.

The sound of the vacuum cleaner stopped. Maxwell could hear faint footsteps from above, as though she were moving here and there about the room. Furniture scraped—a chair, the bedside table.

Maxwell furrowed his forehead for a moment. It came to him. *Dusting!*

He was absolutely nonplussed. To interrupt that build-up for *dusting. . . !*

Maxwell snorted. He chuckled. He laughed out loud. He breathed deeply and chuckled again. *Well, honey,* he thought, *you certainly are going to burn up the whole world, someday. But you've got a few things to learn first.* All of his excitement and tension vanished.

She *was* a sweet kid. If she wanted to buy herself a better life by whoring instead of scrubbing floors, what the hell. Look at the things *he'd* done to make a living. Now that Maxwell felt himself cooled and out of the situation, he was prepared to be broad-minded and indulgent.

"Herr Bergmann?" Renata's voice carried down the stairs. "Herr Bergmann?"

"Yes, Renata?"

"Please."

Maxwell climbed the stairs feeling amused and paternal. Despite years of being the best in his trade, despite the sixth sense that kept him alive through so many treacheries, Maxwell went all the way up to the top of the stairs and into the room before he realized he'd been sandbagged.

Renata stood halfway across the room, looking toward the big window, her back to him. She heard his footsteps on the stairs, heard him come into the room, heard him stop. Slowly she brought her hands up in front of her, slipped the unbuttoned shirt off her shoulders. She let her arms go down to full length behind her, and the shirt fell to the floor.

Again, light through the window made her yellow hair glow. Maxwell could see faint down extending along her neck to a point.

He had been set up.

He didn't care.

Renata turned her head and looked at Maxwell over her left shoulder. Her neck sloped in a smooth curve, its gracefulness compensating for the width of her shoulder. Her shoulders and arms were rounded fully. There was strong muscle there; Maxwell appreciated that. But everything was rounded.

As she turned to look at Maxwell, her upper body twisted slightly, and he could see her firm breast silhouetted against the window.

She's doing it like a stripteaser.

He didn't care.

Renata smiled and turned to face Maxwell fully. She stood erect, her arms at her sides, holding herself to show him her breasts. They were not enormous, as in his dream. His hands would be able to cup them. Renata held her breath. She twisted slightly from the waist, slowly swinging each shoulder forward and back. She looked at Maxwell steadily with an open smile.

She's displaying herself. It's merchandise.

He didn't care.

Renata moved her hands across the tops of her thighs and up to her waist. Very slowly, she unfastened her belt. Very slowly,

127

she pressed the button back through the buttonhole. She lifted the zipper tab with her right thumb and forefinger.

Where did she learn this? It's like a dirty movie. He didn't care.

"Now the other services, yes?"

She pulled down the zipper. The tightness of the fabric spread the sides of the opening apart, but she kept both hands over it. Maxwell had only a glimpse of golden fluff between them.

"Yes?"

All he could do was nod.

She slid her palms inside and around to push the trousers down. Bending, she slipped them to her ankles, stepped forward clear of them, then straightened.

After a moment, Maxwell realized he was about to black out from not breathing.

Renata stood still, letting him look at her. Her waist was slender, her belly only slightly rounded. Her long legs were full but firm.

Then she crossed to him, took his hand, led him to the bed. She lay on it, still looking at him, still holding his hand. She pulled him down to sit beside her, then put his palm against the base of her neck and slowly pushed it to her breast, then over her stomach and down between her legs.

Maxwell's pulse hammered in his ears. All the despair, the fear, the guilt of more than a year—the thousands of hours, uncountable minutes of pain in body and mind and soul suffered alone—all exploded out of him in a firestorm of passion.

His clothes came off. He lay upon her, kissing her, biting her, rubbing his face against her hair, his hands running up and down her body, kneading her, his body writhing on hers. He thrust into her. He twisted and surged. She was warm and holding. She was dark and safe. Deep inside her was comfort. Deep inside her was oblivion.

10

"Your technique, darling, your technique is absolutely marvelous," he said when he was able to speak again.

"I'm not at all sure I like that."

"Why not? It was meant as a compliment."

"Sounds rather studied, don't you think? *Her technique was perfected through years of practice.* Rather connotes professionalism."

"Sorry." Corchran rolled to his side and propped himself on his left elbow. "Let me say, then, that you, as an amateur—and I mean someone doing something purely for the love of doing it—bring to bed a fervency of spirit and a natural, unstudied talent, a degree of artistry that could never be approached by one who was—pardon me—merely in trade."

"Yer not 'arf bad yerself, luv."

"Ta." He kissed her nose. Not her mouth—that would start them again, and he had to rest a while.

It had been a delightful evening: dinner at Rules—smoked salmon, herbed spring lamb perfectly pink, and an excellent St. Julien. Both of them had been brilliantly witty and had played a smashing game of "will-she-won't-she." He was certain she would, though they never had, but she kept it going even after she invited him into her flat. She gave him brandy, then sat in a chair opposite instead of on the couch beside him. She let him finish his drink and say he had to go, then offered him coffee.

"Not this late. I wouldn't sleep."

"But I don't want you to sleep, darling."

All in all, it had been a perfect way to celebrate defeat.

During the first week, Corchran had believed he might win. "Almost forty years," he had said, holding the pages of his digest of Maxwell's career together by one corner. The distance between his fingers was less than a sixteenth of an inch.

"There are volumes in every line," said Minelli.

Corchran shook his head. "Max could have kept the *Sunday Telegraph* readers sitting at their breakfast tables over congealed eggs week after week if he'd sold his stories: how he set up those nets in Silesia, or getting Grigenko out through Danzig. But when we get it boiled down to the important facts . . ."

He waved the file summary in the air and dropped it onto the table. "When I was in school—in my Freshman English class—I had to write an exercise: everything that happened during the first five minutes after I got out of bed one morning. Everything. I put on my socks: what color they were, what they felt like. My pants. What I felt like, what I thought about. Instant by instant. It went on for pages. It was fascinating to realize all the thoughts, the sensations one has without really being aware of them. But ultimately, Frank, in the great scheme of things, all it said was I got up."

"What does this say about Max?"

"Maxwell was originally Maxciewycz; his grandfathers came from Poland and Czechoslovakia. He's a textbook example of the melting pot. And the American dream: father the first to go to high school, Max sent to college. The prosperous family business in Akron. For our immediate purposes: he meets people easily and they like him, and as a result he knows about a quarter of the population of east-central Europe by their first names. But in the past thirty years or so he has had only four really close friends. Three of them are dead."

"When?"

"Oh, way back. The last was in '59. A man named Aldrich.

Actually, one of the others lived longer. Retired to the States in '56; he and Max just never got together again."

"And the fourth was Newlands."

"Right."

"Cheese and crackers got all muddy! I'm surprised he didn't take Max over to meet the Queen. I mean, they could have called up old Blunt and all had tea. These Brits . . . !"

"In this case, Frank, I think that's a little hard."

"Well, you said he suspected, and he still took Max out."

"Max told him he wasn't defecting."

"Sure. Gave him his word as a gentleman. It's all very quaint, and I know you like them, but these Brits . . . I don't think I'll ever get over it."

"I don't think Newlands will either."

Corchran's tone brought Minelli's eyes up sharply. After a moment he said. "OK, Corky."

Corchran went on without the edge. "I think Newlands is right. Whatever we think about his taking Max, he's very sharp. He's sure Max wasn't lying, and he doesn't think Max would defect, anyway. He agrees with my theory: Max has gone off to die."

"Like an elephant."

"Exactly."

"To Tahiti?"

"He doesn't think so. I tried that idea. Newlands said Max might go to somewhere sybaritic precisely because he never has—complete reversal under the stress of dying. But Newlands thinks Max is too much of a Puritan for that."

"A Puritan? I've heard stories about Max in the old days . . ."

"Newlands says Max has to earn his indulgences."

"Ah. Yeah. But he could think just dying was enough to earn—"

"Of course. But what Newlands says makes sense in context of the rest of it."

"What?"

Corchran tapped the file. "He's a sports nut. A physical

131

fitness nut. Memorizes world's records. He's been to almost every Olympics—summer and winter—for the past thirty years. If this were a few years ago, I could have believed he'd sold out just to go to Moscow. He sees them all: World Cup matches, Winter Games, everything. *That's* what he's done with his leaves. He stopped going back to the States when his mother died. He just saves his time and goes to games. And he works out every day. Ted Staros roomed with him for a week in Berlin three years ago while they were waiting for Schirmer to come across, and he says Max did calisthenics for thirty minutes to an hour every morning."

Minelli dropped his eyes to the file and stared at it. "I wonder if he still does them," he said finally.

"Yes. I suppose it isn't the way any of us would choose to go, but for a guy like that. . ."

"Yeah. Well, so. . . ?"

"So? So I think that's a pretty good start for three days! I've found how he got out of England and I've found the thing he seems to be most interested in."

"And?"

"And I don't know where he is or where he's going! True. But I believe it will be to somewhere scenic where he can watch well-developed bodies—"

"Do you think he could be queer?"

"Max? Maybe. Latent. Anyway, where he can watch athletes in action. I'm checking on schedules of sports competitions. If that doesn't work, my next guess will be around the Med. Water sports, bare bodies. Greece, maybe. Olympia! That would fit. Joe Klugman is coming in from Vienna this afternoon—he's been in the field with Max more than anyone else in the last year—and I've got calls in to Ditter and Nash. As I go over this some more, I'm bound to get more names. Someone will have heard Max say something that narrows it."

"Good. OK, Corky, keep at it. Keep me informed."

The next day they heard about Handelsmann.

Because the possibility of Maxwell's being paid in Switzerland was obvious, it had never seemed a likely place for him to stay. Handelsmann's death confirmed that Maxwell had been there: therefore, he would not be there any longer. Corchran crossed Switzerland off the list.

Margaret had become more and more interesting to Corchran throughout the whole mess. He had noticed her before, of course. They made small talk on his way in and out of Minelli's office. She could be very funny. On those occasions when Corchran imagined himself as James Bond, Margaret played Moneypenny. He had considered her reasonably attractive, although shorter and rounder than he preferred, and she seemed a trifle straight. She dressed well enough but would never even try to bring off wearing a Chantilly lace tablecloth pinned with three diamond brooches and nothing else, as his friend Lady Eugenia had done.

But Corchran had no opportunity of seeing Lady Eugenia during those three weeks. Everyone was working flat-out. There was no hysteria, not even the tight-lipped kind: Minelli wouldn't allow it. Minelli shaved and changed striped shirts in his private bathroom and spoke calmly. He didn't order overtime, he just kept giving people things to do, and whenever someone's task ended after close to eighteen hours of work, Minelli would send him away for six.

Except for Corchran, who was a wheel within a wheel. He was given a desk, one phone line, a cot, and use of the conference room for interviews. He had support: his messages went out with Minelli's own priority, and people he wanted to talk with were brought to him. But essentially he was on his own. Margaret, handling his communications, passing people and papers to him as they came in, was the only person other than Minelli he saw regularly.

As he saw more of Margaret, she began to look better to him. He was grateful for her help and her attempts to cheer him, even more so in the second week when he was tired and beginning to doubt, while the pressure began to come off all the others.

By the third week, all that could be found that Maxwell had touched was quarantined. The full implications of his betrayal might never be known, and rebuilding the structures that had been razed would take years. Still, most of the office resumed near normal schedules.

But Corchran slogged on and became increasingly tense and frustrated. As he looked again and again at the pages of dates and names and at the lists that he had written and crossed through, as the writing faded and left him staring at blank despair, Corchran often found himself filling the emptiness with pictures of Margaret without any clothes on.

Remembering, he smiled to himself. He looked at her as she lay on her back beside him. Light from sodium-vapor lamps along the street below her window gilded the rises of her body. She was neither as slender as he usually liked, nor as pneumatically voluptuous as he had imagined her to be during those dreadful hours when he was trying not to admit failure.

Margaret was looking toward the window. "I like a night like this," she said.

"Ra-ther!"

"I mean the weather."

"The weather. Oh. Oh, dear, and I thought . . . Well, I *had* hoped . . ."

"Oh, Corky! I was being poetic."

"Poetic?"

"I was pretending it was fog. A real fog, like in Sherlock Holmes. Of course they don't have those now that there aren't coal fires, but when it's drizzling you can imagine you're in the old London."

"Yes."

"Isn't it nice to think that? That we're in London the way it's *supposed* to be?"

"Yes."

"I like to pretend that London is still as it's supposed to be. On a night like this I can walk through Mayfair—Shepherd's Market—and imagine myself still in the Restoration, coming from cards at Lady Sneerwell's. Or if I'm in Belgravia, I think I'm Lady Uppercrust and have sixteen servants like Hudson and Jean Marsh, and a stuffy old husband, and a new lover each fortnight.

"That's what we'll pretend, Corky! Reginald has had too much port, as usual, and gone home early, and we've slipped away from the ball. Who shall you be? Lord . . . Or perhaps a Viscount—you're too young to be a Duke. Viscount Lustful! And you—"

"I don't like pretending."

"Why not?"

"When you pretend something, you're simply admitting it's not true. I've spent a great deal of time—and money, too—to reach the point where I don't have to pretend anything."

"Sorry. I wasn't implying—"

"Of course not. I'm sorry. Of course it's pleasurable to imagine how things used to be. But I like things as they are, too. And I certainly don't have to pretend *you're* anyone else."

"Thank you. Corky, I didn't mean I had to pretend *you* were someone else."

"Margaret, my ego would never have permitted even a suspicion of that." Corchran smiled to show that all was well. It was. *A little pudgy*, he thought, *but very nice*.

He put his hand over her navel and rubbed gently in a circle.

"So much for poetry," she said and laughed.

"The belly of my love is like a peach, her breasts are golden pears."

"Never mind, darling. You're a poet enough with your hands."

Corchran knew she was right. He liked to think he could play upon a woman like a musical instrument. He improvised a theme and variations. Margaret's body responded to his touch, moving under his fingers as he played arpeggios, then arching up against his palm at the crescendo. He added a little coda, lightly, then lay back to let her take her turn.

She had just begun in an interesting way that promised a quarter-hour of excruciating delight when the telephone rang.

11

"WE'RE SORRY . . . We didn't want to disturb you."

"Disturb me?" Vronsky closed his eyes and kept them closed through two breaths. It never did any good to lose his temper. "But, as you see, I am disturbed."

Nella did, and her eyes were wide with horror at the sight.

"If you'd been up before I left, if you'd *ever* get up in the morning, you wouldn't have to be disturbed," Paul snapped.

"Paul!"

"*I* did not go to bed at nine o'clock," said Vronsky. "*I* was thinking until after three. I needed sleep."

"You've been sleeping for four days!"

"I was tired! I had not slept for two weeks . . ." It was irrelevant. The whole argument was irrelevant. Vronsky took another breath. "Now I am ready to work."

He turned on Nella. "I told you last night. I told you the clouds were parting, the sun would shine again, and I would work."

"Yes, Doctor Vronsky."

Vronsky opened his palms, placing his case clearly before her. "I said that I would begin writing."

Nella could not look at him. "Yes, Doctor Vronsky."

"You didn't tell anyone you would need paper."

Vronsky turned to Paul, turned his head only, as though not quite sure what he had heard. He blinked through his new glasses. "I said I would write."

Vronsky was tempted to sarcasm, to ask whether he was expected to carve his thoughts into the plank walls of the chalet. But he had learned. It was necessary to communicate with such people. Losing one's temper, sarcasm, did no good. It was best to speak slowly, using short words, with perhaps a hint of scorn to focus attention, but smiling so that the person would not become defensive and stop listening. He smiled.

"I said I would write. It is necessary to have paper in order to write." He smiled again. *Q.E.D.*

"Then why didn't you ask us to get you paper before I went to Zermatt this morning? If you thought about it last night, why didn't you say something?"

The suggestion was as incomprehensible to Vronsky as the idea of a new value for *pi*. If he had ever provided for his own needs, that time was beyond effective memory.

"Couldn't you plan that far ahead? I thought you were supposed to be such a great thinker."

"Paul!"

"I say it! What is this? We got to tiptoe around all day so we don't disturb the great mind when he's resting; and after four days, he wakes up, and he can't even figure out that if he's going to write, he's going to need some paper. I mean, the whole world is waiting for him to lead us to the True Socialist Society, and he is going to lead us—well, he's going to write us some directions anyway—except that he didn't think to ask for any paper!"

"Paul, you don't understand a man like Doctor Vronsky. He—"

"Paul can't understand, Nella, because he's—"

"I do understand! These flabby—"

"Never mind, Doctor Vronsky. Paul hasn't got the intelligence—"

"I got sense enough—"

"I'll get the paper for you. I can go down and—"

"You'll what?"

"I'll get Doctor Vronsky's paper for him."

137

"Why should you—"

"Because you won't and he can't. And I appreciate—"

"You appreciate his shit, that's what!" Paul strode to Nella. He seemed to tower over her—more from forcefulness than height. "You act like his servant! Wipe his boots. Wipe his ass, if you could! *Oh, shit on me, boss, I love it!*"

Nella shrank before him. Vronsky stood frozen. The flush suddenly draining from his face.

Paul raged on. "Ever since we got here, you hang around waiting on him like . . . You're nothing but—"

"Don't speak to her—"

"—one of the asskissers—"

"Don't you speak to her—"

"—that keep the exploiters of the working—"

"*Don't you*—!" Vronsky's shout rose to an unintelligible scream as he lurched across and struck Paul's ear with the back of his hand.

Vronsky clutched his hand; Paul rubbed his ear. Both of them were more shocked than hurt. They stared at each other. Then Vronsky burst into tears. Nella moved to put an arm around his shoulder, but he shook away. With his hands over his face, he ran up the stairs to his room on the second floor.

Vronsky was still in his room three hours later when Nella returned with a ream of paper, three boxes of pencils, ballpoint pens, erasers, and some manila folders. She had found where a typewriter could be hired if needed.

Paul sat at the dining table, staring out at the Matterhorn. His Walther PPK and the little Baretta they have given Nella were on the table in front of him, along with a can of oil and a rag.

"You got it," he said.

"Yes." Nella put the supplies into a carved wooden chest opposite the fireplace. "Those didn't need cleaning," she said.

"I know. Neither did the house. I had to do something."

"A girl did the house this morning, while you were gone."

"Oh?"

"She said it was included in the rent. I thought it would seem strange to send her away."

"She didn't see him?"

"No."

"Of course not. Still in the sack."

"Paul . . ."

"You think she's all right?"

"Why shouldn't she be?"

Paul picked up the oil can, put it down, stared at it. "Nella, I . . ." He spoke four languages but had difficulty pronouncing words of apology in any of them.

Vronsky's step on the stair gave him an excuse to stop trying. Paul gathered the guns and cleaning materials and started to rise.

"Paul, wait." Vronsky came and stood for a moment by the table, then sat across from Paul. Paul kept his eyes down.

"I am sorry I struck you." Vronsky's tight lips squeezed at the corners into a rueful smile. "I do not imagine that I hurt you." He rubbed the knuckles of his left hand. "I apologize for having tried to hurt you. I do not wish, ever, to hurt anyone; so perhaps I am fortunate in being such a small person."

Paul stared at the tabletop, embarrassed for Vronsky. Nella stood frozen.

"I have seen the hurt that big people, strong people, can do," Vronsky continued. "Bullies. My country is run by bullies. The police are like that. They stand over people—as you stood over Nella—and they speak to them as you spoke to her. That is wrong, Paul. That is *wrong*.

"Of course, it is not only those who are big who are bullies. In my country the greatest bullies are often quite small. They do not stand over anyone. They sit behind desks. I believe you may know some like that in your own country, Paul; so you know that they are, perhaps, the greatest bullies of all.

"But the way of the bully—big or small—is fear and force. I have been made to fear. I have been held by force. I know the evil of that way, not from theory, but from suffering in fact. I hate it. I must fight against it whenever I see it. We all must fight against it."

Vronsky spoke quietly, at the lower register of his light voice. It was the tone in which he had spoken the last minute of his presentation to the congress. It was the calm voice of total certainty. Paul and Nella stared at him transfixed, as had the three hundred physicists.

"I know you are disappointed in me, Paul. You hoped for a leader, a general who would raise the people as an army, who would lead them to fight and bleed and draw blood, and out of the blood to purify the world. That is not my way.

"Perhaps, sometimes, there must be blood, must be fighting. If so, for that you must find another leader. I cannot do that. I would not, if I could. My way must be a way without blood, without force and fear.

"There are people who believe that force and fear are the *only* way. They are wrong. My work is to prove that and to show what is right; to show that there can be a society, a world without force, with respect among people, with caring for one another.

"If you believe as I do, then help me, Paul. If you believe in the other way, then leave me."

Without taking his eyes from Paul's, Vronsky took a softpack of American cigarettes from his shirt pocket, lit one, inhaled deeply, exhaled. He continued to stare at Paul through the cloud of smoke.

Nella stood behind the chair at Vronsky's right, her hands crossed over the chairback. Tears ran down her cheeks.

Paul rubbed the oily rag back and forth a few inches across the table top. "I don't think you're right, Doctor. I mean, I don't think it works that way."

Then he shrugged, tipped his head. "But what the hell, huh? It should."

"Thank you, Paul."

140

Nella wiped her cheeks with the heels of her hands. "I got paper for you," she said.

"Thank you, Nella. Then I will begin writing."

Vronsky rose. He waited as Nella hurried to the chest and brought back the paper and supplies. He smiled as she gave them to him, then he nodded to Paul and started to go up to his room.

As he reached the third step, he paused. "Could there be something to eat?" he said, and went on without looking back.

At two-thirty the next morning, Nella tapped lightly on the door of Vronsky's room. She had heard him pacing. He would stride back and forth from window to door, then rush to sit at the little table and write.

"Yes? Come in."

Nella tentatively swung in the darkwood door. She remained outside the threshold, just at the edge of light from the small parchment shaded lamp on the table. Thin, in her white nightdress, with dark hair framing her face, she was a wraith.

"Excuse me, Doctor Vronsky. Can I get you something? Some tea?"

Vronsky squinted at her over the glare from the lamp and its reflection from sheets of paper spread on the table. "Thank you, no."

The room was blue with cigarette smoke. Seen through the layers—his thin hair disheveled and standing, the fullness above his eyes and his swelling forehead bright from the light below his face—Vronsky seemed to Nella the incarnation of genius. The fire of creation was within him. More than the gleam of lamplight on thick lenses burned in his eyes. She also saw shadows that deepened the pouches under his eyes. She feared his inspiration might consume him.

"You are working very late."

"Yes. It goes well."

"Oh, I'm so glad!" She clapped her hands, clasping them in front of her like a delighted child.

Vronsky was delighted too. "Yes. The first part is all written.

I am revising now, making it more simple. For every three words I have written, I take out two. I think when it is simplified it will be more effective."

He could see—he was sure he could see—Nella's eyes shining. He was emboldened. "I think it will be eloquent."

"Oh, Doctor Vronsky!"

"Perhaps you would like to read it?"

"Oh, yes!"

"Not now. Later, when I have finished revising."

"Oh, thank you! Yes!"

"A few more hours . . ."

"Tonight?"

"Certainly."

"Doctor Vronsky, you must not work too hard. You must not tire yourself."

"I don't feel tired."

"It is the excitement. You are so excited with what you are doing. But you must not overdo."

"I am not overdoing. I am not tired."

"I can see you are."

"I am not!"

"You see? You are irritable. Because you are tired. You should rest. Then tomorrow your work will be even better."

Vronsky opened his mouth and closed it again. He had been interrupted; he *was* irritable. At the same time, he was pleased with Nella's concern. As he looked at her standing spiritlike in the doorway, he felt suddenly that she was the guardian angel his grandmother had whispered about when they were left alone together.

"Please, Doctor Vronsky, go to bed now. Rest. Sleep. It will be best for you."

Vronsky stared at her. The sentence that was firing his mind before she knocked flickered away. "All right, Nella. Thank you. I will." He smiled.

She smiled back. She reached in to grasp the door handle. "Good night, Doctor Vronsky." She pulled the door closed.

Vronsky stared at the place where she had been. "Good night, Nella," he said finally. It was as though the darkness of wood and hallway were the same, as though she had materialized out of it and disappeared again and might still be exactly there, incorporeal. He put out the light before he undressed and put on his pajamas.

As he was settling himself in bed, he heard a creak of springs and a bump just behind his head. The realization flashed upon him that Nella was not a spirit in the doorway but a real woman in bed, that her bed and his were head to head, separated only by a thin wall. Vronsky held his breath and was sure he could hear hers. He lay still, afraid to move, and fell asleep, finally, flat on his back.

                                                                •

Vronsky astounded Paul by getting up and asking for breakfast at nine-thirty. By noon he had finished his revisions. Nella read the work sitting at the table in Vronsky's room. Vronsky sat on the bed, rocking back and forth and occasionally twitching with nervousness.

The first part was simple and eloquent.

Vronsky had worked inductively. He set out the facts of life in Russia, simple facts presented in a way that at first seemed almost random, uneditorialized: an explanation in three lines of how dissenters are committed and treated in mental institutions, including the physiological sensations caused by the drugs used, followed by a list of people Vronsky knew personally to have been sent there; a paragraph about the fate of one of his students; two lines about shopping in state-controlled stores versus farmers' private markets; two about the homes of the elite and those of factory workers; some statistics; reminders of Hungary, Czechoslovakia, Afghanistan, Poland—and here and there, single sentences about himself and his own experiences. Vronsky wrote as a scientist. He used no adjectives, offered no judgments. He presented data. The pattern was varied and repeated so that each statement was like a single light stroke of a hammer on metal, but each stroke echoed.

Stroke after stroke, reverberations rang together into a swelling alarm.

When Nella had finished the last page she turned to Vronsky with a look of anguish. He believed he understood.

"This is not an attack on communism; only on the perversion of communism. In the next part I will examine capitalism and fascism in the same way. Then I will explain why these evils occur. This is necessary. It is necessary to understand the principles of belief and action which cause the good ideals of any system to become perverted and cause societies to become oppressive. Only when these principles are understood can a new set of principles be formulated."

Throughout the afternoon, Nella worked in her room correcting Vronsky's spelling and punctuation while he paced in his and drafted ideas for the second part. She sent Paul down to Zermatt to hire the typewriter and, in the evening, typed from the manuscript.

Nella worked quickly and accurately and seemed far more in touch with mundane reality than Vronsky. She made him stop and go downstairs to eat the supper Paul had cooked, made him look out at the sunset before they began working again, brought him tea and bread and jam at midnight. Yet, truly, she was intoxicated, almost delirious with a sense of purpose and destiny. Nella had never been so happy.

Again she made Vronsky stop work at three. Again they heard each other undressing and getting into their beds. That physical closeness, though, seemed only the most obvious manifestation of the excitement and intimacy they had shared all day. They had discussed Vronsky's work only in details, not cosmically as a work; yet both felt its importance to be like . . . *Das Kapital* came to mind: a work that would alter the structure of society.

Nella expected Vronsky to knock at her door, to come into her room. She knew the sense of intimacy was not hers alone. She had seen him look at her across the supper table before dropping his eyes quickly, and again while they watched the sunset. She would have expected him to try sooner or later to come into her room, even had they not worked together. That was the way with men, and the looks made her certain.

But Vronsky didn't try.

The third day was more thrilling yet. Vronsky had no first-hand experience with the evils of capitalism, so he relied on Nella and Paul for anecdotes to make the second part parallel the first. As ever, Nella was outwardly calm, but inside she was ecstatic: not only was she a helper, but a contributor!

That night, she got up after five minutes and went to his room.

"Constantin? Darling, darling Constantin." Nella leaned over Vronsky, kissed him lightly. "Wake up. It's morning. It is a beautiful morning. The most beautiful morning in the world!"

It was eight A.M., an hour Vronsky had not seen for many years, except occasionally by order of the State. But it was a tender morning, breathless and flushed as new love, and Nella was determined that they should walk out into it. She prodded Vronsky out of bed and aimed him down the hall toward the W.C.

When they came downstairs, Paul was cleaning his own breakfast dishes. His eyes went wide with astonishment at seeing Vronsky, then narrowed as Nella took Vronsky's arm and—with her eyes downcast but head held high, and with a special smile—led him to the door.

"Where are you going?"

"For a walk."

"You can't go out. *He* can't go out!"

"We won't go far."

"What if somebody sees him?"

"No one will see us. It's very early. And there is no one here."

"Nella—!"

She was wrong.

Nella and Vronsky had walked barely fifty yards along the road when, coming around a sharp bend, they met Maxwell. Nella was still too transported with the rapture of romance and the beauty of the morning to be alarmed.

She offered Maxwell *buon giorno* gaily, with the sense that beauty shared is multiplied. "*Che bello mattino!*"

Although Maxwell didn't speak Italian, he understood that much. But he wished to keep to his German cover. "*Guten Morgen. Schön Tag.*" He would have preferred to say nothing, to have met no one. He enjoyed the freshness and solitude of the early hours. But he was too content on that lovely morning to be rude, and besides, years of habit made him meet people with an expression of openness and cheer. And the radiance these people gave off reached him and made his smile genuine.

"*Guten Morgen,*" said Vronsky automatically.

"*Che belli flori!*"

Maxwell had been picking his daily bouquet. He extracted a mountain avens and—with a little bow—presented it to Nella.

"*Oh! Signor! Grazie!*"

"*Bitte.*"

Jealousy struck Vronsky at the same time as appreciation for the gesture. Both to express that appreciation and to assert his position with Nella he thanked Maxwell too, "*Danke schön, mein Herr.*" He recognized that his jealousy was absurd but instinctive, and began thinking that perhaps instinctual possessiveness was a fact he would have to—

"*Wir sind Nächbaren, ja?*" Again, pure habit: Maxwell had always tried to develop acquaintances, so, despite himself, he called attention to their being neighbors.

"*Ja, ja, so.*" Vronsky continued to analyze his new emotion. "*Sie sölten uns besuchen,*" he said vaguely, nodding, smiling, and beginning to drift away along the road. He would have said something polite in any case, but it was distractedness that led him to invite Maxwell to visit.

12

Maxwell considered trying to use the telescope, but at that range he could probably have examined the hairs in the man's ears and not seen enough of his face in one view to allow for possible recognition. The 10x50s were good enough.

Maxwell had smiled to himself as he watched Vronsky and Nella stroll along the road past him. *Honeymooners*, he had thought.

That would explain why he had seen so little of them in the week since they had come. It wouldn't explain the other man. Well, whatever the details, it was obviously something of a honeymoon.

Feeling both warm and strangely discontent, Maxwell returned to his chalet and began to consider what he would do that day. Perhaps he would go across the slope directly opposite Findeln: to Riffelalp and around to Gornergrat to see Monte Rosa. He used the big binoculars to look that way. He could clearly see the trail going along the slope and around.

Then he remembered the cable.

In Findeln he had noticed a heavy cable drooping across the ravine, over the stream, and into the woods opposite. What was it for? He scanned down over the forested hillside to find where it ended. As he swept slowly around the area where he thought that point must be, he saw the man—only his head and shoulders, the rest of him screened by a branch.

Maxwell fixed on him out of idle curiosity. But then the man

147

raised his hands to his eyes—holding binoculars, too—and looked back.

Maxwell felt a tingle in the back of his stomach.

There was nothing remarkable about a man standing on one of the mountainsides and looking with binoculars at another. Maxwell himself did it every day.

But his stomach tingled. Sometimes his stomach was mistaken, but not usually.

Keeping his view fixed, he backed several steps into the room, away from the window.

After a few moments, the man lowered his arms. But he stayed where he was, looking up at Findeln.

Maxwell brought one of the straight-backed chairs from the dining table. He sat in it the wrong way, so he could brace his elbows.

The man was leaning against a tree trunk. In another minute, he raised his glasses again, looked through them for thirty seconds and lowered them. After about two minutes he repeated the action. His point of focus never varied. He didn't sweep back and forth across the hillside and never raised his view to the peaks above.

Maxwell put down his own binoculars. The tingle in his stomach had been replaced by a feeling like dropping in a fast elevator. The sensation dragged him so far that, finally, it pulled his head down onto his forearms crossed on the chair back.

After some time he roused himself and looked again through the glasses. The man looked back at him.

No, possibly not. Maxwell couldn't be sure exactly where the man was looking; what place he had under surveillance—the true word might as well be used. Possibly it wasn't Maxwell at all.

Perhaps Findeln was packed with people who'd sold secrets and were being hunted.

Sure. Well, possibly.

Maxwell snatched his rucksack from the closet, threw in

some bread and his water bottle, and stuffed a sweater on top of them. He grabbed the 8x30s; the bigger glasses would be too heavy, but he used them once more, just to check. The man was still there.

Maxwell went out and turned up the valley toward the glacier, the way he would have gone anyway; up to where the cut between the Findeln and Riffelalp sides was less deep, then across the stream to pick up the path going toward Gornergrat—above the watcher.

Even walking rapidly it took Maxwell over an hour to reach the place above where the man must be. The man couldn't be seen from the path, and Maxwell almost hoped he wouldn't be there any longer.

Checking in all directions, Maxwell stepped off the path, working down the steep hillside. He could see horizontally but not down very well. Although there was no underbrush, the branches of the lower trees screened that direction.

He made no sound at all as he stepped down on the cushy turf. Great fir tree trunks and blue-black foliage made the sunlight soft and splotchy. All was serene. He moved slowly from one tree to another, pausing at each to check again all around. He got to within fifty yards behind and to the right of the man without being seen.

Maxwell stood three-quarters behind a trunk and considered the implications of the situation. The man was still watching, not tiring himself by trying to hold up the glasses constantly but looking often and long enough to see almost everything that might go on. That confirmed him as a watcher. But he was not watching Maxwell, whom he would have seen leave for his walk. Though the man might remain in place waiting for Maxwell to return, he would not keep up a steady routine with the glasses. He must, therefore, be looking at the chalet next to Maxwell's—the one with the young couple. There were no other houses within the tight sweep of his binoculars.

Maxwell sensed a lessening of weight on his heart; lessening, but not lifting entirely. The distance between the other chalet and his own was small. Someone interested in one could not help but look at the other. Maxwell was confident of his cover, but always careful.

At any other time of his life, he would have gone back to the house, packed quickly, and moved away. The little voice of instinct and experience told him to do that. He throttled it. His determination not to leave the Matterhorn was overwhelming.

He would have to know more.

There seemed to be nothing more to be learned by watching the watcher. The man's clothes were probably made in Sri Lanka and available in any cheap department store on any continent. Unless Maxwell came up and made him speak, there seemed no way to discover his nationality.

Work the other way, Maxwell decided.

He climbed carefully back up to the path, decided the distance to Zermatt was probably shorter by going down from that side, and started off at a fast pace.

When he reached Zermatt, Maxwell found Frau Julen satisfyingly talkative. She let the girl wait on the other customers while getting Maxwell's loaf of bread herself.

Yes, the people in the other house were Italians. No, they were not honeymooners. It was the stocky man with the moustache who was the woman's husband. They were servants of the other man. He was a wealthy Italian businessman who was recuperating in the mountain air from a serious illness. Well, she *assumed* he was Italian, too. The people who hired the house on his behalf were Italian. They had said he was from Milan.

The alarm in Maxwell's stomach grew stronger as Frau Julen spoke. The man he had met that morning might have been pasty and flabby, but he was not ill. And he and the woman were lovers.

When Maxwell left the shop he tried, for a moment, to rationalize his misgivings. The man was a rich businessman, he and the girl were having an affair, they were hiding away with the other man as cover. The wife—or some blackmailer—had them under surveillance.

Everything fit, but his stomach didn't believe.

The man was not Italian. Only at that moment was Maxwell aware of what he had known since the brief conversation that morning. The man's German was good, but the trace of accent was Slavic.

Maxwell went diagonally down the street to the terrace of the Old Zermatt, bought a paper, and ordered coffee.

He found what he was looking for on page three. Vronsky's presentation of his Theory of Forces and his subsequent disappearance had been covered by all of the newspapers in repetitive detail for most of the preceding week. There was no further information, no speculation: no news was the only news, and that was presented in two lines in a special box that summarized each day's nonevents.

It's a hunch, just a hunch, only a hunch, Maxwell told himself, but even that straw was snatched away as he looked up and realized Vronsky was staring at him—from the cover of the international edition of *Time* magazine on the rack just beyond the newspapers.

Maxwell did not have to go over and take a copy to put everything together. He sat for several minutes, numb.

Never in his life had he sat as he did through those moments, without some plan forming, some action working its way through his muscles, preparing him to move.

He would, of course, have to go. Otherwise he would be found—if he hadn't been already.

But he had no place left to go.

He might as well simply end it.

But he wasn't ready!

Anger brought Maxwell's head up. He looked at the Matterhorn; the embodiment of unwavering strength, of immortal steadfastness. He would not leave it!

But how could he . . . ?

Suddenly it came to him. It was as obvious and clear as the mountain itself: he didn't have to go *far*. Not *away*. Someone had found Vronsky, not *him*.

Maxwell almost laughed out loud at his own stupidity. He

151

had only to leave Findeln. There were other chalets around the other side of the chairlift or on one of the other slopes.

He was on his feet at once. He would pack quickly. He could be done in time to come back to town, spend the night in a hotel. He would find Renata, and she could help find a new place.

He would have to have a story, of course; some explanation for Herr and Frau Julen, and for Renata, too. Well, he was good at improvising. He'd think up something on his way back to the chalet.

It was 1:30. In the offseason the chairlift didn't open again for the afternoon until 2:00. He could get back quicker by walking. He visualized the route in segments, estimating times. Even from the center of town, he could get to the path where the trail to Findeln began in five minutes. Five more, and he would be in the forest on his way up to the outlook over the waterfall. Left there, the long stretch . . . Forty-five minutes or less for all.

He climbed rapidly toward the outlook. He was working on a plausible story for leaving his chalet, and his mind did not register the scene until it was too late.

Light hung in the air, suspended in the mist of the waterfall. Coming from a sun still nearly overhead, it seemed to stand in pillars as straight and solid as the great black tree trunks. The constant roaring from the waterfall was more a muffler of sound than a noise in itself. Everything was like a model, meticulous in detail, true to life, but carved: a display in a museum of natural history. Even the men were absolutely still.

One of them had his back to Maxwell, hands folded, leaning his forearms on the rail at the center of the outlook. He wore a navy-blue overcoat, a city coat, tight across his hunched shoulders.

The second man was a dozen paces farther up the path, hard to see at first—a charcoal suit, in shadow, his back against a tree trunk.

Maxwell glanced up to his left. A third man was there. He

had scaled the steep bank up far enough to find a root to brace his feet against. Two-thirds of him was in shadow. His right shoulder and arm had penetrated a shaft of light, and his black leather jacket sleeve gleamed bright and darkly at once.

Purely from a sense of obligation, Maxwell looked over his shoulder. Two more men were coming up the path behind him.

Maxwell walked on up to the outlook. He, too, leaned his arms on the rail.

The man there turned his head and smiled wanly. "Hello, Max."

"Hello, Boris. How are you?"

"Not bad. Not too bad at all."

"You haven't put on any weight."

"A kilo, but I lost it again."

The man Maxwell knew as Boris was cadaverous, his cheekbones high and waxy-bright against the brown patches under his sunken eyes. His wispy hair was white but dull.

"My fault?" said Maxwell.

"I'm afraid so."

Boris was sixty-seven and had only half a stomach. He had been brought from retirement to be Maxwell's contact because he was dying, too.

"I'm sorry," said Maxwell.

"How are *you*, Max?"

"Pretty good. I . . . I had some trouble with my exercises the other day, but . . . I guess I'm better than might be expected."

"I'm glad to hear it."

"I'm sorry you didn't get back to your rose bushes."

"Oh, I did. When I left you in Kensington Garden I went to a safe house, and I was back home two days later. I had nearly three weeks."

"Sorry they dragged you out again."

"Well . . ." The old man shrugged. "So," he said.

"So," said Maxwell. "Constantin Vronsky."

"Yes."

"He's in the house next to mine, up past Findeln."

"Yes."

"Boris, I don't think you're going to believe this, but it's really a coincidence."

"Max," said Boris in a falling tone.

"It's the truth. I've played it straight with you all the way."

"We have hoped so. Frankly, Max, my people are doubting you now."

"Your own doctors examined me."

"Yes. We are convinced about . . . your condition. *I* am convinced, even without the medical report. But what is it, the saying you have . . . ? What a way to go! A last assignment, still to be useful—I understand that. The perfect opportunity to give disinformation. You testify to its authenticity with your death."

"You must have suspected that possibility all along."

"I am sure someone has. I had given my own opinion that you were truthful."

"I was," said Maxwell.

"I wish that were so."

"Well, they won't send you to Siberia."

"No."

"They wouldn't cut your pension?"

"I don't think so. They might, but I don't think so. I'm an old man. I think they will let me go back to my cottage and die. But I would not like to have made such a mistake on my last assignment."

"Why should you care? It doesn't matter anymore, Boris."

"To me it matters."

Maxwell stared at the water, too. His eyes quickly tired of trying to follow the falling droplets, picking one, then jumping back in an instant for another. He let his stare glaze, but his mind raced on.

"OK, you want proof. I've got it for you: Vronsky."

"How?"

"Come on, Boris, you guys are supposed to be the chess players. Figure it out. Turn it around. It *was* an operation. I told the Agency I was dying, and they saw a chance to feed you. Right. So we did it, and it worked. You paid me, you must have believed—at least you thought you might believe me. All we have to do to keep it going is to keep you convinced about me. So what does the Agency do? Puts me next to Constantin Vronsky. Now there's a stroke of imagination! There's cover.

"Of course, you can look at it another way. Maybe we were too stupid to think you might find Vronsky, and me, and get suspicious. Maybe we just blithely closed one operation and started another. We need someone to tie in with Vronsky's defection. And who gets picked? Maxwell, who's dying day by day. Maxwell is sent in to take care of it single-handed. If you believe that, Boris, you'll believe anything."

"Of the possibilities we have considered so far, Max, coincidence is the one we would most like to believe. It is difficult, of course. In our profession, as you know, there are no coincidences, and the simple explanation is never the truth."

"So?"

"So, there is still the question: why are you living next to Constantin Vronsky?"

"Because I didn't know any better. I didn't know it was Vronsky—I only saw him for the first time this morning. And then I saw your man with the glasses on Riffelalp—"

"Oh?"

"Yeah. He was under pretty good cover, but I was looking that way. Anyway, to make it short, I went to town and saw Vronsky's picture on the cover of *Time*. I was on my way back right now to pack up and get the hell out. It's the truth, Boris."

"It is a very good story, in any case. It is possible we may even be able to believe it."

"Boris, all I want to do is get out of it all and look at that mountain and feel like I'm really living before . . . and just check out in my own way, when I'm ready."

"Yes. Yes, I understand. *I* believe you, Max. I hope that will be possible for you. Soon."

The ridges across Maxwell's forehead smoothed. His face went blank again. "Soon?"

"Soon, but . . . not yet, Max."

"Tell me."

"Assuming your relationship to Vronsky is coincidental, it is also fortunate—for us."

"What do you want me to do?"

"Nothing much, Max. Only to keep the eye on Vronsky and tell us what you see."

"Your man on Riffelalp can do that."

"You are closer. Don't be difficult, Max. You understand what is wanted."

"I don't know Vronsky. He hasn't been out of his house . . . I only met him today."

"You should become more neighborly."

"Look, if you want him, why don't you just go and get him? You've done it before."

"If it were only so easy. Be serious, Max. How would you get him out of here? There are no automobiles allowed here. Delightful, isn't it? But inconvenient. Are we to hire one of those electric carts? It would take a fleet of them. Steal them? Can you see us abducting Vronsky and speeding away in a train of electric milk carts at five kilometers per hour? Perhaps we should put ropes around him and march him down the trail here. Or send him down on the chairlift wrapped in a carpet. This place was chosen very well for him."

"Helicopter."

"We are considering it, you may believe. But this matter must be handled with some discretion."

"One cover story in *Time* is bad enough."

"We would prefer Doctor Vronsky to tell the world he has returned of his own free will."

"You could 'liberate' him. Say he'd been drugged, held against his will. He could confirm that, express his gratitude to you for doing what was necessary."

"Possible, but only as a last resort. At this point it seems best to wait until he moves to a place more advantageous to us. This is the subject on which we would appreciate your help."

"Tip you off when I think they're going to run."

"Precisely."

"No."

"Max." Boris spread his bloodless hands apart and clasped them again. "It is required."

"If I don't?"

"Must you ask? We will assume you took money for false information, and take the usual punitive action. I'm sorry, Max. I am."

"Sure, Boris."

"I am."

"I believe it." He and Boris, in a way, had spent their lives together. They had sat up waiting in unheated buildings through the same winter nights, suffered the stupidity of the same bungling superiors, lost friends together, run and hid from the same pursuers, felt the same pride of skill in the craft they practiced. When they had met for the first time a few months before, they had known each other forever. Of course they liked each other. Now they would die together of the same disease, unless—as each knew—it was necessary for one to kill the other first.

Maxwell's hands gripped the railing. Finally he said, "What about you, then? Can you go home now?"

"No. I fear we are in this together, Max. My people know we have a rapport. They wish me to stay, to continue as your contact."

"Yeah. Well, let's hope—for both our sakes—that Vronsky moves soon. How am I to report?"

"Whatever you think best, although . . ."

"Yes?"

"If it would be possible, if you don't mind, perhaps you could come down and see me in the town. The altitude . . ."

"Sure, Boris. No trouble."

"Before you go, Max, you must meet someone. But I want to

157

tell you first, be careful of him. He has always had a strong reputation, but now . . . He was the one who lost Vronsky in the first place. Yes. He must be under suspended sentence. He has done impressive work in the past, so I suppose they are giving him another chance. He is very tightened up." Boris nodded and waved his hands toward the man in the charcoal suit standing up the path.

Nev came down to them. He stopped eight feet from Maxwell, stood squarely, feet apart, weight even between them and a little forward. Although shorter than Maxwell, he kept his head tipped slightly down and looked up from under his dark eyebrows.

Maxwell remained standing as he had been, facing Boris. He turned only his head toward Nev.

"This is Major Nev," said Boris.

Nev made no acknowledgment. He neither spoke nor nodded. He continued to stare at Maxwell.

Sizing me up, Maxwell thought. *Figuring whether he can take me. He probably can. I've got three inches, thirty pounds on him, but he's got twenty-five years on me, and he's not sick.* He countered Nev's intensity with relaxation. *He'd be fast, and go for the gut and the crotch.*

Nev and Maxwell regarded one another, and the other men watched them both, all unmoving in the timeless afternoon.

Finally Maxwell said, "OK, Boris, I'll be in touch," and he walked past Nev and up the path toward Findeln.

13

BACK IN HIS CHALET, Maxwell sat through the long afternoon and into the evening. He sat in the deep armchair by the fireplace, from which he could look through the windows at the Matterhorn.

It was not *what* they were asking him to do that mattered (although he assumed they would ask more later). It didn't really matter that it was *them*. He was past caring about that. It was having to do anything at all: to think, to act, to be concerned. He shuddered with revulsion.

By seven o'clock, those thoughts had risen and engulfed him. He made a decision. He would not do it; he would not be forced.

He started toward the bathroom to take a shower, but it was already late. He'd have to skip showering and changing clothes or he'd miss the sunset. He went to the kitchen instead.

There was no steak. He had planned all along on having a good steak. *Screw Corchran*, a steak was what he wanted. There were wursts, schnitzel, a pork chop.

He didn't have the right wine, either. It was to have been a very good Pommard or Chambertin. The best he had was a medium-priced Medoc.

None of it's right!

He slammed the refrigerator door and stood staring at it for a moment, seething. Then he jerked it open, snatched out a chunk of cheese and slammed the door again. He groped around in the lower cabinet, found the Medoc, and opened it. It wouldn't have time to breathe properly. He reached into the cabinet over the sink for a glass. His hands were shaking, and he fumbled against the glasses. One fell and smashed.

Shit! Shit! Shit!

He slammed his fist down on the counter beside the sink with all his strength. A jolt of pain flashed up to his shoulder.

He kicked the cabinet under the sink, once, twice; on the third kick, the door cracked and broke inward.

He grabbed another glass, snatched up the bottle and cheese and stormed out onto the balcony.

He drank a glass of wine quickly. It tasted sour at first, bitter at the end. He poured another.

There isn't even any sunset! The western slope had gone pale white and paler blue until the Matterhorn seemed transparent, fading gently like a Victorian maiden lady.

He couldn't even *die* the way he wanted!

Laughter mocked him on the soft air.

Maxwell strained around in his chair and looked off behind and to his right. He could see Nella and Vronsky on the balcony of their chalet. They were facing each other, pelvises pressed together. Vronsky had his chubby hands at either side of Nella's waist, and she leaned back from him. She seemed to be tickling his face with her forefinger. She laughed again.

Damn them! It was their fault! Vronsky's fault! No one would ever have found him if Vronsky hadn't come! *You bastard!*

He was unable to imagine exactly what he would do to Vronsky if Vronsky were in his hands; none of the specific images that half formed seemed horrible enough.

If they hadn't come, if they were gone—

At that instant, Maxwell knew what to do.

He had looked at the problem backwards—worrying about the Russians trying to run him instead of dealing with how to make them stop. As always, his subconscious had come through with the answer: *Get rid of Vronsky.*

He didn't have to die yet. He would have to work for a time, but he could make the time short. The Russians wanted to know when Vronsky would leave. Maxwell was sure he could give them the news they wanted very soon.

He felt as though a wind had blown choking fumes from around his head. He breathed fully. He rose from his chair and walked over to the side of the balcony.

"*Guten Abend,*" he called cheerily.

"*Guten Abend.* Good evening," Maxwell said, smiling broadly.

Paul nodded in return but continued to block the foot-wide space between the heavy door and its jamb.

"Do you speak English?" Maxwell asked.

Paul nodded again, but offered no word of encouragement in any language.

Maxwell refused to be offended. "I'm your neighbor."

Paul was unmoved.

"I was invited to visit," said Maxwell. Then, lowering his voice but widening both his grin and his eyes, he added, "Doctor Vronsky invited me."

"Who?"

Maxwell seemed not quite able to suppress the grin, but he narrowed his eyes knowingly. "Oh, I think you heard me."

"*Momento,*" said Paul. He shut the door abruptly.

Maxwell heard him move away into the chalet, call "Nella!" and then, more faintly, "Dottore!"

Two minutes later, Paul was back. "Please," he said, bowing Maxwell into the house.

Maxwell strode in. He heard the door closed and latched behind him. He assumed Paul stood by it, his hand on the pistol in his pocket.

At the foot of the stairs, Nella stood with her hands held up at her chest, fingers twisted together.

"*Bono sera, Signorina,*" Maxwell said. "That's all the Italian I know. Do you speak English?"

"Yes. A little."

"Well, you remember Doctor Vronsky invited me . . . This morning, Doctor Vronsky invited me to come over for a visit, and, well, here I am."

Maxwell grinned at her, then turned to include Paul as well. "Look, I know you must be pretty upset about my coming here like this. But I did hope I could meet Doctor Vronsky. I mean, really meet him. Officially. You see, my son teaches—"

"Who are you?" Paul spoke levelly but without threat.

"Oh, I'm sorry. My name's Howard Bergmann. I'm from Ontario, Canada. I'm . . . sort of vacationing here, and—"

"How did you know Doctor Vronsky is here?"

"I saw him." Maxwell looked bewildered. He turned to Nella. "This morning, remember?" He turned back to Paul. "I didn't know who he was then—"

"I told you he didn't recognize him!"

"No, I didn't recognize him. But when I went down to Zermatt this afternoon, well, there was Doctor Vronsky all over the cover of *Time* magazine." Maxwell raised both hands and waved them reassuringly. "Don't worry, I haven't told anyone, not a single soul. Your secret is safe with me. I figured you must be up here hiding away from the Russians. Well, I can assure you that's fine with me. I'm a capitalist, myself."

Unimpressed by that declaration, Nella and Paul continued to stare at Maxwell, who took a breath, drew himself up and went on in a more serious tone. "Look, I know I'm intruding, and you're suspicious of me. I know you have to be. I came over here for two reasons. One of them is selfish. I really would like to meet Doctor Vronsky. But the other reason's not."

Maxwell turned directly to Paul. "You people should be more careful. You shouldn't let him go out. I thought maybe you didn't know about the *Time* cover, so I came to tell you."

"He does not go out again. That—this morning—that was a mistake."

"OK, but I just thought you should know."

"Thank you."

"Thank you! Oh, thank you so much!" Nella had been nearly frantic with fear and guilt.

"Anything I can do. Maybe I should put it a little stronger: I really do not like the Russians." Maxwell allowed himself to speak with total sincerity. "I've had some business dealings with them, and I do not like the way they operate, and I do not like them personally. So if there's anything I can do . . . Well, just let me know."

"Oh, thank you. We are very, very grateful."

Paul was less effusive. "We are grateful, sir, but I think we will not need your help."

"I hope you're right. And don't worry, I'm not a gossiper."

Maxwell turned back to Nella. "Would it be possible for me to meet Doctor Vronsky? You see, my son teaches physics at Calgary, and he'd be so pleased . . ."

Nella's feelings were torn, but Paul had no hesitation. "Perhaps another time. The Dottore is working now."

"Sure. I understand. But we are neighbors, so maybe there *will* be another time." Maxwell started toward the door. Paul opened it for him, bowing slightly, still on guard.

At the threshold Maxwell paused again. "I really mean it, about helping. I've been in business for a few years, and I know what it's like to be in a tight place. I'll keep out of your way, but I'll keep an eye out for you, too."

He nodded once to Paul, went back to his own chalet.

Maxwell awoke early. He dressed and exercised in semidarkness. When it was light enough, he began checking with his binoculars. The man was there again, in the forest across from Findeln. He would be useful soon.

Maxwell ate breakfast, checked on the watcher, read a little. It was too early to go over to the other chalet again.

He actually jumped when the doorbell rang behind him. It had never rung before. He hadn't even known he had a doorbell.

He opened the door carefully, standing mostly behind it,

163

and swinging it against his braced foot in case someone should try to throw it inward.

No one was there.

He opened the door wider.

A stout woman was walking up the road away from his chalet, pushing a bicycle. She saw Maxwell looking after her.

"*Poste*," she called.

Maxwell looked at her stupidly.

"*Poste!*" The woman pointed toward the doorway.

Maxwell hadn't realized he had a mailbox.

There was an envelope inside. It was properly stamped, the stamp cancelled by hand with ballpoint pen strokes. It must have been given to the woman after she started her round, not sent through the post office. Maxwell stared at it and felt his insides go soft.

The letter was addressed to him at Chalet Elise, Findeln. To Charles Maxwell, Esq.

14

THIS TIME there was no feeling of soaring as the gondola carried him up over the mountainside. He did not delight in the line of other gondolas drifting down and passing on his left like strung beads. He did not gaze in awe at the Matterhorn.

Maxwell saw nothing. He breathed regularly, and for part of the way up he did isometric exercises to relieve the tension while getting his body ready for action.

He didn't expect action. Relief was more important. They wanted him to be tense, that's why they had done it this way.

Dear Max, We're up at Blauherd. Won't you join us? No signature.

Maxwell saw them as the gondola swung up over the last rise and into the station. Three of them, away from the building, by the parapet. As Maxwell came out, one of the men moved away and took position forty feet from the others.

Maxwell walked up to the pair. They all looked at one another for several moments.

"Long time no see," said Corchran.

Maxwell remained silent.

Without looking away from Maxwell, Corchran gestured toward the Matterhorn towering over the lower slopes and the valley and the tiny village below. "Truly magnificent," he said. "You really did find the place. I never would have thought of it, but now that I see it, it's obvious."

Maxwell remained silent. *Sometimes the only thing you've got is what they'll give you.*

Corchran was annoyed. He had expected Maxwell to be off balance, but Maxwell stood with his palms stuck down into his back pockets, his feet planted and apparently taking root.

"I don't think you've met Bob Dolby," said Corchran, inclining his head toward the other man.

Maxwell swiveled his glance a degree or two to look at Dolby but made no change in his expression.

Dolby remained equally blank, then nodded his head slightly as though affirming something to himself. "Charley Maxwell, the famous double agent," he said. His voice was gravelly. The sound came as a surprise, because Dolby was young and skinny and intense looking, and wore glasses. Maxwell would have expected a nasal tenor.

"Well, Charley, who're you selling today?"

"Max doesn't like to be called Charley, Bob."

"I'll call the sucker anything I want."

"Don't be unpleasant. Max is a sick man."

"Not as sick as he's going to be."

"Don't be too hard on him, Bob. When you understand what kind of a guy Max is, what he must feel, dying, being eaten up inside—"

"I understand he's a traitor. Don't give me any shit about understanding, Corchran."

Maxwell moved his hands from his pockets and folded his arms across his chest. He let his gaze drift off to the panorama. He was feeling better—not much—but some.

Are these guys serious? he thought. The tough-and-friendly team approach was ridiculously obvious. What it meant, though, was that they were trying to work him. They hadn't shot him; they weren't just going to haul his ass back and lock him up. They wanted something out of him. That didn't give him much, but maybe something.

Because he was looking away, he missed the instinctive twitch of Dolby's eyelids. Maxwell caught the body movement barely in time to tense his muscles as Dolby punched into his solar plexus.

"Look at me when I talk to you, Charley!"

The punch was meant only to shock him, not to take him out, and Maxwell was able to brace against it. Still, it bent him and rocked his footing. He came up gasping.

Dolby and Corchran had sprung back to avoid any counterblow.

"Dolby! You don't have to—Max, I'm sorry. Are you OK? Bob, he's a sick man! Max, I'm sorry. Bob's from Langley. They're all uptight—God, Bob! You don't have to hit him!"

Maxwell straightened, breathing carefully and rubbing his stomach.

"Come on, Corky. Let's cut the games. What do you want?"

Corchran held the look of concern before he answered. "Bob wants to get you back and debrief you."

"What do *you* want?"

"I told him we should be satisfied if you just gave us a list of what you sold the Russians. Considering your condition, I said we should be satisfied with that."

"If?"

Corchran paused for a moment. He sighed.

"Right, Max. If. If you help us with something else. One last little assignment. Something you might think of as settling your account?"

"Tell me."

"Do you know who your neighbor is down there?"

It was Maxwell's turn to sigh. "Constantin Vronsky."

"You do know?"

"I saw his picture yesterday on the cover of *Time*." Maxwell was becoming bored with the story.

"We're worried about him," said Corchran.

"Why?"

"The Russians will try to get him back, if they can."

"So?"

"He's the greatest physicist in the world."

"Theoretical, Corky. He doesn't make bombs."

"Yes, he does, in his own way. Have you ever read any of his papers? The political ones?"

"No."

"You know about them."

"I know about them. First he blasted western European social democracy, and the Party gave him a prize; and then he blasted the Party from Lenin on down, and they sent him to Uzbek or someplace."

"Exactly. He's been silenced for the past seven years. We imagine that by now he's got a lot to say."

"Like Solzhenitsyn."

"Right. With more focus on him because of his theory."

"So take him home with you. Let him live up there in Vermont with Solzhenitsyn. They can shoot off their mouths together."

"We'd love to have him, but he doesn't care for us any more than he does the Russians."

"What's your angle, then?"

"Let him go off wherever he wants and fire at both sides. We don't care what he says about us. Everyone knocks us, we're quite used to it. But they all know that when there's an earthquake, or the Russians start massing troops, Uncle Sam will be there. The communists are the ones who can't take criticism, especially from one of their own. We want the world to hear what he says about them."

"What do you want me to do?"

"Make contact with him, keep an eye on him. You're in the perfect position. Let us know if you see anything suspicious so we can offer discreet assistance if needed."

"The Swiss police could do that."

"The Swiss will settle the problem by moving Vronsky out, whether he has a place to go or not. They might send him back. Undoubtedly they'd be pleased to have Vronsky work in Switzerland as a scientist, but they're not happy about political writing. Violates neutrality, you know."

"You checked."

"Of course. I understand it was done on the ministerial level, hypothetically. We inquired on Vronsky's behalf, just in case we should discover where he is."

"So you're just playing nursemaid."

"Correct. And you will advise us how best to do so."

"And if I do?"

"If you do and if you give us that list, when this is over we'll leave you here to . . . enjoy your retirement."

"And if I don't?"

"I think you will, Max. You don't want to leave this place."

"You think you can extradite me? You going to kidnap me?"

"No, Charley," Dolby croaked, "we'll just help the Zurich police solve a murder."

Maxwell stared at him for a moment, then off toward the Matterhorn again.

"I wasn't going to bring that up, Max," said Corchran.

"Yeah," said Maxwell.

Maxwell paid no attention to the view going down, either. His intuition was trying to tell him something, but he couldn't sense what.

He tried to sort all of it out. The Agency had found him. That was bad. But maybe it was good, too. They seemed to be willing to let him off. He didn't trust them, but it was a chance. And he could use them to get himself off from Boris.

He hadn't told Corchran about Boris. It hadn't seemed—
That was it!

Maxwell felt a sudden rush of excitement and relief—like a projector lens being focused: it didn't matter what the picture was so much as that it wasn't blurry.

From the Sunnega end of the Gondelbahn, he went directly to the chairlift and down to Zermatt. He called from the post office, then went to the Old Zermatt. He sat inside this time. Boris came ten minutes later.

Boris ordered hot chocolate. When the waiter had gone, he

laced his fingers together, rested them on the table top and smiled at Maxwell. "Progress so soon?"

"Some. I've made contact with the bodyguard and the girl, not with Vronsky. But that's not why I came."

Boris inclined his head and waited with an expression of pleasant attentiveness.

"I need to know, Boris. How did you know Vronsky was here?"

Boris's expression did not change for several moments, then he shrugged. "I assume we heard from some source."

"You mean he wasn't tracked. It wasn't detective work. Somebody told you."

"Oh, I really do not know that, Max. I am not part of this affair, except for talking with you."

"I need to know, Boris."

"Why?"

"I can't tell you."

"Then how could *we* tell *you?*"

"I mean, I don't know for sure. But I have a reason."

"Max, assuming this information concerning Vronsky had been received from a source, we would hardly reveal who or where it was."

The waiter brought Boris's hot chocolate.

"Boris, you have a problem."

"Oh?"

"You won't trust me. Sure. From your point of view you *can't* trust me. But you *have* to trust me."

"To a point, Max. Of course."

"To a point. Right. Number two: It's *me* you're dealing with. It's me you're using. If you just wanted to get somebody to report from closer to Vronsky's house you could have—you probably could hire the girl who does the housecleaning. You want *my* reports—even though you don't really trust me— because I'll find out things nobody else will find. All right. Now I'm telling you I need to know this in order to be effective. Now you tell me, or the deal is off, and you can try to do anything you care to about it."

Boris unlaced his fingers and tapped the ends together. "I see. I will tell Major Nev. He will ask his superior." Boris allowed the corners of his mouth to curve slightly. "Major Nev is in almost constant communication with his superior. I will return an answer to you."

"When?"

"Perhaps this afternoon. Certainly by tomorrow morning."

"How? If I have to keep coming down to Zermatt I won't be able to watch Vronsky."

"I understand there is a small cafe at Findeln."

"Yes."

"I would suppose they have a telephone. Call me."

It was just before noon, so Maxwell was able to ride the chairlift back up before it closed for the long lunch break. By the time he walked down from Sunegga to the chalets and got the papers from his, it was past twelve-thirty. He moved in and out of his house with a display of urgency in case anyone was watching from next door.

"Let me in. It's important," he said.

Paul wore no jacket this time, but he would not have tried to hide the Walther in any case. He stood aside carefully to let Maxwell pass.

Maxwell went into the house, put the papers onto the table, stepped back, and stood with his arms folded so Paul could see his hands. "First, read these."

Paul came to the table and pushed at the papers without really taking his eyes from Maxwell. He picked up the Canadian passport.

"That may not impress you," said Maxwell. "I guess those can be faked. But it's something. Look at the letters."

Paul put the passport back onto the table, picked up the letters—four of them stapled together at the upper left corner.

"You'll see that I inquired about renting my chalet last October. I contracted for it in December. I don't know when you arranged for this house, but if it was after that, then that should tell you I'm OK."

Paul glanced at the letters, flipping them in one hand to see them in sequence. "And for why do you show me these things?" he asked.

"Why are you carrying that gun? Look, Mister . . . Mister?"

"Paul."

"Look, Paul: I spent thirty years making and selling machine tools—tools for precision metalwork; sold them all over Europe. Now I always tried not to get involved with politics—with political situations, you understand, but I know a little bit about international intrigue, if you know what I mean. Now I meant what I said last night about wanting to help you, but I'm not so dumb as to think I can just come in here and have you believe what I have to tell you."

"What do you have to tell us?"

"I was down in the village this morning. I had a cup of coffee in the Old Zermatt. There were a couple of characters sitting at the corner table. They didn't look like skiers, and they were talking Russian."

Nella gasped. She stood halfway down the stairway, a hand up to her mouth.

"Do you speak Russian?" Paul asked in a tone of polite curiosity.

"No. Just 'hello' and 'goodbye.' But I told you I've done some business with the Russians, and I know what the language sounds like."

"Perhaps it was Polish."

Maxwell uncrossed his arms, let them swing at his sides for an instant, then rested his fists on his hips. "OK, Paul. Maybe it was Polish. Maybe they were Englishman talking backwards, so it just sounded like Russian. *I* thought they were Russians, and I thought you'd want to know."

"Paul, they have found us!" Nella leaned across the banister rail, speaking in Italian.

"What did she say?"

Paul ignored the question. "What did the men look like?" he asked.

"One of them was an old guy—seventy, seventy-five; white

hair, thin—looked like he'd been sick. The other was stocky—
your build, maybe a little taller. Black hair cut short around his
ears, thick eyebrows—he kept his head down, looked from
under them. He needed a shave—"

"Isn't that the one—?" Nella's eyes were wide.

"Nev." Vronsky's voice came from the second rise of stairs,
behind Nella. He came down to her, his eyes on Maxwell.

"Dottore . . . !" Paul moved swiftly toward him, without
turning his back on Maxwell.

"Good morning, sir. Mister . . . ?"

"Bergmann. Howard Bergmann."

"Dottore! Please go back up—"

"Never mind, Paul. Mr. Bergmann already has seen me, and
he will not attempt to hurt me—certainly not while you are
holding your pistol."

Paul suddenly brought the pistol to waist level, pointed at
Maxwell.

Maxwell seemed not to notice. "Doctor Vronsky, this really
is an honor. My son—"

"Perhaps you can tell me about your son another time.
Would you tell us now more about these men?"

"I don't have any more to tell you. I didn't want to seem to be
watching them, so after I finished my coffee, I just left. Then I
came straight here."

"It is very kind of you to be concerned for me. May I ask, Mr.
Bergmann, what are you doing here? I mean, in this place."
Vronsky gestured vaguely, indicating Findeln—or that general
area of the universe.

"I'm recuperating. I had a heart attack last summer. Angina.
Been pushing too hard for too long. My doctor recommended a
long vacation, plenty of exercise, good air."

"I would have thought the air would be too thin."

"Well, I was on oxygen at first, of course, but now—I guess
it's a new theory: make the system work, build it up."

"Ah."

Maxwell continued to look at Vronsky, smiling slightly, his
face open. The three stared back at him, not smiling.

"Well," Maxwell said at last, "that's all I have to tell you now. I guess I'd better go home and have some lunch."

No one moved. Paul continued to cover Maxwell with the gun.

"That is, if you don't mind," Maxwell said. "I don't think you ought to shoot me," he said. He put his hands behind him, slowly, sliding his palms into his hip pockets. He nodded at Vronsky and Nella, then at Paul. Then he walked slowly to the front door and let himself out.

"We must move!" Nella was almost breathless.

"No," said Paul.

"No? What else can we do? They have followed us! They know we are here! We must get Constantin to safety!"

"Where is that?"

"Somewhere! Not here!"

"Not anywhere I know. Where would we take him? How would we get him out of here?"

"We have to do something! We can't just—"

"Nella." Vronsky spoke quietly. "Paul is right. We cannot move without knowing where or how."

"Maybe we don't move at all. Maybe we get some help, fortify this place. I know half-a-dozen men—with them we could hold out against— What are they going to do? Start a war?"

"I wish to leave as quickly as possible, Paul. And I don't want any chance of fighting. But you are right. We cannot leave without a plan."

"Constantin—"

"Nella." Vronsky smiled at her, brushed his fingertips back and forth over her upper arm. "There is danger, yes. But there has been danger all along. We must think carefully before we act." He turned back to Paul. "You can contact Professore Bentivoglio?"

"I can contact someone."

"You must do so. Say the men must come from Italy now, with or without the official permission, and take us away."

"I will have to go to the village to the telephone for long distance. I will have to leave you."

Vronsky shrugged. "We have no choice."

"Right. I'll make some lunch and then go."

"Go now. Nella can make my luncheon."

Maxwell watched Paul leave. Then he made his lunch. Afterward, he checked the man on Riffelalp and sat for a while staring at the Matterhorn, letting himself drift and ponder.

Vronsky finished the tiny omelet and poked at his salad. "Couldn't I have another egg?" He asked in a small voice.

"It is not good for a man to eat many eggs, Constantin. I have read that in all of the magazines. Especially when he is a little overweight. Eat your salad."

"I don't like salad."

"It is good for you."

Vronsky sighed, poked again. He was hungry, but didn't care to argue. His mind was racing. He stared at the window, letting his eyes go out of focus. Nella sighed too, loudly, with exasperation at his refusal to eat the salad. She was about to reprimand him when she noticed his preoccupation. Quietly, she removed the dishes.

"Blue," Vronsky said.

"What?"

Almost startled, he began to explain. "There are chains: people, events leading to now. If one sees them as . . ." He drifted away again. "Blue could break," he said.

Russians surrounded Paul.

As he came down the path from the waterfall and into the fields, two of them fell in behind him. They were disguised as fat German tourists with walking sticks.

When he passed one of the cafés he saw a busboy sweeping the terrace steps watch him, head swiveling slowly, then nod to the thin man standing in the doorway across the street.

He was aware of the man in the black leather jacket sitting

175

outside the post office pretending not to notice when he went inside.

Hey, compare, get hold of yourself. He was making himself a joke. Cautious, yes; he should be cautious, but not make a joke of himself.

Paul gave the operator the number and stepped into the booth. When the call went through he reported the situation tersely and hung up. He received no instructions and had expected none.

Everything has to go through channels. It would be ninety minutes before he could call back.

He realized he was ravenous. He went to the nearest café and ordered the full roast pork dinner. At least he would get a meal out of the trip, one he didn't have to cook.

"I will have to see you."

"Does that mean you're going to tell me?"

"Perhaps."

"What's the game, Boris?"

"We must talk."

"We're talking."

"Not on the telephone. Max, I must see you."

"I've been there once today already, Boris. Things are moving here. I should—"

"It is necessary that we speak in person, Max. If you wish, I will walk as far as the waterfall again."

"OK, Boris. It'll take me about thirty minutes."

"For me also. The distance is shorter, but uphill."

Maxwell reached the waterfall first. After several minutes he saw Boris below, starting to climb the leg of the trail leading up. The old man walked slowly and carefully but still had to pause for half a minute after every three.

Maxwell turned away. He felt a mixture of pity and revulsion.

I should have gone all the way down, he thought guiltily. Yet his anger was at Boris as well as himself: a loathing, an instinctive desire to punish Boris for being infirm.

When he reached the overlook, Boris stood for several moments, wheezing and clutching the rail with both hands to steady himself.

Maxwell waited, not looking at him.

"I'm sorry to make you come down here," said Boris, at last.

"*I'm* sorry, Boris. I shouldn't have made you come up."

"Ah, well. My physician says I should take some exercise each day. No matter, I have the information you requested."

"But."

"But, I must exercise judgment before I give it."

"What?"

"Why do you want to know this?"

"I told you I had a good reason."

"That is not a good reason for us."

It seemed to be trading time. "I don't have to be here, Boris. I didn't have to meet you this morning. You have no leverage on me anymore—the Agency's in town."

Boris pursed his pale lips for a moment. "So?" he said. "Then why are you here?"

"Goes 'round and 'round, doesn't it? I'm sure they know you're here."

"Did you not tell them?"

"No. And they didn't ask. That's the point. I think they think I'm working for *you*. But you think I'm working for *them*."

"Are you?"

"I think so. I think they expected me to tell you they're here. And now I have."

"Why?"

"Because I'm working for *me!*"

Boris gave no sign, but he was shocked. Maxwell's vehemence was the only overt emotional expression he had ever seen the big man make.

"I want to find out what's going on here, how I'm being used. So I can get the hell out of it!"

Both of Maxwell's hands were clamped around the railing. He glared across his shoulder, his chin thrust forward at Boris. "Now you tell me something," he demanded.

"Under these circumstances, Max—"

"Boris, *don't you*—" Maxwell broke off. He straightened, taking a breath and looking up through the dark fir branches at the pale afternoon sky.

"Boris," he said calmly again, "this big nose isn't just for decoration. I detect a peculiar aroma. Now, maybe I'm wrong. Maybe this is just what it seems: you guys trying to get Vronsky and our guys coming in to stop you. Maybe. I don't think so. If I have some more information, I may be able to find out for sure. Now, maybe my suspicion doesn't interest you. Maybe you're satisfied. But if you're not, how are you going to find out? Now, I can go talk to Corchran, try to get something out of him. Tell me, Boris, if you decide you are interested, who are *you* going to talk to?"

"And if you find something, Max, should we believe you will tell us?"

"If I think it will do me any good, yeah."

Boris deliberated. "Very well," he said. "We received information on Vronsky's location from a double in *your* Rome office."

"How did he get it?"

"You know the deviationists are in control of the Party in Italy. They are trying to get Vronsky into that country. Somehow there was a leak, and it reached your people."

"Is any of this true, Boris?"

"Possibly so."

"Then why did you tell me? I mean, you should have gone back to your major, talked over my people being here, decided whether you would trust me. You should have made me call you again in two hours."

Boris smiled broadly to reveal his fine, blue-white, plastic teeth. "We have already considered, Max. We do not trust you. Oh, we do recognize the possibility that you are truthful, but our primary assumption is that you are not—that you are working for your side—still or again. Nevertheless, we are interested in what you tell us. Or ask us."

"You're willing to chance losing your man in Rome?"

178

"A gambit."

"Yeah. OK."

"Is it likely I will see you again?"

"Depends."

"Yes."

"If I am with the Agency, then you will see me, because they'll use me to feed you. That how you figure?"

Boris simply smiled again.

Maxwell nodded. "Sorry I can't say 'no,' so you could go home again."

"Well. This is a beautiful location."

"I thought you liked the seacoast."

"Oh, of course. And it is much warmer. But the mountains are very interesting. Very grand."

Maxwell couldn't see off through the thick woods, but he looked for a moment anyway.

"Yes," he said.

Paul felt better after eating, but he still did not feel calm.

Just as he stepped out from the thick doorway and blinked against the bright sunlight, someone darted back into an alleyway between two buildings to his left.

A child shouted and was answered by another. Had the figure been only a child?

Paul walked toward the post office, keeping close to the side of the street. Suddenly there was a crunch and *thunk* behind him!

He whirled, flattening against the storefront, his hand going toward the Walther stuck in his waistband under his jacket.

With a whine the electric delivery truck accelerated past him, its blue-coveralled driver staring at Paul in surprise.

Paul made his second call. Instructions: Stay. Help would come.

Still the feeling of threat would not leave him. Paul walked past the sparkle and riches displayed in shop windows, past the gaiety of signs and colored carvings—the glitter and paint of a greedy old woman, he thought.

A flash caught his eye. A window swung closed just as he looked up.

Two men dressed in skiing clothes stood at the next corner looking at him. They turned away when he stared back but watched as he passed.

Take it easy, he told himself. But at the chairlift, his control almost broke.

Two hikers, side by side, were just lifting clear of the station roof as he came up. They rose against the sky, swinging slightly.

The thought of hanging immobile above the earth—where anyone could pick him off—paralyzed him.

He felt a flush of anger at himself. He stomped up to the window, slammed down his coins and snatched the ticket as it was passed out under the grille to him.

Then fear swept back against the anger as the attendant slammed the safety bar across Paul's lap, locking him in place, and the chair jerked up into the air. He was helpless! Totally exposed! Couldn't run, fight, hide . . .

What's the matter with you? You getting old? Right, the Russians are here. Right, they probably saw you. So? You think they're going to shoot you in the chairlift right in broad daylight? You're going out of your mind!

Paul forced himself back into the chair and made himself look away from the ground and off to the Matterhorn.

Half a mile up the mountainside, the lift crossed a service road that ran up to Findeln. The man standing there waited patiently until Paul cleared the shoulder below. Then with both hands he raised the silenced long-barreled pistol, tracked Paul as he swung overhead, took precise aim, and carefully fired two shots before the chair was shielded by the roadbank on the uphill side.

15

MAXWELL SAT at his dining table. He didn't have to write much. In truth, he hadn't sold a great amount. He knew the Agency would be more hurt by what it must have done when it found out about him than by what he'd actually given. Still, he took his time, putting down every detail. He knew also that interest would be high concerning anything else the Russians might have asked for, or any indication they already knew something he told them. He tried to put down everything, so there would be nothing left worth hounding him for.

From time to time he evaluated the light hitting Riffelalp from the westing sun. He wanted to wait as late in the day as possible but still give them plenty of light by which to see.

At four-thirty he decided it was time. He took the 8x30s, held them under his arm as if hiding them, and crossed to the other house.

Nella opened the door.

"*Bono giorno*," Maxwell said in incorrect Italian, "May I come in?" Then he checked his smile. Nella's cheeks were wet, her eyes puffy.

"What's the matter?" he asked.

"Please, come in."

She stepped back from the door, against the wall, away from Maxwell as he entered. He looked at her questioningly, but walked into the house. Then he halted abruptly as his gaze came around to the figure on the table.

Paul lay there.

Maxwell's eyes darted to Vronsky sitting beyond the table, then back to Nella. He decided she might be frightened enough to shoot, but he didn't think she would be able to hit him with the little automatic in her shaking hand.

He did worry about Paul. Paul held the Walther in his right hand. It was as steady as the table on which he rested his forearm. It pointed directly at Maxwell's stomach.

Paul was without shoes or trousers. In shirt, shorts, and socks, he half reclined, leaning on his right elbow. His upper left thigh was stained red-brown. Strips of cloth torn from a bedsheet were wound around it. The remains of the sheet lay on the floor along with his bloodstained trousers. There was more dried blood on his face.

"What happened?"

"I have to tell you? Somebody shot me. In the chairlift. When I was coming back from town."

Maxwell looked at him steadily. He looked down at the gun, then back again. "It wasn't me."

"Did I say it was you?"

"I get the impression you think so."

"I think. I do think. I think, somebody knows I am coming back from town. That means somebody knows I go to town. Now, why do I go to town? I go to town because you tell me the Russians are there."

"I think you'd better let Doctor Vronsky do the thinking. I didn't tell you to go to town. I told you the Russians were there. I kind of assumed you might think that was a good reason for *not* going to town. You might figure they'd see you there. You might figure, now, that's how they knew you were coming back."

"Where were you this afternoon?"

"I took a walk."

"Oh? Where?"

"Down through Findeln, into the woods and back."

"Not to Zermatt or over by the chairlift?"

"Just down through Findeln and back."

"You see anybody there?"

"Yes."

"Oh?"

"Yes. That's what I came to tell you. I saw somebody. *From* there. You can see him from here, too." Maxwell gestured with his head toward the window. Moving slowly, he took the binoculars from under his arm and extended them toward Paul. "But you'll have to stop pointing that gun at me if you want to look."

Paul regarded him for a moment, then let the pistol dip as he shifted his weight. He sat, swung his legs over and down to the floor, and slid himself off onto his right foot.

"How bad is that?" Maxwell asked.

"Didn't hit the bone. Went right through, along the side."

"How big a hole?"

"Small."

"Your cheek?"

"Splinter. First shot went through the top of the chair next to me."

"Good thing he was such a lousy shot."

"Yeah, I guess so."

Using the table and then a chair for support, Paul hopped over to the window. He leaned against the couch back, continuing to hold the pistol and never looking totally away from Maxwell for more than an instant.

"OK, where?"

Maxwell came to him and handed over the binoculars. He gave directions.

"*Si, si.* Yes, I see him."

"What is it, Paul?" Vronsky had sat quietly in a sidechair by the fireplace. The thin stream of smoke from his cigarette rose straight up beside his head.

"A man. Watching. Yes, he has binoculars. He's looking at me."

"Can he see us?" Nella came into the room.

"No. I don't think so. Not back in the room. Not when it's this dark. At night, yes, with the lights on."

"Possibly in the morning, too," said Maxwell. "When the sun is coming in."

"What should we do?" Nella was not panicky, but she was very frightened.

"Nothing."

"Doesn't this make a difference?"

"No, Nella." Vronsky spoke calmly. "This means that we must be even more careful, but that is the only difference. We have yet no other place to go, and since they are watching, and shooting, it would be unwise for us—only three of us, alone—to try to escape. We must stay."

Maxwell was dismayed. "Look . . . ," he began tentatively, "I don't want to get into this . . . I mean, to make suggestions." He looked at Paul. "I wouldn't want you to hold me responsible for anything. But it seems to me . . . Well, you're pretty vulnerable here. And there's just three of you. Even four, if I can help—that isn't much—"

"There will be more." Nella felt better to be able to tell him.

"You're getting reinforcements?"

"There are men coming. Comrades. From Italia. They will be here—"

"Nella." Vronsky broke in, still calmly. "We expect them very soon," he finished.

"Well . . . good," said Maxwell. "Good. Well, I'll keep an eye out from my place. If there's anything I can do . . . Just give a yell."

"Thank you very much, Mr. Bergmann. I am grateful for your concern."

After his supper, Maxwell sat trying to think it through. The plan had slipped and was out of hand. His own efforts to scare Vronsky into running had backfired, and there were things going on that didn't fit.

He sat, or sometimes got up and paced, until the room was

quite dark. No lights came on next door, and Maxwell kept his own house dark to give a sense of sharing the danger, even though he felt none.

He was used to waiting to see if the axe would fall. Yet he had some trouble going to sleep, and then had bad dreams. At first the dreams were vague and incoherent, with brief appearances by Boris, Corchran, and the three next door, as well as many old acquaintances and a number of people he had never seen before but distrusted. In the deep of the night he had the jelly dream again.

He was lying on a bed in a hospital. His insides—all his guts, organs, bones and muscles—had turned to soft and slimy jelly. His skin seemed healthy; it was tight, but when he tried to move, it quivered. He couldn't move, and when he strained, the jelly squeezed and oozed out of his eyes and nose. He tried to call someone but could only make a sort of gurgle. He tried to call louder.

The fat little fellow nibbled daintily. He held the piece of bread up in front of him and took small bites, chewing them rapidly. Corchran reached forward and rubbed his stomach. Leaning back, he saw Maxwell standing just above him, on the path.

"What do they call these, here?" Corchran asked.

"Marmots."

"They look like our woodchucks."

"Same family."

Corchran tossed away the last piece of croissant, and the marmot waddled after it.

Corchran smiled at Maxwell. "That's a nice looking sweater. Icelandic?"

"Yeah."

"Must be warm."

Maxwell decided to play it Corchran's way. "Yours looks good, too," he said.

"Thank you. Fair Isles."

185

Corchran's sweater was white, a heavy cabled roll-neck. He wore a deep-blue nylon windbreaker. His trousers were gray wool, rugged and full enough for hiking, but trimly cut with leather piping around the pockets.

Maxwell tried to think what Corchran looked like an advertisement for. The picture wasn't quite right from above, from the path. A photographer would go to the other side and down, catch Corchran looking upward, his windbreaker against the snow of the Matterhorn, his gleaming blond hair against the azure sky.

Maxwell didn't like to think of Corchran seen against the Matterhorn. *Cologne*, he told himself. *Men's perfume*.

Corchran breathed deeply. "One needs a good sweater in the mountains at this time of year. Rather a nip in the air these mornings." He breathed again, taking his time. "Invigorating, though."

Maxwell waited.

Corchran swept his gaze slowly to the Matterhorn and then on around to the peaks across the valley. "Truly magnificent," he said.

Maxwell resisted the suggestion. He kept his eyes focused on Corchran.

Corchran took a final deep breath. He decided his control of the situation was established. "Well," he said without turning, "what have you got for us today?"

"They're scared, but they're not moving."

"Oh?"

He should have turned, Maxwell thought. *He's interested in this—he's supposed to be.* "Yeah, I told them the Russians were in town, watching them. And then somebody shot the bodyguard—Paul."

"Really?" Corchran did turn then, but too late. Maxwell no more believed his surprise than his previous indifference.

"Yeah."

"Did they kill him?"

"No. No, they had a marksman. Flesh wound in the thigh, scratched his cheek."

"You believe they didn't intend to kill him."

"Well, it would have been pretty hard not to, wouldn't it? Hanging there, only thirty, forty feet up. You could use a grease-gun, even a .45 automatic, and empty the whole magazine in the time it took him to go over. Even with a .22 target pistol—which is my guess—you have to be pretty good to hit only the side of a thigh instead of the center of the body. Right?"

"Just trying to scare him."

"Right. But it didn't work."

"Nerves of steel? Will of iron?"

"Orders. They're scared, but they've been ordered to stay. Reinforcements."

"Who?"

"I don't know. Coming from Italy, I guess."

"How? When?"

"I don't know. They don't really trust me. That's as much as I could get yesterday. I'll try for more when I get back down there."

"Yes. Anything you can. Keep up the good work."

Corchran smiled encouragingly, but Maxwell simply stared back without expression.

"I could do better if I knew *what* I was working on."

"You know all you need to, Max."

"I know more than I need to."

"Oh?"

"I know you knew the Russians were here. You knew it yesterday when you asked me to watch for them. I know you think I'm working for them. I know you wanted me to tell them you're here."

"Did you?"

"Yeah."

"Then I guess we were correct."

187

"Corky . . ." Maxwell threw up his hands. "I don't know. Why try? They think I'm working for you. What else would explain my being here, next to Vronsky? You think I'm working for them; what else would explain it? I'm caught! God, I'm caught in the middle, and neither—"

"*I* think it's a coincidence, Max."

"You do?" Maxwell was stunned: first by his surprise at being believed, then by hope.

Corchran went on matter-of-factly. "Of course. We've made inquiries. You booked your chalet months before Vronsky came here, before the Russians knew he was here."

"Well, God in heaven, Corky, then—"

"That doesn't mean you're not working for them, Max. You weren't working for them on this when you booked your place, but now . . ."

"No! No, Corky! I don't have anything to do . . . Why should I?"

"Why should you in the first place?" Corchran shot back. "You have your reasons, no doubt; sufficient unto *you*. Maybe they're paying you, maybe they're blackmailing you. I don't know. I don't really care. I do know they brought in Algernon—your 'Boris'—your own special contact, and you went directly to see him yesterday after you left us."

"I *knew* you'd know he was here! I *knew* you'd expect me to see him!"

"And you did."

"I didn't try to hide it! I needed to know . . . I just . . . For God's sake, Corky! I'm not working for anybody! I don't want to, I just . . ."

Maxwell's arms shook with tension as he held them out toward Corchran, fists clenched, straining.

Corchran stood there, apparently no more affected than the white mountain peaks in the still morning air.

Maxwell realized he would not be free. All the horror of his illness came upon him as he had imagined it, as he had dreamed it when he would not let himself imagine: he was powerless, weak, and there was nothing he could do. He sank down onto a rock.

"I just want to die! I just wanted to go away and die! I don't want any more of it. It's worms—snakes, all wrapped and twisted together. All of you! I don't care! I don't care about . . . Thirty-eight years! God! My whole damned life! For what? It doesn't matter! I don't care what happens to any of you! I just want to live in peace—get away and live . . . Oh, God, it's always the same! Nothing makes any difference. Work, fight, try . . . I've had it! I'm finished! I just want to live for a little while, to . . . *live!* I just . . ."

Maxwell slouched as he felt his insides liquifying. There was no escape, no release. They had hunted him down and would never let him go.

It was not possible for Maxwell to cry. His nerves and muscles no longer knew that response to pain. He sat, head down, and stared through a blur at the moss by his feet.

Corchran uncrossed his arms and shoved his hands deep into his trouser pockets. He looked high above where wisps of cloud were just forming. Finally he spoke. "OK, Max. I believe you. I believe you."

He waited until he was sure that Maxwell had heard.

"I believe you, but it doesn't make any difference. Believing you doesn't make any difference—but what's going on here, that *does*. That does matter. So, I'm sorry."

Corchran kept his eyes up, not wanting to look at the big man slumped before him like a rotten tree stump.

"I'm genuinely sorry that what's happening to you made you do what you've done. I'm sorry you feel what you feel. But we've got a job to do here. It's your rotten luck to be caught in the middle of it, but you are, and you're going to help us. Then we'll leave you alone. I promise you that. We'll go away, I promise."

Maxwell's right arm hung down along the rock where he sat. After a moment he swung his hand back and forth lightly, rubbing his knuckles against the rough stone.

"What do you want me to do?" he said at last.

"Just what you're doing. Keep an eye on Vronsky. Keep in contact with the Russians. Tell us."

Maxwell sighed. He managed to bring his head up—first, to look down the slope at an outcrop of rock, glorious in its invulnerability, then at the tree tops below, and, finally, across the valley. He kneaded his forehead and cheeks as cover for wiping his eyes.

When he was ready to look at Corchran again, he asked, "What is it, Corky? What's really going on here?"

"I told you."

"You lied."

Corchran simply shrugged. Maxwell looked at him steadily.

"You'd better tell me," he said. "I'm not *really* working for you now, taking whatever I'm told, not asking, not trying to figure, just doing my job. I'm not working for them, either. I told Boris that. I told him I'm working for *me*. Now, I'll help you, if that gets you off my back, but I'm more likely to be of help if I know what you really want."

"I've told you. Get close to Vronsky. We may want to get a word to him sometime. For now, just get close."

"OK, Corky. You want me to get close by telling him it was you who shot Paul?"

Corchran paused an instant too long.

He doesn't have the rhythm, Maxwell thought, *the instinct. He thinks first.*

"What do you mean, Max?"

"Come on, Corky. Paul was shot to scare him. To scare them all into making a break."

"Very likely, from what you say. I imagine that's precisely what our opposites want, for Vronsky to make a break so they can nab him."

"Right, Corky. But they want to make sure that when he runs they *will* nab him. They don't want him to get away, and they don't want it to be messy. Their whole point in trying to use me was to find out how and where he'd run before he ran.

They wouldn't have tried to spook him; not yesterday, at least. And your using me to tell Boris you're here—what's the point of that? You want me to tell Vronsky about that?"

"We wanted them to know about us so they'd think twice before—"

"Bullshit! It's bullshit, Corky. How sick do you think I am?"

"Maybe sick enough not to be taken into confidence."

Maxwell leaned back, slipped his fingertips into his trouser pockets, and regarded Corchran. "OK, Corky," he said. "OK, we'll leave it. Do you mind satisfying my curiosity about something else?"

"If I can."

"What are *you* doing here? This isn't your area."

"I'm here for you, Max. Minelli assigned me to try to find you. In the process I got to know a lot about you. They believed I'd make a good control."

"How did you find me? I've been around long enough—you never traced me."

"No. As a matter of fact, finding you was quite a surprise. When Minelli called me . . . I think I'll not go into the effect Frank's call had on me."

"So how did you find me?"

"We found Vronsky, and there you were."

"Yeah. That's what I thought."

Maxwell watched the marmot. It had finished the croissant and decided the danger in Maxwell's outburst was past. It approached again, pausing a dozen feet away, ready to flee, its nose twitching. It looked at the men first with one eye, then with the other. A fat marmot, even in the spring of the year. Maxwell guessed it was fed well by hikers. It took a tentative step forward, then back again. Maxwell sensed it was playing hard to get.

"My next question ought to be how you found Vronsky," Maxwell said, "but I already know that."

"You do."

"Yeah. From Boris."

"He *told* you? Why?"

"I asked him."

"And he told you?"

"I said it was important."

"Your opinion must carry weight."

"It does. I told him it was important for me to know because I smelled a rat. I told him if I found *where*, I might let him know—if it was in my interest. I guess the chance of finding out what I'm interested in was interesting to him."

Maxwell looked at the marmot. It came forward two more steps, then sat.

"How old are you, Corky?"

"Thirty-two. Why?"

"What kind of work do you usually do for the Agency?"

"Why?"

"Surveillances? Contacts? Takeouts? What? Recruitment?"

"Why?"

"Because you are very bad at this part. You better go back to whatever you usually do, or get a desk to fly, because you're never going to make thirty-five if you stay in the field."

"Sorry I don't meet your exacting standards. May I ask what particular faults you find?"

"You don't feel it from the other side. You don't feel yourself in the other guy's place—what he feels, thinks, what he *should* feel. For example, you shouldn't be surprised at Boris telling me how you found Vronsky. OK, maybe a little surprised. You should want to know *how Boris knew* you found Vronsky. That's what you should have asked me. Even if you know you've got a penetration in the Rome office, you shouldn't let me know. You know why?"

"I'm not going to miss this chance to learn from the master."

"Because now I'm going to think that if you know about the penetration, you're using it. It's a *triple*—true or blind, it doesn't matter—and you're using it to feed the Russians. If you know Rome is penetrated, then you wanted them to know Vronsky is here."

"Fascinating. Do you do those Chinese puzzles—boxes inside of boxes? When you think up something like this do you ever sneak up on yourself from behind?"

Maxwell snorted, smiling at Corchran with one side of his mouth. He turned back to the marmot. He whistled. The marmot sat up on its haunches.

"You can construct it other ways too, Max: we didn't know about the penetration until after he told about Vronsky. Or another: we did know, but we let the word about Vronsky go through—figuring we could protect him—so as to maintain the conduit for other purposes. That's the trouble with these games, Max, you can invent anything."

"You're right, Corky. That's why I don't spend much time playing them. But I do get hunches, and I trust them. You don't like to lie, do you?"

"I . . . No. I don't."

"Now I believe that was a true statement. You started to think about it, and then you decided it was a safe question, so you told the truth. I could tell. I can tell about you, Corky. Let me tell you: the only way to be successful—to survive—in this business is not to care about the truth. You know what you're supposed to think, what you're supposed to feel and say. You work with what the other guy is supposed to think. You get the real truth about a situation that way. If you try working in terms of the truth as an idea, you're in trouble. Now the truth here is that the Agency found out where Vronsky was hiding and fed it to the Russians. And the truth is you're not protecting Vronsky, you're trying to stir things up. Now, you can tell me why, or you don't have to—but don't expect me to be a good little soldier and do what you say without thinking about it or trying to work my own angle."

Maxwell held Corchran's eye for a moment, then turned back to the marmot. It had dropped to all fours again and crept three steps closer. "You got any more bread?" he asked.

"No."

"I don't have anything either. Tough luck, little guy."

The marmot sat again. It neither saw nor smelled food, but it remained hopeful.

"OK, Max. When all else fails, try the truth—as they say. It's not your area, but you know what's been happening in Western Europe. The trend is toward the left: France, Italy, Spain. Even Germany. But it's chaotic. First the socialists are falling apart, then two years later Mitterand wins. Communists almost in the Italian government, then out again. They're fragmented—right wing, left wing, Eurocommunists, Stalinists, Maoists, Trotskyites, moderates, crazies. The closer they all get to power, the wider they split. Now after Afghanistan, Poland, the divisions are even greater. So at the one time they're stronger than ever, they're also potentially weaker. And at this crucial moment, Constantin Vronsky makes his appearance upon the stage of history. A certified genius, the mind that reconciled the strongest and weakest forces in the universe and proved them one. A man who is also an ideological theorist, who is prepared simultaneously to revitalize the spirit of communism while cutting it away from Russian control. It's enough to make a Eurocommunist believe in the efficacy of prayer."

"But it doesn't do much for either the Russians or us."

"You have it."

"So we want them to take him back."

"Correct again."

"But not in their own good time."

"You win the cigar. Naturally, they want to take Vronsky with a minimum of fuss. Well, we're not enthusiastic about the 'revitalization of communism' part, but we're all for discrediting Moscow."

"Got it."

"So you see, Max, our interests coincide here. You and we have a joint desire to see Vronsky depart as soon as possible."

"And the Russians."

"And the Russians. The only disagreement with them would be over technique."

"He doesn't have much of a chance, does he?"

16

THERE WAS NO TROUBLE at the border. All the documents were in order. The four men were given permission to enter Switzerland as "guest workers." They looked like workers. Even the small, young one was tough and wiry. It was unusual for men who came to work on the roads in summer to have their own cars, but the Fiat was eight years old. Its color had faded like that of worn, work-blue trousers. Yet it seemed well cared for and had correct registration and insurance forms. Probably third or fourth hand, a good buy, brought back into condition by its new owner. He looked like a man who would be a competent mechanic. All four of the men had regarded the border guards—first Italian and then Swiss—with stolid disinterest. They showed neither nervousness nor elaborate unconcern, either of which mark amateur smugglers.

There was no trouble going through the Simplon pass. Several times, other cars darted past as they came out of a curve, and once a blond young man with dark glasses and driving gloves swerved his Lancia Zagata into the wrong lane and shot blindly past in the middle of a tight hairpin. Two-pitch air horns blared his anger and contempt at the caution with which the Fiat was driven.

Despite that caution, they made good time. Getting from Milan to Zermatt would be the quickest part of the operation. The greatest delay had been in deciding who could be sent, locating them, and getting them together. The man with the scar on his chin, asleep in the right rear seat, had been driven up from Naples in the night. Then there had been some time spent over the documents. Still, they would probably reach Zermatt with little trouble by late afternoon, a little more than twenty-four hours after Paul had called.

Though the men did not know it, trouble began as they slowed to pass through the village of Ried bei Brig, where two men sat in an Opel sedan, parked beside the road. One of them looked back toward the oncoming traffic, watching through binoculars for cars with Italian license plates. He saw the Fiat two hundred yards before it reached him, so both he and his partner were able to look carefully at the four men as they passed. Then he spoke into his hand-held transmitter.

The Italians passed through Brig. They would pick up the Rhône Valley highway there, only nine kilometers from Visp. At Visp, they would turn into the Mattertal.

Moving slowly, they went onto the access ramp. Suddenly there was a bang as the right rear tire blew out. The car pulled, but the driver was able to control it, and they came to a stop on the shoulder. All four men got out to assess the problem.

They were not especially concerned. They were, after all, on a public highway. It was broad daylight.

The driver opened the trunk, gave the young man the orange safety triangle to unfold and place down the road behind the car. Cheap-looking valises came next. The man with the scar took out the jack, and the other two began to get the spare wheel free.

When the Opel stopped behind them, the young man assumed at first that the men inside intended to offer assistance. He waved to indicate that none was needed.

The man in the passenger seat of the Opel had already rolled down his window. He watched ahead. His driver used the rearview mirror.

The traffic was regular but not heavy: two cars coming, close together. On the highway itself there were perhaps three cars in any given kilometer—counting those moving in either direction—but they were too far away and going too fast for anyone in them to see clearly.

As the two cars passed from behind, the driver grunted. No other car was turning onto the ramp. The passenger swung open his door and stepped out behind it so that he was screened. He brought up the submachine gun he had been holding across his lap, poked it through the window opening and leaned his elbow on the door.

It seemed purely arbitrary whether he should first shoot the man working the jack at the side of the car or the young man who was walking up the road. He selected the young man.

At that moment, when the target was being chosen and sighted, the man with the scar glanced up. He was accustomed to danger, and to action. He responded instantaneously. He shouted, throwing himself sideways from his knees to the ground and rolling under the car.

The shout was too late. It came to the young man at the same time as the roar from the submachine gun. He understood neither. Four heavy-caliber bullets in a close group slammed into his back and tore out through his chest.

The gunman kept the trigger squeezed as he swept the gun back and forth across the small arc necessary to spray the two men at the trunk of the car. They spun and jerked like marionettes with twisted strings, then fell across each other.

Their bodies made a screen for the man under the car.

He lay on his back, staring up at the underside of the car. He did not think about his chances or what he should do. He waited, ready. It was like soccer, which he had played as a young man. He had been goalie. The ball is passed down the field toward you; it will come at you—you wait, and when it is time, you jump.

He heard the crunch of gravel on the road as the Opel rolled forward.

The car moved slowly, blocking the line of sight between the bodies and a Mercedes that was coming up the ramp.

The driver of the Mercedes flashed his lights and swept by

muttering about idiots who would pull out just at the moment of his approach.

The Opel stopped parallel to the Fiat. The gunman opened his car door again. He leaned down to his right, holding the back of his seat with his left hand. In his right he held the gun. He held it flat, just above the ground so that he could fire under the Fiat. It would kick and pull, so he made sure his grip was firm. Accuracy was of little importance.

The man with the scar rolled out from under the car and came to his knees, facing up the ramp. He spun around, keeping low, and—as the gun roared and bullets richocheted from the road under the Fiat—he ran, crouching, down the ramp.

Past the tail of the car, he straightened and sprinted. A yellow VW was accelerating up the ramp toward him. The man ran to meet it, waving.

The driver braked and swerved. The runner jumped back and forth, trying to keep in front of the car, to make it stop for him. But the driver swerved again and, frightened, tromped on the accelerator and sped past. A hundred yards up the ramp he slowed once more, his mind reacting to the images of one man running toward him while others lay in the road. He stopped and looked back.

The Opel was in reverse, its engine and gears screaming, speeding backwards after the running man. He cut suddenly across the shoulder and jumped into the field beside the ramp.

The Opel slewed around at an angle across the road. The gunman leaned through the window again and fired.

The runner tried to zigzag, but within three steps he was cut down.

In the VW the driver sat stunned. Then he crashed the car into gear and raced away. He would stop at Glis and notify the police. By then, though, the Opel would have completed its turn, gone wrong-way down the ramp, and disappeared.

17

"TEAR GAS?" said Maxwell.

"No way," said Paul. "How they going to get close enough to throw a canister? No tree, no bush; we got an open field of fire."

"Two pistols: you can't protect all four sides at once."

"When the others come, we can."

Paul sat on the couch, his injured leg out straight. He faced the large window and glass door leading to the terrace on the Matterhorn side of the house. He spoke over his left shoulder to Maxwell, who stood by the east window. Vronsky sat to one side of the west window, and Nella watched to the north through the small pane in the front door.

"I sure hope they come soon," said Maxwell.

"You afraid?" asked Paul.

Maxwell returned his look steadily for a moment. "Yes," he said, "and I hope you're afraid too, because if you weren't, I'd have a poor opinion of your smarts."

Both men were surprised when Vronsky spoke. "I am not afraid, Mr. Bergmann." He brought up his cigarette and took two quick puffs. Seeing the expression on Maxwell's face, he smiled. "Nervous, yes, but not afraid. I do not think they will try to take me from here by force, not just now."

"I hope you're right."

"Paul is right. Such an attempt would require a battle. I do not think they wish to kill me, so they would hesitate to shoot into this house. On the other hand, Paul and Nella would—I am afraid—shoot them. While Nev might accept casualties, he would not like the problem of dealing with them. Nor would he like the noise."

"You have to sleep sometime. And when it's dark . . ."

"Of course. And I am grateful to you for helping us watch now, too. But when our reinforcements come . . ."

Vronsky broke off, puffed at his cigarette again.

"What's wrong?"

"No." Vronsky gave the slightest negative shake of his head. "I am sure all will be well."

It's not working. Maxwell had not truly expected it would work, that he could increase the pressure enough to make them bolt. *Well, it was a try. At least I'm inside now.*

While Corchran took the list of sold information and went off to report, Maxwell had sat hidden behind the rock outcropping below their meeting place. He was still reading Vronsky's dossier half an hour later when Corchran came back for it.

"Interesting?"

"If these are good translations, the guy can really write."

"He did them himself. You saw from the personal data that he's fluent in five languages. Apparently the Party wanted the first article—the one on Western Socialism—to have definitive translations. So he did them himself. I guess he felt the same about the second."

Maxwell checked his watch. "You didn't go down to Zermatt."

"I'm fleet of foot."

"You guys have a place up here. With a radio, or just a phone?"

"We keep in touch."

"Don't be cute, Corky."

"Don't be overly inquisitive."

"I might need to reach you."

"Then you just step outside your house and stretch, like before."

"I might want you to come there to me. If this heats up . . ."

"OK. Take out your handkerchief and blow your nose."

"How long after that?"

"About ten minutes."

Maxwell had sat alone for the rest of the morning. Occasionally an idea for action would occur, and he would be tempted to move, but his sense of the rhythm of the operation prevailed. It was better to let his neighbors stew by themselves for a while.

When he did go back, as though returning from the village, he told them about seeing more Russians. He went so far as to say he had seen Nev at the top of the chairlift.

Paul and Nella were already watching to the north and south, and simply by going first to one side and then taking station at the other, Maxwell had manipulated them into the four-corners watch. He did it purely to make them feel threatened all around.

Now it seemed pointless, and he was getting bored and tired. "Well, if you're convinced this Nev won't attack now, we don't all need to keep standing here. We can probably see anything coming for a while just by looking north and south. We can take turns, and when it gets dark—"

"They'll be here by then." Paul was confident.

"You're sure?"

Paul looked at his watch. "They could be coming into Zermatt by now."

"Well, I'll stay until they get here."

"Thank you, Mr. Bergmann," said Vronsky. "Your concern for me is very comforting."

Maxwell found himself surprisingly tired. He moved away from his window toward one of the armchairs, then changed direction and went to the door. "Why don't you sit for a while?" he said to Nella. "We can trade off."

"No, thank you. It is more better I do something." She had seemed calm, but she giggled with nervousness.

"How did you get into a thing like this?"

Nella told him.

"Really? Makeup for the movies? That must be very interesting."

She giggled and shrugged.

"Well, you must meet interesting people. Do you work with any stars? Mastroianni? Sophia Loren?"

"Oh, no. The company I work for is very small. We make the films about the West. The 'gunslinger.' "

"Ah. I see."

"One time . . . when I am *apprendista*—I do not know the English—when I am learning, I help makeup to Clint Eastwood!"

"Really!"

"Yes!"

"What was he like?"

"Oh, I do not know him . . ." She giggled once more and dropped her eyes.

"What's the matter?"

"I think he is like you: inside very . . . *risoluto*."

"Well, thank you." Maxwell glanced at the Baretta in her hand. "You know how to use that thing?"

"Paul has shown me."

"You ever shoot anyone?"

"No."

"You think you could?"

"If I must."

"Well, you probably won't have to. Are you frightened?"

"Yes."

"I'm sure it will be all right."

"Yes."

"You're sure you don't want to sit for a while?"

"No, thank you."

"Well, then, I will."

By six-thirty the tension in the room was growing thicker

than the blue from Vronsky's cigarettes. Two hikers had passed at four o'clock. After that, no one. No movement, not even a breeze stirring the wildflowers. As the sun tracked toward the western side of the valley its rays cast long shadows from the chalets, from the buildings down in Findeln, from boulders. The angle flattened further, and minor variations in contour seemed to rise out of the mountainside. Even hummocks of grass loomed. Nothing moved, yet in the heavy stillness, every object seemed as though it were alive and waiting.

"So, they got off later than I figured," said Paul after checking his watch for the second time in five minutes.

"Were they bringing weapons?"

"No. They were just going to wait 'til they got here and pick up rocks to throw."

"I mean, maybe they got stopped at the border. Searched."

"Why?"

"Routine check. I don't know."

"Nobody finds anything *they* have in a routine check."

"Who would know they were coming, Paul?" Vronsky spoke from the depths of the armchair where, for two hours, he had sat without motion except for the regular swings of his hand with a cigarette.

"I don't know. Whoever sent them. The Professore, maybe. Probably the big cheeses in the Party. Only a few. Why?"

"I think there is a weak place, a break, somewhere in Italy."

"In Italy!"

"Yes."

"Can't be!"

"How did Nev find us? He did not follow us that first night. Therefore, he must have been told by someone who knows. But the only people who know are in Italy."

"Not anyone in the Party!"

"Perhaps not. It would depend on what side chains there are, what points of contact. But someone, somewhere—in Italy."

203

"Maybe you've got a spy," offered Maxwell.

Paul would not believe. "Not *that* many people knew where—"

Vronsky sighed. "Someone knows," he said with controlled annoyance.

"What will you do if they don't come?" asked Maxwell.

Paul slapped his hand on the couch beside him. "They'll come! Hey, Nella. How about you make us another omelet?"

Nella started hesitantly to move from the door. Maxwell rose to take her place.

"Could there be something other than another omelet?" Vronsky asked plaintively.

"That's all Nella knows to cook."

"I'm sorry, Constantin."

"Would you like me to cook something?" said Maxwell. "I'm not too bad."

"That would be very kind. I do not know what we have—"

"There's some *cotoletta*. Cutlet."

"Anything except omelet."

"Sure." Maxwell smiled at Nella and went to the kitchen.

"Finish your spaghetti, Constantin."

"I've had enough."

"You should eat more. You must keep up your strength."

"Every meal, we have spaghetti. I wish sometimes there could be potatoes."

Paul snorted. "You want potatoes, Dottore, you should carry them up on *your* back."

Maxwell sensed that the bickering was carried on more by habit than by real antagonism. Certainly, he felt no anger behind it. To the contrary, for the first time all day, everyone seemed relaxed and contented.

Eating had made all of them feel better, even though the sun had dropped behind Gabelhorn and shadows grew and spread and joined, advancing stealthily, creeping over their refuge.

The high thin clouds which had screened the intensity of blue all day now gradually reddened the evening sky. As though kindled by that first warmth, the Matterhorn seemed to ignite and glow from within.

"Ah! So beautiful!" Nella breathed deeply and shook her head from side to side. Her own face glowed in response to the color; her forehead and cheeks were flushed, her eyes gleamed.

"*Alpenglühen*," said Vronsky. "Alpenglow. I believe it is caused by the refraction of light through ice crystals."

"It is so beautiful."

"Yes." Vronsky patted her hand, and they smiled at each other.

In contrast to the sunlit snowfields and ice-covered cliffs—now brilliant orange-red—crevices and eastern faces seemed cobalt blue; shadowed, yet not dark, not cool.

The four of them sat silently, Paul still on the couch, holding his wineglass, his plate on the floor beside him, the others at the table. They had rationalized leaving the door unguarded, and now—for the moment—forgot the danger. Vronsky and Maxwell sat at opposite ends, their chairs turned to face the window. Nella leaned on her forearms between the men but closer to Vronsky.

The shadows, deepening in hue but never less vivid, were shapes and lines to move the eye up and down the mountain's surface. They made it seem to move, to flicker. The mountain was fire—not taking color from the high clouds, but lighting them from heat and life within itself.

Yes, Maxwell thought, *this is how it should be, how I knew it would be.* A sense of calm filled him; an acceptance beyond resignation. Peace.

This will be the way. Here. Looking at that. An evening just like this. The good meal, the last of the wine. And the mountain, burning.

Nella sighed. "So beautiful," she said again.

205

Paul sipped his wine, then Vronsky, Nella, Maxwell. The sequence was unconscious, but it was as though a communion cup had been passed.

"Yes," said Vronsky. "Yes, a lovely place to recover from illness, Mr. Bergmann."

"What?"

"A lovely place to regain your health. To prepare again for life. After your angina, I mean."

"Oh. Yes."

"I understand why you chose to come here. I believe I feel much the same myself: as though I had been ill for a very long time—near death; but now, to rest, to enjoy such natural beauty, to regain one's strength—and then to go back to work."

"Work?" Maxwell was stunned. He tried to recover himself. "Yeah. Yes, of course, you must be anxious to get back to your work. Although after your theory—well, I don't know what you're going to work on. From what I read in the papers, you seem to have about wrapped it all up."

"Thank you. But that is not the work I mean."

"Oh? What else? My son will be very interested."

"My political work. My social philosophy. I believe that is where I am to make my greatest contribution."

"Yeah?" Maxwell was annoyed at the interruption in his contemplation of the mountain, annoyed at Vronsky's self-importance, most annoyed—even repulsed—by the thought of work. It was like an alarm clock shocking him to rise before dawn on a cold morning. "You have a theory about social philosophy, too?"

"I am developing one."

"Good luck."

"The subject seems to displease you."

"I'm not much on theories. On social theories. Marx and Lenin had theories; I guess you know pretty well how they worked out. Mao had a theory—it about tore China apart. Pol Pot had a theory, and it's killed off half the Cambodians. Khaddafi's got a theory. I'm not really much on theories."

"You said you were a capitalist. Capitalism is a social and economic and political theory, too."

"I . . .I've been for capitalism because it works, as a way to make a living. I don't believe in it as a *theory*. The people who take it that seriously are probably as bad as any of the others."

"Ah. I see. I agree with you, Mr. Bergmann. Yes. That is precisely the problem. My theory will not be a theory in that sense—a doctrine to be professed or burnt in the name of. I mean it in the scientific sense, as an explanation of cause and effect. By showing how certain kinds of behavior—"

"You'll what?" *Easy, easy,* Maxwell tried to tell himself.

Vronsky was startled by the vehemence. "I will show how society can be changed into the kind—"

"I'll show you how you can fly. Grow wings. I'll show you how to live forever. Don't die! Things don't change."

"They do!" Vronsky thought for only an instant. "Slavery. There was a time when slavery was accepted. Now—"

"Now we call it other things. Your country's got the gulags. In South America they've got péons . . . Paraguay . . . South Africa. We've got migrant workers. Most workers—most people—sure, we're paid, we're free in a sense, but—"

"Mr. Bergmann, if you cannot see the difference between those things and true slavery, as it used to be accepted, then you are either ignorant or—"

"The difference isn't *that* different!"

Vronsky let out the breath he would have used to complete his sentence. He stared at Maxwell for a moment, then turned to look out of the window again.

"Constantin . . ." Nella put her fingertips on his arm.

"Mr. Bergmann . . ." Vronsky turned back again. "I do not agree, but put that to the side. Let us say you are correct. Let us say there has been no change in human life—no true change; that we are our savage ancestors with their hair trimmed. That does not mean no change is possible. We can *imagine* change. We can imagine something better. Look at that mountain, Mr. Bergmann. Look."

Maxwell shifted his eyes to the Matterhorn again. The fire was deepening like old red coals, and the shadows were dark purple.

"What do you see? What is the shape of that mountain?" Vronsky paused. "How does it seem to you? Some people call it a lion—the back there along to the west; the head up, facing east. It is said to rear, to thrust up triumphantly. Do you see it that way?"

"Yes."

"No. It is a giant bell. It is a pointed hat. It is a symbol of tyranny—a great mass, a force, spreading, flowing downward, pressing down from a narrow pinnacle of authority; a weight, heavy, oppressive, crushing all beneath it. Can you see those things?"

Maxwell looked. He made himself see from the top downward. "Yes."

"But that is not what you have seen before, what you wish to see. And what you wish to see is what truly matters. If you see that mountain as heavy and ominous, you will be dismayed by it. If you see it as lifting up, you will be uplifted."

"So?"

"So we can change how we feel, and act—how others feel and act—on the basis of what we see and how we see it. If we can imagine change, if we believe change is possible, we *can* change. Even if we are unsuccessful—if we can imagine something better, then we can hope to achieve it."

"I guess I'm not much more on hope than I am on theories."

"You must have hope!" Nella's voice startled all of the men. "Without hope there is no life!" She strained toward Maxwell for a moment. "Please . . . Please . . ." She broke into Italian.

Vronsky put his hand over her clenched fist.

"Nella begs you to have hope. She begs you. And she is right."

Maxwell tried to manage a smile for her. "I'll try. I guess I don't see much to be hopeful about."

"But that is it!" said Vronsky. "The hope must come from within, not from what you see! The hope comes because you can imagine, and you try, and you work!"

Vronsky squeezed Nella's hand, and she stared at him, following every word in the unfamiliar language, then turned to Maxwell, nodding affirmation, then back to Vronsky again as he rushed on.

"If you have no hope, still you try. And that you try is reason for hope!"

Nella gazed at Vronsky.

The weepy kind, thought Maxwell. Yet despite himself, he was moved by her emotion. He fought against the feeling, but it spread through him, through the transparent peacefulness. It solidified, and weighed him down.

"Well, I'll think about that, Doctor Vronsky," he said.

They let the argument subside in the dim twilight, each lost in private thought as the color of the mountain deepened further against the darkening sky.

"Hey!" Paul broke in suddenly. "Hey! Hey!"

"What is it?"

"Look. Look down there."

Maxwell, Vronsky, and Nella sprang from their chairs and to the window.

"Look." Paul pointed.

Coming out of the gloom around the buildings at Findeln were four men. Their faces were dark, but they were faintly back-lit, blue-violet, from the mountain. They walked steadily, deliberately, up the path toward the two chalets. When they made the turn below Maxwell's they looked up, keeping the light on them so their faces could be seen. The first smiled and waved.

"It's them!" Paul shouted. "I told you they'd get here!"

18

MAXWELL SHOULD NOT have left the binoculars where Renata could notice them, on the deep sill of the window by the bed. It had been natural to do so, putting them down while he rubbed his eyes, then leaving them when there was no point in looking longer.

He had begun watching as soon as he returned to his own house the night before; not constantly like the shifts of Russians across on Riffelalp or their American counterparts hidden somewhere on the Findeln side. Once night had come fully he couldn't see anything anyway. He checked once when he woke at three o'clock and began again shortly after dawn.

The side window in the bedroom gave him the best vantage. He could see well into the downstairs living room of the other chalet—at least half of it—and a little more of the nearer upstairs bedroom. He could see the bed clearly. Vronsky and Nella were in it, still asleep, when he had looked last. At eight o'clock, two of the Italian men had left the house, wearing empty rucksacks, presumably to get supplies in Zermatt.

Maxwell had put down the binoculars, rubbed his eyes, and gone downstairs. He had paused on the doorstep to stretch, then walked out of sight along the road to confer with Corchran.

Corchran had known of the Italians' arrival, of course, from his own watcher, so it couldn't have been surprise, exactly, that Maxwell sensed in his manner as the two of them assessed the situation. Maxwell felt there was *something*, but perhaps it was just an aspect of the annoyance they both expressed at the prospect of Vronsky's digging in. They agreed there was nothing to do for the moment but to wait and see.

On the way back to his chalet, Maxwell realized it was Saturday again. Renata would be coming. As always when he thought of her, his feelings were mixed.

When he had learned fully of his sickness, and for the year afterward, he had felt no lust. That had partly been due to the medication. But also he wanted to be alone. By himself, he still could feel life strongly, but every relationship and human contact was without future, emphasizing the imminence of death. Suddenly Renata had made lust one of the sensations of life again, in a way without committment or obligation.

She was in the chalet when he returned. She had gone first to Vronsky's but had been sent away.

Maxwell went directly to embrace her, placing one arm around her shoulders; his other hand, behind her pelvis, pressed her against him. She seemed surprised, amused, and pleased all at once.

They had gone straight up to the bedroom.

"What do you look at?" she asked, picking up the glasses.

"I was looking at the mountains," Maxwell said casually, "but now I want to see—"

"These are very good quality," Renata said, adjusting them for her eyes. She leaned against the window frame, trying to look at an angle toward the Matterhorn. "I think you see the mountains better from the other window."

"We'll look at the mountains later. Come on, Renata, we don't need to play games this week."

Renata scanned in an arc. Maxwell tried to think how to stop her without being obvious. It was too late.

She gasped.

"What is it," he asked.

She lowered the glasses from her face and stared at Maxwell

wide-eyed, her jaw dropped in astonishment. Then her expression changed. She lowered her eyelids and smiled lopsidedly. "So? This is what you look at."

"What?"

Still smiling, she extended the glasses toward Maxwell. "*Ja,* this is a most interesting outlook."

Maxwell came across the bed, took the glasses, and looked—as Renata had—at Vronsky's chalet. From his own habit, he glanced first at the living room, but a movement caught his eyes, and he focused on the bedroom. Vronsky and Nella were no longer asleep. He looked for a moment, then turned away.

Renata laughed.

Maxwell knew he was blushing. "Renata, I haven't been . . . I don't . . ."

She laughed again. "Do not be embarrassed. I will not tell."

"I really do not get my kicks by watching—"

"Why not? It is very sexy to watch.'

"I'd rather do it than see it."

He put down the glasses and, pulled Renata over and down onto the bed again. He lay across her, kissing her neck and shoulders. He got her sweater off, tried to loosen her trousers. The zipper stuck.

"Wait. I do it."

She sat up, unzipped the trousers, and began to slip them off. "You don't like to see? Should I close the curtain. Make the room dark?"

"I don't like to see other people."

"Is it not exciting to know at this moment they also—"

"I've got all the excitement I can handle right here."

"Well, I do not mind a little more." Renata took up the glasses again.

"Dammit, Renata! Get the hell back here and—"

"Ooh-la-la! Oh, *das ist schön!*" She giggled. "Here."

Clenching his teeth in annoyance, Maxwell swung his legs over the bedside and took the glasses. *Look at the peep show, and get her back in bed,* he thought.

It took an instant before he could recognize what he saw. Then he realized that Nella was lying across the bed, her head away from him. Her legs were over Vronsky's shoulders as he knelt on the floor, his head in her crotch.

Maxwell threw the glasses down on the bed.

Renata laughed. "Is that not very pretty?" She came up to Maxwell as he stood barefoot, with a flush blotching down his bare chest. She put her palm against his abdomen. "You do not think it is nice?"

Maxwell saw in his mind the white flab around Vronsky's waist as he squatted ridiculously. The whole picture made him unaccountably angry. "It's not my style."

Renata suddenly slipped her fingers inside Maxwell's waistband, reaching down to clutch him. She laughed again. "Yet I think you think it's sexy."

She pushed him gently, forcing him back to the bed. She unfastened and pulled off his trousers and caressed him. "I think you like it if I do it that way."

Maxwell's disgust overpowered his throbbing excitement. "Is there an extra charge for that? There usually is, isn't there?"

For an instant Renata's slight smile was gone, and her eyes narrowed as though flinching. She recovered. "We do not speak of that."

"That's right. We've never talked about that. Don't you think we should?"

"I think . . . I think it is nicer not to think of it."

"Nicer?"

"I do not like to think about the money now."

"Well, don't you think we ought to get the contract settled? After all, you might be putting all this out for nothing."

Renata looked at Maxwell steadily. "You are rich. I please you. I believe you will be generous."

"What if I don't pay? What if I flip you five francs and say, 'Thanks a lot, kid'?"

Renata was kneeling beside Maxwell. She took her hands away from him and folded them in her lap. She continued to look at him for a moment. "Then I thank you for teaching me."

213

"Teaching you what?"

"To be a better judge of people. I think now I am a good judge. I think now I can know who will cheat, with whom I must write a contract. I wish to make no business with such people. If you teach me I am not a good judge, then perhaps another time I do not make a more serious mistake. So I thank you."

"Doing business that way is risky."

"I think it is the best way, if one is a good judge."

Renata sat on her heels, quite still. The light from the window was soft through her fluffy hair and on her smooth skin. She was so slender and lithe, so young. Yet she was strong. It seemed to Maxwell that her fully opened eyes and slight smile were as old and knowing as a sphinx'.

"You judge you can trust me."

"Yes."

"I guess I should thank you."

They stared at each other for a moment.

"Do you . . . Why . . . ?" Maxwell stopped. He looked up to the ceiling.

"What?"

"I was going to ask you why you were doing this, and if you liked it. But that's stupid. I know why you're doing it—you want the money. And every wh— Every woman tells the man she likes it."

"*Ja*, I like it. Why not? Everybody like it, *ja*? I do not do it with everyone. Only with three men before. I must be careful—Zermatt is a small place. And the right man—he must be trustworthy, he must be rich, *ja*, but I must like him . . ." She looked away for the first time, as though this were the shameful admission. "I must think I would like it with him even for no money." Then back to Maxwell defiantly. "I do not do this with a man I do not like. I do not want money so much as that! I am yet young. I can wait. One, two years more, then I leave Zermatt."

"What will you do then?"

"I go to Zurich. I study business—much I know already.

Then I buy clothes, a little jewelry. Then I find where are the rich men, and I go there."

"Same line of work again."

"Only at first."

"I see." Maxwell felt a great sadness. He wasn't sure whether it was because of the likelihood that Renata would fail in her ambition, or the sense he had that she would succeed. Again, she reminded him of Eric Handelsmann, for whom—though he felt no guilt—he did sometimes grieve. Like Handelsmann, she saw the world and accepted and dealt with it. But her ambition and determination were only other names for hope. That made her seem so young, so vulnerable. He sighed, looking up again.

"You are no longer angry."

"No."

"Good." She watched him for a moment, trying to understand his mood. She ran her finger along the side of his leg, but he did not respond. She folded her hands and waited.

"Renata . . . How much money were you figuring on making before you could leave here?"

"Perhaps thirty thousand francs. To pay for school, to live for a while . . . Why?"

"Oh, I just wondered. That's a lot of . . . housecleaning."

"Tenne pays well. I save. It is not all housecleaning."

"Have you ever thought of taking a loan?"

"I have no security."

"Maybe from someone who trusted you. Maybe from a friend."

"No one gives money without security."

"Well, I might."

She leaned forward abruptly. "You? Why?"

"Maybe I'm jealous, thinking of all the other visitors you're going to have to . . . work for." He said it sarcastically, so they'd both know it wasn't true.

Renata laughed, bent, and kissed Maxwell's knee. She laughed again. "For so much money I would give to you an exclusive contract."

215

He turned away in sudden anger. "I wasn't asking for a contract."

"For what, then?"

"Nothing. I was just talking about a loan. I didn't say anything definite, I was just asking."

"I see." She sat back on her heels. Maxwell was looking away from her, so he did not see her eyes fill. "Thank you." she reached out and touched his knee. She looked away, too, then, in a moment, spoke in her normal tone. "I do not look for such a loan. I earn my money." She leaned forward. "Please?" He did look at her then. "What I do . . . It does not give me shame. To take money, without work, without giving something, *that* would give me shame."

"Then why don't you want to talk about the money?"

"Making love should be about love, not about money. If I pretend, then it is. When I serve at Tenne, I pretend the customers are my guests—in my house. Then I like to serve them. It is always nicer to give something than to sell it."

"But you need the money. You take it."

"So. Why does this make you angry?"

"I don't know. I guess I don't like pretending things. I guess I like to deal with the facts."

"It is a fact I need money. It is a fact I wish for love. I deal with those facts."

She had sat back on her heels again, facing him directly. Her hands were together on her thighs, neither displaying nor concealing her sex. She seemed to present her entire being to him with that honesty. She seemed . . . Maxwell did not actually try to find a word, and the concept was one he would not have thought appropriate for a woman who took money in exchange for her body—but what she seemed to him was *wholesome*.

He reached toward her, and she leaned into his arms. He held her for a moment, then brought her gently down onto the bed. He held her tenderly, and they lay so until holding was not enough, and each had to give everything to the other.

216

19

"WHAT'S WRONG?"

"It's not working."

"I mean, what's wrong with it that it's not working?"

"How should I know, Nella? I'm not a man of electrical knowledge. Dottore, you should know about these things."

"Only in theory, Paul. I'm sorry."

"Yeah. The theory. Hey! Either of you guys know about radios?"

"Sorry, buddy. Not my line." The young man at the big window turned, smiled, and shrugged.

The older, heavy one, called Parducci, looked into the room from his place at the front door and shook his head a single time in negation. Paul could not remember his having spoken since the four had arrived the evening before.

"It was working fine yesterday. This morning I turn it on— nothing."

"Have you tried it in another outlet?" Vronsky asked.

"Yeah. I thought of that."

"I'll bring down mine," offered Nella.

Both of the men at the windows heard, but neither looked back to the table where Paul, Nella, and Vronsky sat.

"No rush now. No news again before noon."

"I'll get it anyway. But the batteries were weak."

Nella took her plate and cup to the kitchen, then went upstairs to her room.

"You slept late this morning," said Paul. His voice was neutral, but there was the hint of a smile.

Vronsky colored slightly, finished his coffee. "We were very tired. From the tension yesterday."

"Yeah. Good to get relaxed."

Vronsky changed the subject. "When should they be back?"

"Lunch time. They went down early to be there when the shops open."

"Do you think they will have any trouble?"

"No. They aren't going to take the chairlift."

"Someone might wait for them in the forest."

"What do you think, Vito? You think your buddies could get ambushed?"

The young man laughed. "We can hope. They try to surprise Bonnario and Ricci, they get a surprise themselves. Take out some of the opposition, maybe."

Suddenly from the top of the stairs came a startling sound, the heavy chords of Liszt's second *Hungarian Rhapsody* made thin, as though the grand piano had been shrunk and put into a tin can. Nella spun the dial as she came down with the little radio in her hand. On another station she found a man and woman singing about the agonies of unrequited love. She put the radio onto the table. Vronsky regarded it with distaste.

"The batteries have rested," she said.

Vito and Parducci did turn to look into the room this time, focusing first on the radio, then—for an instant only—letting their eyes meet.

"Do you think they *will* receive new instructions?" asked Vronsky?

"Who knows, Dottore. A situation like this, anything can happen. Or nothing. They call this morning, they call tomorrow. It doesn't matter. We're safe now, and as soon as we get the word, we go."

The song ended, and a man's voice came on speaking rapidly and authoritatively in German.

"What does he say?" asked Nella. "Is it the news?"

"It's only the weather. We don't get the news for another hour."

Corchran had already heard the news. When he got back to base—one of the chalets in the group up near Sunegga—Dolby told him.

"It was on the eight o'clock—just after you left to meet Maxwell."

"Do you suppose *they've* heard?"

"Vronsky? No telling. Just have to wait and see. Jack hasn't seen any activity, so we assume all's well." Dolby nodded to the man at the window who had the chalets below under watch.

"What did it say?"

"Not much. Who did it, or why, still unknown. Checking with Italian authorities. Police confident. All the usual crap."

"They know more than they're saying?"

"Not from what we can find out so far. I put a call through as soon as I heard. They found weapons in the rocker panels."

"Well." Corchran nodded to himself. "I wondered what the hell was going on when Max told me the reinforcements had arrived. I couldn't believe Nev would let them through. I thought maybe our boy in Rome hadn't gotten the word back to him. You think we should tell Max there's been a switch?"

"You think he doesn't know?"

"I'm sure. I really believe you're wrong about Max, Bob. I don't propose trusting him very far, but I'm sure he's not working for the opposition."

"Maybe. Maybe not. I don't plan on trusting him at all."

"Well, trust or not, should we tell him?"

Dolby pondered for a moment. "I don't think so."

"If we don't tell him, he won't know what to watch for. He thinks they're digging in."

"He's supposed to watch for *anything*, anyway. If he's square, he'll tell us whatever he sees. If he's not, I think it'd be better if he didn't tell his contact we know they cancelled those guys' checks and that they're bouncing their own."

"They'll know we heard it on the news."

"Maybe not. I mean, they won't know we know, any more than they know we fed them the tip-off in the first place. Maybe they'll figure they can beat us out by moving quick, before we know for sure."

"Today?"

"If I was them, I'd go tonight."

"Hey, Paul, how about you watch for me while I put on some lunch?"

"It isn't even noon."

"I'm hungry. You hungry, Parducci?"

Parducci grunted, proving, at least, he wasn't a mute.

"You want me to cook?" Paul offered.

"You keep off that leg. You just come sit here by the window. I need to move around anyway."

Paul hobbled to the couch and took up his old position.

"How's it doing?"

"OK."

"Hurt much?"

"Only when I dance."

Vito went to the kitchen and began looking into the cabinets. "Didn't we bring up some clam sauce? Parducci, you want some spaghetti with clam sauce?"

Apparently expecting no answer, Vito opened some cans and a package of spaghetti. He put a pot of water on the stove and moved back to the table.

"You get any good disco on this?" he said, picking up the radio and spinning the dial. He found only the classical music program again and some regional oompah-oompah.

"The other station's the best. Leave it back there."

Vito returned the dial to the soft-pop and put the radio back onto the table, near the edge.

"What they doing up there?" he asked, jerking his head toward the stairs.

Paul looked at him for a moment. "Now they're working," he answered with a straight face.

"Oh?"

"The Dottore's writing a book."

"What about?"

"Politics."

"Yeah? Any good?"

"Yeah."

"You read it?"

"Some of it."

"What's he say?"

"He says Lenin and Stalin and all the Russians, and all the capitalists too, he says they all got their heads up their asses."

"Oh? But he don't."

"Right."

"You believe him?"

"Maybe."

"You think he's really that smart?"

"Maybe."

"He don't look very smart."

"No."

Vito returned to the kitchen, put the spaghetti into the pot to cook and turned on the heat under the sauce. He began to set the table.

"That Nella . . . She must think he's pretty smart, or something."

"Yeah."

"She let him screw her?"

"Why don't you ask her?"

"No offense."

"Sure."

Vito got silverware.

Paul checked his watch. "Turn up the radio, will you?"

"You like this song?"

"It's almost time for the news."

"Why you so hot to hear the news?"

"I just like to know what's going on. Turn it up."

Vito turned up the volume, went back to the kitchen and took the two-litre bottle of wine from the refrigerator. "Hey, Parducci, you want to eat first, or do you want me to eat first?"

"You eat."

"Or you want I should fix the plate and bring it there?"

"Eat."

"OK." Vito drained the water from the pot of spaghetti and served a large portion out onto one of the plates, then poured sauce over it. He picked up the plate of spaghetti with one hand and plates of bread and butter with the other.

Chimes sounded on the radio, then a series of ticks, then a tone.

"*Guten Mittag. Hier spricht Kurt Stammelweisse mit der Mittagsnachrichten,*" the authoritative voice spoke from the radio.

"What's he saying?"

"It's the news."

"What's he say?"

"He says it's the news!"

"It's in German."

"Of course it's in German!"

"You understand German?"

"Yeah, I understand German. Now shut up and let me listen."

Vito caught the wine bottle under his right arm, pressing it against his ribs. He walked unsteadily toward the table.

"*Die Valais Kantonalpolizei ansagten dass noch nicht haben sie einen Schlussel zu verstanden die Morden gestern der vier—,*"

Suddenly the wine bottle started to slip from under Vito's arm. He lurched to the side to hold it, tipping the spaghetti plate. Spaghetti began spilling. Righting himself, still trying to hold the bottle, he dropped his forearms onto the table. He released the bread and butter plates with a clatter, then swung

222

his left hand over to clutch at the bottle while lunging to get it onto the table. His elbow struck the radio, knocking it to the floor. Trying to keep his balance, he shifted his feet, and his heel smashed down.

Maxwell sat in his living room, staring out at the Matterhorn. Moisture in the air veiled the mountain, flattening it. But whether he looked out through the window or closed his eyes, Maxwell saw the womens' faces: Nella's and Renata's, one then another, one becoming the other.

First, he saw Nella's face as he had seen it that morning when Renata first handed him the binoculars—it had been a face transfigured by pure, almost holy love. Then he saw her body, naked in the act of sex, sanctified by that love. The vision aroused him sexually, and the face became Renata's. He again felt desire for her—not only physical—and finally an overwhelming sense of his sickness.

Maggots crawled inside his body, consuming him. He acknowledged them for the first time outside the dreams over which he had no control. For the whole year he had accepted death like winter, a fact to be dealt with, and he had dealt with it pragmatically. Now he knew death was not a season to be gotten through, to be coped with or faced down.

He called Renata back into his mind; he tried to hide again inside her but could not obliterate the cold he felt in his guts. Then Nella returned to him: her resolution, her courage, her intensity of hope. Then again Renata, determined, honest.

How could he despair? How could he let himself give in when he had the inspiration of those pure—

Bullshit!

He was letting himself fall in love. He was letting himself be infatuated with an idea. He was inventing them out of his need. *Pure!*

He again saw Nella and Vronsky copulating, saw Renata and himself. Saw Nella on her back, with Vronsky's head between her legs. That toad. That flabby white slug!

223

It was Vronsky's fault! Vronsky's and Nella's fault, both of them, all of them! He would have gotten through it all, right up to the end. He could have gone out strong and clean, if *they* hadn't come with their fear and hope and work and love and . . . death. They had brought the sense of death and forced it into him!

I want to go. All along I have wanted to go. Yes.

Vronsky saw increasing light as though he were in a tunnel approaching brilliant sunlight. But something was wrong.

"Do they feel better now?" asked Nella.

Vronsky took two more steps, stopped, wiggled his toes. "They are still very stiff."

"New boots are always stiff. But do they still rub?"

"No. The extra stockings help."

Nella came to him, got down on her knees, took hold of Vronsky's right heel. "Let me feel it again."

Vronsky moved his foot up and down.

"Yes," said Nella.

"Can I take them off now?"

"Don't you think you should wear them through the afternoon to break them in?"

"They are heavy."

Nella considered. "You shouldn't tire yourself. But perhaps you should wear them for another two hours. There will still be plenty of time to rest before we go. Try on the jacket."

She brought over the new orange-colored down jacket and helped Vronsky into it. "There." She smoothed it over his shoulders, pulled down at the bottom. "Zip it up. Here, let me. Now put on the hood."

"I don't think I shall need a hood."

"It gets very cold at night. We will be walking for many hours. You will need to keep your head warm. Let me tie it."

She pulled the drawstring tight. Only Vronsky's nose and eyeglasses showed at the hood opening. "Good," she said.

She stepped back and regarded him. "Good." Then she

smiled. "You look very handsome, Constantin. You look like a mountain climber. You look as though you could climb the highest mountain in the world."

"Can I take it off now?"

"Of course."

Nella helped Vronsky out of the jacket. She folded it carefully and put it onto the table beside the red one they had brought for her.

Vronsky stood as she had left him, staring vacantly at the window.

"What's the matter, Constantin?"

"Nothing."

"Aren't you pleased that finally we shall escape?"

"Of course, but . . ."

"What?"

"I am only surprised that *all* difficulties were overcome so quickly."

Paul was surprised too. His surprise saved him, later, when Vito came back.

Paul hadn't wanted to make anything of the business with the radios. His relief at being reinforced, his confidence in the men he saw as ordinary soldiers like himself, comrades truly, whose competence he could trust—those feelings had forced his suspicion into hiding.

It made sense: pressure caused by the Russians had broken the blockage in Rome, and Vronsky's permit was granted. Things always happen at the top when they have to—never before the crisis comes; that would be too easy—but finally they happen. It made sense. Since Vronsky was no longer hidden, he should be taken out. It made sense to take him out that night, under the protection of four good men, just when it looked like they were digging in. It made sense to leave Paul behind. He really had no choice—he couldn't have walked far. It had all made sense.

But Paul was troubled. He was not given to extensive self-analysis, but he was aware that his misgivings were partly from being left behind. Vronsky had been his charge—a measure of the respect in which the Party held him. He felt the lifting of responsibility as a demotion. It was not as though his mission were completed, or even that he had formally been relieved. Bonnario had come back with his own orders: Vronsky was taken up, not handed over; Paul was not discharged, just left behind.

But there was more. Beneath the rocks of rationalization which Paul had piled up on it, his suspicion lurked, and pounced out on little things, and fattened. Vito hadn't seemed surprised at the order to leave at once. Paul felt he had pretended to be surprised. And every time Paul had tried to draw the others into conversation—innocent talk among old troopers about where they came from, who they had worked for and where—he had found evasion. And then the lack of clear instructions for him to follow when they were gone: Move around. Go out, come in, turn lights on and off. Make it look like all of them were still in the house. Ordinary enough. But nothing more. Nothing about how long to wait or where to go when he did leave. What should he say if the Russians caught on and stormed the place and took him alive? Bonnario's briefing had been a joke.

So Paul did not go back and sit on the couch after they left at ten that night.

Nella had squeezed his fingers, then impulsively kissed his cheek. Vronsky had shaken his hand and thanked him. Parducci had grunted, Bonnario and Ricci waved *ciao*. Vito had punched him twice on the arm. Paul had waited until they all were moving away on the road—Ricci out ahead, then Bonnario just in front of Nella and Vronsky, the others guarding behind—then he closed and locked the front door. But he did not return to his couch.

"Paolo, hey Paolo!" Vito held his head close to the glass door. He called in a low tone, sure he could not be heard as far away as the next chalet where the Canadian lived.

226

He paused, knocked lightly. "Hey, Paolo! It's me, Vito. Let me in. The Dottore forgot some papers. I got to get them. Let me in."

"Paolo?"

Vito waited again, then knocked.

What in shit's sake is the matter with him?

He had come to the house perfectly innocently, not as if he were trying to hide. His hands had been empty—he had kept them out in front so Paul could see, if he had stayed at the door and was looking. Vito hadn't slipped the automatic with its long silencer out from under his jacket until the last instant, when he was sure he was out of sight of the little window. He held it now, down by his right leg.

"Paolo!"

He couldn't be asleep. Maybe he's in the crapper.

Still careful that the gun should not be seen, he moved around to the side of the house. Very carefully, he peered in at the bottom of the west window.

The night was dark, partially overcast. Stars could be seen, but they were blurry. Vito could make out the table near him, but he could see little else in the room. He looked toward the big window. He could see its mullions and the shape of the couch in front of it. Paul was not sitting there, he was sure; he might have been lying . . .

Vito stood for a moment, indecisive.

Then he ducked beneath the window and worked his way to the south side. The thought of standing silhouetted outside that large window gave him pause. But he decided to brazen it out. He hiked up his jacket in back, stuck the gun barrel down into his waistband, and stepped in front of the window.

"Hey, Paolo," he said, smiling, though he knew his face couldn't be seen. He waved at the darkness inside the room.

He tried the glass door. It was locked, as he expected.

Fear was growing inside him, as though he had swallowed a balloon and it was being pumped up with cold air.

He put both hands up to his forehead, shielding his eyes, and leaned against the glass. He could see part way back into the room. Paul was certainly not on the couch or in any of the chairs. Vito could make out the table on the west side and the carved cabinet on the east. He could not see the stairs or into the kitchen.

Vito stepped back around to the side of the house.

What the hell is going on?

He thought about going back to the others, getting further instructions from Bonnario. But what could they do? They couldn't leave Vronsky and the girl, they couldn't bring them back and kill Paul in front of them. Maybe he should just cut out. He could say . . . No, he couldn't say that. They'd find out.

He could tell the truth and let Bonnario decide.

He could look like an asshole, that's what he could do. Sent back to take out one old fart—crippled at that—who didn't even suspect, and he couldn't handle it.

Paul had to be in the crapper, or upstairs.

Vito went back to the front door. He took out the gun, again holding it low. He looked in through the lower corner of the small four-paned window, but saw no more than before.

He knocked louder. He rattled the door handle.

Finally, in desperation, he changed his grip on the pistol and, with a single sharp blow, smashed the lower right pane, above the latch.

Vito waited. Surely that sound would bring a response.

"Paolo?"

"Hey, Paolo, you in there? Hey, buddy, I know you must be in there. Hey, it's all right. It's OK. It's me, Vito. I just had to come back to get some of the Dottore's papers."

Silence.

"The Dottore, he left some papers."

Silence.

"Hey, man! What's this shit! You hear me?"

Silence.

"Hey, I got to come in. You hear me, now, it's OK. I just gotta come in for a minute."

228

Silence.

The balloon filled Vito's whole chest. He could hardly breathe. He held the gun ready in his right hand and reached in cautiously with his left to press down the door latch from the inside.

Paul stood in the alcove closet to the left of the front door where it was hinged. He had not been able to see Vito peering in through the glass, but he could clearly see the hand as it moved over the shards of glass left in the bottom and side of the broken pane.

Suddenly, Vito's arm was grabbed and yanked down, his shoulder pulled into the opening. He half gasped, half screamed as the points of glass bit into his armpit.

Paul had seized Vito's arm with his left hand and hauled it down and in. Simultaneously, with the barrel of the Walther in his right, he tapped the thumblatch on the door handle and jerked Vito's arm with all his might. The door swung in, pulling Vito off balance.

Vito tried to get his pistol around the partly opened door. As his hand came through the opening, Paul brought the Walther smashing down, crushing the point of the radius bone just back of Vito's thumb.

Vito screamed as the gun fell from his hand.

Still holding Vito's left arm through the window, Paul stepped partway around the door. He struck again with the barrel of his gun, first on the bridge of Vito's nose, then again full strength at the joint between his right clavicle and humerus, paralyzing Vito's right arm.

Paul released his hold on Vito's wrist and let him slump through the doorway. He grabbed Vito's collar and dragged him into the room, next to the stairway.

Vito never quite lost consciousness, but the successive shocks of pain had rendered him incapable even of any instinctive action. For the first minute after Paul dropped and left him on his back, Vito could only lie on the floor and moan.

Paul went back to the door, checked the road outside, then

kicked the door shut and locked it. He picked up Vito's gun.

The blows to Vito's wrist and shoulder had left his right arm useless. He tried to raise himself on his left. Pain from the glass cuts shot through his shoulder socket, and he could feel his shirt hot and wet against his side. He tried to gasp for breath, and his head rang. He struggled, but he could force neither body nor mind to action.

Suddenly, Paul was back, kicking Vito's left arm out from under him. Paul stripped off his own belt and looped it around Vito's neck. He twisted a figure eight, pulled Vito up to a sitting position against the bottom banister, and buckled the belt around it. Then he hobbled to the kitchen and brought back a towel and one of the straight chairs. He sat to Vito's right and threw the towel onto Vito's chest.

"OK, buddy," Paul said, "tell me."

With his left hand, Vito wiped blood from his nose and mouth. Then he cursed, repeating his limited repertoire of obscenities between racking, gasping breaths.

Paul waited him out.

"OK, buddy. I heard you. Now you tell me."

"What is this *for!* What do you do this to me *for!* You crazy? Oh, God!"

"Tell me, Vito."

"Tell you what! I come back to get some papers—"

Paul leaned over and with a snap of his wrist brought the barrel of the Walther down lightly on Vito's shin.

Vito gasped.

"What for is this?" Paul held up the silenced automatic. "Why this? You came ready, huh? In case I want to keep those papers for a souvenir and you have to take them? Don't shit me, buddy."

"I ain't shitting—"

Paul snapped his wrist again, this time striking Vito's kneecap.

Vito's gasping moan was throttled by the belt around his throat as he jerked up against it. Paul waited until he could breathe again.

"Which do you think hurts worse—the shin or the kneecap? I think the kneecap, myself. You want to try them both again before you decide?"

"Bastard! Bastard!"

Paul struck twice, quickly: shin and kneecap.

"There. Now of course I'm still hitting you pretty lightly."

Vito tried to hold out. He took two more blows, harder ones, before he cracked.

When Vito had finished, Paul sat back for a moment, regarding him, considering what to do. Then he moved quickly, before Vito could understand, and shot him through the head with the silenced gun.

20

THE SOUND brought Maxwell suddenly awake. He was disoriented for a moment, then realized he had fallen asleep still dressed, still sitting in the armchair facing the window.

As he tried to remember what had awakened him, the sound came again—an urgent knocking at his front door. Instantly he was fully alert.

His door had no window. He stood with his back against the wall to the left and asked who it was.

"It's me—Paul. Bergmann, open up!"

Standing back so that it could not be flung against him, Maxwell opened the door and at once swept it back six inches to shield himself as he saw Paul with a gun in each hand.

"What is it?"

"They got the Dottore. And Nella."

"Who?"

"The Russians. I need your help."

"What happened?"

Paul told him.

"What's happening now?'

"They're taking the Dottore down to the Russians." Paul stifled the fury that had almost driven him off alone, hobble-running in pursuit. He spoke urgently but without rushing. "They said it was instructions—to get him out tonight. They're going to walk all night, take the road and trails all the way down to Randa, where the car was left. That's the story, and that's what they're going to do, but the Russians will be waiting to meet them."

"Four of them?"

"Three. One came back to put me out. That's how I know."

Maxwell appraised Paul for a moment in silence. "So?" he said.

"So I need you!" Paul's control almost gave way. "You been making big noise about helping! You been making out you got steel balls! OK, now help!"

Maxwell's control was firm, but a wild exhilaration was beginning to well inside him. They had taken Vronsky! Away! Vronsky's capture meant his own freedom!

"How?" he asked.

"Go after them. They'll be going slow, waiting for Vito. They can't go fast with the Dottore, anyway. We can catch them."

"Let's go."

Maxwell's decision came instantly. He had to go, of course, to seem to make the effort. *Make haste slowly and come too late*, went through his mind. Shakespeare. Maxwell didn't know what play, but James Newlands had said it once, and Maxwell often had reason to remember and follow the advice.

He grabbed his down jacket from the closet, and stepped out.

Paul extended Vito's gun. "Here. You know about this?"

Without answering, Maxwell checked the safety, the magazine, the chamber. He strode off along the road.

In less than a minute it became obvious that Paul could not keep up. At best his stride would have been shorter than Maxwell's, but he could not stretch even that far. It wasn't the pain alone that stopped him—he had, after all, gotten out of the chairlift with the wound new and burning; he had held his jacket over it to hide the bleeding and walked all the way down to the chalet with every step like a hot poker jabbed against his thigh. He could have endured the pain, but the muscle would not stretch. The pain told him if he tried to make the muscle stretch, it would tear and refuse to carry him at all.

"I got to go slower."

Maxwell looked back. "You think we can catch them?"

"Maybe they stop and wait for Vito."

"How much lead have they got?"

"Half an hour. But maybe they stop and wait."

Maxwell shortened his step. He felt as though he were merely strolling. He breathed deeply of the cool night air. He felt the flow of adrenalin, the excitement, but over it was a great sense of relaxation. There was hardly any chance of catching them at that pace.

"Bergmann . . ."

"Yeah?"

"Maybe they don't wait. Look . . . You think you could go ahead? I mean . . . I don't mean you should try to take them alone, but maybe you could see where they are. Maybe you could do something to slow them until I come up."

Maxwell considered for a moment. "OK." He started forward again.

"Bergmann, I mean it. Don't try to take them alone. I'll be there, if you can just slow them." Paul swung his leg as briskly as he dared, trying to make the pain cover the guilt and shame he felt.

"OK," Maxwell called back over his shoulder. *Don't worry, old buddy*, he thought, *I am not going to try to take them alone.*

The road was surprisingly bright. Maxwell could clearly see it passing under the chairlift and around a shoulder. He estimated the distance at which he might first make out the group ahead—he didn't want to blunder upon them—by glancing back to check the distance at which he could no longer see Paul. Perhaps, though, he would see the group from farther away.

If he saw them.

Maxwell let his intuition work on that one. Should he stay ahead of Paul but never reach the others, and say—truthfully—he had never caught them? "Too much of a lead. They didn't wait for Vito, maybe took a shortcut."

Or should he sight them, tail them to make sure they got down the way they planned?

At three hundred yards, Paul's figure was lost against the cut where the road had been leveled through the hillside.

Maxwell quickened his pace slightly. He was probably up to four miles an hour. He estimated that Vronsky and Nella could not be moved at more than two. Depending on the accuracy of Paul's estimate of their lead and whether they stopped to wait for Vito, he could expect to see them in less than twenty minutes. Then he could shadow them down to Randa.

It would be first light by the time they got there. Vronsky and Nella would not be worried, though, presuming they had left the Russians far behind. Maxwell would find a way to hang back and watch as they were taken to the parking area. Whether Nev and his men actually made the pick up then, or made a transfer to a closed van farther down the valley would not matter. Once he saw them put into a car, Maxwell could kiss Vronsky off and be free.

Suddenly waves of shock and fear swept over him, as though he had almost stepped into a pit in the middle of the road.

Corchran!

No! Corchran, Dolby . . . *They* didn't want Vronsky out that way, the easy way. And if Maxwell let it happen—they would never believe he hadn't known, hadn't been working with Nev. Maxwell was appalled at his own stupidity, that his relief in thinking of Vronsky gone had so blinded him.

If he could get word through . . . They might get down to Randa first, mix it up.

Damn you, Corchran! You stupid bastard! If you had told me where you were . . .!

Maxwell could only make contact by going back to his house and doing something to attract the attention of Corchran's watcher.

You clever asshole! You wouldn't trust me, and now you're screwed! We're both screwed!

But he couldn't go back past Paul.

Kill Paul.

Maxwell halted and looked back. The plan formed itself

immediately: Corchran and Dolby to mess it up in Randa; Paul's death tied to that—killed by Vronsky's abductors, whom he was pursuing.

Maxwell moved to the side of the road. He leaned against the bank so that his darkly clothed figure would be lost against the dark earth. He peered back along the road, then shifted his focus ever so slightly to the right so that his peripheral vision would see Paul's movement.

He hunched his shoulders, tensing them for a moment, then relaxed. He went over it: Wait for Paul—five minutes. Back to the chalet—fifteen. Signal. How? Wave a light? Might as well flash Morse in the clear—who's there to hide from? Wait for Corchran—ten minutes. Thirty total so far. Corchran to confer—surely he would carry a radio! Another five minutes. Altogether, not too long.

Maxwell thought he detected movement. He continued to look just to one side.

Corchran could call out the troops, get to Randa—

No cars! How would they get to Randa? Did trains run at this time? Even if they did, the Russians would see them.

Bad plan.

Second team? Reserves brought in for the intercept? There should be a backup stationed farther down the valley, but was there?

They should have told me!

The movement was definite. Maxwell shifted his focus: he could see Paul's shape in the distance even with the center of his vision.

There's probably a back-up. If not, we can come back this way and follow them and probably catch them by the time—Probably!

Maxwell despised and feared "probably." He had seen men die of "probably." He pushed himself away from the bank and swung again into his stride.

He would have to stop them himself.

The road wound around the slopes on the eastern side of the

valley, dropping gradually as it went north. Occasionally a side road branched, one going down to Zermatt, others to widely scattered clusters of chalets or hamlets of haybarns and cabins for summer herdsmen. It passed into darkness, through a treed area, then out again. Farther below, the mountainsides were almost completely forested.

Maxwell moved quickly but with care. Anyone nearby would have heard the crunch of his boots on the pebbles, but his step was too light to carry far.

In ten minutes he saw them. He stopped. A quarter-mile away, the road curved to the left around an outcropping of rock lighter than the road bank. The first figure passing across the rock had caught Maxwell's eye. He waited. Three more shapes passed. Then—after a space—the last.

Maxwell sensed the speed of their walking and started on again at that rate. He moved closer to the inside of the road, hoping to blend himself into the darkness there.

How to do it?

They would surely hear if he came up behind.

Maxwell looked above him. At that point, the bank was not high, and he could see it sloping down ahead of him, meeting the road before it rose again toward the outcropping. The hillside was grassy.

Could he run on the grass quietly and get above, even ahead of them?

He decided to wait. When the road entered the forest below, he might be able to move through the trees quickly and get ahead more safely. There were miles, hours, before he had to act.

No: Paul was coming, moving slightly faster than the group. Unless his leg worsened . . .

As he walked on, Maxwell again considered waiting, letting Paul come up, and killing him. He might have to do that. If he did, he would. But he had enough scruples left not to kill if he didn't have to. It was bad enough that he might have to kill Vronsky and Nella.

It came to that, finally. His own peace, his remaining life, depended on getting rid of Vronsky. But he couldn't let the Russians just take him. And he couldn't arrange the kind of incident that would satisfy Corchran—a public abduction with witnesses: an abduction both messy and successful. The only thing he could improvise was to kill them all there on the mountainside and let the police and newspapers put the story together. Paul would have to get the credit or blame for it.

Maxwell hoped he would be able to avoid killing Vronsky and Nella himself. He assumed the men taking them would have orders to abduct if possible but kill if necessary, to prevent escape. He might only have to deal with three. Given his assets of surprise and a silenced gun, the odds were reasonable.

He paused for a moment and checked carefully behind. Paul had been outdistanced again. Maxwell went on, shadowing the group ahead.

He had almost decided to try the approach from above. Then he came to a place where the road turned right, opening a large view ahead. He could make out the group, walking steadily and in formation as before, and the road beyond them. It dropped down and then reversed direction. Undoubtedly it turned back on itself again somewhere below, but no matter. He had found the place.

Keeping low, Maxwell crossed the road and started to let himself down the hillside. It was steep. He had to go down sideways, touching the ground from time to time for balance.

When he reached the bottom, he estimated he was five minutes ahead of the group. He began looking for cover. Down the road another hundred yards he saw rocks: one huge boulder, its base buried in the mountainside; three more, almost man-sized, leaning against it. He got behind them, peered around, squatted to explore the spaces and chinks between them. The place was perfect.

He stood for a moment, visualizing, then went through it in slow motion. He stood with his back to the main boulder, looking over his left shoulder and just above the rock on that side. He would see them coming. He would let the point man pass, then the second with Vronsky and Nella. When they were on the other side of the boulder he would pivot, rest his extended arms on the side rock, and shoot the rear guard. At point-blank range he could kill with one shot. Then he would roll, his back against the big boulder, and shoot the second man—also close—over the other side rock. The point man would be moving by then, running across the road or down it. Even if he was stupid enough to stand and return fire, it wouldn't matter. Maxwell dropped to his knees, aimed through a chink across a field covering all those possibilities. Vronsky and Nella would either freeze or run down the road; it wouldn't matter. The point man would shoot them, or Maxwell would; it wouldn't matter. The rocks were a fortress, and he had eight bullets. He would command the situation.

Maxwell waited, making himself calm, listening. He heard nothing, but suddenly the first man was there, coming silently out of the darkness. The man moved smoothly, bending from the waist, his head and shoulders swinging to one side, pausing, swinging again as he looked and listened.

Maxwell flattened against the rock and waited. He heard the soft scrunch of sand as the man passed. Then he heard the next three approaching and a low call. "Ricci, *momento.*"

The first man stopped. The others came up to him. The men spoke together, a few words only, quietly, in Italian. Then one of them spoke to Vronsky and Nella. Maxwell could understand none of the words, but he understood the meaning.

He heard Vronsky and Nella come up to the other side of his boulder scrape against it, and sigh.

Maxwell understood. They were resting. They would group around and against the boulder. He would have no idea of their configuration. He no longer had command.

Very carefully, he let himself down onto his heels and leaned his back against the boulder. His right elbow rested on his knee, forearm straight up, the silenced pistol pointing up past his forehead. He held it firmly but gently, finger at the side of the trigger. He tipped his head back, resting the point of his skull against the cold stone. He took a deep, careful breath.

Nella and Vronsky murmured together. Their words were meaningless to Maxwell, but he could hear the solicitude in her voice.

Nella was worried about the fit of Vronsky's boot. He assured her that, though stiff and heavy, the boots were not rubbing. She worried about his fatigue. He assured her that he was not really too tired. She said that when they reached Italy he must begin to take some regular exercise. He agreed. He said many things would be changed when they reached Italy. She worried that he was cold. He was not cold. The one thing that truly concerned him did not worry her. He was in agony for a cigarette. The points of pain at either temple were beginning to bore through to meet in the center of his head. He wanted to ask Bonnario if now, in that shelter, the small fire of a cigarette would still be a danger. But the fear of increasing the contempt he knew Bonnario already felt for him was finally greater than his need for nicotine.

Ricci went silently down the road, keeping his sixty-foot lead. He squatted there, in the middle of the road, resting his legs but still swinging from the waist from time to time, alert.

Parducci had closed in from behind, but then he turned and paced slowly back uphill. He would walk all night and all the next day, too, if necessary, as long as he never stopped to let his old legs stiffen.

Maxwell heard Parducci move away. His heart pounded. He could feel blood racing through every artery and vein, except where the pressure was constricted behind his knees. Squatting was bad. His legs would go to sleep, but he had no choice. He closed his eyes for a moment, lifted his head away from the rock, rolled it from side to side to reduce the tension.

The night air was refreshing. Maxwell realized he had no idea of the hour. Nights like this, with no moon riding across them, were timeless; totally serene and silent, with no wind, no crickets, no human sounds. But for the low voices on the other side of the rock, Maxwell would have let himself drift thoughtlessly into this sense of eternal peacefulness.

Bonnario said something. Maxwell heard him move around the main boulder and up along the smaller one on the downhill side. Bonnario stopped beyond it, facing away from the road. He started to unzip his fly. Automatically, he looked right and left.

Even under dim starlight, Maxwell could see his face clearly. He must have been in his mid-thirties, handsome as a Renaissance prince: curly dark hair framing strong features. A large nose, long and straight. Full lips, the upper a sharply cut M with arched sides. The lips began to open, and the heavy eyebrows to rise in the frozen microsecond that he saw and comprehended Maxwell.

Without lifting his elbow, almost languidly, Maxwell tipped the pistol thirty degrees to the right and shot him. The bullet went in under Bonnario's strong jaw and came out the back of his head.

Maxwell thrust himself to his feet. Keeping his left hand against the boulder for balance, he swung around.

Twenty-five feet up the road, Parducci had heard the pop of the silenced gun. He did not instantly recognize the sound, but he was turning to look.

Maxwell rested both hands on the rock, took aim, and put three bullets into Parducci's chest. He could have continued with his original plan but did not know that Ricci was down the road. Not counting on any remaining element of surprise, but having no choice, Maxwell stepped around the boulder to face downhill.

Ricci's reflexes were quick. He too had heard the first shot and looked back to see Bonnario fall and Parducci fling out his arms and sprawl backward. Ricci whipped his own gun from his waistband, and—as he saw Maxwell's shape come around the rock—fired two shots at it while springing up and wheeling to sprint down the road. He ran three steps, then cut right toward the outside of the road. As he approached its edge he bounded into the air, intending to leap over, strike the lower hillside and roll down to cover.

The first shot went past Maxwell's right ear. The second richocheted from the rock by his left shoulder. Maxwell ducked back, then out lower, on one knee. He saw Ricci running, brought the gun up with both hands again, took aim, and began firing. The first two shots went wild, as Ricci cut to the side. The third caught him at the height of his leap. He jerked to one side and twisted as his legs went on churning in the air. As he struck the ground on his knees, Maxwell hit him again.

Maxwell spun back to check Parducci, then rose. He regarded Vronsky and Nella cowering against the boulder. His gun was empty. He nodded to them almost absentmindedly. He walked around the rocks and up to Bonnario's body. He rolled the body onto its back with his foot, then took Bonnario's pistol from his belt. He put the one he had been using in his waistband.

Maxwell walked down the road to Ricci, then up again— nodding once more as he passed the boulder—to inspect Parducci. Finally, he came back, Bonnario's gun still in his hand, and stood in front of Vronsky and Nella.

Paul heard the two unsilenced shots. The sound carried up the mountainside on the gentle current of air rising from the valley. Cracks, snaps almost, not loud, but unmistakable to someone who knew what they were.

Hearing the shots stopped him in midstride. He stumbled as his wounded leg took the shock of a step out of rhythm. He paused only for an instant, then lurched forward again, trying to push himself faster, gasping at each step.

His leg felt as though the skin had been flayed from it. The wound had opened again. He had felt the warm trickle of blood. He had paused for a moment and stripped off jacket and shirt to bind his undershirt tight around his thigh. The cold air had been like a gentle hand on his sweating chest and back. Clothed again, he had started walking as fast as he could, before he heard the shots.

He tried to run, hopping on his good leg. It was no use—the effort took more breath than he could drag into his lungs, and the gait was too awkward. He nearly twisted an ankle. He could only walk, wheeze, and curse, and feel the pulse pounding in his leg and hear it roaring in his head.

It might have been the sound in his head that made him miss—at first—the other one from above. It was like a large, speeding bumble-bee. The second time, it registered.

Paul stopped, half crouched. He twisted, looking back and forth. He knew the sound—bullets going over his head. He jumped to one side, spinning, trying to find a place to hide. There was none. He was at the place along the road where Maxwell had considered going up the hillside, where the grassy slope came all the way down to the road. He was being shot at from higher up the mountain, and there was no bank to get against.

He hop-limped two steps down the road. Sand and dust spurted up from the roadbed just ahead of him. He twisted and lurched to one side. Behind him, the slope on the outer edge fell away more steeply. If he could make it back there he might get over the edge and roll to safety. It was essentially the same plan Ricci had tried.

Paul stumbled back up the road. Eight or ten meters might be far enough. The spurts of sand chased him, then stopped as though outrun.

Then they began again, one after another, so rapidly that Paul's eye saw them as a continuous line, like a snake racing in S's down the road toward him.

Maxwell looked down. Vronsky's and Nella's faces were pebble gray against the darker boulder. The red of Nella's jacket seemed the same hue as the rock, and Maxwell's own suntanned hand was like slate. Snow on the high peaks set the light end of the color range; the gun in Maxwell's hand marked the dark. A black-and-white photo. An old movie. When he pulled the trigger, black lines would trickle down from the corners of their mouths.

And then Technicolor again for him! Blue skies; vibrant green grass; flowers in every hue—that explosive inner glow; golden sunlight to sit in, warming his soul while he looked at the violet mountains, the orange and magenta sunset, the fire-rose of alpenglow. He would be free to sit and . . .

. . . *and die.*

An instant, an eternity: Vronsky and Nella were too shocked and terrified to have any sense of time; Maxwell was too overwhelmed by conflicting emotions.

Their death for his life.

His *life?*

His death.

Their life for his death.

Maxwell stared at them for just over thirty seconds. Then he slipped the safety on the pistol.

21

"WAIT!" Maxwell's voice was low but sharp. Nella and Vronsky halted, looking back at him. "Wait a minute."

Maxwell moved past them and continued cautiously up the road, crouching, ready to jump. He could not tell what the dark shape ahead was, but it should not be there. He slipped the safety off the pistol.

On the way back toward Findeln, Maxwell had told Vronsky and Nella about the substitution of their "reinforcements," and about the planned abduction. Nella had licked and bit her lips, but—to Maxwell's surprise—Vronsky showed no nervousness at all.

"What must we do now?" he had asked.

"Meet Paul and go back to your house. If we can hide the body of the guy Paul shot, then you're just about where you were two days ago. It'll take a while for the police to find the ones I hit and connect them with you—if they ever do. You can contact your people in Italy again, get some genuine help."

"If there's a break—a leak there . . ."

"I think this time we can avoid anyone finding out that someone's coming to help you."

Vronsky had looked sharply at Maxwell for a moment but said nothing.

Maxwell moved toward the shape carefully, his pistol held well out ahead of him. Because of foreshortening and the way the figure lay twisted, he had to get within fifteen feet before his eyes resolved the picture and he recognized Paul.

Still crouching, Maxwell turned his head slowly and scanned the downslope to his right, the road ahead, the hillside above and to his left. He could see no one. He swiveled around to look back toward Vronsky and Nella. They stood as he had left them, at the side of the road, looking up toward him.

Should he yell for them to run? Where to? They were a hundred feet beyond where the bank began to rise again. And was there any safety if they reached it? They were exposed. They were all completely exposed.

They had been exposed for several minutes. They could have been shot at any time.

Maxwell straightened. He walked back to the others. *How much can they take*, he wondered. There was no way to break it gently.

"It's Paul. He's dead."

Vronsky's jaw dropped. Then he closed his eyes and sighed. Nella stared at Maxwell for a moment in disbelief, then at the form lying on the road ahead. Suddenly she ran to the body and dropped on her knees beside it. When Maxwell and Vronsky reached her she was kneeling with her fists clutched between her thighs, rocking back and forth, sobbing. Vronsky went down beside her, trying to give comfort. Maxwell continued standing, scanning the hillside again. He could see nothing, although the nearby slope offered little cover. Whoever had shot Paul must have been farther away, using an infrared scope and a silenced automatic rifle.

Grouped together the three of them were an easy target, but Maxwell was not worried. They had been almost as easy before, and no one had shot at them.

After several moments they were able to raise Nella to her feet again and go on. She moved as though asleep, leaning against Vronsky, her head turned into his neck, still sobbing.

Maxwell was careful. He kept ahead of the other two, listening and watching, especially when they passed through the short section of trees. But he did not really expect trouble, and there was none.

When they came to the chalets again, he took Vronsky and

Nella past them and down the path to Findeln. At the upper end of the hamlet was a small chapel, made of stone, big enough to serve Mass for a dozen people. Maxwell led Vronsky and Nella inside. He latched the door and took a place by the small window facing the path.

"Sit down. Try to get some rest. We'll wait here until it's light." Maxwell checked his watch. "That should be in about two hours."

"Then?" asked Vronsky.

"Can you get in touch with your people in Italy?"

"I don't know . . . Nella?"

"Yes. I can call." She sat upright in one of the simple pews, her hands clasped in her lap. "I will go to Zermatt and call with the telephone."

"No!"

"No," Maxwell agreed. "You can't go alone. But we can't stay here. In Findeln, I mean. Not without Paul. Not unless you get some more help. What we'll do is make your call from the phone at the cafe here in Findeln."

"There is a telephone here? Then why didn't Paul—"

"Paul wouldn't have used it—even if he knew about it. There's no way of being sure it's secure. And if anybody knew he was calling from it, it wouldn't have been. But we only have to call once, get one answer. Maybe they'll send help. Probably they'll just move you. There must be a thousand places in Switzerland just like this one."

Vronsky stared for a moment at the altar—a plain shelf, bare except for a wooden crucifix. "No," he said at last.

"No? No what?"

"No, I will not move to another hiding place in Switzerland."

"Doctor Vronsky, you haven't got an awful lot of choices. Staying here is the least—"

"I will not stay here. But I will not hide, either. If I wished to stay in Switzerland, there would be no need for me to hide. I could walk down to Zermatt now, to the protection of the police."

"Well, that is true!" Maxwell was amazed by the simplicity of the obvious. "All you have to do is to retire from politics and they'll probably make you an honored citizen and watch over you day and night. And nobody on either side'll care anyway."

"Retire from politics? What do you mean?"

Maxwell was tired. He had not spoken carefully. "I mean, what you were saying the other night about your social theories."

"What about my social theory?"

"I mean, I'm sure you can stay in Switzerland as long as you don't publish any social theories."

"I do not follow you. Why should my theory—"

"Doctor Vronsky, the Swiss are very careful about their neutrality. I don't think they'd want to give you asylum so you could write things that would upset political situations in other countries. I don't think they'd like you writing things that would upset the Russians—or the Americans, either—which I guess is what you want to do."

"Mr. Bergmann, the Swiss are a very proud and courageous people. They are jealous of their freedom and independence. I suppose they would not permit me to engage in illegal acts, but my writing . . . There is no question but that I could publish what I wish to write. I believe, Mr. Bergmann, that you have been badly misinformed about the Swiss."

Maxwell started to retort; then he pondered for a moment. He decided that he had indeed been misinformed. "So, your problem is solved," he said.

"No. If I were to stay in Switzerland, simply writing and doing no more, I would . . . It would be as though scattering seeds upon the wind. That is not enough. I intend to plant them and to take a hand in making them grow. I have wished to do that, always. I believe that is my destiny. And now . . . And now, I have a special reason, a special debt."

"What?"

Vronsky pressed his right hand to his forehead, squeezed his skull between thumb and fingertips. He massaged the flesh over his eyes.

"Paul looked for a leader. Someone who would take action. I will never be the leader he thought of, because I will not use the methods he assumed were necessary. But I will act. I will not go into hiding, I will—"

"Constantin," Nella put a hand on his arm. "Please—"

"Don't interrupt me!" Vronsky jerked his arm away. "I am not afraid!" He paused. "That is not true. I am afraid. But I will not hide."

He dismissed the idea with an abrupt wave. His hand was shaking.

"Maybe you'd better get some rest before you decide what you're going to do," Maxwell observed. "You're kind of on edge."

"I apologize. That is true, forgive me. Forgive me, Nella. I have given up smoking."

"Constantin?"

"When?"

"Tonight. When I saw Paul. When I decided to go at once to Italy."

"Italia!"

"What!"

"To Italy. If I can—however I can. Paul was right: I should appear in Rome and announce myself."

"They'll send you straight back."

"I do not think so. I will speak first to the press. What I say will be heard all over Italy, all over Europe, the world. I do not think the government will dare to send me away after I have spoken." Vronsky smiled. "I am not a fool; I have had too much experience with governments to be naive. I will not make it impossible for them to keep me, but what I say will make it impossible for them to make me go."

Nella broke into tears again and began talking excitedly in Italian. Maxwell couldn't tell whether she was afraid for Vronsky—remonstrating with him—or thrilled with his decision. Or both.

Vronsky smiled at her, patted her hand, forced a word in

edgewise from time to time, but he kept his attention on Maxwell.

"How do you intend to get to Italy?" Maxwell asked at last.

"I do not know. I do not know how I am to escape from *here*. But my destiny calls me." Vronsky paused, looking directly into Maxwell's eyes. "I believe you will help me. And after seeing you tonight, Mr. . . . . Bergmann? . . . I believe you will find a way."

22

"WHAT'S HE GONNA DO?"

"Probably wait until it's light. Probably figures they'll be safer when other people are up and around."

"Then?"

"How should I know?"

"You're supposed to be our expert."

"I'm not his psychiatrist. I know a lot about him, but . . . I know enough about him not to presume I know what he's going to do from one moment to the next."

Corchran and Dolby stood at the window of their chalet, staring down at Findeln where they could just make out the tiny chapel. A third man sat, elbows propped on the window-sill, looking through night-glasses.

"See anything yet?" Dolby asked.

"Nothing."

"Keep on it. I don't want that bastard out of sight for a second until we get Vronsky and the Russians set up again." Unable to savage the true object of his fury, Dolby chewed briefly on his tongue. "That bastard. I should have told Fox to take him out, too."

Corchran's distaste for his colleague flared into momentary anger. "What you should have done was tell Max we had Vronsky's escape *covered*. I imagine he thought he was doing us a favor."

"The whole idea of using him was stupid to begin with. He already proved we can't trust him."

"What he proved last night, Bob, was that he's not working for the Russians. Not on this, anyway."

"What he proved is *nobody* can trust him. Dolby gave a quick snort. "Yeah. Boy, if he thought he had trouble with us, just wait 'til the Russians catch up with him."

Closing in.

Maxwell leaned against the east wall of the chapel looking diagonally through the window there and up the mountainside. Moving down silently toward the chapel, soon to surround it, was an army of ghosts. Wisps of mist were rising, joining overhead into cloud. Maxwell took a deep breath and felt an inner surge—instinct slipping him smoothly into high gear.

"Doctor Vronsky. Nella, wake up. Nella?"

Maxwell's voice jolted Vronsky, who realized he must have been dozing sitting upright on one of the wooden benches. "What?" Vronsky blinked, turning to peer through one window, then the other. "It's not light yet."

"Not yet. Soon. But a fog's coming up. A few more minutes, we're going to be in the clouds."

"Ah. Yes, of course. We can leave here without being seen!" He *could* play this game, too.

Maxwell regarded him obliquely for one moment. "We can try," he said.

"But the telephone . . ." Nella wondered if they could have forgotten.

"No. Better not." Vronsky's delight grew with the realization that action also involved logic. "There has been a break in Italy. If no one knows our plan, then no one can reveal it."

"Right, Doctor. And they can't say no either. Nella, do you have some friends, someone you can trust—outside the channel you've been using? When we get across, you call them."

Vronsky clapped his hands together with joy. "Wonderful! We shall slip away into the clouds and leave Nev twiddling his fingers, waiting for us in Randa."

* * *

Nev's hands lay in the crooks of his folded arms. He moved them only slightly to check his watch. He assured himself he was not nervous. Clouds had formed over the valley, below the tops of the peaks. The light was gray; it had no direction; it brightened imperceptibly. Time was hard to judge.

But it was time!

They should have come into the town just before dawn, the Italians making a great show of caution. They should have come into the parking area, two of them close to Vronsky and the woman, the other two spread, all ready for attack. But there would be no attack. Undisturbed, they would reach the blue van. They would drive away. At the next town they would pause, still on guard, while one of them brought coffee from a café.

Nev took pleasure in the thought of doing it with coffee.

But it was *time!*

Even allowing for some delay if Vronsky proved to be more of a weakling than Nev's contempt had already judged, they should have arrived before now.

Nev refused to panic, but finally—forced to some action—he lifted his radio, pressed the button, and said one word.

Immediately, Kusnich answered. One word of acknowledgment, one of negation.

What could be wrong? The watcher back on Riffelalp had seen the Italians signal when they left Findeln and had reported all well before he went back down to Zermatt. Could Vronsky have broken a leg? Anything was possible with that little pile of cat puke. But Bonnario would have found some way to send word.

But it was *past* time!

Nev knew he would have to do something. He was deciding what when he saw Dobrinsky hurrying toward him. Nev threw open the car door and bolted out. No one was awake to see him, and he didn't care anyway. He ran toward the station and the phone booth Dobrinsky had been covering. He snatched up the dangling receiver.

"Nev," he said. As he listened, his face drained and his eyes grew bright with anger. "Enough! The helicopter! Get it down here at once!"

23

WHIRLING BLADES pounded the air, their sound beating Vronsky's eardrums. The three figures turned away, half crouching, as though trying to hide from the machine settling almost upon them like a giant insect.

What would it be like, Vronsky wondered. Would it be like an airplane? He could tolerate airplanes. If he sat next to the aisle, never looking out the window, he could tell himself he was riding in a bus. Would a helicopter be tolerable, or would it be like that ultimate horror—no, being lowered out of the window had been the ultimate horror—that penultimate horror, the chairlift?

He had ridden the chairlift. He was proud, though still shaken. Seeing it scoop up passengers, bear them off dangling in space on the thinnest of wires, understanding the sensation he would feel, Vronsky had nevertheless forced himself to walk onto the platform, turn his back, and allow the machine to seize him. Nella had ridden in the chair beside him, squeezing his hand. He had been grateful for that. He might have fainted otherwise.

Maxwell had shepherded them down the trail to the outskirts of Zermatt in almost total silence and taken them into the village only far enough to find a telephone. He refused to say whom he called. Then he took them out of town again, going up the river. When they came to a small forested area he took them off the road and told them to rest. By lying down, they could be out of sight of the road while remaining near it.

Vronsky was infuriated. "What are we doing?" he demanded. "What is our plan?" He was suddenly finished with being led through life without explanations.

"We're trying to get to Italy," Maxwell replied curtly.

"I appreciate that. May we know where is Italy?"

"Right over there." Maxwell gestured.

"I presume you mean on the other side of the mountains."

"Right."

"And how do we get there?"

"Walk."

"Walk! Is there not a helicopter in the village?"

"Right. And Nev has one too. That's such an obvious way to get you out, he's had it covered all along."

"Surely he does not follow every time the machine flies about the mountains."

"He would if it headed for where he knows you are."

"But now he does not know."

Maxwell paused for a moment. "We have to assume we've been seen going this way."

"Ah. So. Walk."

"Yeah. If we could ski, we could ride lifts right up to the ridge and ski down the other side. You *don't* ski, do you?"

"No."

"That's what I thought."

"So we must walk from here to Italy?" Vronsky was still incredulous at the prospect.

Maxwell took a breath and sighed to control his annoyance. There was no rational reason for his unwillingness to explain. In truth, though, he knew his plan was weak. Subconsciously he wanted to avoid recognizing that by making it public.

"We don't have to walk all the way. There are lifts—a chairlift, cableways—straight up onto the glacier. One down the other side. We'll only have to walk a few kilometers between."

"Ah." Vronsky stared off in the direction Maxwell had indicated. He could not actually see the mountains through the trees, but he visualized the route. "You say the cableways go straight . . . Are there many? Do they go to different points?"

"No. They just make a line up to Klein Matterhorn."

"Ah. Then that is clearly the most direct route for us to take."

"Yeah."

"And you believe we have been observed? We will be followed?"

"Yeah. That's why it's only a chance."

Vronsky continued to stare into the trees. After several moments he spoke again. "In science . . . When one finds the answer to a problem, almost always the solution is seen to be clear, simple, even obvious. It is the most direct route. It seems so when looking backward after the problem is solved. One does not solve the problem at once, though, because at the beginning other routes seem more obvious."

"Yeah." Maxwell was amused at Vronsky's deliberation. "In my business we call that a red herring."

"Red herring? A fish?"

"Yeah."

"A red herring. I wonder why? However, would it not now be possible to—"

"Misdirect them."

"Precisely."

"I would if I could, Doctor Vronsky. Standard operating procedure. But I haven't been able to figure—"

"Excuse me. Is it not possible . . . Everyone believes that the shortest distance between two points is a straight line. You say that the cableways go straight toward Italy. Is it not possible that once we were seen to be started along that line . . ."

"*Then* the helicopter."

"Precisely."

Maxwell looked carefully at Vronsky, who blinked back through his thick lenses. Vronsky's fingers were fumbling at his lips. He looked as vague and ineffectual as usual, but Maxwell began to revise his estimate.

"That's good thinking, Doctor Vronsky. But since the helicopter would still be coming to where we'd been seen to go, I don't think Nev would be fooled."

"Ah. But it would seem to be better than no attempt at all, would it not?"

Maxwell's eyes narrowed slightly as he considered the implications of Vronsky's suggestion. "Just possibly . . ."

A single person came along the road. Maxwell rose and went to meet her. Nella was astounded: she recognized the girl who cleaned their chalet. Maxwell spoke with her for over ten minutes. She gave him a package and left. The package contained croissants.

"Is that girl going to help us?" Nella asked.

"Yes. She's going to try, anyway."

Quickly, they finished eating. Maxwell led them to the chairlift, and they rode up to Furi—the liftstation and hamlet on the near shoulder of the long ridge that runs toward Zermatt from the Matterhorn itself.

At the instant his passengers were aboard and buckled in, the pilot lifted away. The helicopter hovered, pivoting to face down the valley. Bright red, brilliant in the clear morning light, it jumped at the eye in contrast to the green slopes below.

Suddenly, Nella gasped. "Look!"

Maxwell and Vronsky snapped their heads to the side to see where she pointed. They saw nothing at first. Against the woods and lawns, the dark blue-green of the other craft was almost indistinguishable. Only its motion revealed it as it rose in a swift arc, swinging up from the town and around to the west.

The pilot of the Air Zermatt helicopter saw. He kept himself fixed in space for a moment while he considered. On one hand, Christoph Rass was a professional pilot. He flew for business, not for adventure. Of course, anyone who chooses flying for a career must be somewhat daring, but driving a helicopter through the air currents of the high mountains had already provided more thrills than a forty-year-old man with two children should expect. He was a good commercial pilot in part because he avoided risks. On the other hand, Rass had been in the Swiss Air Force for over ten years; he would be yet, but for a wife who nagged about the danger.

He had been surprised about the identity of his passengers, to find he was not simply carrying an executive called from holiday by urgent business. He had been excited to find himself involved in an adventure.

He considered. The other helicopter was coming, clearly to follow, perhaps to try to intercept. He knew he should set down again directly, make his passengers get out, and have nothing whatever to do with whatever was going on. The most that professional responsibility might require would be to take them to the Zermatt heliport and put them off there in safety.

Nev's helicopter was sweeping in a curve that would bring it up to Furi from the northwest.

Rass advanced the throttle and pushed the stick. Pivoting half around again and banking, he dropped over the side of Furi and sped southeast through the ravine between the low ridge from the Matterhorn on his right and Plattelen on his left. Then he bore farther left, turning east, climbing only slightly as the land rose beneath him, keeping close to the shielding cliffs.

Nev's first instinct told him to keep high. As his machine arced over Furi, his pilot started to drop into the ravine also, but Nev motioned him to maintain altitude.

A moment later, the Russians hovered at three thousand meters over Plattelen. Nev peered southwest, up the Furggbach. His pilot looked southeast, toward the narrow glacier-cut gap between the mountain masses. But it was Grabov, sitting behind Nev, who saw. He struck Nev's shoulder, pointed left of where the pilot was watching. A red dot had moved out from behind one ridge. It popped up over another to its right and dropped out of sight again, heading east into the little valley between Riffelberg and the Riffelhorn ridge.

The early-morning clouds Maxwell had used to screen their

departure from Findeln were rising and dispersing as the sun climbed higher, warming the air. Still, the clouds lay in cottony patches swaddling all the peaks above three thousand meters. The top of Riffelhorn knifed clearly below them, but beyond, the Hohtäligrat ridge was sheathed.

Nev understood at once that he must modify his tactic. He could not simply keep the advantage of altitude, watching from above and behind, certain that no matter how his quarry darted for cover from ridge to ridge, eventually it would have to climb over the mountain tops to escape.

The Air Zermatt machine was large enough for eight passengers, its power engineered for load. Nev's smaller one was meant to carry only three and the pilot swiftly. Its nose dropped as it raced in pursuit.

Rass was already at maximum forward speed. Yellow-green grassy hillsides and splotches of gray and brown rock flashed past below, but the other helicopter closed swiftly, a falcon after a pigeon.

Ahead, the east-west blade of Riffelhorn; naked rock, too sheer on either face for vegetation to mask its vicious sharpness. At speed, it seemed to cut directly at them. Rass dodged left, and the ridge went slicing past.

Suddenly, just past the peak, Rass lifted. Combining the power of his machine and an updraft from the sun-warmed meadowy mass of Riffelberg, he soared over the sharp edge and disappeared below it.

Just approaching the peak, but farther to the left and higher than his game, Nev's pilot saw and duplicated the maneuver. The little chopper leapt up, tipped and slid to the right over the edge, and then—with gut-tearing swiftness—fell, caught in the downdraft along the shadowed cliff, toward the glacier five hundred meters below.

Rass had countered the downdraft he knew would be there. He lost some altitude, but used power to control his descent and to swing away from the cliff and the intensity of the downward pull. Rising again, he turned back and up.

Points of cliff seemed to hurl themselves at Nev. After the

first instant he had lost the sense of falling. Now he felt himself suspended while jagged edges flashed by. He was aware of something knobby pressed into the backs of his shoulders. The knobs were Grabov's knuckles gripping Nev's seat. Only the pilot escaped paralysis. He had not expected the downdraft, but he knew what to do about it. He fought as Rass had, forcing his machine away from the cliff as it fell, lessening the downward drag. He swung out in a deep parabola, flattening less than a hundred meters over the ice, but in control again. Scanning around and upward, he saw the red helicopter disappear into cloud over Gornergrat. He went straight up after it.

When he came above the clouds, he saw Rass about one and a half kilometers away, at his altitude, passing just beyond the peak of Hohtälli.

And Rass saw him. He dropped into the cloudbank. To his right—five hundred meters—the Gornergrat-Stockhorn ridge; to his left—three hundred meters—clouds thinned into the gap between Gornergrat and Rothorn: altogether, a little less than one kilometer of cover. But spurs ran north from Stockhorn, through the clouds. At his distance from the ridge, they should be below. Should be.

Rass went up quickly, just to the top of the clouds. He saw the top of the Stockhorn cablelift directly to the right and knew the northern spur running from that point would be safely below. But suspended above it was a dark and shining globe. Instantly, Rass ducked back into the cloud.

Hanging above the ridge, Nev's helicopter tracked east, facing north where the flash of red had been seen, where it must appear again. From the final summit of Stockhorn ridge ran the highest spur, first snow covered, then, lower, a rock escarpment, the whole line of it rising above the clouds almost to where the clouds ended. The quarry had been caught in a three-sided box: it had to lift into sight to go over ridges to the east, south, or west or leave cover to go north.

They waited. The white glare became intolerable. Their eyes ached for the spot of red.

"Down." Nev gestured.

A moment of blankness, then a gray shadow-world: the ice-field below seemed almost murky in contrast to the brilliance still in their eyes.

The red machine was scarcely two hundred meters away.

Rass had dropped into the cloud, then gone through it. He had seen the box, as Nev had, but with a ceiling. He hovered for a moment, considering. His hunters would be above, waiting for him to come up, as he must eventually.

But must he? What if he flew directly toward that high north-running spur, then along it? If he went low enough and close enough, he might keep a few wisps of cloud to screen him as he rounded the end and came back again under solid cover for twenty kilometers.

He moved parallel with Stockhorn and with Nev's machine. Then he started to swing away.

"Rass! Behind, to the right!"

Up again, back into the cloud.

The Russians went up, too, jammed into their seats: full power, thrusting through the cloud, popping up above it.

"He's still inside!"

"Down!"

Canopy white, then gray again, then clear. They hung just below the cloud, as though stuck to its underside.

"Up!"

Again through limbo into blue-and-white brilliance. Nothing.

Nev gestured. Pivoting, always facing toward the center of the boxed area, the helicopter moved in an arc to its right and took station over the center of the spur. Nev could look down past the edge of the cloud and see its end. The trap was closed.

They hovered. They waited.

"You think he's going to try to wait us out?"

Nev did not reply.

They waited, fixed in space, rocking gently as the pilot compensated to hold position in the shifting air. He could hold position; the ridge below would mark any tendency to drift.

But the other craft, presumably unseeing as it was un-seeable—could it hold its position inside the cloud cover by seat-of-the-pants sensation alone? Could the pilot be sure he was not slipping toward one of the cliffs? Must he not come up to check?

"But he could drop down, check his bearings, go back in," Nev's pilot speculated aloud.

They waited.

"Could he have gotten around," the pilot inclined his head to the right, indicating the end of the spur, "before we got in position here?"

Nev did not reply.

They waited.

"How long can he stay there! How can he expect to get out?"

Nev did not reply. *How long?* He concentrated on keeping his sense of time steady, not speeding, not letting tension force him to move too soon. But even his governed sense said *too long. How can they get out?* How would *he* get out?

Suddenly he snapped his fingers and pointed.

Rass and his passengers were allowing themselves guarded optimism. As minutes went by, it grew to exhilaration. Rass had flung his machine up into cloud and toward the northeast, then hovered and waited. Finally, he dropped just enough to see. Up again, barely within the bottom layer of cloud, he moved toward the Stockhorn ridge, lowering for instants to check his bearings. Close to the ridge, he turned west—opposite the direction he had taken since the beginning of the chase. He remained at the bottom edge of the cloud, creeping carefully as close to the mountain as he dared.

After they had skirted the Hohtäligrat again, they all breathed with relief. When they passed back along Gorner-grat, someone made a joke, and they laughed. They were almost giggling when—swinging well away this time—they went by Riffelhorn.

And then Nev was there. He had waited until they cleared the Horn and were beyond the cloud over it, and then motioned his pilot to sweep out from the other side, to rise and pounce from behind. Rass knew only when the dark machine buzzed down over his canopy and rose again to hang directly in front of them.

Instinctively, Rass dropped. The other helicopter dropped, too, holding its place just ahead, just above. Rass slipped to the left and tried to rise. Nev's pilot darted on, rose in a tight banking pivot, and returned to the same relative position. Then he began to settle, as though to push against the forehead of the larger machine.

Rass lowered the nose of his craft, dipping backward, then suddenly he dropped, using full throttle and the acceleration of his fall to try to escape forward and under. Nev's pilot flung up in a high backward arc, a curve complementary to Rass's, and came down again just above his nose.

"He'll kill us!"

"He'll kill himself, too!"

"I don't think he cares!"

"I think we have lost the game," said Rass.

24

THE MACHINE SETTLED and stopped with a soft bump. The door rolled back, and they stepped out. Black despair, white death: Vronsky had thought the bleakness of gray steppe over which he had looked each winter was cruelty absolute, but no longer. That vastness had been simple indifference; it now seemed gentle compared to the viciousness of rock like claws, teeth of ice.

"You do believe there is yet some chance?"

"There's a chance."

"How? How much?"

"Depends. If they fake Nev out and get away and he thinks he's lost us, we're home free. If he follows them . . . It all depends on how long it takes him to find out."

Nella had been as gleeful as a child. They had played a trick, they were getting away. She had been filled with delight and elation throughout the cableway ride up to the summit of Klein Matterhorn. Suddenly the implication struck her. "What will happen if he catches them? Would he . . . ?" First, horror at what she could imagine, then guilt. "Would he . . . ?"

Renata, too, looked to Maxwell. The question had been obvious to her from the beginning. But now that it had been asked, she was forced to acknowledge her own fear.

Maxwell gave the answer all wanted. "I don't think Nev will do anything to them. He doesn't have anything to gain. Except revenge, maybe, and he's too much of a pro for that—at least where it could cause him trouble. But Renata's brothers are used to taking risks." Maxwell looked from Nella to Renata. "They understood the risk when they took the job."

Renata nodded slightly. "We all understand the risks. We are satisfied."

But she knew she did not understand, truly. This man, whom she liked, whom in moments of ecstasy she had loved, had asked her help. And offered money; much money—but, because of the danger, earned money. Her brothers had accepted for the money and were satisfied. She was not satisfied. She had always been honest with her men and herself about her feelings and their money. But she did not understand why this man was helping the Russian doctor, and she was not sure she knew why she was helping him.

Although he was accustomed to service, Vronsky was overwhelmed. "Fräulein . . . I cannot express . . . That you and your brothers should have such concern for me. I shall prove worthy of what you—and all—have done for me. In time, history will know."

Renata took a breath to speak but stopped herself. If Bergmann, or whoever he was—the name on the letters to the bank in Zurich which he had given her and her brothers was Martins—if he wished to do good in secret, she would not betray him. She shrugged and looked away.

"I think we should get something to eat." Maxwell was glad to change the subject. He was not sure why he wanted Vronsky and Nella not to know about the money. For the first time, he felt a sense of shame. That was curious, since—for the first time—he was using it unselfishly. But because of that sense, he avoided thinking about it. "Renata, you go in. We don't have time to stop. Get us something we can eat while we walk."

While we walk. Vronsky looked from the station terrace across the snowfield to the cone of Testa Grigia, where they would take the cableway down to Italy. Not far, it seemed: the lifts—half a dozen of them—carrying skiers to various points on the glacier were quite clear; the skiers themselves clear—not simply specks at a distance, but figures with arms and legs. Vronsky felt confident. They were yet in danger, but they *could* walk out of it.

For one instant, when the helicopter door opened and the three men stepped down, Nev considered killing them. He stood with his pistol in his hand, and as he saw the men he understood that he had been tricked. His hand tightened, and he almost shot all of them. Without a word, he motioned to Grabov, vaulted back into the machine, and—gun still in hand—jerked his arm up.

Sick with failure, he pondered for a moment as the helicopter gained altitude. How far back did the trick go? Only to the American, Maxwell; only to Furi? Or farther: was it the CIA, finally acting after watching so long with no discernible objective? Had they orchestrated it all, and were they now taking Vronsky out by another helicopter or hidden under a wagonload of cheese? Nev evaluated two directions: Maxwell taking Vronsky south, or the CIA planting that *mis*direction while taking him north. Which should he cover? Could he deal with both? He pointed to Zermatt.

Line-of-sight from Klein Matterhorn to Testa Grigia had been a fraud. They couldn't walk that way, there were cliffs between. And there was no trail. A way, perhaps. Renata claimed to know a way and led, shuffling through snow half up her shins. Vronsky staggered after. Despite Renata's efforts to break the snow, he sank in at each lurching step. The headache he had felt from lack of nicotine had faded. He remembered it only as a gentle pulsation, as soothing as a massage compared to the constant agony now inside his skull. Despite the dark goggles Renata had brought for all of them, the glare knifed through his squinted eyes and slashed his brain like a hot knife. Heat. Who would have expected such heat in this place of ancient ice. His jacket was tied around his waist. His shirt collar was open, but sweat soaked him.

267

"Halt!" A shout from behind, from Maxwell.

Vronsky sank to his knees, slumped sideways into the snow, thrilled with dumb relief. He dragged half a dozen breaths into his burning lungs before gaining enough curiosity to turn.

Eight paces back, Nella was on her knees retching. Maxwell leaned over her, his hands on her shoulders. The figures were semitransparent to Vronsky, like an overexposed photograph. Another figure appeared, and he realized vaguely that Renata had passed him.

"What is it?" Then she answered her own question. "Altitude sickness."

"Yeah, him too. They can't take the height."

Nearly twelve thousand feet above sea level: even sportsmen in top condition need two or three days to acclimatize themselves. Vronsky and Nella's bodies, unaccustomed to strenuous exercise at any altitude, were starved for oxygen.

Maxwell and Renata looked steadily at each other, sharing a grim understanding. She spoke the impossibilities for both of them. "Get them oxygen. Take them down quickly. Carry them." She shrugged. "Go slowly, rest often."

Maxwell nodded. Renata went to her knees beside Nella, put an arm around her shoulder and spoke a few words in Italian. Maxwell walked forward to Vronsky and stood looking down at him.

Part of Maxwell was glad. He tried to keep that secret from himself because it was shameful. But it was true—he was tired. Not just the altitude. Not just hiking through the night, the lack of sleep, the effort now of walking in snow. He was tired *inside*.

Off to his right loomed the Matterhorn: lord of the cruel land. Maxwell had planned to come to it slowly over the weeks, looking first from Findeln, then closer from Gornergrat and Zmutt. Finally, when he seemed to have earned the right, he had hoped to approach this near, possibly even to set foot on the lower ridge of the mountain itself. That would have been much later, toward the end, when he was ready. Now he was not ready and was approaching in weakness. He had lost his own strength without gaining fully what he needed from the mountain. The white ice and stone of the terrible majesty rebuked him.

Up from Zermatt, up toward the mountains: Nev's last try. He did not think of it as his last *opportunity*. He had failed; he had lost Vronsky three times. When he returned to Russia, he would be summarily tried for gross incompetence and executed. Perhaps, if finally he succeeded in capturing Vronsky, they might only send him to labor camp for fifteen years. Nev preferred death, not only because it would be easier but because he deserved it. His career, ambitions, and hopes were ended; his life was ended. Those losses meant nothing. What made him stone-cold and heavy was loss of self-esteem.

There was another private helicopter in Zermatt, probably the CIA's. It had not moved. No unusual freight had gone by rail or electric cart down the highway. No ambulance. No heavily-veiled old women. Nev knew himself to be a failure, but not totally incompetent. Even while waiting in Randa or chasing decoys around the mountains, he kept his watchers in place. They watched yet. Unless they saw Vronsky very soon, though, their next instructions would come from other authority.

Nev used his own last authority to raise his helicopter and carry himself, Grabov, and Dobrinsky back to the high peaks. Neither reason nor instinct assured him Vronsky would go that way, but the likelihood was obvious, and the last that Nev could cover himself.

Whump-whump-whump-whump, pulsing inside their heads. At first the sound seemed like the rush of blood. Even as it resounded from the mountainsides, each thought it might be an hallucination projected from the agony of two hours' stumbling and lurching across the snowfield.

"There!" Maxwell pointed.

The helicopter was below them. As it moved from behind the ridge past Gandegg, the trick of echoes that had synchronized rotor noise and heartbeats faded. Pitch and rhythm rose to the sound of rapid strokes on a snare drum. The machine skimmed above the glacier four hundred meters below where they stood. Though far away, the dark speck was like a bullet which sped-up vision could see shooting toward their eyes.

A flash of red: a skier went by in front of Maxwell. The color and motion pulled his eyes, and drew him back to action.

"Move! Keep moving! We've got to get down to the ski lift." A hundred meters beyond them was the top of the Plateau Rosa lift. Skiers dropped from it and stood to wait for companions. "We've got to get in with those people."

Through his pain and dizziness, Vronsky understood. They must move quickly, hide before they were seen. But he couldn't run. How could he run? He tried. Like a year-old toddler, leaning forward, feet thrown out—steps too long, too short, thrown to the side.

"Slower! Go slower!" Maxwell called. "Take it easy, Vronsky. Don't call attention to yourself."

Vronsky stopped, bewildered. Renata moved past him, setting a pace faster than before but yet too slow. Vronsky knew it was far too slow. The missile swelling along its trajectory toward them: they must flee from it—but slowly! So slowly they would never reach—

Not toward them, exactly. As the helicopter neared, they could see its direction was to Testa Grigia. It reached its destination, hovered, faced away from them, and descended.

Maxwell took the lead, bringing them among the skiers. He left Vronsky and Nella next to a group of four and went on for several paces, indicating that Renata should follow.

"I don't think this is good enough. There really aren't enough people coming up this lift to cover us for long. Anyone watching will see." He looked farther down, to where the two Ventina lifts ended.

Renata followed his gaze. "Yes, more people; but it is—what?—three hundred meters away. And it is *closer* to Testa Grigia."

"Yeah." Maxwell turned back to the other couple. The group of skiers had departed, and Vronsky was leading Nella toward another. But those, too, shoved off and dropped away as he neared them. Vronsky stood, turning back and forth almost in panic.

"We can't go back," Maxwell said. "There isn't any place to go to, and we'd never make it if there was, and we'd be exposing ourselves. We can't stay here. Down there, it'll be harder for them to see us."

"But easier for them to make recognition if they do see."

"Yeah." Maxwell gestured for Vronsky to come to him.

Maxwell varied the pattern: sometimes all four of them together, sometimes separated, the distances between them changing. It wouldn't work, he knew, if they were being watched continuously. But with the skiers gliding by, sweeping braided zigzags around them . . .

The peak of Testa Grigia was half a cone rising from the glacier immediately around it, but it was below their elevation. Looking down, they could see the hotel and the other buildings, including the cableway terminus. They could see the helicopter parked between the hotel and station.

Would that machine rise, hang in the sky, rotate slowly to see them? Imagining that motion, seeing it begin at every succeeding moment, made moving toward it all the more terrifying. It would not fly on wings—birdlike in appearance, at least. In its supernatural defiance of gravity, it seemed inexorable and monstrous.

Vronsky tried to obliterate that image. He tried to control the dread of moving toward it, which seemed to slow each step more than sinking into snow.

"What will Nev do?" he asked. "Will he simply inquire for us and leave? Or will he wait?"

"He'll probably just check and leave. No reason for him to stay there. If he doesn't see us, he'll probably assume we've gone down already."

"Have you seen my friends? A tall man, big, older; and a

271

small, round one—with eyeglasses? An Italian woman with them? We were supposed to meet here, but I have been delayed. Perhaps they went down on the cableway? Perhaps there is someone else I should ask? Ah, all passengers must show tickets here. I see."

When they reached the top of the Ventina lift, Maxwell allowed himself some confidence. Skiers deposited by the lifts, others coming down, pausing—a crowd milling. "Keep the picture changing, we've got plenty of cover. We can wait until they leave. We'll be OK. How're you feeling?"

Vronsky closed his eyes for a moment. Although he was brimming with gratitude, the question seemed to him incredibly stupid. "Badly," he said.

"You think you can make it?"

"I must."

"How are you, Nella?"

Nella tried to smile; the tight movement of her lips might have been understood that way.

Maxwell squeezed her shoulder. "It'll soon be over. They won't stay there all afternoon. Don't worry, just hold on." He touched Renata and began to move away.

Renata looked toward the sky, then down along the ski lifts. Where the lifts started it was bright enough from reflected light, but it seemed blue; it was in shadow cast by Testa Grigia. "How much longer do you think they wait for us?" she asked.

"I don't know. I wouldn't think much longer. But even if they wanted to wait to see if we're still coming . . . Maybe an hour. Two at the outside."

"We cannot wait so long."

"Why?"

"The lifts—they are closed from 1400 hours."

"What!"

"The afternoon . . . It becomes too cold, later. After 1400 hours, it is too late to begin a ski trip."

Maxwell thrust out his watch. "It's 1:30 now!"

* * *

"And you have been on duty here all day? You have no time away for the midday meal?" Nev recognized that the man did not like questions, did not like him. Nev waited, taking half the space in front of the window while two American girls bought cableway tickets. Then he persisted. "So, someone takes your place. Please, could I speak to him?" Nev had to wait further.

Insane. It seemed insane. Vronsky's mind did not reject apparent insanity. He knew it sometimes had its logic—like sailing west to reach the Orient. He must have faith in the incredible proposition that walking down toward Nev was the path to safety. He understood. He walked. But the sense of madness grew, meter by meter.

Walking was easier. A great tracked machine had crawled up the slope between the lifts, packing the snow. Vronsky still stumbled, but less often, and sank less into the snow. The pain in his head was as severe as before, but he was no longer faint. He could see the people on either side of him clearly. Was it possible they would make a screen sufficient to hide him from Nev?

It's possible, Maxwell thought. The line of skiers gliding up might shield them. Renata was keeping as close to the left-hand line as she could while remaining on packed snow. Someone sweeping a glance from Testa Grigia might not see them through the spaces between the skiers going up and distinguish them as walkers coming down.

A group of girls went past in pairs, giggling shrilly, shouting to each other along the line. But unlike Vronsky, Maxwell did not look at them. Maxwell watched the people at the bottom and judged the possibilities by their number. There were a dozen, sometimes twenty; as those ready first took the lift, others came down from the higher runs. But the average number was decreasing. Knowing the lifts would close in ten minutes, those skiers who had to return to Zermatt began to do so.

When no one else was allowed to join the group at the bottom of the lift, and when the last of those waiting there had

273

ridden past, then Maxwell knew that he, Vronsky, Nella, and Renata would look like bugs pinned and wriggling on a great white wall.

". . . but I have been delayed. Could my friends have checked into the hotel here? Ah, only by reservation. Could they have waited somewhere? Perhaps I might ask . . ."

Vronsky seemed able to make it. But Nella . . . She had fallen twice. Left alone, she would stray as though delirious, wobbling off into the path of the lift. Maxwell trudged with his arm around her waist, trying to make supporting her look only casual and affectionate. Nella seemed like a mechanical doll, putting one foot out and then the other, but she could not be hurried. They had, perhaps, two hundred meters to go.

At the bottom, a couple was starting to ride up. They tossed their blond heads back and grinned at each other. A man with silver hair stood with his arms around two young women. He patted their bottoms to send them to the lift and followed. He was the last.

Maxwell's eyes shifted continually from those skiers to the buildings at Testa Grigia. The hotel now blocked the helicopter, but Maxwell still believed he would see it rise at any instant. That belief had been born of hope that the machine would leave while there was cover, however slight. But as those last five skiers moved toward him, Maxwell knew with the certainty of despair that *now they'll start to leave.*

Renata turned for instructions, but Maxwell could give her none. There was no going back or staying. They must proceed to where their enemies waited.

The two girls passed, talking animatedly to each other at once. The older man passed. He had a face the color and texture of an old boot. He flashed very white teeth and waved his arm at Renata and her companions.

Then they were alone. Skiers swung in their wide traverses over the glacier, but they were off to the side of the lift. Renata halted until the others caught up. Obviously, there was no further point in pretending they were not in company. "So?"

It seemed incredible to Vronsky that they had not been seen.

"We'll have to assume that we have been." Maxwell answered without taking his eyes from the buildings at the summit. "I guess they must figure, why come after us when we're coming to them." He let his glance move to the cliffs which emerged from the snow at the southwestern base of Testa Grigia. "On the other hand . . ."

"Then let us go!" Inspiration struck Vronsky with the joyous clarity it always brought. "There are people there. It is a public place. This is not Russia. What can they do?"

Maxwell used his years of practice in controlling surprise. "Well, Doctor Vronsky, they can try to force you into that helicopter. It would be messy, but by now they're past caring. And—"

"But—"

"And if we make too much fuss about it, I think they'll just kill you. Then they'll fly away, and I don't think they'll give a damn about what anybody says about it."

Vronsky was shocked beyond speech. He knew the measures his masters could use. But never, at any time since he first contemplated escape, had it occurred that they might kill him. Kill *him*.

Maxwell took up his previous thought. "But if they haven't seen us . . . Let's move!" He crossed under the lift-lines, heading toward Testa Grigia, but toward the left. "Come on!"

He spoke back over his shoulder. "If they *haven't* seen us . . . If we can get against that cliff on the back side, they *won't* see us."

"What then?"

"Who knows?"

Nev sat on the restaurant terrace of the hotel. He had questioned all of the waiters. There was no one left to ask. No, Vronsky had not come there or gone down on the cableway. It was too late to believe that he would come. The route through Testa Grigia had been the obvious one, and Maxwell had somehow been more subtle.

Nev sat at one of the small metal tables and stared off at the northern mountains gleaming in afternoon sunlight, because there was nothing else to do. He ordered tea and drank it, sitting like the other customers with his back toward the bright sun. From the perspective of the young man two tables to Nev's left, who turned his head frequently to speak to his girl friend, the four figures out on the slope seemed to perch for a moment on Nev's right shoulder. Then they were blocked as they moved lower.

25

NELLA LAY UNCONSCIOUS. When they had reached the cliff base and paused, she had crumpled. They feared she had gone into shock, but she seemed simply to be asleep. Vronsky cradled her shoulders in his lap, her head on his chest. He tried to think, to plan, but in the moment while he caught his breath and tried to organize his thoughts, he drifted away too.

Maxwell longed to sleep as they slept. He was sick with weariness. Ordinarily he would have been in shape and prepared to go through it all again. But now he was dying. Not in six months—which could seem like never—but now. If they escaped Nev, he might see those six months. But death would not come at a moment at the end. He felt himself dying at that instant.

Renata studied him as he stared ahead. He was not simply weak and unused to exercise. No: he was strong and powerful, all she wanted a man to be. There was something wrong with him. Suddenly she was aware that he was ill, that he was suffering. Yet he persisted, not merely like the woman and the little doctor, dumbly, because they were prodded or led. Left alone, those two would have slumped and remained helpless. They moved by this man's will. And she knew it was only by will that he kept himself going.

"Who are you?" Renata was sitting beside him, leaning back against the rock. Their shoulders touched in an unconscious intimacy.

Partly, Maxwell was too tired and sick to care anymore. In larger part, he wanted to be honest. He admired her. She was smart, she was tough. She saw the picture, made her choices.

"Charles Maxwell," he said. "People call me Max. I used to work for the CIA."

"Ah. So." Renata nodded to herself.

"I'm retired. I got pulled into this by . . . coincidence. Accident." Suddenly, Maxwell could hold himself in no longer, "I'm dying. I came here to die. Cancer. Six months. I . . ." He pushed his goggles up, was momentarily blinded by the direct sunlight. He pressed his hands over his eyes and leaned his head back against the rock. After a moment, he wiped his eyes and pulled the goggles back down.

Renata put her hand on his upper arm and leaned her head on his shoulder. "When this is over, I come to stay with you."

"That would be nice. I don't think I'll be able to go back to Zermatt."

"I will find a place."

"That would be nice." Maxwell touched her hair. Then he roused himself. "But this isn't over yet."

"What can we do?"

"I can't understand why they're still up there! It doesn't make any sense. I thought if we got this far we could just wait until they left and go up. But if he's going to stay . . ."

"A, he has seen us." Vronsky's voice startled Maxwell. "A sub 1, he waits for us to come. A sub 2, if we do not come to him, eventually he will come for us. B, he has not seen us. B sub 1, not having seen us, soon he will leave. B sub 2, although he has not seen us, he believes we yet may come. He will wait. C, whether or not he has seen us, he waits there for some reason not directly related to our present position. It is not necessary to speculate on this reason." Vronsky saw the situation entirely, the possible moves all at once. He separated and enumerated them for the benefit of his companions. "Summary: we do not know whether he has seen us, nor can we make any reliable evaluation of whether he will leave soon, stay all night, or come here. *Conclusion:* we must attempt to leave this place for somewhere other than Testa Grigia." Vronsky lifted his fingers nearly to his mouth before remembering he held no cigarette in them.

"How?" Even as Maxwell spoke, he was leaning forward, looking to left and right. "Is there any other way down to Italy?"

"Theodulpass," Renata gestured to her right.

"Where?"

"To the north. From farther around this cliff you can see it. It is one, perhaps two kilometers away."

"It goes to Italy?" Vronsky shifted in excitement, and Nella stirred and moaned without waking.

"We are in Italy. Since we came across the ski lift."

Vronsky stared out, both thrilled and shocked. He had expected a land of warmth and bronzey sunshine. Below and around him were the same sterile ice fields and barren mountain peaks of the hell he had suffered all day. But perhaps it had been only purgatory. Far below, through the haze, the land seemed rounder and green.

"Is there a trail from here to the pass?" Maxwell could make out none.

"There is no pathway, but one can walk. In winter there is skiing all the way to Cervinia. Now, on this side of the mountains, the snow goes not so far."

"Is there cover? I mean, how far do these cliffs extend?"

"Only around the peak here. From the peak—even the cableway—someone could see us; but from lower—the hotel—I think not until we reach the pass."

"Let's go."

A waiter passed, and his presence reminded Nev to sip his cognac. Alcohol was not his vice; he rarely touched it. He could not have been sure why he had ordered the brandy at all. There had been a sense that he ought to order something after he finished his tea if he was going to continue to occupy his table. He could not have said why he continued to occupy it. He did

279

not delay leaving out of any hope or out of fear. He knew his end; he welcomed it. Yet he sat slackly, staring off at the mountain peaks, which had paled until they were blue in the distance, and let images come into his head.

He had almost finished the cognac, without tasting any of it, when Dobrinsky came to him.

Maxwell could not resist looking over his shoulder at every third step. They had been in clear sight of the cableway terminus almost as soon as they moved on after resting and getting Nella to her feet. She was better. It was Vronsky, now, who seemed to be more in trouble. His mind was clear enough, but he looked to be nearing the end of his strength. So was Maxwell—he had to acknowledge it. Yet he felt they must try harder, move quicker.

Ahead, the ground dropped more abruptly. Perhaps when they reached that place they might regain cover. It seemed incredible to Maxwell that they could have gone on so long without being seen, much less possible that their luck could continue.

Yet as he looked back for the last time that he could see Testa Grigia summit, before they rounded a shoulder and went into the place where the little pass was scooped between ridges, the sky was clear and empty. They slipped and stumbled down until they reached the saddle. To left and right, snowfields dropped and widened away like spilled sugar. Directly ahead, cliffs rose again—one line going west, the other rising higher to the north—the two joining in a point toward them. Rock and ice showed on either side, but the point was snow covered. Obviously, their way led up it.

Then they heard the helicopter—Maxwell first, because he had been expecting to hear it, then the others heard. They all froze for a moment, looking up and back.

Maxwell recovered. "Move! Keep moving! Try to get to that cliff!" He lurched forward, half carrying, half dragging Nella. She held to him and tried to help propel herself.

Alternately warmed by the southern sun and frozen again, the snow base was firm. Only the top six inches was soft, and some of that was packed under the pressure of their feet as they tried to run. Yet they sank at each step and slipped and tripped. They couldn't really run, but they plunged and staggered, fell to their knees and threw themselves forward again.

The drumstroke sound swelled to a roll. It tumbled like an avalanche down the mountainside behind them; it billowed, filling the air, and crashed back from the blue-steel sky. It whipped them, and they writhed and scrambled, trying hopelessly to flee it.

They did reach the cliff before the awful engine came down upon them. The helicopter had to land behind them, where the terrain was more nearly level. Nev was out, dropping into the snow, before the machine touched down. Dobrinsky came almost as quickly, while Grabov took a moment to squeeze past the pilot.

Renata, still leading, went diagonally up the slope, not directly up its snow-covered center but toward the left-hand cliffs.

The slope was not extremely steep but angled enough to force them down on hands and knees.

Still erect and bounding, Nev and his men were catching up.

Vronsky's breaths were shrieks in his throat. Renata turned, saw him open-mouthed, feet churning, pawing through the snow behind her. She twisted back toward him, seized his upper arm, dragged and then pushed him past her.

Maxwell cocked his right leg under himself, dug his toe into the snow, took hold of Nella by the shoulder and waistband, and heaved her along like a heavy sack. Nella crawled on as fast as she could. Renata took her hand and pulled to help, and as she went by, followed after, pushing Nella's rear.

Maxwell had to give himself two lung-filling gasps before he could turn, fling off his goggles, and rise half-up in front of Nev. Nev never stopped. His thick thighs drove him, and he kept his momentum. Still below, he shot his left hand at Maxwell's solar plexus. Maxwell struck it away, aiming for Nev's wrist joint which he knew he could break if he hit it correctly. But Nev expected that and twisted his hand, taking the blow against the heel and moving with it. Then he swung his own right low and upward, a stiffened claw toward Maxwell's crotch. But Maxwell had expected *that*. He changed from cut to grab, caught and twisted Nev's jacket cuff, and pulled. At the same time, he fell backwards, kicking his feet from under himself and down. He didn't catch Nev's ankles, but using the angle of the hillside and Nev's momentum, Maxwell pulled him off balance and down.

For a moment they lay, Nev on top of Maxwell, their hands locked together, straining, trying each other's strength. Maxwell lost. Holding Maxwell's hands down against the snow, Nev raised himself on stiffened arms. Then suddenly he released Maxwell's wrist and smashed the heel of his right hand against the side of Maxwell's head. Red-yellow flashed inside Maxwell's skull. He tried to roll away from Nev, who completed his own roll the other way, his right arm wound back across himself, and whipped the knife edge of his flattened hand across and down. If the cut had struck Maxwell's thorax it would have killed him. Maxwell was half turned away, and the hand caught the base of his skull, just behind the ear. Nev struck once more, and Maxwell was still.

Nev scrambled to his knees, ready to give another blow. At the periphery of his vision he saw a shape rush up at him. He twisted. It was Dobrinsky.

One glance assured Dobrinsky that Nev needed no help, so he sprinted on, slipping and sliding. Pulled away from the heat of combat, Nev focused again on the point of the chase: Vronsky. Nev wanted to reach him first.

Vronsky was running on knees and shins, his arms flailing. Sometimes he managed to get his feet under him and rise and throw himself forward for three steps. Then he would fall full length again. He came to a place where he could either go on up to the top of the cliff or nearly horizontally along a two-meter wide terrace between tiers of rock. He took the latter. He was able to stand upright and almost run, lurching, with his right hand against the upper wall for balance.

Nella never was able to get to her feet. Renata crawled behind her, pushing, trying to help her rise. When Dobrinsky reached them, Renata rose to face him. He charged upward, and as he struck her shoulder, knocking her to the side, she seized his arm with both hands, clutching it to her with all her strength. Dobrinsky tried to shake her off. She clung to him, falling, hanging on, dragging at him. Dobrinsky reached around, embracing her, and lifted her clear of the ground. He tossed her downhill, but she held to him. He slipped. They fell together, tumbling and sliding a dozen feet. As they stopped, he broke her grip, swung back and slapped her once with full force. Then he pushed himself away and started climbing again behind Nev, who had passed them.

When Maxwell could see again, it was only a searing whiteness, which his eyelids shut out instantly. He tried to open them and tried again, not sure why he persisted. Finally he was able to force them to stay open. The blank whiteness gradually resolved into grains, which somehow he knew were of snow. Then something dark appeared to break the uniform glare.

As Grabov's foot swung forward, Maxwell caught it with the arm that had been outstretched in the snow. He rolled onto his back and seized Grabov's ankle with his other hand as well, pulling Grabov off balance. Grabov hopped, twisting so as to break his fall and come down away from Maxwell. Then he kicked backwards. Maxwell ignored the kick to his thigh and slashed with the oaklike edge of his palm down onto Grabov's kidney. Grabov arched with pain but still twisted to face Maxwell. Maxwell ducked and drove a jab into the point where Grabov's rib cage divided. Jabbing again, the second motion blurring with the first, like a snake striking, Maxwell hit straight to Grabov's throat. Grabov fell back and away. Maxwell tried to raise himself, to give whatever final blow might be needed, but could not. He lay in the snow, staring at the hard sky, while Grabov writhed, unable to breathe ever again.

Vronsky stood facing the cliff, both hands against it. He looked back and saw Nev start along the ledge after him. Vronsky shuffled sideways two paces. The ledge was narrowing. It had dwindled to less than half a meter, and it tipped downward. Vronsky pressed his chest against the cliff; still he felt he would topple backward. Slowly he rolled against the rock so that his back was to it. Nev came after him, steady as a cat. Vronsky took three more dragging sidesteps. He kept his eyes fixed on Nev in horrified fascination. The angle of the ledge was increasing under his feet. Snow covered it. Vronsky knew he would slip. His feet would shoot out from under him. He tried to find something in the rock behind him to cling to. It was smooth. Nev came on. He held his eyes as fixed as Vronsky's. Vronsky stepped to the right again, and then again, and then once more. He looked down to check his footing. One more step, and the ledge would be narrower than the length of his small foot. He looked out in front of himself and moaned in terror.

Nev saw. He looked at the horror twisting Vronsky's face and understood. And he was thrilled. He longed to push at Vronsky. Only with a finger tip, not enough to budge him. A little jab, then wait five seconds. A poke. Wait ten. Harder pushes, longer waits between. He fantasized slipping his hand between Vronsky's shoulder and the cliff, ever so slowly, as though to pry him off; watching Vronsky twist his mouth and gurgle as he tried to plead. But Nev restrained himself. He allowed only five seconds to look into Vronsky's eyes and smile.

Something stung his shoulder. Nev wheeled around, surprised, more annoyed than hurt.

Nella lay where Nev's blow had thrown her. Her arms were outstretched toward him. They shook, and she could not see clearly, and she would have been a bad shot in any case. The second, third, and fifth bullets missed Nev completely. But the fourth went through his right lung, the sixth through his neck, and the seventh hit him in the eye.

The little snaps from the Baretta broke a spell. The Russians all carried pistols; none had used them. They had hoped to take Vronsky alive, and it was undesirable to leave his companions' bodies lying around. Maxwell had assumed, without having to think about it, that they would observe the rule *we won't shoot if you don't*. It was customary. And since their guns outnumbered his, the rule had been in his favor.

Now it was broken.

Maxwell tried to raise himself. Renata had scrambled down to him and lifted his head in her arms. His head was clear—or nearly so; but he couldn't seem to gather the strength to lift his shoulders and sit up. Again he tried, straining his will as much as his muscles. Renata lifted, and at last he was able to bring himself upright. He twisted around to face uphill.

Legs churning, Dobrinsky rushed high enough up the slope to see Nella lying in the snow where the ledge began. He had stopped for an instant at the first shot, seen Vronsky against the cliff wall; seen Nev standing, one hand out, looking incredulously back the way he had come; seen him stagger and fall sideways over the cliff. Dobrinsky had started running again, his hand digging inside his jacket for his pistol. When his shoulders reached the terrace level, he stopped, spread his feet, and aimed.

Maxwell tore at his pocket: he had jammed Bonnario's gun in there. The butt was caught under an upper corner. Maxwell tugged. It would not come. He yanked, but the jacket rode up to his chest. In desperation, he grabbed the outside of the patch pocket and jerked with all the strength he could find. The pocket ripped downward, sending a flight of feathers wafting out onto the snow. Maxwell caught the pistol.

The first shot made Dobrinsky arch his back as though trying to touch shoulder blades together. The second spun him half around. At the third, he toppled, struck the slope, and slid his own length downward, leaving streaks of red melting into the snow behind him.

Maxwell held his aim, but Dobrinsky had dropped his weapon, and he lay still.

Then they all heard the roar of the helicopter. Its engine had run continuously, ready for instant takeoff. The machine leapt from the ground.

Maxwell spun around. He saw his first two shots spider-web the canopy. As the helicopter flung itself upward, he fired four more times at its underside, not sure what he had hit.

The helicopter continued rising, banking, and swinging itself away out eastward over the glacier. Maxwell watched it, his heart sinking. There would be no escaping the men it brought back from Zermatt.

But the machine kept swinging around, its arc carrying it toward the south, toward Klein Matterhorn. Then it rocked, swung back north, banking to the left more and more sharply. It turned completely to its side and stalled. Its nose dropped, and it corkscrewed to crash and explode, sending sheets of orange flame streaking across the ice.

26

ROSE AND PURPLE-BLUE: the western faces of the peaks to the right and behind flamed with the alpenglow Maxwell loved. The shadows were rich and thick by contrast. Where it was dusk down in the valley far beyond, the lights of Cervinia sparkled against the shadows like jewels in a velvet box. But still high on the grassy hillside, Renata, Vronsky, Nella, and Maxwell glowed with the color of the sun they seemed to walk straight toward.

"Why must we go on?" Vronsky had demanded. They had been at the top of the cliffs above the pass, moving along what Renata said was the trail, when Vronsky's mind emerged from hiding. He had fallen once more, but this time, he consciously refused to rise as Renata tried to help him.

Maxwell realized that the flood of adrenalin his own sick body had been able to produce under the stress had worn off, too. Nella dragged on him, her little weight more than he could support farther.

"All right," he said. "We'll rest here." There was a rock outcropping that would provide a semblance of cover.

Vronsky lay in the snow, only his shoulders and head raised against the outcropping. "Surely the danger is over."

Nella lay curled against him. Maxwell and Renata sprawled on either side. All three—even Renata—waited in the pathetic hope that Maxwell would say their ordeal was ended.

"It's not over." Maxwell had to speak slowly, three breaths

287

for his body before one could be spared for words. "Ten min-
utes . . . I guess only ten minutes more, outside . . .
Helicopter up from Zermatt . . . Police . . . Investigate the
crash. We're lucky. He got pretty far out before he went down.
They may not come this way. But they might. See those bodies.
See us. And Nev wasn't the only one after us. There are others.
We're not safe from them yet."

Despite the danger he felt still tracking them, Maxwell did
allow ten minutes rest. Toward the end of that time, Vronsky
spoke again. "I am glad for this. This day. I have been thinking:
it is a purgatory. A test. I am—I have been—a theoretician.
Now I go to a world of action. To be a leader. The pain, the
fear, enduring, overcoming . . . After this day, I shall be
ready. I shall have earned the right."

Nella smiled weakly up at him and reached to touch his face
with her hand. Vronsky smiled back at her.

Maxwell looked at them and said nothing.

Then Vronsky raised his head and caught Maxwell's expression. "Ah." He smiled at Maxwell. "That must seem amusing to
you. And vain. I am hardly the hero of this day. I have been
nothing in comparison to you, my dear friend. But I have been
much in comparison to me—to my old self. It is that which
gives me confidence for the great work I must do."

Maxwell was too tired to mask the disgust with which he
turned away.

"Why do I offend you?"

"People with missions are a pain in the ass."

"I do not understand."

"People with missions are always starting out to save the
world, but it always seems to turn out the only way to do that is
to have a bunch of people die killing a bunch of other people for
the cause."

"I will not permit anyone to kill—!"

"You're sitting here now because she killed Nev! And I killed
those other guys! And last night! And Paul! There are dead
bodies lying over half of Switzerland because of you, and you
haven't even gotten started on your 'work' yet!"

Vronsky opened and closed his mouth several times. He stared at Maxwell, then covered his eyes. When he revealed them again they were filled with anguish. "I will try—I will do everything I can—"

"Yes, Doctor Vronsky." Vronsky's earnestness softened Maxwell. "I believe you will try."

The two men looked directly at each other for a moment.

"I believe . . ." Vronsky began again. "I believe that one must try to do good in the world. One must try to do whatever one can. Otherwise . . . When one comes to the end of his life he will look back and realize he has not lived at all."

Maxwell stiffened.

Vronsky went on, trying to reach him. "That knowledge must make death horrible. One must live for some principle. You say you do not believe in missions, in causes. But you must have some principle by which you live, some principle that leads you to do all you have done for me."

Maxwell stared off toward Italy as Vronsky had done. "I guess," he said at last, "I guess my principle is that people ought to leave each other alone."

"Yes, but men must live together in societies . . ." Vronsky let his words trail off. Then, "I assure you, my friend, I shall think always of what you have said. To the extent I do exert influence . . . But I believe that when the causes of society's evils are understood, means may be found . . ." He gazed off into the afternoon sky, trying to make the vision clear.

Nella looked up at him in adoration.

Maxwell watched them and said nothing. Renata's eyes met his. He saw in her face the same blank neutrality but also the same shrewdness of assessment, the same mixture of judgments. He sighed to himself. The sense of lost possibilities that had been with him vaguely all of the past year had become clearer in the last two days and now was focused and sharp. But he *hadn't* met her sooner, under different circumstances. There was no point to thinking about it.

He fished in an inside pocket, found a pen and two folded sheets remaining of the paper Renata had brought for him to write the letters to his bank. He wrote another, briefly, folded it, and handed it to her. "Keep this for me. If we get out of here all right, I'll want it back."

Vronsky's attention was brought back to immediate practicality. "What must we do now to get out of here?"

"Keep walking. Down that ridge." Maxwell nodded to the right.

"To Cervinia?"

"No. We'll cut away before we get there. Go to one of the smaller places on the outskirts. Find a gasthaus. Nella can call her friends. I don't think at that point anybody will be able to trace you."

"Ah," Vronsky sighed with relief at the prospect. "And then what? Will you come to Rome with me, my friend?"

"No. I . . . I'll probably go back to Switzerland—someplace—and . . . finish my vacation."

Vronsky studied Maxwell for a moment, then turned to Renata. "And what will you do, Fräulein?"

"Renata will be going to Zurich," Maxwell spoke before she could. "She'll be taking a course in economics—finance. She's come into some money, an inheritance. If she invests it right, she ought to be able to build it up so she can live pretty well without having to work too hard."

"How fortunate for you, Fräulein. While I cannot, in theory, approve of such wealth, I wish you every success. Sincerely."

"Thank you." Renata looked levelly at Maxwell as she spoke.

"Will you not first come with us to Rome? I should like somehow to thank you for all you have done."

"No. Thank you. I shall also return to Switzerland. I wish to rest for a while before I go to Zurich."

"Ah." Vronsky's tone was neutral, and he did not turn to Maxwell knowingly, but suddenly and surprisingly Maxwell was embarrassed. "I guess we'll all know what you're doing," he said to cover. "Tomorrow Italy, next week the world."

Vronsky smiled. "Perhaps a little longer. First, I must finish my writing. He patted his chest. "It is here. I have half, Nella has half." He smiled again. "We are testing to see if it wears well. I must finish it, and while I do that, I must develop plans for practical action. After the attention that will be generated by my arrival in Rome, the world will probably hear little of me for a year or two."

"And then you'll start everyone marching to a brighter tomorrow."

"I shall try to lead people to walk that way."

"Yeah. OK, I guess it really doesn't matter to me. But if any of us are going to see tomorrow, we'd better start walking out of here. Right now."

Soon after they started again, they did hear a helicopter, faintly, far away on the other side of the ridge. It did not come to the pass, and Maxwell assumed it was the police. Perhaps the bodies would not be found until skiing time the next day.

In half an hour, they had gone below the spring snowline and were walking a clear trail through rocky scree. The going was easier, but their fatigue was such that they hardly noticed. After another hour, the ground was grassy, the highest slopes where cows might graze. Ahead, to one side and over the shoulder of the rounded ridge on which they walked, they could see the roof of a barn.

Then that sound again. It was far enough away, faint, echoing from the cliffs, that it seemed to come from all directions. All of them heard it, stopped, stood looking up and around. This time Renata saw it first. It was back and to their left, following the line of the cableway down to Cervinia.

"Down! Get down! Get down!"

The helicopter continued on its line, passing them in the distance. Apparently they were unseen.

"Up! OK, it's OK. Come on, we've got to keep moving. We've got to find cover."

They were nearing the barn when the helicopter turned over Cervinia and started back, this time following the trail—which showed distinctly through the green pastures.

"Run! Run! Run for that building!"

They ran as best they could. Vronsky caught Nella's hand, tried to pull her. When they left the path to go over the crest and down toward the barn, they both fell and tumbled. They came up again and went on, Nella leaning on Vronsky and hobbling. Maxwell tried to sprint and suddenly felt as though he had been hit with a sandbag. *The wall*, he thought. He could not seem to push himself even one more step. He leaned forward, tried simply to move his legs to keep from falling downhill. He felt as though he were encased in lead while trying to run through a mountain of sand.

There was no hope of reaching the barn before being seen. The helicopter shot overhead, pulled up and banked, came back over them again. Then it completed its circle and settled by the path, on a level patch out of their sight over the crest of the shoulder. Vronsky and Nella stood transfixed looking back. Renata ran on, but when she checked over her shoulder and saw them and Maxwell halted, she stopped, too.

The small barn was L-shaped. It was really two structures: a rectangle about twenty feet square and a smaller square off of one corner. It was old, walled with black-brown planks, with spaces between, knotholed. Maxwell assumed the floor was earthen. It was four inches deep in relatively fresh manure, so he couldn't be sure. The reek was almost overpowering.

He stood in the manure, just inside the doorway—a simple opening, wide enough for a cow, without any sort of closure. He checked to make sure there was a bullet in the chamber of Bonnario's gun.

He waited. The door faced uphill. Half the picture it framed was grass, now gray-green in the dusk. Above were deep blue sky and the peak of a mountain, which was incongruous, since no rises up to it were visible. A faint rosiness still touched a westward ridge, but the bulk of the mountain was that passionless blue. Its shape was vaguely familiar. Suddenly it struck Maxwell that he was seeing the Matterhorn from the other side.

He was glad for that. For one moment he allowed all thought, all fear, to drain out of him and the mountain's peace to fill their place.

Then they came, spread widely: six of them, over the rise, against the skyline—like Indians in a Western. They were careful but evidently did not think it necessary to surround the barn first. As they came down, the flank men moved ahead so that they all formed a semicircle. Four of them carried submachine guns.

Well, the games are over, thought Maxwell. "Hold it there!" he shouted.

The men halted, all but two dropping to one knee and bringing up their guns.

"Max? It's OK, Max."

"That's right, Corky. It's OK. You just stay there, everything's OK."

Corchran took a step toward Dolby and spoke with him. They appeared to argue. Then Corchran called out again, "Max, can we talk?"

"Talk."

"Let me come down, Max. Let me come down and talk to you there. It's for your own good."

Maxwell deliberated for a moment. The last tinge of warmth faded from the mountain.

"OK, Corky. Come talk. Always glad to talk with an old friend."

Corchran started down the hill.

"Cor-kee . . ."

Corchran raised his hands and bowed in a gesture of exaggerated apology. He went back to Dolby, faced Maxwell again, removed the pistol from inside his windbreaker, and handed it over ostentatiously. Hands still up, palms outward at shoulder level, he moved slowly down to the barn.

He paused at the doorway. "Charming," he said.

"It suits me," Maxwell said. "Come on in."

With obvious distaste, Corchran put his fine boot down into

the manure. Maxwell swung up his pistol and jabbed it into Corchran's side. "Easy, now." He ran his hands over Corchran's body.

"I wouldn't try to fool you, Max."

Maxwell stepped back. "OK."

"Where are they?" Corchran, his eyes adjusting to the gloom, looked around. He could not see into the L. He started to move toward it.

"Stay!"

"I just wanted to meet—"

"Stay!"

"OK, Max."

"I know what you're here for, Corky."

"We merely want to assist Doctor Vronsky in—"

"Bullshit. Cut the bullshit, Corky. We've got enough of it in here already. It's come down to it. You tried to set up the Russians—to let them take Vronsky, but messy. Then you tried to set me up—followed us down from Findeln. I knew you would. You tipped them which way we were going. Everything crashed, and now it's come down to this: you've got to take him out yourselves."

"No fooling the old pro, is there? We're going to do it, Max."

"And me too?"

"We don't want that. I don't want it. You are a shit, Max, but . . . I've been over your whole record. We owe you a few. At least enough not to put you down, here, now. You really are one of the old soldiers. I'd like to see you fade away—or at least take it on your own terms."

"You're a sweetie, Corky."

"I didn't have to come in here, Max. Dolby thinks I'm stupid. He just wants to blast the place. But I don't want you to end this way. I mean it. Max . . . Both of us—our families came over on the boat. They were all dirt poor. Poorer than dirt. And they all made it. Your family's got a solid business in Akron. My great-grandfather started a business, too; my grandfather made a million out of it, and my father can't give it away—which he does—as fast as it comes in. And I'm grateful,

294

Max. Not for the money. Not just for the money. I'm grateful to a country that makes that possible. And you should be grateful, too. Ask your grandfathers if you shouldn't be grateful. If you could find any relatives in Poland or Czechoslovakia today, they'd tell you."

It was growing darker in the barn, but Maxwell could still see the intensity in Corchran's eyes. Outside, the men with their guns were fading to colorless gray as the grass had done. Soon it would be difficult to distinguish them from the rocks as they crouched, still.

"That's why I should let you kill this guy?"

"I told you, Max. You've read his stuff yourself. Since you've been with him you've probably gotten some more of it. He's a genius, but he's an evil one."

"Come on, Corky; he's a fat little—"

"He got *you!* Sick old Maxwell: can of worms, all you want is to die in peace. He got you to cut off every bridge behind you, possibly get yourself killed for him. And you probably don't even believe the crap he spouts. What's he going to be able to do with people who do believe? I don't mean he's satanic, Max. He thinks he's doing good. Quite possibly he thinks he's the Messiah. And other people will think so too. That's why he's a threat to us. To America—not wave-the-flag, my country right or wrong. To America the Land of Opportunity, the Home of the Free . . . And you know it *is* that, Max."

Maxwell was silent for a moment. "You really are a true believer, aren't you, Corky?"

"With all my heart and soul, Max."

"And the others? What about the girls?"

It was Corchran's turn for silence. Then, "Sometimes you have to do really rotten things for the right reasons. If you'd let the Russians get him . . ."

"Yeah. If they'd gotten him, they might not have cared what a couple of girls said. They could always get him to deny it. But if we do it, and the word gets out . . . People might think we're just as bad as they are."

"Which we are not! That's the point! That's the essential

295

point. It's a complex world, Max. Choices are not easy, but you have to make them."

"Yeah."

"Come out with me, Max."

"No."

"Why! Why are you doing this? If you don't care about your country—about those values, then what *do* you care that much about?"

"I don't know . . . Why did you come in here?"

"I told you."

"For me. Decent."

"I try to be. We all try. My personal sense of decency didn't conflict with the greater good."

"The 'greater good'."

"I don't care how it sounds. There is such a thing. You know it."

"I *don't* know, Corky. I guess that's my point. Vronsky may think he's the Second Coming, like you say; and most of what he says *is* horseshit, but . . . He's a nice little guy. And they make a lovely couple. I guess I couldn't think of anything I wanted to kill them for."

Corchran studied Maxwell, tried to make out his face in the deepened shadow. "OK, we'll let the girls go."

"No deal."

"I promise you. I'll *make* Dolby. We'll let them get down the hill into those trees. In a couple of minutes it will be too dark for us to find them again; you can see for youself."

"No deal."

"We have all the cards, Max."

"Play with yourself, then."

Suddenly, Corchran stiffened. "Shit!" He turned and started toward the now totally dark L.

"Hold it, Corky!

Corchran ignored him.

"Hold it!"

"They aren't there! You . . . ! I came down here to save

your ass, and you suckered me!" Then with a sigh and a nod, "You clever old bastard."

Maxwell smiled to himself. He remembered the parting when he'd sent the others on. Renata had looked at him for an instant. It was only an instant, but Maxwell felt they had told each other all they could have said. Then Renata had taken Nella's hand and Vronsky's arm and pushed them along. Nella had been too tired or frightened to understand. Vronsky hadn't understood at first, either. He had started downhill saying, "A good plan . . . delay, change direction . . ." Suddenly he had turned, his eyes wide, his mouth open. He actually had taken a step back toward Maxwell before Renata had caught his arm again and dragged him after her.

Corchran wheeled and started for the door. "It's getting dark, but we'll—"

Maxwell stepped sideways, barring the doorway, pistol up, held with both hands. "Not in another couple minutes."

"I haven't got a gun, Max."

"Mistake."

"Dolby hears a shot, he'll know. Max . . . This isn't what you sold out for. This isn't the way you planned it. Don't make us kill you. You don't want to die here, in a pile of shit!"

"It seems as good a place as any."

Corchran stood still. "I came here to try to save your life, Max."

Maxwell showed no reaction.

Corchran decided. "I'm going now."

Maxwell jerked the gun upward toward him. Corchran halted. "Dolby!" he shouted.

Maxwell fired point-blank. Corchran seemed to fly backwards, both hands at his chest.

Dolby shouted back, "Corchran! Corchran!"

Maxwell turned to face the door.

There were almost five seconds of silence. Then Dolby screamed again. "Maxwell, you rotten bastard!" And all four machine guns began firing at once. The forty-five-calibre bullets tore through the old barn siding as though it were paper. They caught Maxwell at chest level. He dropped to his knees.

Looking out through the door, he did see the Matterhorn once more before falling forward.